D0659381

This book is dedicated to my parents, Robert (Bob) Charles Macomber and Martha Jane (Janie) Macomber, who instilled in me a love of books and of exploring beyond those far-off watery horizons

The Honor Series
By Robert N. Macomber

At the Edge of Honor
Point of Honor
Honorable Mention
A Dishonorable Few
An Affair of Honor
A Different Kind of Honor
The Honored Dead
The Darkest Shade of Honor
Honor Bound

POINT OF HONOR

the continuing exploits of
Lt. Peter Wake
United States Navy

Robert N. Macomber

Pineapple Press, Inc.
Sarasota, Florida

Copyright © 2003, 2011 by Robert N. Macomber
First paperback edition 2005

All rights reserved. No part of this book may be reproduced in any form or by any means, electronic or mechanical, including photocopying, recording, or by any information storage and retrieval system, without permission in writing from the publisher.

Inquiries should be addressed to:

Pineapple Press, Inc.
P.O. Box 3889
Sarasota, Florida 34230

www.pineapplepress.com

ISBN-13: 978-1-56164-345-5
ISBN-10: 1-56164-345-9

The Library of Congress has cataloged the hardcover edition as follows:
Macomber, Robert N., 1953-
Point of honor / Robert N. Macomber.
p. cm.
Sequel to: At the edge of honor.
ISBN 1-56164-270-3
1. Florida—History—Civil War, 1861-1865—Fiction. 2. United States—History, Naval—19th century—Fiction. 3. United States Navy—Officers—Fiction. I. Title.
PS3613.A28 P65 2003
813'.6—dc21

2002014307

10 9 8 7 6 5 4 3 2

Design by She Hicks
Printed in the United States of America

Preface

We're sailing with Lt. Peter Wake again. He is in his second year with the East Gulf Blockading Squadron and facing a multitude of professional and personal dilemmas afloat and ashore. Peter Wake is not the same man who arrived in Key West from New England as a volunteer naval officer in May of 1863. Like the rest of the nation, Peter Wake has been through too much to ever be the same.

The war, sadly, is far from over. It is now the spring of 1864, and everyone, in both the North and the South, has given up hope for a quick end to the bloodshed. Indeed, throughout the Northern states the sickening litany of casualty lists is producing second thoughts for many citizens about the wisdom of continuing to force the South to stay in the Union. If they want to leave the Union that badly then let them go, some are saying. Does the nation have the will to stay the course and win total victory? National politicians are debating that very thing.

On the other side of the conflict, the Southerners are exhausted. They are fighting because they must defend their home soil, but the enthusiasm is gone, along with the naïve hope of formal recognition by Great Britain and France. Too much of the Confederacy has been captured, too many thousands of men killed and wounded, too many homes and towns destroyed for anyone to feel they will have a total victory. By now they are hoping for a partial gain of some manner of independence, at least a grudging cessation of the hostilities so the Yankees will just go away. Some sort of agreement is hoped for so the people of Georgia and Tennessee and Virginia can return to a semblance of peace and try to rebuild what they have lost.

Florida is in an ironic position by 1864. Previously considered a nice but nonessential sibling in the sisterhood of Confederate states, Florida is the South's sole remaining largely unconquered food-producing region east of the Mississippi, the main breadbasket for the large Rebel armies fighting the Federal forces in Georgia and Tennessee. Beef, in particular, is Florida's most important contribution to the Confederate war effort, and thousands of head of cattle are shipped northward by priority rail each month.

Florida's coastline is still somewhat important, with hidden places remaining where the occasional small Rebel blockade runner can bring out small quantities of cotton and run in equally small shipments of foreign munitions and manufactured goods. These runs are not productive enough to matter much in the overall war but do influence local events in the peninsula. Generally speaking, however, the U.S. Navy has made blockade running on the Florida coast much more dangerous than it was the previous year.

In fact, the navy has been instrumental in transforming its efforts in Florida from a backwater blockade to an offensive invasion at several points along the Gulf and Atlantic coasts. Working closely with the army authorities, naval operations have succeeded in enabling Union forces to break up the food production capabilities in different areas of Florida. More substantial invasions to capture the heart of the state are being thrust ashore against numerically weaker Confederate defenders.

But with all that effort and naval support, Tallahassee remains the only Confederate state capital east of the Mississippi not captured during the conflict. Each time the Federal forces have tried to get close, they have been defeated by a ragtag rabble of the frontier Floridian home guard along with some regular Confederate army units that have been moved back into the state.

This is the situation that Peter Wake faces as he leads men through the inhumanity and confusion of war. The conflict becomes continually more complicated. This year of the war will find Wake making decisions at sea that will bring him the unwelcome attention of his superiors and decisions ashore that will have profound risks. Wake will also have to make bittersweet decisions of the heart. But no matter what, Wake will remain steadfast, and his decisions will be made based upon that most simple point of character he has ingrained deep in his soul: honor.

Come aboard. The anchor's hove short, and the sails are unfurled. It's time to get under way. There's a war on and we're needed out there.

Your most humble servant,
Robert N. Macomber

Acknowledgments

Again my thanks go to the other two writers of the Parrot Hillian Writers Circle, Roothee Gabay and Dian Wehrle. They have been aboard with Peter Wake for his whole career, and I hope they ship over for the next cruise.

There are three nonfiction authors who deserve a "Bravo Zulu" notation. They are Dr. George Buker, who wrote *Blockaders, Refugees and Contrabands;* Lewis Schmidt, who wrote the four-volume work *The Civil War in Florida—A Military History;* and John Viele, who wrote *The Florida Keys*, a three-volume work on the history of those unique islands. These are excellent books that I recommend to anyone who wants to know the true story of that fascinating time in this fascinating place.

And a special thank you to Dena Macomber.

—Bob Macomber
Off the coast of Florida
13 September 2002

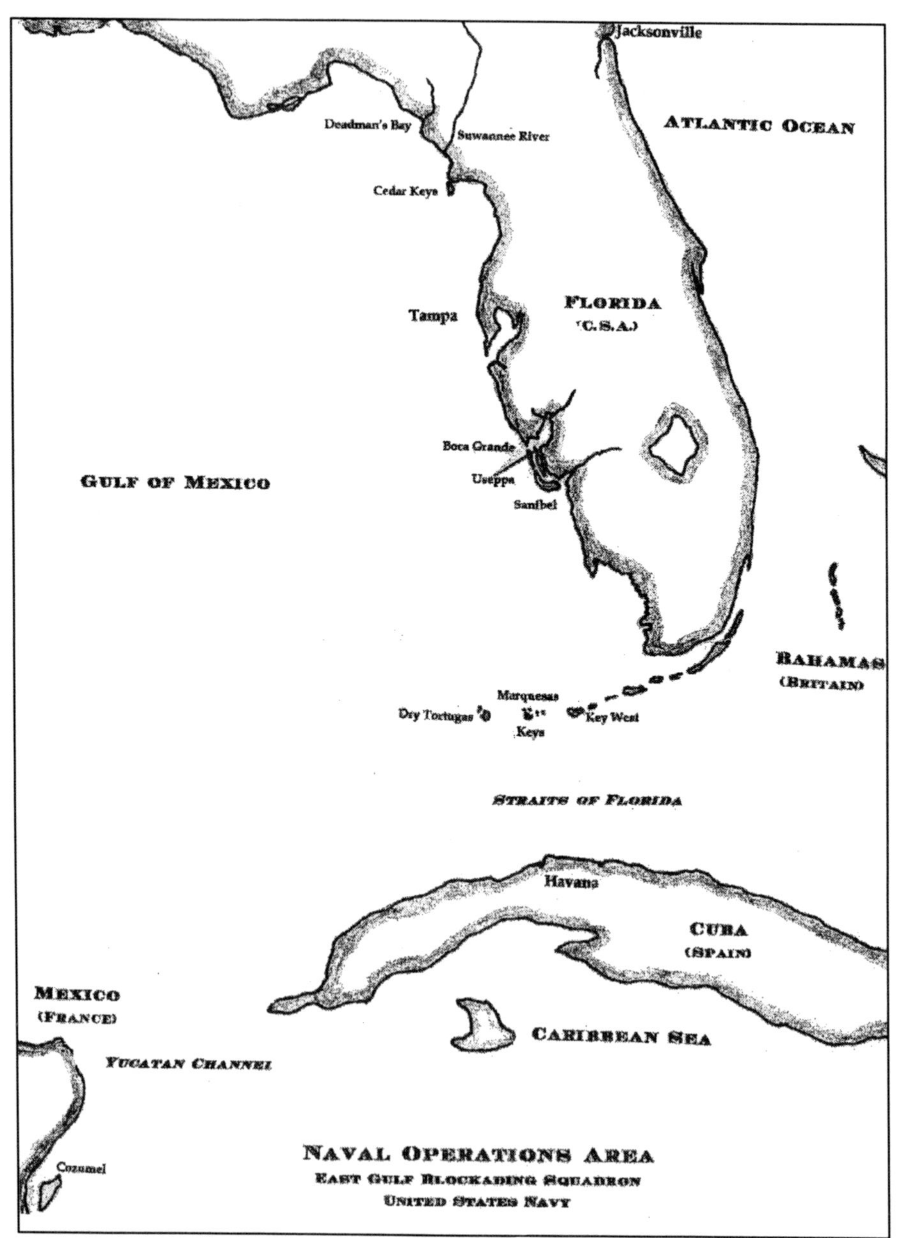

Jacksonville
ATLANTIC OCEAN
Deadman's Bay
Suwannee River
Cedar Keys
Tampa
FLORIDA
(C.S.A.)
Boca Grande
Useppa
Sanibel
GULF OF MEXICO
BAHAMAS
(BRITAIN)
Marquesas
Dry Tortugas
Keys
Key West
STRAITS OF FLORIDA
Havana
CUBA
(SPAIN)
MEXICO
(FRANCE)
CARIBBEAN SEA
YUCATAN CHANNEL
Cozumel
NAVAL OPERATIONS AREA
EAST GULF BLOCKADING SQUADRON
UNITED STATES NAVY

1
Desperation

The grotesque war raging far to the north of them frequently provided a topic of conversation for the soldiers and sailors at the fortress but no actual sense of threat. The real enemy in the Dry Tortugas was the dazzling tropical sun. Its breathtaking heat and blinding glare could make a man slowly go crazy with skin rashes and hallucinations or cause a sunstroke that could kill him outright. Rank or position provided no protection in this place—senior officers and newly enlisted men were struck with egalitarian efficiency.

It was all so cruelly strange to the pasty, white-skinned boys from the Maine or Pennsylvania or New Jersey regiments. They hadn't joined up for this, had never even imagined a place like this existed. Not long after each man's arrival he would start to curse the incessant pounding of the sun, and by the time a week had passed he would despise the shadeless coral rock islands and those sadists in Washington who had sent him this godforsaken place. The boy from up north who used to love the warmth of the spring sun was now a man who hated it as his mortal enemy.

"Gawd, how I hate everything about this damned hell-hole!

Smell the stink o' the place. Ya'd think the poor army sods ashore would have better latrines than that. Half-wit fools can't even get that right!"

Able Seaman Thomas Mason, sweat soaked and grimy, looked over at a privy on the dock a hundred yards away. Frustration vented, he bent down to seize a crate addressed to the army regimental staff ashore and, grunting out additional opinions about the soldiers of the garrison as he lifted, manhandled it to the edge of the gunwale with a crash. Mason lay over the top of it, catching his breath. Slinging a wave of slimy perspiration from a stubbled face, he gazed aft and sneered between gasps. From a gig alongside, a figure in a dark blue uniform had arrived on deck. The brass from the buttons and insignia gleamed in the steaming glare of the sunlight.

"Ah Lordy, Jackson, see what the United States Army in all their glory done sent us now? Will ya look at that little boy back there all dressed up like a officer. Ya know, maybe it's a girlee by the look o' him, come ta think on it. Gawd, no wonder they can't get it done up in Virginia, little boys like that leading the army."

White, the coxswain standing by the foremast and supervising the unloading detail, heard the comment and quickly silenced Mason, who was supposed to be helping Jackson sway down some gear into the workboat. The captain wanted to weigh anchor in an hour and they didn't have much time left. And making fun of officers was never a good idea, especially when they might hear it.

"Mason, never you mind the army, it's the ever lovin' navy you're in and the navy that'll have your hide! Now shut your damned hatch and do your work, and mind that fall tackle there. Jackson, ya poxy idiot, get that damned thing lashed up proper and swayed over!"

With that said, White turned aft and examined the object of Mason's sarcasm. Shaking his head and smiling, he found himself in silent agreement with Mason's comment. The officer did look pretty pathetic.

The badly sunburned army second lieutenant who was the unknowing subject of Mason's assessment looked distinctly uncomfortable as the *St. James* rolled with slow rhythm in the low swells of the anchorage off the fortress. Hanging onto a nearby shroud for support, the young man appeared to have little military experience and absolutely no confidence. Sweating profusely in his heavy wool formal coat and hat, he stood on the deck of the naval schooner trying to convey, as professionally as he could, a request from his colonel ashore to the captain of the vessel, Lieutenant Peter Wake of the United States Navy. Tanned and wearing a cool white duck cotton shirt and trousers, Wake's lean frame swayed easily with the deck as he listened to the army officer's awkward recitation of the message. The blinding sun made the army lieutenant's eyes squint, accentuating his less than imposing appearance. The naval officer's face, by contrast, was in the shade of a broad-brimmed straw hat, haggled from an ancient Bahamian weaver woman in a Key West tavern four months earlier. Wake, uncertain whether the lieutenant's discomfort came from the nature of the request, the roll of the deck, or both, almost felt sorry for him until he thought about what the man—boy really—was asking him to do.

The lieutenant explained that the 52nd New Jersey Artillery, stationed there at Fortress Jefferson in the Dry Tortugas Islands, had managed to lose some of its men. Five of them, to be exact, had evidently decided to take "French leave" and head somewhere, anywhere, other than the notorious Dry Tortugas Islands. Wake stared at the lieutenant for a moment, wondering how you could lose five men out in the middle of nowhere in the Gulf of Mexico, but was distracted by some whispering forward. Around him the crew of the schooner snickered about the army's problem and were offering ideas as to why the men had left the desolate outpost. The bosun of the schooner, Rork, standing with arms akimbo on the foredeck, soon put an end to their fun by putting them on the windless to heave the anchor rode short. Rork was not in a good mood. The crew knew the look on the bosun's face too well. Wake returned his gaze to the unfortunate youngster before him.

"How in the world did they leave the islands here?"

"The Colonel thinks they took an old rowing boat that was on the beach at Bird Key. Nobody thought it would float. Thought it was pretty much rotted out, sir. But I guess they somehow patched it up and made it float. Musta' made a sail too."

"You say they've been gone for three days? Why didn't your people go after them right away? Well, they're probably dead by now."

"Colonel said that he didn't want nobody else goin' off in a little boat and gettin' killed themselves, sir. All we've got are the garrison's small boats. Colonel's pretty mad about all of this. Said to ask the navy to go over to the Marquesas Islands and see if the boys made it over to there. He really wants those men back, Captain."

"Very well. Tell him I'll check those islands for his men. If I find them, we'll bring them back here for the colonel to deal with as he sees fit. Tell the colonel I don't think we'll find his men alive though."

With that said Wake dismissed the lieutenant, turned and walked aft toward his cabin ladder, glancing at the tall square-framed bosun.

"Rork, get her under way for the Marquesas. The ebb should carry us out of the anchorage a bit. Have the anchor ready in case we need it in a hurry to keep off a reef. I'll be below for a minute."

Descending the ladder to the cabin, he listened as Rork roared out to the crew in his deep voice with the Irish brogue.

"Aye aye, sir. All right now, lads, you heard the captain. Turn to and lay on the halyards. With a will, boys! Let's send 'em up an see what she'll do."

In his airless cabin Wake sat at his desk studying the chart of the islands in the Marquesas group. If those men had made it to that archipelago, over forty-five miles away against what little wind there was, then they'd had better luck than most. The Dry Tortugas were surrounded by very dangerous water, filled with bewildering swift currents and uncharted coral reefs. There were many ways for the deserters to die before they made it to the dubious safety of the uninhabited Marquesas Islands. And once they made it there, if they did, there was no fresh water or help. Only mangrove jungle. Those islands were as desolate as the Tortugas.

Wake tried to puzzle out exactly what had made them try it. Didn't they know the odds? Had they any maritime experience? He remembered when the 52nd New Jersey had arrived two months ago he heard that they were from some place inland in that state and were angry at being assigned to the bleak and barren Fortress Jefferson. Probably the fugitives had no idea of what they were doing. Probably, in fact, they were dead.

His patrol station for the ninety-foot-long *St. James* included the Tortugas, the Marquesas, and the western Florida Keys. He had been assigned this station for three long months, since April. The year 1864 was over half gone, and Wake was sick of this duty. Beyond the mind-numbing routine of patrolling the area for blockade runners, message relaying between Key West's Fort Taylor and Fort Jefferson, and the occasional special mission to go to Havana for dispatches, there wasn't much to do in this patrol area.

Wake sighed and involuntarily touched the scar on the side of his head, a memento from when he had had a much more active station on the coast of the mainland last year. The blast of the cannon during the fight with the Rebs on the river was still absolutely clear in his mind. As was the pain of the wound inflicted that morning. He flinched as he recalled the chaos of the fight and the carnage afterward. Part of that scene of carnage were members of his own crew lying on the deck of the sloop *Rosalie*, dead or wounded during the battle. It seemed a long time ago and far away. Wake realized there was no such danger from the enemy in these islands. He dragged himself up from the desk in the torpid heat and made his way to the main deck again, where he found himself amidst the bustle of the crew's laboring at the pinrails around the masts.

The main and foresail were up and drawing slightly on the zephyrs of wind coming in puffs from the southeast. As the crew set her jibs, the schooner came slowly around the eastern side of the fortress. Wake glanced at the parapets and saw a group of officers standing together talking. He recognized one as the messenger lieutenant, who listened as a man who appeared to be Colonel Grosland, commanding officer of the 52nd New Jersey Artillery, was speaking and waving a hand in the youngster's face. Then the colonel pointed at the schooner.

The voice could be vaguely heard across the water but the words were not discernible. Wake could guess at what they were, however. Grosland was a martinet in love with his uniform but never satisfied with his people's efforts. Wake had met him a month before while at the fortress and not liked his condescending attitude. This war was bringing out men like Grosland in all the services—those with no experience or capability leading other men, much less leading them through difficulty and danger. A place like Jefferson would be even more of an ordeal with a man such as Grosland in charge.

Fort Jefferson had been built over the last twenty years on an island in a small group of scattered coral islets known as the Dry Tortugas, seventy miles west of Key West. And dry they were. There were no fresh water wells on the islands. The three hundred men of the garrison relied upon huge cisterns on the parade ground and under the walls of the fortress to gather enough water in the rainy season to last for the rest of the year. Surrounded as they were by some of the most beautiful salt water imaginable, the army rationed fresh water among the souls assigned to the fortress.

Fortress was an appropriate term. Wake had never seen anything like it. Jefferson was huge. It was known as the Gibraltar of the Gulf because of its size and the emplacements for a potential of 450 guns. At the moment, they held only six ten-inch Columbiad cannon, along with a couple of small howitzers by the docks. Wake knew from his reading of the *New Era* newspaper at Key West that the massive walls designed in the forties were already outdated. Reports of battles pitting naval vessels against forts in Charleston and on the Mississippi had revealed that much. Modern rifled naval artillery such as those very Columbiads would make short work of the faded brickwork of the fortress—a mere façade of strength, like so many façades that Wake had seen thus far in this awful war. Colonel Grosland was its human counterpart.

Still, Wake had to admire and respect the men who planned and actually built this edifice of war in the middle of a tropical sea. The efforts and expenses made were unparalleled. But there was an ugly side to the fortress as well. Almost two hundred army prisoners were held here, Union Army prisoners who had committed some of the worst military offenses known. Fortress Jefferson was so notorious in the army, Wake had heard from an engineer captain at the island, that soldiers under sentence of death could have it commuted to hard labor at Jefferson as it was considered the same. The labor battalion worked on the never ending project of improving the fortress. They lived in stifling cells under the walls and eked out their lives toiling in the brutal sun under the eyes of a garrison that was under a similar, but shorter sentence. Periodically the regiment on garrison duty would be replaced by another, so that each only served six or eight months at Jefferson. But the prisoners never left.

Fortunately, Wake had the freedom to leave. As the *St. James* ghosted away from the immense brown brick walls that rose out of the bright green waters, the crew of the schooner could see the soldiers of the garrison, and a few of the prisoners, watching them sail quietly away. It was the same every time. The men of the fortress always stopped their work and stared at the schooner. It was always eerie.

It took two days to cover the distance eastward to the

Marquesas. The wind was light and from varying directions the whole way. Twice they anchored when the wind died and the current started to sweep them southward. By the time the *St. James* anchored off the westernmost island of the group, the crew of the schooner had thoroughly cursed the 52nd New Jersey Artillery, their colonel, and their deserters.

The Marquesas Islands were a uniquely formed group. Unlike the Keys of Florida, which stretched out westward in a string of islets for one hundred fifty miles, the Marquesas were a circle of islands around a central shallow lagoon. The lagoon averaged only about a fathom or less deep, with brown and green grasses covering most of the bottom. Deeper, smooth-bottomed swash channels snaked their way in varying shades of blue all over the lagoon, giving a contrast to the colors of the grassy shoals. When viewed in conjunction with the thin, white sand beaches backed by the tumble of dark green mangrove jungle, the whole effect on a brightly sunny day was one of a dazzling spectrum of colors.

In addition to the beautiful colors, the Marquesas had some of the most fantastic water Wake had ever seen. In fact, offshore from the islands it appeared that there was no water there at all, for the schooner was apparently sliding through the air over a perfectly seen bottom ten feet down. The shadows from the moving ship and her sails covered the sand and coral below like the shade of a large bird gliding over a meadow. The brilliant creatures of this intriguing world would scamper or flit away from the shadow as it approached them, providing an endless source of fascination for the crew, most of whom had never served in the tropics before. As wonderful as it all was, it was also disconcerting, for the depth perception of most of the men was thrown out of scale upon first seeing this splendor. Many times they yelled for the helmsman to head up and avoid a coral head, only to find they were deceived by the transparency of the liquid underneath them when the suspect reef would pass mockingly beneath the warship.

Wake knew his men were exhausted from the humid heat and the exertion of working on the baking deck. A soon as the anchor was down and holding, he told Rork to let them swim for a few minutes before taking the ship's boat through the islands to search for the soldiers. The grateful sailors immediately stripped down, jumped overboard, and were transformed into energetic boys exploring the amazing world below them in the startlingly clear waters. Their shouts and splashes made Rork and Wake smile when the two glanced at each other.

"Well, Captain, I'd venture a nice swim will do the lads good before their row today." Rork's thick Wexford Irish accent flavored the words.

"Yes, I do believe it's a good tonic for the men in this heat. The soldiers will still be there an hour from now, if they're alive."

"I agree with ya, sir. Nary a one could be breathin' after that journey, I'm thinkin', sir. Hell of a row from the Tortugas. 'Specially for farm boyos not used to this heat. This ol' Irishman ain't used to it neither, sir!"

"Give the men another twenty minutes, then send off a boat's crew. Have them row all the way around the islands on this side of the group, we'll search the other side tomorrow. Check anything that looks odd. If those soldiers are here, they'll be needing help by now."

"Aye, sir. I don't much think they're here though, sir. Me thinks the poor beggars are most likely in the belly of some sharks somewhere."

"Probably you are right, Rork, but we've got to confirm that they're not here. If they are, the Tortugas might even look good to them by now. Wonder what the colonel will do to them if he gets them alive?"

"No way of telling that one, sir."

A half hour later the pleasant noise of the men relaxing in the water gave way to the somber sounds of the boat crew rowing away from the schooner. Armed and looking serious, they were like all sailors told to go after deserters. They had no qualms about dragging those men back to their duty and would show no mercy to any deserter who did not surrender. Wake had seen it happen other times at Key West and was always amazed at it. One would think sailors would sympathize with the deserters, but they never did. Instead they despised them as weaklings that made extra work for the others.

For the thousandth time, Wake marveled at the discipline of the navy. That men could, and would, work in such conditions without mutiny showed the tremendous contrast to the merchant marine life he had known up until the year before. As hard as life was for a merchant sailor, the harsh realities of naval service were worse. That he, in his mid-twenties, was the undisputed master of these sailors' lives gave Wake a chill down his spine. It was such a long way from his previous life aboard the coastal schooners of New England.

That thought took him to another, more melancholy one. The previous year, while stationed at Key West and before commanding the *St. James*, he had fallen in love with a woman named Linda Donahue. Daughter of a rabid anti-Yankee Key Wester now languishing in a prisoner-of-war dungeon in Boston's Fort Warren, Linda still lived in Key West with her pro-Confederate uncle. The strain of carrying on a love affair with the enemy of her family had proven too much for Linda, and one day four months ago she had told Wake it had to end, that she couldn't take it any longer and their love could not endure the hate that was all around them on both sides of this dreadful war.

For those four months Wake had not been the same man. It was as if he'd had a leg amputated and still had the ghost feelings of the severed member. He loved and desperately needed Linda. He was not able to get through a day without thinking of her, and routine things would somehow bring her to his mind, saddening him. His periodic visits to Key West for supplies or orders were a constant pull upon his heart to go near her house and maybe just see her in the distance. But his will power had managed to overcome his heart, and he had not burdened her with his presence since that day.

The sun had sunk low into the western sky when Wake,

lying under a shade awning on the afterdeck, was shaken from his reverie by a gunshot in the distance on the lagoon side of the island closest to them. Rork, who was stretched out by the twelve-pounder amidships, leaped to his feet and peered at the island in the failing light.

"Quick, Dumfrey, get your sharp eyes up the mast and spy out what would be happenin' over there with our lads. Did ye hear that, sir? 'Twas a gunshot, sure as Jesus, sir."

"Yes, I heard it too, Rork. Get the anchor hove short and the furl lashings off her, in case we have to move quickly."

Dumfrey ran to the shrouds of the mainmast and ascended them to the crosstrees, scanning the eastern horizon in segments. With no sighting, he climbed to the very masthead, clinging precariously. Seconds later he cried out.

"Captain sir! I see the boat over on the lagoon side with a bunch o' men in the shallows around it, sir. Can't tell who's who, but it looks like some o' them is prisoners, sir. Trussed up, like."

Wake looked up at the eighteen-year-old Dumfrey and realized his understanding of what was happening was entirely through the boy's eyes and interpretation. Dumfrey was from Vermont and had been in the navy for five weeks. He'd only been on the *St. James* for two.

"Anyone lying down, Dumfrey? Can you see if anyone is wounded?"

"Yes, sir. Now I see one man in the boat lyin' down, like, sir. Could be wounded."

Rork, standing by his captain, had gotten the remaining crew working to make the *St. James* ready for weighing the anchor. The dinghy was being repaired in Key West and there was no second small boat to go ashore. He looked over at Wake.

"No way to support the lads, sir. Just have to wait till they come back. But it sounds like they're all right, by Dumfrey's eyes."

"I hate this waiting, but you are right, Rork. We wait."

Fifteen minutes later, as the sun was making its daily show of farewell on the western horizon, the schooner's boat was seen coming around the point of the island. It was pulling steadily for the *St. James*, and from two hundred yards away the men on the schooner's deck could hear the coxswain, White, calling the steady cadence to the men rowing. In the growing darkness there was no discerning the condition of the men aboard, and all hands on the deck stared without a sound at the boat until Rork bellowed out.

"White! Are ye all right?"

"Nay, Bosun! Man shot!"

The bosun's voice stirred the others to action and a dozen pairs of arms reached out to fend off and hold as the boat finally came alongside its mother ship. The lantern shed light into the well of the boat. A collective gasp exhaled from the crew looking down. At the same time a wail came up from the boat's floorboards. A writhing man was down there doubled over and clutching his guts, which were spilling out of his hands like a nest of slimy snakes. Two sailors were trying to hold the man down and stuff the glistening intestines back into the gaping wound in his belly, while several others were prodding three skulking men up from the bows of the boat to climb the hull of the schooner. The prodding was being done with their cutlasses and not too lightly. White looked up from below at his captain.

"Only found four of them soldiers, sir. They said the other's dead on the beach on the northern island. These ones walked to this island through the shallows. Molloy had to shoot this one, sir. Damned sorry, but nary a choice."

Wake saw, as he listened to White, that the three ambulatory deserters were now lashed to the foremast and the sailors were trying to get the wounded soldier lifted up on the deck. Gentleness was not employed as they finally threw the now screaming man up after several failures at being more delicate. Wake looked again at White.

"All right, White, come up and tell me what happened. Rork, try to get a dressing on that wound and bind it up. Use some of the laudanum to quiet that man."

Both men acknowledged Wake, with Rork adding that White had better get the ship's boat cleaned up before any of the mess set in. White told the ship's boy to start on it as he climbed up the main chains to the deck and walked aft with the captain. When they reached the stern White stopped, took off his canvas hat, and stood quietly waiting.

"Go ahead, White. What happened?"

"Well sir, Molloy and Hill were walking around the shallows on the lagoon side of the island, looking for them deserters like ya told us all to do. I had three others walking around on the windward side, on the beach there, looking too. Me and the boy was at the boat, waiting for 'em all to come back."

"Yes, go on. How did they end up shooting him?"

"Well, sir, I sorta seen it myself, 'cause the curve of the island let me see the boys walkin' through the shallows over there. They's a walkin' along and suddenly like, a man jumps outta the mangroves an' on Molloy with a cutlass or bayonet or somethin', sir. Saw it my ownself. Molloy starts a hollering and Hill starts a wadin' back to him, but Molloy finally shot the son of a bitch with his pistol while they's a wrastlin'. Hill waren't close enough to help ol' Molloy afore that bayonet coulda' done its duty, so Molloy shot 'im and I woulda' too, sir."

"And the others?"

"They's a hidin' in them mangroves too. When Molloy used his pistol they came outta there, hands high in the air and beggin' not to shoot them too. Made 'em all drag their friend back to the boat and put him in. They started to get bowed up when we put them three in the bow, so I had the lads keep cutlass points on 'em to keep 'em quiet like. Sorry he ain't dead, sir. Know what a pure chore it'll be, but Molloy only got one shot off and it crossed his belly, lettin' his guts out. Molloy's a new man, sir. He's a feelin' poorly 'bout it right now."

"I see. Tell Molloy he did his duty and defended himself, White. I'll talk to him later. Meanwhile get the boat and schooner cleaned up. Lay back on the rode and get her ready for the night.

I want two men guarding the prisoners at all times. Send Hill to me."

While Rork tended to the wounded soldier, who was still alternately crying and screaming despite the laudanum, Wake surveyed his crew. Still no pity showed toward the deserters, who had made the ultimate mistake of showing violence to the men who were doing their duty to apprehend them.

Instead, the sailors were congratulating Molloy on the fact that at least he had hit his target from a distance of six inches and berating him that he couldn't make it a kill shot from that range. Molloy, a quiet young man in normal circumstances, was smiling at his crewmates but not joining in the laughter. When the others weren't noticing, he occasionally looked up to the foredeck where Rork was finishing up his dressing and binding. Wake made a mental note to definitely speak with the youngster and went below to his cabin.

Hill arrived as Wake was lighting his lamp. A skinny man, around thirty, he looked and smelled like he had never known a bath. He ran a filthy hand through his greasy hair to get an errant curl out of his eyes then stood as straight as the cabin overhead would allow.

"Sir, Seaman Hill reportin', sir."

Wake sat at the small desk and eyed him for a moment. Hill tried to look away.

"Hill, tell me what happened. Tell me straight, Hill."

Hill tried to stand still and looked at the chart on the desk.

"Well, sir. That ol' soldier jes' jumped Molloy in the mangroves. I's ahead a Molloy, an' turned when I heard the splashin'. Deserter man was comin' at Molloy with a bayonet or long knife. Got him up close too. Molloy said to 'im 'get back!' an' the soldier kept acomin' with that big blade, so's ol' Molloy shot him in the gut. That stopped him.

"Then they's a bunch o' other ones in the groves, an' theys' all give up right away like. No fuss from them. Molloy had no choice on it, sir."

"Where's the knife, or bayonet?"

"We looked, sir, but couldn't find it. Gotta be there, under that silt 'n sand."

"Very well, Hill, thank you. Send Bosun Rork here."

Wake turned his attention to his pen and paper as Hill climbed the ladder to the deck above. He would have to start on a report detailing all of this, with statements from the sailors and from the deserters. From the looks of the wound, the gut shot deserter could well be dead by the morn, and the documentation of all of this would best be started now, while it was all fresh.

Rork's bulk filled the room as he slid down the ladder and turned to the captain. He was bent almost double due to the five-foot headroom. Blood stained his shirt. His eyes looked weary.

"Rork, sit down and take a load off your feet. How's the wounded man?"

"Not good, sir. He'll probably go by tomorrow. I've seen 'em last longer, but not much. He's a bit more tranquil now, Captain. I put a Irish lullaby on his head to make him forget the pain."

After serving with the bosun for almost eight months, Wake by now knew that an "Irish lullaby" was a stout blow from a strong fist to a head, intended to knock the recipient out cold.

"And what of the others? What did they have to say?"

"They made a pot o' noise, sir, most of which had no sense. They did tell the story of their venture. Seems they had no idea exactly where they were, 'cause the ship that dropped their regiment off at the fortress in Tortugas steamed there in the night. Didn't know the distance. They thought Key West was just a ways to the east. Sail a bit with the wind at your back and the magic city would come over the horizon!

"Fools they were, Captain. A wee bit o' water and some biscuits. They all were scared proper by the time they spent a night alone in a leakin' sailin' skiff made for a day's sail o' reef fishin'. Was prayin' to Peter and Paul, they was, by the sound of their story. Drifted by the wind an' set by the current across to the Marquesas. Not knowing where they was, o' course, and landed on the island three days later, damned near dead, all of them. No water left 'n no food. One soul drank the sea water and ended his days on the beach of another island, twistin' in the guts. Buried the poor bastard on that island where he fell. Rest sat there for a couple o' days more, till they saw the darlin' *St. James* come along like an angel to save 'em.

"Said they was glad to see us, an' was made up to go back to their regiment. Had quite a bit enough of the life o' the carefree deserter an' buckaroo."

"Really? Interesting . . ."

"Even more curious than that, sir. Said that the one layin' gutshot came out to talk, an' got shot by our boy Molloy. Two o' them twarn't talkin' on it, Captain, but the oldest o' the lot lashed up there, the man named Dobert, he said it looked like the sailor shot the soldier by mistake. Got startled and the pistol fired."

Rork stopped talking and looked across the dim cabin to his captain.

"Bring them one at a time back here, except the wounded one, of course, and we'll get statements. It'll be a long night, Rork."

"Aye, that it will, Captain. No rest for the wicked or the weary!"

With that the bosun lifted himself up the ladder while Wake returned to his penmanship in the yellow-tinted gloom. The evening moved slowly, with two of the prisoners talkative about how they had stolen the boat and fled the hell of Fortress Jefferson but silent about the shooting, and Dobert strangely devoid of emotion as he described how his companion became mortally wounded.

Next, Rork brought White, Hill, and Molloy down separately. Each gave a sworn statement reciting what they had previously said. In the end, Rork and Wake sat at the desk and spoke of the situation.

"Well, sir, it looks by the face o' it that our lads should be believed. Accident or in battle, the man was a deserter who got shot, and if he dies on the 'morrow he may be luckier than those who live to see Jefferson and that colonel again. Methinks that those men will have a hard way to go, an' may plan better the next time they decide to go cruisin' through the islands. If they live past the punishment! You have a problem with it, sir?"

"No, Rork. You're right. A deserter deserves whatever he drifts into. Doesn't really matter, does it? It'll get written up, and that will be that. Get some sleep. We sail in the morn to bring the gallant colonel his wayward boys."

The scene on the deck the next morning was one not likely to be soon forgotten by the men of the schooner *St. James.* The wounded man, full of laudanum and rum, was lolling around on the deck, his leg lashed to a ringbolt, and the other prisoners were staring at him with a look of dread in their faces. Wake thought that it might well be a valuable lesson to the younger members of his own crew about the consequences of military, and especially naval, discipline. So far on this ship, Wake hadn't had to resort to any serious discipline, a result he related to Rork's ability to lead men through example and deterrence. Still, it was good that those who had not seen such discipline be treated to this sight.

The wind sprung up from the southeast after sunrise, and the *St. James* sailed on her best point with the air on the port quarter. With six knots of speed she was making good time to the west and the Tortugas Islands. None of the sailors would stand or sit near the prisoners, and the wounded one, now known to be named Drake, had a broad area of deck to himself. His dark, soaked dressing oozing blood onto the deck made the sailors cringe and curse, not from the pain, but from the work to holystone the wood clean again.

As the day went on, the taboo area around Drake diminished in size, until the crew fairly stepped over and close to him as they did their chores. He became just another of the deck fittings, without value or respect. As if he were already dead.

The prisoners lashed to the foremast sat sullenly throughout the day. As deserters, they were not even allowed the amenities that enemy prisoners would be allowed. No periodic freedom to stretch their legs. No regular food or drink from the crew's mess. Just enough water and rock hard ship's biscuit to sustain life until Jefferson. Staring at Drake, their eyes appeared to look at him with envy, for at least he was without pain or fear.

In the mid-afternoon the lookout sighted the walls of the fortress rising out of the sea. As eerie as it was when they would depart Jefferson, Wake couldn't help but be impressed each time he returned. Despite the unsavory and sad aspects of the place, it did hold some spell over him.

An hour after first sighting the Tortugas, Drake stopped rolling around in his stupor on the deck. Rork went over and felt his neck for a pulse, made the sign of the cross, and walked aft to report to Wake that the prisoner was dead.

"Should we bury him here at sea, sir, or take him to his regiment?"

Wake muttered in reply. "Regiment." He walked over to the windward rail for some air. The business of catching deserters like they were stray dogs did not appeal to him. He hated it.

Dozens of men, some in blue uniforms and others in dirty gray rags, lined the walls of Fort Jefferson and its main dock when the *St. James* anchored off the fortress later in the afternoon as the shadows were starting to lengthen. The same young flustered army lieutenant arrived at the schooner in the garrison's boat and awkwardly climbed up the side to the main deck. He stared at the prisoners, three alive and sullen, one dead and serene, lying on the foredeck. One could almost imagine a slight smile on Drake's lifeless face. The lieutenant finally turned to Wake.

"Sir, the colonel presents his compliments and appreciation for capturing the deserters. He said to say he was sorry for any inconvenience the voyage to the Marquesas to capture this scum has caused you. My soldiers in the boat will take them from you now. But I see only four. Did they resist, sir?"

"Yes, Lieutenant. This one," Wake pointed to Drake, "resisted. The others gave up. One had died of thirst. He's buried out there. None of my men were wounded."

"Well, thank God for that, sir. The colonel, he wants to invite you to be his guest for dinner, sir. Says the army would like to show the navy its hospi . . . hospitality, sir. I'm to come and get you at sunset."

"Thank the colonel for his invitation, Lieutenant, but I am tired and would not be good company, though I am sure that his table would be splendid. I have written a short summary of the events of the capture and death of your men. I just completed a copy, which you'll get now, before we leave."

The lieutenant looked positively scared.

"But sir, the colonel has invited you to dinner! You've got to go, sir. He's invited you to dinner with the senior officers of the regiment. He expects you to be there, sir! I'm supposed to bring you. You can't leave now!"

"Lieutenant, I am tired and not in the best of outlooks right now. Your deserters are in your boat and so should you be. Tell your colonel that the exigencies of the service deny me the pleasure of his table and company, and that I must and shall depart. Now. Good evening, sir."

Wake turned away and watched some of his crew start to clean up the large dark stain on the deck. He noticed that Molloy was not among them.

"Rork, weigh the anchor and let's get her moving along. I want to be out of the fortress channel by the time it gets completely dark."

When it became clear that no one would look at or talk to him, the army lieutenant finally moved to the edge of the deck. He went down the side without a word and the boatload of misery made its way to the dock. Rork met Wake aft by the tiller.

"Leavin' outta' here in the dark, Captain? It'll be a wee bit dicey dancin' amongst those reefs tonight."

"No, Rork. We'll sail out of the fortress channel and anchor after dark inside the reefs by Garden Key. We'll cross the outer reefs in the morning light."

"Aye, sir," said the bosun, who saw but did not understand the odd look on his captain's face. "I was a wonderin' why the sudden departure with the dark comin'. No disrespect intended, sir. Are ye all right, Captain?"

"No, Rork. I'm not all right. But I'll start to be when we get away from this hellish place and its damned puppet colonels and dungeon atmosphere. And I want that stain off her deck! God, I feel like I'm on a stinking slaver."

"Aye, sir. By morn she'll look as clean an' pretty as an' Irish bride at the altar, sir! Know whatcha meanin' about the slaver. Takes a bit out o' a man to go after one o' his own, even if they are just a bunch o' army pogues. Had to do the duty, though, sir."

"I'd rather be going after the enemy, Rork. It's cleaner work."

"Aye, we all agree on that, sir."

The two of them turned their attention to the immediate issue of sailing the schooner away from the fortress in the gathering dusk, and no more was said about the stain or what caused it. Both of them knew there would be more stains, and there was nothing anyone could do about them, except clean up afterwards.

2
The Stream

The *St. James* was entering upon one of those glorious days that Wake loved in this part of the world. He had never seen anything like it sailing the North Atlantic off the New England coast. There the sea's beauty derived from a terrible majesty, but here it was the intermingling of the clear and delicate water colors with the soft forms of the islands and reefs that lent a beauty that could not be described adequately in letters back home to his parents in Massachusetts.

St. James was east of the Tortugas Islands, sailing directly into a rising sun on a close reach with the trade winds sending a gentle, but steady, flow of air from the south southeast. She had almost all of her wardrobe showing as the sails took in the wind provided and pulled her forward through the emerald seas around her. It was one of those mornings that makes a man thankful to be exactly where he is, and Wake took in a lungful of the clean warm air, stretching his lanky frame to its furthest extent. The feel of the sun and wind on his face, combined with the smells of the galley and the salt air, made him feel alive. The toes of his bare feet flexed on the smooth wood of the deck and his fingers wrapped around the tarred main shrouds that rose up to the mast cap high above. Wake felt all of his senses heightened, reveling in them as he looked around to see what was what since he had gone off watch eight hours earlier.

His survey of the decks this morning took in McDougall, the gunner's mate, and his party cleaning the bore on one of the twelve-pounder deck guns. McDougall was a quiet and serious man, of more years than anyone else aboard, who knew his business with cannons. His graying hair and low growling voice showed his authority far more than any insignia of rank. He had sailed in all the seas of the world and would occasionally tell of things he had seen and done, especially on the Anti-Slavery Patrol in the forties, inspiring silent reflection in all who heard. McDougall and Rork, both Catholic Irishmen, were the two senior petty officers aboard and the solid pillars around which the rest of the crew formed.

Farther forward, Beech, the spindly framed cook, was emerging from the foredeck hatch with a pot of coal ash cleaned out from the galley fire below, preparing to toss it leeward. He nodded to his captain as he made his way across the heeling deck.

Wake was glad that he had Beech. The man was a decent cook who made the provisions they were issued actually edible, unlike most of his counterparts in the navy. More importantly, he made the fish, crab, and lobster they caught aboard while patrolling taste absolutely delicious, the stuff of fine dining establishments, which is exactly where Beech used to work in New York City before joining the navy in an effort to avoid dying in the mud somewhere in Virginia or Tennessee for some intangible Union cause.

Wake still remembered the all-night poker game at the Rum and Randy Tavern, a rather jaded establishment on Turner Lane in Key West, where he had won Beech from the lieutenant commanding the ordnance ship stationed in the harbor. As the game neared dawn, the other remaining man at the table had exhausted anything of value to bet with. He finally said that he had a cook aboard his ship who had been a chef up in a New York dining room. The final bet of the game was the cook's assignment versus Wake's case of Cuban rum and forty-two dollars, which itself had belonged to the ordnance ship captain at the beginning of the evening. Wake smiled at the memory of Beech reporting aboard the following day. The cook had not been happy at all about his new assignment on a small schooner, nor the method of his transfer to her, that took him away from the comforts of Key West.

Wake turned his view to the after deck of the ship, where four seamen were rubbing the deck spotless with holystones near the port main shrouds. Patient explanations of how to steer a "small" course were being made to a new seaman at the helm by Faber, the bosun's mate. Faber was something of an unknown quantity to Wake, having just shipped aboard three weeks earlier. Somewhere around twenty-four or so, with a face that looked perpetually pained, Faber had so far shown the competence of an experienced seaman if not the leadership of a veteran petty officer. He had made bosun's mate a month before reporting aboard and had last served on a steam gunboat in Tampa Bay. Serving aboard a schooner in the Florida Keys was certainly quite different.

All of this activity and invigorating atmosphere reminded Wake that he had not yet had anything to eat. As he descended to his cabin for a bite of breakfast, he saw Rork coming aft on the main deck and motioned for him to follow below. Wake wanted to go over the provisions with him.

Seated at the small chart table in the commander's cabin both men started at the grouper fish, potatoes, and gravy laid out by Beech. Wake, fork in hand, was the first to speak.

"Rork, wher're we at on the provisions? Especially water."

"Aye, Captain, we're down to six o' the small casks, plus the wee one in the schooner's boat, o' course. Other provisions are still good. Not sure how many, but I'm sure that we have at least ten o' the salt pork left, and as many o' the biscuit. Fruit, o' course, is gone. A wee bit o' the beer left. Water's the thing, sir."

Wake didn't like that. They had used up too much water already. But in the heat of the tropic summer, the men had to consume more water or die.

"All right, it looks as though we'd better put in at the squadron for more water. How are those casks doing? Are we losing some through leakage?"

"Aye, sir. Some, but not as bad as we've had before. I just looked at the six o' the little devils still full. Nary a drop around 'em leakin'."

"Right then, back to Key West. Weather should hold."

"Captain, with this lovely little wind she'll do nicely. Key West by the morrow's night perhaps, I'm a thinkin'. A bit o' a beat upwind if the wind goes back to the east, but she'll point high enough if we're behind the reefs in the calmer water."

With this decision made, Wake returned to what was left of the meal before him, swilling down a mug of coffee and then wondering how much water was used to make it. If the weather changed for the worse, or the wind died, all hands would be put on short rations by tomorrow morning. Six small casks of water for twenty-five men would not last long.

Sunset in this part of the ocean was always an event. As they roared along eastward, heeled over and beating upwind in long tacks toward Key West, the men of the *St. James* stopped in their work to admire the free display of God's artistry spread out on the horizon behind them. Wake never halted this practice, for he believed that enjoying the tranquillity of a tropical sunset was one of the few benefits available to men subjugated to the disciplines and dangers of naval service.

This was one of the memorable ones. There were just enough cottony trade wind clouds to provide a moving canvas for pastel colors to be projected upon, and the luminescent glow of the sun as it slid downward made the waters to the west dance like glittering jewelry. Even the toughest of the men appreciated this demonstration of beauty and appeared to be pondering inward thoughts as they swayed with the movements of the ship and gazed far off into the receding light.

Wake always wondered what they were thinking, but no one ever talked during the last few minutes of a sunset. It was as if each owned a part of it, possibly the only thing of beauty he had ever owned, and it was an unspoken taboo to disturb his communion with the sun's last moments.

Close to the horizon, golden hues were giving way to bright rose and faded pink, while at the zenith above, the colors were turning from darker royal blue and greenish-gray into violet-black. On the upper eastern arc of the sky the first, and brightest, stars were starting to glimmer in the early night void. Only two or three initially, then more as the blackness spread. Almost touching the bowsprit forward, the moon, seemingly twice as big as when seen from land, started to erupt from the sea, a faded spot of orange tinged with yellow. It was as if the watch had changed in the heavens, the sun going below decks and the moon coming on duty, smiling hello to its companions on the deck of the schooner. It was one of those moments sailors remember forever. When they'd grown old in some dreary place, wondering where their course in life had led them, this sunset would appear in their mind and remind them of the wondrous sights of the world they had once seen.

And then the surreal beauty of the cosmos around them changed in a stark instant.

"Sail ho!" The lookout aloft cried out and pointed to the southeast.

"Schooner to the east, hull down. Wing an' wing downwind, sharp on the wind'ard bow!"

Wake shook himself from his reverie and looked over to Rork standing at the transom. The bosun nodded, and turned his attention aloft to the lookout.

"Has she altered course, son?"

The surprised reply came immediately. "Aye, she has, Bosun! She's done a flyin' jibe an' goin' on a port broad reach, a bit more southerly now! She ain't that old army supply schooner, neither. She's new to me. Looks to me like she spotted us an' turned tail."

Rork looked back at Wake, the two minds ruminating the same questions. Do they chase? For how long? What about the water? *St. James* was close hauled on a port tack. The chase could take a while. Rork knew better than to say it aloud. It was not his decision. It was the captain's. Wake saw them all watching him.

"Bear off, Bosun Rork! Bear off and after her. She's probably up to no good, and we'll have to see."

"Aye, sir. All hands to your sail stations. Faber, I want her turned off the wind smoother than a baby's coo. You take the helm. Stand by the sheets, lads! No time to lose, we've got to close her so's we can catch her in the moonlight. 'Twill be a glorious chase, this one, me lads!"

By the time the moon had ascended fully up above the eastern horizon, *St. James* had borne away from the wind and was crashing along to the south on an intersecting course for the unknown schooner. Both were moving fast, and the distance between them rapidly diminished from seven miles, to five miles, to maybe three. The moonlight cast a silver tint over everything as it rose higher in the sky. Depth perception in the off-light suffered as the men of the *St. James* tried to gauge whether they were still gaining in the chase.

The lookout aloft, now one of the younger sailors with better eyesight since Wake was taking no chances in the night, yelled out his observation.

"Deck there, she's turnin' more southerly!"

"Follow her around, Faber." Wake was busy trying to gauge the point of interception, now made more difficult by the course change. *St. James* was now reaching, still on a port tack, with the suspect vessel ahead and to windward of her.

Rork had arrived at the same conclusion.

"Cuba. She's trying to get to Cuban waters, sir. Thank God she didn't go north into Quicksand Shoals. Be the devil to follow her through those at night."

"Yes, Rork, I'm thinking the same. And we need to stay right on her through the night. I want the big fisherman stays'l sent up. We're too far away from her. We've got to speed up."

"Aye, sir. We'll put it on and see how she'll take it."

"And Rork, all hands are on short water rations as of right now."

Wake regarded Rork's expression and laughed. He spoke loudly for the crew's benefit.

"And just imagine how much prize money that schooner will bring!"

"Aye, me Captain! Enough quid for me whole family to cross ta' America an' live like the nobles they should be! Short water now, an' rich bastards later, sir!"

The men around them were grinning, for they had all been quietly adding up their own share from the future sale of the strange schooner at the Admiralty Court in Key West.

St. James, like a beautiful thoroughbred doing precisely what she was created for, kept up her race to the south into the deep waters of the Straits of Florida—and away from the pleasures of Key West.

The night should have seemed long, but the intensity of the chase and the constant evaluations of *St. James*'s speed made the watches go quickly. The wind backed to the east and held. The moon took its time to cross the sky, allowing the men of the *St. James* to watch their prey edge slightly to windward with each roll of the sea. Gradually, they changed position to windward until they were behind the mystery ship, keeping in her wake throughout the night.

Near the end of the last watch White, who was the petty officer of the deck, noticed that seas were changing. Though the wind was the same—from the east at a strong breeze—the waves started to get higher and steep sided.

It was a sure sign of their location. The schooner had entered the largest river in the world: the Gulf Stream. It stretched from North America to Europe and was deeper, longer, and wider than any other flow of water on earth. Misunderstood and feared for centuries, it was only recently that seamen had measured its current and temperature. Matthew Fontaine Maury, originally of the United States Navy, lately in the Confederate States Navy, had been one of the first to study the Stream and its effects upon ships and the sea. Such concepts were far from the minds of the watch on deck; all they knew or cared was that the schooner was no longer riding over the seas. Now she was fighting them.

St. James was no longer surging along, with water sluicing past the leeward starboard gunwale. The ship was now crashing into each wave and slowing with each collision. Both the pursuer and the prey were having the same difficulty, and the question soon became which one of them would shorten sail in order to reduce the strain on the hull and rig.

Rork and Wake conferred at the stern while holding onto the taut main sheet as the deck bucked beneath them. Wake raised his arm and gestured out over the crazed sea. He yelled above the sounds of the complaining wood and canvas.

"It's the Stream!"

Rork's face showed he didn't understand.

"I said, it's the Stream, Rork. We're in the Gulf Stream!"

The bosun nodded and shrugged his shoulders. "It kicked up fast, sir. How much longer, do ye reckon?"

"It's the opposing wind against the current. As long as the wind's easterly it'll stay this way. All the way to Cuba, or near to it!"

"She'll not take this much longer, sir. The big stays'l 'll have to come down. Look at the masts jerkin' with each sea!"

Rork's point was valid. The masts were jerking and grating at the deck. Sounds of wood creaking from the spars and hull were getting louder. The lookout aloft had long since been ordered down as the mast tops were whipsawing around wildly.

Two hours until dawn. The chess game of the chase had gotten more difficult with the added dimension of fatigue on ship and men. Wake had to hold on to the main backstay to keep upright. He looked again at the big fisherman stays'l bellying out from the fore and main masts and solidly full of the wind. He couldn't wait any longer.

"Bosun, take that stays'l down!"

"Aye, sir. They'll have to shorten too, sir."

The crew turned out on deck with all hands working to douse the ungainly stays'l. Bringing it down to the deck in some sort of organized effort failed when most of the enraged and wild canvas escaped over the lee side and dragged in the water. Now soaked, torn, and twice as heavy, it fought all attempts to get it aboard for half an hour, until they finally managed to manhandle the sail onto the deck. A dozen men lay collapsed upon it, heaving their breaths while they passed furling lashings around it.

Wake went to the foredeck and watched the suspect ship until dawn. She had not shortened sail, and her motion was apparent even in the moonlight from this distance. *St. James* had calmed down a bit, and was not as violent or rapid in her bucking through the waves. But the other schooner was fighting the wind and the seas every foot of the way. Wake didn't know how she kept her spars in her, but it soon was obvious that her over-canvassed masts were not pulling her away from the pursuing naval vessel. Wake leaned on the sampson post, holding on as his schooner plunged through the seas. He stared at the other ship, willing himself into the mind of her captain. Peering across three miles of moonlit water, for hours he watched every move of the other, trying to glean some clue as to who she was and what she was up to. One thing was certain; her commander was competent and strong willed. He would not surrender until the very last minute.

Dawn flooded the sky with a depressing gray light that diffused the silvery shades of the moonlight and made observation of the lead ship more difficult. The moon was faded but still overlooking the scene when the sun reappeared, coming up from the horizon and making the main and fore sails stand out in golden contrast to the dark gray western background. All hands on watch, except the helmsman, crowded the foredeck to see if anything had changed with their rival.

She was still there. A little closer even, but still not close enough.

Old McDougall even deigned to come forward and look at the ship he might be called upon to destroy. He stayed for just a moment, gazed at the other vessel in his noncommittal way, and returned amidship to his guns.

As he passed by Wake he muttered his opinion without stopping. “In this sea, Captain, a quarter mile with solid shot should put ’em in the mind to heave to. Be a bitch ta’ board though. God be with the bastards who have to do that.”

Wake smiled, amazed that McDougall had just said exactly what he had been thinking. There could be no boarding in this sea. They would both have to sail to calmer water for that. And there was no calm water around, except for some bays on the forbidden coast of Cuba.

As if on cue, the lookout standing in the foreshrouds just off the deck said, “Believe that’s land over yonder, boys. Yep, land ho, dead ahead!”

“Dammit, Hutch, make a proper report to the petty officer of the deck!” Rork’s voice took everyone, including Wake, aback. Hutch, the lookout, duly chastened, repeated his information in the prescribed manner to Faber, who had the deck watch. Rork sat down next to his captain.

"Cuba and them Spaniards, sir. Wonder what she'll do now."

"Time will tell. I may break this off if the wind doesn't ease. We're getting pretty far to leeward from Key West. I'll decide at noon."

"Aye, noon it is, sir."

By noon the day was bright and the sea had laid down a bit. Both schooners were still sailing to the south, and the mountains of Cuba were clearly visible. He knew distances at sea were deceiving, but Wake thought they would be in Spanish territorial waters by sunset. The distance between the two ships had narrowed to a mile. Within gunshot for a twelve-pounder but not accurate range in those sea conditions. Since daylight had arrived *St. James* had been flying her ensign but the mystery ship had no colors showing.

Rork stood at the leeward rail, leaving the windward to his captain as custom dictated. The decision had to be made, and made then. And only one man aboard could make it. Wake crossed the deck to the low side.

"Rork, we stay on the chase. Serve the beer until it runs out. Then cut the water rations in half again and serve that. Put the beer and the water in the pantry locker and secure it. There's room in there for it, right?"

"We'll move some of the salt pork barrels out and put the beer an' water in there, sir. "

"Very well. And set the big stays'l again once it's repaired."

"Aye, sir."

Wake studied his second in command.

"You're uncommonly silent, Rork. Why?"

"Well, Captain, I'm thinkin' this here is a uncommon situation, sir. This could go well for us all, or bad for us all. Either way, we're all in it, sir."

Wake nodded agreement and descended into his dark den of privacy. He was exhausted. Lying down on his bunk for just a moment's rest slid him into a sleep that occupied four hours.

"Deck there! A big lugger is coming out of that bay ahead!"

The sound of the lookout's report startled Wake's dreaming mind and he sat bolt upright, almost cracking his head on the beam above. By the time he had reached the main deck, most of the crew on watch was staring off to the south, pointing at a two-masted triangular-sailed vessel standing out to sea, straight at *St. James* and the other ship. The Cuban coast was only three or four miles away. Abruptly, a spot of color appeared in the after rigging of the new vessel: the gold and white colors of the empire of Spain. The lugger was naval, and she was now steering directly for the schooner ahead of *St. James.*

With a determined countenance, Rork shook his head and turned to his captain, who had just come up to the foredeck.

"Captain, I'll be a sheepherder in Bantry if it don't look like the dago navy will be protecting our friend there. Probably escort them into harbor so's us yanks don't violate the precious sanctity of Spain's waters! Won't have her afore she reaches their protection. More's the pity too, sir. Me relatives in Eire would've loved it here. Luck o' the ever bleedin' Irish."

Wake, who usually tried not to show great emotion in front of the crew, believing it lessened the trust they had to have in him, gave in to his frustration.

"Damn, Rork, I think you're right. She'll just make it. Damn it all. Make ready to come about. We'll just head home the minute they come up to her."

But Rork was not right. The fleeing schooner did not rush into the protecting arms of the Spanish Navy. Instead, moments after the lugger had shown her official colors, the mystery schooner bore off to the west and put her sails out wing and wing again. *St. James* was close enough now, less than a mile, that Wake could look through his glass and see figures on the fleeing ship setting more sail.

"By Jesus, Mary and Joseph! I'll not fathom that move,

Captain!"

"I don't either, Rork, but let's follow her around and bear off the wind. And get everything aloft that will catch air! Maybe we won't turn around after all."

Now a puff of smoke showed from the Spaniard and the dull pop of a cannon shot came across the water. A splash erupted two hundred yards behind the other schooner.

"Well, I'll be a son of a bitch! 'Tis the damnedest thing I've ever seen, sir! The dagos are goin' after her."

"Now I've absolutely got to see what's aboard her, Rork. This is getting very interesting."

With all hands in the evolution, *St. James*'s crew completed a very dangerous jibe and brought all sail wing and wing. Every sail aboard was sent up and spread out on either side of the ship as the chase continued to the west with the wind from astern. She rolled to her beams but stayed under the control of the men, for now it took two at the helm. Everyone in the crew was excited as they watched the other ships, pondering the reasons for the actions of the lugger. Wake stared at the Spaniard, waiting for a shot to come his way. But none were fired toward the American naval vessel. Only the mystery ship was a target of the Spanish—three more times.

Their course was now along the Cuban coast, heading for Mexico. This far inshore there was a westerly countercurrent of the Stream that assisted all three vessels in their progress. The two schooners slowly outfooted the lugger, and by sunset she was a distant third place in the bizarre race. Wake went down to the table in his cabin and pulled what charts he had for this area. The drawer held only small-scale general charts with no details of harbors and bays.

The lack of decent charts reinforced the irrefutable fact that he was taking a huge chance. He was leaving his patrol area. His ship was short of water. They were obviously involved in some sort of situation with the Spanish Navy and heading along the coast of a foreign power. Hopefully, and from what Wake could tell, probably, they were outside the territorial waters of Spain. But what exactly was the situation?

Had Spain declared war against the Confederate States while *St. James* was away from Key West? But the other vessel flew no colors. Or did the Spanish know that schooner and have some other reason for trying to capture or destroy her? Wake knew in his gut that the schooner ahead of them was no run-of-the-mill blockade runner. Something was different about her, and he had sensed it from the beginning. The competency of the captain and crew in complicated maneuvers, the determination to carry sail in rough seas, the veering off from the Cuban coast—it all added up to something important, but Wake couldn't deduce what. He did decide that it was important enough to risk the lives of his crew by running extremely low on the water supply. They were going to continue west and capture that ship and the men upon her, wherever they fled.

At the western end of Cuba stood a notorious cape called Cabo San Antonio. Beyond it, across the 150-mile wide Yucatan Channel, lay the coast of Mexico. That much Wake knew from charts and other naval officers. He had heard that the channel was home to a ferocious current moving north between the two coastlines, as well as a southeast wind that came up unimpeded five hundred miles from the South American mainland. But he had never sailed this far west along Cuba and knew he was going fast into a dangerous confrontation blind. The young ship commander thought about the variables of their situation, and how his superiors would later view his decisions, as the schooner raced through the night on the heels of the ship ahead. The range between them had closed to half a mile, the faded moonlight of the last watch making it seem a bit more.

In the light of a swaying lantern in his cabin he and Rork

were studying the skimpy chart of the area. Wake stabbed the chart with a finger and looked at his bosun.

"I place us here, ten miles from Antonio and off the Colorados Labyrinth Islands, by best guess."

Rork stabbed his own finger at a notation on the chart.

"I agree, sir. On deck in the moonlight a minute ago I thought I saw that last island on the chart there. O' course, I been wrong afore. An' I don't want to make the acquaintance of those reefs!"

"Well, I think we're both right on this. Just wish it would calm down enough for a decent sight with the octant. I hate dead reckoning in this strange area. I don't know the currents here."

"Captain, it looks like she might be headin' for goin' round Cuba. Maybe makin' for Jamaica. Or maybe Mexico. Our water won't last near long enough for that, beggin' your pardon, sir."

A larger than usual wave thudded into the quarter of the ship right by Wake's back, and he lurched across the table as the hull dropped away.

"Yes, I know that. We'll turn if we can't get her by the morrow's night. We've got to get her though. There is something going on here. We must get her, Rork."

"Can we go into a Cuban port for provisions an' water?"

"Only certain ones. None around this part of the coast. We'd probably be taken into custody."

"Jesus above! The luck o' the Irish is holdin' for this crew. The devil is laughin' tonight."

"Now that the beer's gone, how much water's left?"

"Four of the small ones, sir. One was drunk today, and the boat's cask is still there an' full."

"Four small casks for twenty-five men, and we're two or three days from Key West. It's going to be very close. Damn. "

Wake looked at Rork's eyes and suddenly felt much older than his twenty-five years. Then he remembered the date: the 25th day of June. It was his twenty-sixth birthday. He did not tell Rork.

The Gulf Stream hit them again. The genesis for that mighty river started here where the currents of the Caribbean were compressed between Cuba and Mexico and shot out into the Gulf of Mexico and the Straits of Florida. Cabo San Antonio got its reputation from sailors who quickly found themselves in extremely dangerous conditions after they left the lee of Cuba. Antonio was the last protection they had from the current and wind roaring up from the Caribbean. Just after dawn the men of the *St. James* followed their mystery ship out beyond the cape. The Spanish lugger was nowhere in sight.

Fortunately the wind and current were both from the southeast as they roared around the cape. That meant that they did not have the same mountainous seas from the opposing wind they had faced in the Straits of Florida. But it did mean that while they were sailing fast, steering to the south by west, they were actually being carried off by an unknown amount to the north and west. Wake was finally able to get a sun sight at noon. Rork went down to the captain's cabin to see the results of the calculations that would show where they were.

The discussion at the chart table, as Wake completed his mathematics off the celestial tables, centered around the current's direction and strength. That Antonio was still apparently close off their port quarter did not bode well. The current must be very strong. The enemy must now either tack and sail back toward Cuba in order to go eventually to Jamaica, or continue southwesterly and end up in Mexico.

Mexico . . .

Rork didn't quite understand the implications of that destination, so Wake explained the rather dire connotation of the word. He explained that he hoped that they would not sail to Mexico. A more perilous international location could not be found in this part of the world. The Mexicans were currently fighting against French Imperial forces in some of the remote areas of the country, the central region having already been under French control for two years. In July of '62, a puppet Mexican government had voluntarily given up its sovereignty and declared in favor of Archduke Ferdinand Maximilian Joseph, a brother of the emperor of Austria and a subordinate of Emperor Napoleon III of France. However, the newly appointed emperor of Mexico was not doing an effective job of pacifying the country he ruled, even with substantial French military support.

Wake told Rork he had read in the Key West newspaper that Maximilian, as he was known to the world, had finally landed in Mexico with his wife Carlotta a month earlier. He had decided to run his empire in Mexico from that place and legitimize his claim to the new monarchy. Meanwhile, the Mexican patriot Juarez continued to fight on in the northern mountains. The Monroe Doctrine against foreign invasion of the Western Hemisphere sounded magnificent, but in the reality of the Civil War the Americans knew they did not have the strength to eject the Imperial French forces and looked the other way in humiliation. Wake remembered that in the fall of 1863 there had even been some speculation among the officers at the Russell Hotel that the French navy might take pre-emptive action against the lone outpost of Key West, which sat astride their lines of communication to Mexico. Rork recalled the petty officers wondering the same thing at their tavern in Key West, the Anchor Inn. Thankfully, that scare had passed without event.

And if all this wasn't enough, the Mexicans themselves were not especially enamored of Americans since the war eighteen years earlier, which had resulted in a Yankee invasion of their capital and the annexation of over half their country into the United States. Wake didn't know all of the nuances of the political climate in Mexico, but he knew enough to be very concerned. Rork nodded pensively as he thought about the weight on his captain's shoulders.

They discussed the possibility of the mystery ship going into Mexican, now considered French, territorial waters. What could the *St. James* do? The French were supportive of the Confederacy since it drained the U.S. Navy away from confronting them. Would Wake run afoul of a French Navy warship? Even if he did not, might there be a diplomatic protest against a U.S. Navy ship in French waters? Rork knew the protest might take a while to get back to Key West, but when it did it would not be pleasant for Wake to endure. Hot pursuit would not apply, since they did not have evidence at this time that the ship was their enemy, even though no one on *St. James* doubted it at this point.

Whatever the eventual outcome, they were only a short distance from the coast of the Yucatan Peninsula of Mexico, and the decision would have to come quickly. Wake resolved to settle the question of this obvious enemy vessel then and there, and let the powers in Washington deal with the consequences later. After all, he was in a desolate stretch of the Caribbean now and pretty much on his own. Wake said that for some reason he could not cipher, this chase had seemed personal from the beginning, a sentiment that Rork echoed.

The long discussion of currents and winds and political whims gave way to the mathematical establishment of their position, or as close as a celestial sight on a pitching deck and a somewhat trustworthy chronometer would allow. Wake fixed their location as approximately twenty miles southwest of Cabo San Antonio, steering south and sailing at over seven knots an hour. He estimated the current at almost five knots. He further estimated that the time for a tack to the east, in order to beat upwind to Jamaica, would occur in about ten hours. They would continue to follow the suspect vessel. Rork grimly agreed and departed the cabin to exercise the crew at weapons drill one more time, more to occupy their minds and keep them from thinking about the water supply than to improve their skills.

Rork placed McDougall in charge of this drill. The gunner's mate wasted no time in pleasantries, quickly lining up on deck amidships the off watch as well as half those on watch. Each had a cutlass and pistol in a belt or rope around his waist and a musket in his hand. McDougall decided that they may as well fire five rounds from each of the firearms in the direction of the schooner ahead. There was little possibility of a hit, but it would definitely improve morale.

As each man fired his pistol and long gun, the latter in rapid reloaded succession, a cheer went up from the others. They had started the cruise with enough ammunition for thirty rounds apiece of musket ball and twenty for each of the pistols. The ten rounds the sailors got to fire focused their attention on the enemy and its future capture and sale. Like a tonic, it made smiles appear and humor return among the men of the *St. James.* Wake couldn't help but smile also, especially when he thought of the reaction to all of this aboard the ship ahead.

The sunset that evening, the fourth of the chase, brought the men back to melancholy thoughts. On a ship as small as *St. James*, the whole crew was aware of the consequences of their situation, which became the topic of subdued conversation before the mast as much as in the cabins aft. Each of them knew that the ultimate factor was not whether they would or could capture the other schooner, it was if the water would last until a port could be found. They also knew that they were somewhere far outside their patrol area and were going into a situation none of them could predict or control.

As if mocking them, the sun failed to display its usual splendor in farewell, obscured by a trade wind squall line miles off to leeward, the only one they had seen in days. No one stood on the deck and gazed off to the western horizon. Instead they sat up forward around the fore hatch and silently watched their opponent sailing steadily onward ahead of them. No laughter or boasting about spending their prize money. The thirst was starting to hurt. The crew was growing quiet. Both Rork and Wake took note of it.

The whole crew on deck awaited the calculations of the noon sight and the subsequent position. The night and following morning had produced no change in the weather or the relative places of the vessels in the pursuit. The noon position would be the first new information available. From McDougall to Kane, the ship's boy, they all waited and watched the after deck hatch for their captain and bosun to emerge from their conference in the cabin below.

"Well, sir, what do ye think?" Rork looked nervous.

Wake looked up from the table, holding down his navigation instruments with one hand and the miserably meager chart of the coast of Yucatan, Mexico, with the other. Everything on the table was threatening to go over to the deck from the gyrations of the schooner in the now beam seas.

"I think we should see land on the bow soon. Says here there are low sandy hills on the coast, and we should be close to a place called Cozumel. It's a large island off the mainland. I'm pretty sure we are finally out of the damned current now and making good speed over the bottom."

"Captain, I'll be blessed by the saints above! 'Tis appearin' that you were right as rain. Mexico it is. An' now we'll have ta deal with the slimy frog navy, if they show."

"I hope not. We don't need that. I just want to capture that bitch ahead of us and get some water ashore and leave for home."

Rork didn't show the shock of hearing his usually polite captain swear, but he felt it and knew it was a manifestation of the tension they all were feeling. The previous night his captain had made the final momentous decision to continue the pursuit. They were down to three casks of water, not even enough to last the voyage back to Key West. Capture the schooner or not, they were going to have to find water on this coast somewhere. That meant going ashore without permission in a country that was opposed to the Americans.

Wake knew he was in a perilous situation, both physically and politically. He had left his patrol area and endangered his crew and his ship. The only positive way out of this was an immediate capture of the other ship with a valuable cargo aboard. Wake resigned himself not to think about any repercussions, only about the enemy and the water.

The captain and bosun went up on deck and stood by the helm facing the crew that had assembled without being called. Normally, a captain would not brief a crew on the ship's position or decision making. He would order, they would obey. But these were not normal times. These men were on the border of being sick from diminished water intake in the brutal tropical summer sun. And they soon might be faced with a fight for their lives in a naval battle with an unknown enemy. They deserved to know the situation. Wake's voice was dry and raspy as he got right to the point.

"Men, we are off the coast of Mexico. We are going to capture that schooner ahead, one way or another. After we do, we will re-water somewhere on this coast. Right now we have enough water for three more days. Not enough to sail back, but enough to look for water here.

"Today we will sight the coast. Today we will get that ship. We will solve the riddle of this chase. We all saw her reception by the Spanish. There must be someone, or something, on her that was worth it to that schooner's crew to flee this far. We're going to find out what, and we're going to do that today. Rest easy. We may well have to fight her soon."

The crew said not a word. No emotion played on their faces to show their thoughts. They just turned away and went to their watch chores or off-watch rest. Rork's face transformed from serious contemplation to his normal easy smile.

"Aye, Captain Wake. A rougher row to hoe we've not had, but this one will smooth out. I'll see about getting some more rags aloft to catch this breeze an' speed the little darlin' up a bit."

Three hours later they sighted a low blur ahead. Both vessels had borne off the wind slightly and were now rushing on a broad reach over the port quarter, heading more westerly. The blur started to stretch across the entire horizon, with a few bumps scattered along it. The news cheered the men, particularly the younger men who were new to the navy and had not sailed this far away into foreign waters.

The schooner ahead maintained a distance of around a half mile, which fluctuated periodically. McDougall stood by the foremast and eyed the other vessel from the moment land was spotted. Half an hour later he came aft, put a knuckled hand to his brow, and respectfully requested permission to speak to the captain. Rork walked over and joined them.

"Beggin' ye's pardon, Captain, but I've been a thinkin' on that one over there. With our new point o' sailin', maybes we could alter course, ju' a wee bit to windward, an' I could get off a shot. We'd lose ground, sure as a whore smells rotten, sir. But not too much, I'd wager. What've we lost, sir?"

Wake nodded and glanced at Rork.

The bosun sighed. "Worth a try on the gun, sir. But McDougall, my good countryman, what would the bishop say o' your blashemy against the fairer sex. Aye, methinks you're wrong lad, for I once knew a trollop down Wexford way, in Rosslare to be precise, who smelled of roses from her sprit to her counter, an' all between!"

The three of them broke into laughs. Even old sour McDougall chuckled, his face crinkled into an unaccustomed gap-toothed grin as he retorted to his brother Gael.

"Rork, you son o' Eire, ye've got the advantage of youth upon me, lad. For I'm not able to even remember a trollop, rotten or sweet, so many years have passed since that pleasure was mine. So I'll bow to your lordship's wisdom on that one, an' spare a laugh on it too!"

Laughter subsided to smiles, with the rest of the crew staring aft in curiosity at the three men. Not a few of them were smiling too at the sight of old McDougall showing humor during this most serious of times. Wake was grateful to both of the Irishmen for their ability to lighten the tension and return the focus of the crew to the enemy. McDougall soon had the gun crew searching the shot locker for the best specimen. The entire crew grasped the idea at hand and went to their stations for sail handling or gunnery.

The boy Kane at foremast lookout let out a squeaky shout. "Deck there! Her crew's moving about. Somethin's happenin', but I don' know what yet!"

Wake grabbed Rork's arm. "Quick Rork, now before she does something! Head her up!"

"Aye, Captain. Head her up, lad. Stand by ta haul your sheets an' lifts! Haul in!"

Immediately the *St. James* swerved to the left three points and headed farther up toward the eye of the wind. She quickly heeled over and picked up speed. Now they were crashing along, the wind over her deck increased, which made the noises of the sails and rigging louder also. Every man was intently eyeing McDougall and his deck gun crew. The old man was sighting along the barrel now, calmly issuing orders to his crew of six men to adjust the traverse and elevation of the gun. No one else was talking, though all were wishing he would get on with it and fire, for though they were going much faster on this point of sail, they were also heading slightly away from the other ship. It had to be done to free up the gun's ability to fire forward since *St. James* had not altered course, the forward mast and rigging would have continued to mask the gun's sights. But it was taking too long.

Boom!

Smoke covered the schooner for an instant before being blown away on the wind. Twenty-five minds willed the shot to go to the enemy ship. Twenty-five pairs of eyes never left the target. The splash was a satisfactory hundred yards to the starboard of the prey. A cheer of "Hurrah!" went up on the *St. James* as all hands waited to see what the other ship would do. This was when most blockade runners would heave to and accept their fate. But nothing happened.

"Bring her back down to the course and stay on her tail, Rork. McDougall, good shot, man. Make another one even better."

As she came back down to her previous course and lost speed, the gun crew reloaded. McDougall got everyone ready and nodded to Rork.

The order was given again to head up into the wind, and once more the ship sped up and heeled over. This time the gunner didn't need as long to aim, and the gun went off before most in the crew anticipated it.

Boom! . . . and another splash in line but two hundred yards too far aft of the target. It earned another cheer, this one more hoarse.

Kane shouted down from the foremast. "Deck there, sail bearing broad on the looward bow! On the horizon line. Comin' out from shore. Schooner or lugger, sir."

Wake didn't care at this point about any other intruder in his battle. He wanted that ship.

"Keep firing, gunner!"

The gun crew reloaded as fast as they could, with McDougall slowing them down to do it properly. Rork surveyed the approaching ship from a perch in the starboard main shroud ratlines.

"I can see her, sir. Beating out from shore. Be a long while afore she's out to us. By my reckon, we're in open waters anyway, sir."

Boom! Another cheer announced that McDougall had gotten closer.

Wake had to admit after this shot, however, the need to get

St. James back on course behind the target to close the range again. This was all taking too long. They slowed down back on the original course as the gunners reloaded.

Kane yelled out again. "Deck there! There's another one of 'em coming from that big point o' land to port, sir! Ship four points on the port bow. Looks like a lugger rig, like we seen off'n Cuba, sir!"

The large point of land to port, still probably eight miles away, was Cozumel Island, according to Wake's determinations. What looked like a point of land was actually an island. On it was the largest town on the coast. He now wondered if it also had a naval presence there. The sail coming from that direction could be seen from the main deck now. It was coming on fast downwind. The *St. James* had to capture that ship ahead *now*, before the others arrived to protect her.

Rork landed on the deck from aloft with a thud and strode over to his captain.

"Getting' jus' a wee bit interestin' sir. A bit like the marriage party o' a orange an' a green Irish when the two families finally meet. Could be drinkin'. Could be fightin'. No way ta' tell till you're right in the middle!"

"Good God, Rork. How does Eire ever get along without you?"

"A wee bit more boring, sir!"

In spite of the situation, Wake laughed. He then told the helm to bring her up again. McDougall was ready and bent over his gun, sighting and waiting for the roll of the ship. For just the right moment . . .

Boom! . . . but no splash could be seen. Questioning looks at McDougall were met by a slight smile and an upraised hand and index finger, like a teacher requesting attention from his students.

Then they saw it. The wind had carried the sound away so that they could not hear it. But they all saw it and cheered wildly, jumping up and down on the deck and slapping the old man on the shoulders.

The mainsail of the other ship slowly ripped across its belly, with the leeward shrouds whipping around behind it. Soon the sail was severed all the way across from the luff to the leech, flapping thunderously like an enraged wounded animal. Forward of it, the foresail also showed damage, with a smaller tear on the leech where the shot must have passed through it also.

For several seconds the men of the *St. James* stood mesmerized by the destruction they had rendered. Rork soon put an end to that.

"Stand by, the boat's crew! White, get your men and boat ready for boardin'!"

Wake ordered McDougall to reload with cannister shot and have several men with muskets ready on deck to cover the schooner as they approached. He was taking no chances with the other captain, who had already proven his mettle.

As they swept closer to the damaged vessel they saw a red flag hoist up to her main masthead. It shivered and then flew straight out in the wind: the red ensign of a British merchant ship. Figures swarmed around on her decks as they backwinded to the jib and hove her to, wallowing and waiting for the *St. James* to come up to her.

Wake stood by the helmsman and watched his crew as they went into their various evolutions. McDougall and his crew reloaded the deck gun and got the musket men ready. White and his boat crew started to sway the ship's boat out on the fore gaff tackles, as Faber and the rest doused the foresail and readied the mainsail to come down. Rork turned to Wake.

"Request permission to lead the boardin' party, sir."

"Permission granted. Get her under way as soon as possible. I want to get out of here before those two arrive."

Rork followed Wake's gaze to the rapidly approaching ship at windward, and then the one farther away to leeward. The windward one looked to be a large lugger, as the lookout had said. No flag was yet shown on her. But she was heading directly for them and was only a mile or so off. Half an hour at the most, and she would be there. The one to leeward was still too far away to classify, but it was apparent that she was steering for them too.

Soon they were fifty yards to windward of the British vessel and hove to in the undulating seas, swaying out the boat. McDougall came aft.

"Sir, jus' one wee thing. They haven't surrendered proper like yet. Still got the limey ensign showin'. Want me to send 'em some lead an' convince 'em to lower that damned red rag?"

Wake couldn't believe it. McDougall was right. According to the rules of war, they hadn't properly surrendered. He could legally fire into them. Rork scratched his head and lurched over to the shrouds, cupping his hands around his mouth.

"Schooner there! This is the United States Ship *St. James*, and you are captured! Properly surrender this instant by haulin' down that ensign!"

A British-sounding voice came back across the water from a gray-haired man standing at the mainmast by the tangle of the destroyed sail and rigging. "This is a British ship, the *Wendy* of Devon, and we do not surrender. We've done nothing wrong to surrender for. You fired into an innocent ship. You will pay, sir. You will surely pay when London and their lordships of the admiralty hear of this outrage!"

It got very quiet on the *St. James*. The bustle of the crew doing their tasks stopped, and all of them looked to their captain. Rork turned around and faced Wake.

"Orders, sir? Shall we board her?"

The cramps in his stomach spread to Wake's bowels. Nerves in his skin were twitching. Everyone was watching him. He set his jaw, clenched both fists, and fought to overcome the urge to turn and run from this disaster. There was nowhere to run to anyway. There was only one decision to make.

"Rork, tell them we are boarding, and if they show any resistance they will be shot."

When that message was roared over to the other ship, the activity in Wake's crew resumed. Soon the boat and crew, all eight of them armed to the teeth, were on their way across the rough water. Everyone in the crew was watching their progress, except fourteen-year-old Kane, still on lookout at the foremast crosstrees, who brought their attention back to windward.

"Deck there! The lugger to windward has sent up an ensign, sir! Don't know it. Red, white and blue stripes. Big stripes, sir."

Wake looked to windward and saw the big lugger, now a half mile away, sailing fast with battle ensign streaming and two deck guns manned and ready. She slid downwind ahead of *St. James* and rounded up close to the other schooner, which was now being boarded by Rork and his party. As the lugger, as big as *St. James*, came up into the wind, Wake saw the ensign fluttering out astern of the mainsail.

It was the tricolor of the French Navy. . . .

The sailors around Wake grew hushed again, as their captain gripped the pinrail by the mainmast and stared at the French deck guns aimed directly at him. A commotion on the prize vessel caught his attention and he shifted his gaze over to Rork's boarding party.

He could see that they were rounding up the crew and herding them forward. Rork and another man, Jackson it looked like, were yelling something to the water on the far side of the schooner, out of Wake's sight. Jackson was raising his musket and aiming at something in the water, stopped from firing apparently by Rork's uplifted hand. Faber called Wake's attention back to the Frenchman off their bow.

"Sir, what'll we do about her? Looks like they're sayin' somethin', but I don't parley the French lingo."

Faber was correct, the officers on the afterdeck of the lugger were excitedly yelling something toward the *St. James*, but Wake couldn't understand French either. Now the officers were pointing at something in the water, in the same direction that Rork and Jackson were. Some action was taking place on the far side of the enemy ship, where the French and the boarding party could see it, but Wake could not. He was on the point of swearing aloud in frustration when Mason, up on the foredeck, yelled out.

"Escapin in' a boat, sir. Look at 'em! There's a couple of 'em getting' away! Wan' us ta shoot 'em, sir? I think we could get 'em from here!"

Suddenly, a small boat was seen emerging from behind the captured vessel, the three men in it rowing madly in the direction of the French ship. Wake didn't need command of the French language to know that the Frenchmen were cheering on the escapees and taunting the Americans.

"Should we fire, sir?" asked Mason again. Wake wasn't sure what to do at this point, but decided against using the guns.

"No! Wait for now!"

Wake strode aft to the binnacle box and got his telescoping glass. Focusing on the fleeing boat, he examined the men in it. None of them appeared armed. One was black-skinned and another was white with flaming red hair and beard. The older one, on the after pair of oars, was the closest to the *St. James* and the easiest to see. They were getting very close to the French ship, and Wake knew they were safe under the French Navy's protection. As the boat came alongside the lugger, the red-haired man stood up and made an obscene gesture toward the Americans, throwing the French crew into a pandemonium of wild shrieking and yelling. Wake could see the French officers laughing. The man in the stern of the boat, dressed better than the other two, immediately pulled the red-haired one down in a disapproving manner. That older man looked familiar to Wake, but as he was trying to place him in his mind Faber tugged his arm.

"Sir, I said Rork is trying to yell over to us, sir. Oh, here comes our boat."

The *St. James*'s boat was returning with only three men in her. Rork, still on the British schooner, was trying to yell something and was pointing to the boat alongside the French lugger. With all the noise from the Frenchmen, Wake could not make out what Rork was saying. Faber brought Wake's attention back to the lugger.

"Sir, looks like they're leavin'."

The French vessel, her jibs starting to fill as she swung around, was hoisting the small boat aboard. Wake could see the older man from the escape boat standing on the lugger's afterdeck with her officers, all of them looking right at Wake. Rork's bellowing was continuing from the prize vessel, but Wake could only catch part of it. He could tell Rork was upset and was pointing to the departing lugger.

" . . . onders! . . . onders!"

And then it came to him. He couldn't believe it. Rork was yelling 'Saunders'. Instantly he turned his glass on the lugger and focused on the men at the stern, still standing together laughing. He saw him and recognized him now: John Saunders, one of the most notorious blockade runners in Florida, Cuba, and the Bahamas.

Saunders had first come to Wake's attention in '63 off the coast of Sanibel Island on the west coast of Florida. He had deceived Wake then and made a close escape through a false story. Wake had last seen him in Havana the year before and had instigated the Spanish authorities to capture Saunders and destroy his shipping organization in Cuba. However, somehow Saunders had escaped the Havana dungeon and gotten out of Cuba, for Wake had later heard of him in the Abaco Islands of the Bahamas. That had been six months ago, and no later intelligence of his whereabouts was known. Until now.

From the demeanor of Saunders it was clear that he recognized Wake also. By his enthusiastic reception, it was also clear that Saunders was known to the French on this coast. Suddenly several events of the last few days became clear. The Spanish had recognized Saunders' vessel too, but without the warmth of the French. Perhaps he had replaced his Havana depot with one in Mexico, guarded over by the French Navy. Who knew what they had stumbled upon? Wake leaned against the mast and kept the glass focused on the man who had evaded him in three, now four, countries. He still couldn't believe it.

"Sir, Bosun Rork presents his respects and has a message for you, sir!"

White was alongside in their ship's boat and calling up to the captain. Wake reluctantly lowered the glass and nodded at White as the lugger started to diminish in the distance, sailing downwind toward the other ship still approaching.

"Sir, Bosun Rork says to tell ya that there was a fella named Saunders, said you'd know the one, sir, who's on that limey schooner when we's boarded her. Said ta tell ya, sir, that the Saunders fella and two others, a negra an' a limey fella, jumped inta a boat an' rowed like hell over to the froggy navy ship. Did it afore we knew it, sir. Couldn't stop 'em, sir. Bosun Rork looks powerful mad about it, sir. Said he knew the bastard too, an' thought he was dead. Said he was a Reb runner ya got once down in Havany."

Though he already knew all of this, Wake suddenly felt exhausted.

"Very well, White. Did the bosun say anything about the men you did manage to capture? And what about the ship? Any cargo?"

"Aye, sorry about that, sir. I was gonna get ta that part of it. Bosun Rork wants ya ta come see what's aboard of her. Says there's mun . . . munitions, I thinks it is, sir. Guns an' the like. Said you'd be pleased on that!"

Wake looked around his ship. McDougall and the gun crew were still at quarters and ready to fight. Others in the crew, like Mason, were still armed with long guns. Each of them appeared confused at what was transpiring and were looking at Wake. He didn't blame them. He wasn't sure at all himself what was happening.

Feeling forty years older, he lowered himself down the side and into the boat in the rough seas. White's crew rowed him over to where Rork stood waiting for him. The bosun helped him board the schooner. Rork looked as tired as Wake felt. His appearance reminded Wake that they were down to about two casks of water.

"Welcome, sir. Guess you know by now. That bastard John

Saunders was aboard her an' got away in the boat. Didn't know in time to stop 'em, sir. By the time we saw 'em, they were up to that Frenchy lugger sir, an' the lads surely would've hit her if we'd fired. Decided you'd not want *that* kind o' war started, sir! Sorry as hell, sir."

"All right, Rork. What *did* you find on her? White was saying something about guns."

"Aye, guns there are, sir! We made the jackpot o' the derby here, sir! They're all laid out below in munitions crates, jus' as pretty as you please. Limey scum here was takin' 'em into Florida so's the Rebs could kill some more o' us. Arrogant limey pile o' dung who says he's the captain got quiet when we found them beauties, sir. He's as silent as a whore in church now, sir!"

"Please tell about the men found aboard her."

Rork told about the seven men left in the crew who were on deck when he captured the schooner. Four were British Bahamian citizens with their papers, two were probably Cuban, and one sounded like a rebel American. None resisted. The Cubans and American had no papers. Rork had not had time to search the vessel yet, what with all the confusion.

"Rork, is there any water aboard her?"

"No time ta see yet. We'll look an' see right now, sir."

A search of the *Wendy*, for that was her real name, revealed that she had ten casks of water stowed in her hold, next to the guns. An excited howl went up from White when he found and counted the casks. Rork made him check each one for purity. They all seemed potable. Yelling the news over to the *St. James* produced cheers in reply. For the first time in several days Wake felt as if they could make it out of this predicament in good shape.

By this time the sun was starting to descend, but still two or three hours from its set. Even with the drifting from being hove to, the two ships were still several miles off the Mexican coast. Wake decided it was time to get off this coast and sail away before the French got any ideas regarding infringement of their sovereignty and returned. Wake called Rork and White to him at the stern of the prize and gave his orders.

"Rork, you are appointed the prize master. Keep five men with you to sail her. Now, first, get the prisoners over to the *St. James.* I want them shackled on the main deck. Next, get some water over there. We all stay on short rations. After that, I want you ready to sail. We need to leave before the French get ideas. Can you jury-rig that mains'l?"

"Captain, we'll get her sailin' straight away, quick as a rabbit from the hounds."

"Very good. Oh, and search the cabins and every space for any intelligence immediately. I want everything accomplished by sunset. As soon as all that's done, we set sail to the nor'east and Cabo San Antonio. Any questions?"

Neither petty officer raised any.

"Then let's get things done here and get away from this damned coast and those Frenchies!"

Rork nodded his head in agreement. "Aye, sir. We'll get that done in a pig's wink! You'll be lookin' good ta the high Admiral himself when ya bring in this darlin' as a prize to Key West. Not ta mention the fine bit o' prize money she'll fetch on her sale."

Exhausted as he was, Wake had to smile at the optimism of his bosun. "Rork, right you are. Now all we have to do is actually get there!"

Wake had seen the island of Key West come over the horizon many times during his year in Florida, but no landfall was as welcome as this one. It had been three days of hard sailing, with the fair wind and current boosting them along at speeds over the bottom that Wake found hard to believe. Now the famous Stream was helping them, and the assistance provided by that river in the ocean gave Wake the fastest sailing he had ever experienced, sometimes up to eleven knots. *St. James* was moving so fast that he constantly checked his celestial fixes, thinking that an error had been made.

Even with the tremendous speed of the schooner in the perfect weather and current conditions, Wake dared not rescind the water rationing. Since the issue beer and rum had given out, the cask water was all they had. The water had been rationed to all hands equally, even the prisoners, and only four casks were left. It had been very close.

The search of the *Wendy* had revealed some papers, including a letter from a Mr. Thomas Clyde of Nassau that was addressed to a Mr. R. Jomeiene, location not written. Clyde was introducing John Saunders to Jomeiene and commending him as a good contact for future transactions, the content of which was also not explained. Other papers had to do with the registry of the schooner in Nassau and a bill of lading for lumber from Andros Island in the Bahamas to Havana, dated a month earlier. No papers mentioning the rifles were found. Jomeiene sounded like a French name to Wake, though he wasn't sure. It all started to fit.

The rifles were new British Enfields complete with bayonets. Ten were packed in straw in each crate, and twenty crates were stowed in the main hold, enough to arm two or three companies of Confederates. There was much speculation among the men and the petty officers about the destination of the rifles, but no absolute proof was found.

As the ships sailed east toward Key West, there was also much speculation on the value of the *Wendy* and her cargo. The conjecture was in the end settled by McDougall, who listened to all this for two days and finally said, in a voice that was quiet and deliberate, that he thought she was worth every bit of three thousand dollars and would have been worth more if they hadn't had to fire into her. He further offered the opinion that the cargo of rifles was worth about four hundred dollars to the United States government and three to four times that to the government of the rebel states. After McDougall had delivered his considered opinion, the discussions on both ships turned to the ways in which a sailor could spend his share of that money in a port like Key West. The debates culminated in a general consensus that the purveyors of rum and women in Key West, and there were many, would be as happy as the sailors of the *St. James* to see the *Wendy* arrive in port.

In fact, the only people who would not be happy at the sight of the *St. James* and the *Wendy* sailing into the harbor at Key West were the seven prisoners shackled and lashed to the pinrail of the foremast. None of them would talk to Wake beyond stating that they were a legitimate crew with a legitimate cargo bound from the British Bahamas to French Mexico and were the victims of a piratical act by the U.S. Navy. None would talk about Saunders' escape or even why he was aboard the British schooner. The captain, an aptly named stick of a man called Reeks, repeatedly told Wake that the British Consul would make an immediate protest and soon Wake would be the one in custody.

Each day both vessels hove to, and Rork came across by ship's boat to compare both dead reckoning and celestial calculations with his captain. For several months Wake had been teaching Rork the art of fixing one's position by celestial observations and the mathematical tables, but the bosun wasn't yet confident enough to rely upon his own work on a long voyage. Wake and Rork reviewed their daily positions, and the course to Key West in case of separation, but thankfully that possibility never came to pass.

Mid-morning two days later, both ships were sailing up the main channel to the island of Key West. Passing the brown reefs that opened like deadly jaws off both sides of the channel, the schooner and her prize entered the jade waters close by the harbor. The deep blue waters of the Stream were behind them now. The dangers here were not from huge waves but from those jagged reefs just below the surface. The wind became light and confused out of the northeast as they approached, requiring the vessels to short tack up the final leg of the channel. Wake was glad the wind had held until they had found the island. The cask water would not have lasted if they had drifted in light airs out on the Stream.

St. James and the *Wendy* finally arrived in the harbor with the crews listening to the melancholy sound of the Fort Taylor regimental band playing the "Annie Laurie," which it had recently learned and played at its weekly Saturday concerts for the town.

Carter, concentrating on steering at the helm, felt so elated at returning to Key West and its pleasures that he spoke to his commander without being asked a question first.

"Must be Saturday if the band's aplayin', don't cha think?"

This breech of naval etiquette startled Wake, who was equally focused on Carter's steering, but he took it as a sign that the morale of the crew was lifting at their safe return. He didn't reprimand Carter, but in his men's apparent joy Wake did wonder silently if the crew had ever doubted their captain's ability to get them back alive. He knew that their captain certainly had had those doubts.

Glancing aft toward the prize a hundred yards astern of them, he saw that Rork was matching their every move at the almost same moment, tack for tack. The two ships presented a beautiful sight to the people ashore as they glided quietly up the channel in unison, like well-trained wild animals performing in a circus.

Rork, smiling his big grin, leaned out from the main shrouds of the *Wendy* and waved at Wake. Smiling and waving in return, Wake wondered how Rork had felt in those gut-wrenching moments with the French guns ready to blast into them several days ago. Rork never showed fear and Wake was envious of that strength within him, remembering how his own bowels had cramped into knots at that terrifying moment. He wondered if his fear had shown to the crew around him.

"Course, sir? We're at the anchorage."

Carter's voice brought him back to the present and the tricky job of anchoring two ships in the crowded area off the naval docks.

"Yes, well, Carter, steer for that steamer over there and we'll anchor astern of her. Luff her up when we get abeam of Tift's building."

"Aye aye, sir. Luff when abeam o' Tift's building ashore."

Faber, standing with the anchor detail on the foredeck, called aft to his captain.

"Ready with the anchor, sir. Ready with the jibs an' fores'l."

Wake nodded his acknowledgment and replied. "Very good, Faber. When we pass the steamer and the Tift building ashore, we'll luff up and drop the hook."

As Wake gestured to Rork to follow their lead, his eye caught the flash of a glass reflected in the sunlight coming from the squadron's headquarters building. Turning to examine the spot where the flash glared, Wake saw a man in the second-story window with a telescope to his face. It was aimed at the *St. James.* Faber called again from the bow, while stepping over one of the prisoners laying on the deck.

"Abeam now, sir."

Carter brought the helm over and the schooner swung to windward. The ship started losing steerageway as she glided forward, all her sails flapping a protest at being deprived of the wind. As she edged closer toward the steamer just two hundred yards off their bow, the time came for the anchor to be cast.

"Let go the anchor!"

At the captain's order the men on the foredeck cast off the lashing holding the anchor to the gunwale and a splash was heard. Soon the schooner was drifting sternways as the crew paid out the rode through the hawsehole on the starboard bow.

Behind them the *Wendy* was doing the same evolution and falling back on her own hook. Wake couldn't help a smile when he thought of the unknown official in the window watching a naval schooner and her prize coming in from sea and providing such a professional show as that just done. The man in the window was probably the admiral or the chief of his staff—Wake couldn't tell at this distance, but that window was the admiral's.

Whoever it was was probably envious of the commander of such a lovely vessel that had the freedom to go to sea and do what the navy was there to do. Wake thought it must be hell to sit in there and watch others bring in captured enemy ships.

"Holding firm, sir!" came from the foredeck as Faber watched the men belaying the rode on the sampson posts. The lazy coils of the rode were thrown down on the prisoners who were still shackled by the fore pinrail. Wake called to the men at the foremast.

"Douse the jibs and foresail."

Immediately the sails slid down the forestays and the forward mast. Wake turned to the men at the mainmast.

"Lower the peak and halliard. Douse the mainsail, men."

The quiet beauty of the two ships tacking in unison up the channel was now replaced by the swearing and grunting of both crews as they fought to control the heavy canvas along the booms and bowsprits. Furling the sails under the eyes of the squadron called for special care, and the men of the schooner and her prize made a proper harbor stow of the sails, with which no admiral could find fault. Twenty minutes later, when all was completed, Faber came aft. He glanced ashore at the admiral's offices. The flash of the glass was gone from the window.

"Said an' done, Captain. They're all a jealous o' the ol' *St. James* today! Shall I have the gig swung out for you?"

"Yes, Faber. And send a message to Bosun Rork. My compliments on a fine display of seamanship, and I'd be pleased if he would ready himself to accompany me to report to the admiral in half of an hour."

Faber's eyes crinkled into a slight smile but his voice betrayed no emotion as he replied and turned away, continuing to oversee the many chores that needed to be done every time a ship came to anchor.

Wake surveyed the harbor and thought about his upcoming meeting with the admiral. The capture of the *Wendy*, and her neatly packed instruments of death, was a significant victory in this squadron. But the method of that capture would be open to debate at the least, and possibly censure or even worse discipline. Once again Wake went through everything in his mind, and once again he decided that he had made the correct decisions at the times he had made them.

He touched the scar on the side of his face as he leaned against the railing and looked at his prize floating docilely in the harbor. He thought of all it had taken to get her and knew it was worth it. And very shortly he would find out if the man with the glass in that window would agree.

3
Home Port

"Sir, Lieutenant Wake and Bosun Rork, of the naval schooner *St. James*, reporting upon arrival at the port." After making the announcement, the senior yeoman turned on his heel and left the room, securing the door with a thud behind him.

Wake and Rork, dressed in the best uniforms they had, which admittedly were not as clean and pressed as those of the staff officers ashore, stood at attention just inside the office and waited for acknowledgment of their entry. Two men of senior rank were standing next to the table under a window on the other side of the plainly furnished whitewashed room. Turning from the chart they were examining, the admiral and the captain, grim-faced, studied Wake and Rork. Through the open window they could see vessels moving through the harbor. It was this window that had shown the flash of the telescope when *St. James* was sailing to her anchorage. One of these men was probably the man Wake had seen in the window.

The older of the two, Admiral Bluefield, spoke first. The coat of his uniform was draped over the back of his desk chair and his shirt showed no insignia, but his imperious demeanor was warning enough of his rank and position. Bluefield's mouth turned into a sneer and his words came out in a slow monotone as his eyes held Wake's in an intimidating gaze.

"You're late, Mr. Wake. The supply cutter came in from Jefferson two days ago and said you had left there early last week. No one has seen you."

The room became silent and Wake could feel his face turn crimson and heated. He opened his mouth for a reply but stopped. Bluefield was not through yet.

"I saw that you came in today with a prize. That is always good, but it does not excuse your leaving your assigned area without permission. Mr. Wake, you may have impressed my predecessor but you do not impress me, sir. I'll have no rogue ship captains going off for plunder and personal gain while the business of the squadron is left undone. And I'll be damned if a pup of a schooner skipper will desert his area without a very good explanation!"

This time the silence after the statement was long enough that Wake realized he should make some sort of answer. He tore his gaze away from the admiral and glanced at the other man by the chart table, Captain Morris, the chief of the squadron's staff. He had replaced the previous chief of staff, Johnson, who had served the prior squadron commander and then Bluefield. Rumor had it that Johnson had besieged Washington with requests to transfer away from Bluefield, finally being rewarded with command of a division of monitor gunboats at Charleston a month earlier. Morris, tall and thin, almost gaunt, had a noncommittal look that showed Wake was on his own. Rork cleared his throat. Wake tried to sound respectful and confident.

"Yes, sir. I understand that quite well, sir. There was good reason, sir. I'll explain the circumstances of the capture and my absence, sir."

The admiral glanced at his second-in-command as he sat down with his hand still on the chart. Morris followed suit.

"Morris, this will only take a moment. Then we'll get back to that plan."

Bluefield bored in with his cold gray eyes on Wake again and his voice took on a lower tone.

"Wake, get on with it. And quickly, man. We're busy here with important matters."

Wake found himself comparing Bluefield with the predecessor in this room, Admiral Barkley, who had died of fevers and consumption several months earlier. His death came just a week before his transfer north for medical recuperation would have been effected. Wake truly missed Barkley, a respected commander who had been somewhat of a father figure to him. The old veteran sailor had grown to trust the young man with responsibilities usually given to more senior officers. It was Barkley who had seen to it that Wake had been commissioned up from a sailing master of a small sloop gunboat to a lieutenant. It was Barkley who had given Wake command of the *St. James.*

Both admirals were in their sixties, somewhat overweight and graying. Both had done at least forty-five years in the navy. But there the similarities between the two flag officers stopped. Where Barkley was self-confident but polite, Bluefield was arrogant and usually mean-spirited. It was not so much what the man said, but how he said it and the look in his eyes when he conveyed the words. It was as if he hated his assignment and the men under him. Wake had seen little of the new admiral but did not like what he had observed.

Bluefield, it was rumored over drinks among the junior officers at the Rum and Randy Tavern, had been refused a more active command in this war because of his demeanor during the war with Mexico twenty years before. The story was told by a lieutenant commander who claimed to have heard it from an old gunner on the *Octorara.* It seemed that Bluefield, then a lieutenant himself, had refused to go up a river by ship's boat to reconnoiter a Mexican fortified position without an army patrol along the river bank in support. This had the effect of angering his captain and embarrassing the commodore of the squadron on that coast in front of his army counterparts. Bluefield, it was further said, only made admiral recently because of the death of senior men above him. This command was given as some sort of favor to a politician who was a friend of Bluefield. To Wake's knowledge, the admiral had not commanded a ship in almost fifteen years and had been stationed at naval yards since then.

"I said get on with it, man. Are you deaf as well as incompetent?"

"Sir, I was just forming my thoughts."

Again Rork cleared his throat, this time also nudging Wake slightly with his boot. Both were still at attention.

"Sir, it is true that we left Fortress Jefferson a week ago bound for this port. It should have been a two-day passage, but we spied a strange vessel just east of the Tortugas and fell in to inspect her. However, she refused to submit and instead sailed off to the south, toward Cuba. We chased her, close behind. Her behavior was very suspicious, and I felt that we should continue the chase to determine exactly what she was about in our waters."

Wake paused for a breath, glancing at Morris, who was staring out the window at the ships in the anchorage. Bluefield had no time for a pause.

"God's teeth, man, get on with the damned report!"

"Aye, sir. Well, we chased her across the Stream and down to the Cuban coast. And then the Spanish Navy came out to intercept us."

"Oh Lord above. Tell me you did not run afoul of the Spaniards! Do we have a problem with them now? Were you in their waters?"

"No, sir. We were just outside their waters by a mile or two. No problem with the Spanish at all. In fact, they fired on the schooner we were chasing and she fled from that coast, heading along the countercurrent westbound. Couldn't understand why the Spanish did that at the time, but events solved that riddle for us later, Admiral."

Wake now had the admiral's, and Morris's, undivided attention. They would be responsible for anything Wake did with a foreign power. He could see their minds calculating what damages they might be called upon to explain or mitigate.

"By this point I knew, sir, just knew, that the schooner was something of substantial value and needed to be caught. So we continued the chase and ended up on the Yucatan coast of Mexico."

The reaction of both senior officers was an identical gasp and a tightening of their hands upon the chair arms. No one said a word for a moment until Bluefield nodded for Wake to resume the story.

Wake, assisted occasionally by Rork, then told the details of how they came to capture the British schooner as the French Navy bore down on them.

"And so, sir, we sailed into the harbor with the *Wendy* about an hour ago. Upon my return to the ship I will get the armaments off her and over to the armory ashore for safekeeping. My reports have been given to the yeoman for your review, sir."

During the time taken by the explanation of the capture both Bluefield and Morris were silent as they listened to Wake. They made no sign of approval or disapproval of his actions. Indeed, Morris had been silent the entire time since Wake's arrival. Now, following the culmination of the narrative given him, the admiral marched over to his desk and picked up a piece of paper lying atop a stack of reports. Thrusting it at Wake, the sneer returned to his face. Bluefield's voice picked up an octave and he jabbed his finger in the air at Wake and Rork.

"Wake, the capture was a damn lucky thing for you. That is, if what you say is accurate and you've not gotten me in some insane mess with the dago or frog navies! That luck that got you that schooner just might have overshadowed your impertinence in gallivanting off to Mexico. Mexico, of all places. Can you believe it, Morris?"

Captain Morris shifted in his seat and said nothing but nodded and adjusted the spectacles on his face while Bluefield returned to Wake.

"But that luck doesn't compensate for your insulting one of the senior army officers of this area! Read this correspondence, young Mister Wake, and now explain that!"

Wake took the paper from the admiral's hand and focused on the writing. It had a grandiose letterhead proclaiming it to be stationery of Colonel Jonathan Grosland of the 52nd New Jersey Artillery. As he read it, Wake felt anger surging within himself.

17th day of June, 1864

My Dear Admiral Bluefield,

I find myself writing this missive to you in exasperation over the conduct of one of your junior officers, a Lieutenant Peter Wake, who commands a schooner in these waters. His behavior unfortunately and regretfully necessitates this memorandum.

He and his men were requested by me to search for and return some miscreant deserters. He did this duty quite reluctantly and, upon receiving an invitation to my table at the Regimental Officers' Mess afterward, cast Disrespect upon this Officer and this Regiment by making impertinent and discourteous remarks to a junior officer of this Regiment regarding the said invitation.

This kind of demeanor indicates a lack of discipline, which in these times of peril for our Republic, shows that a man might not be able to do what is necessary for the attainment of his assignment. It was said and done in front of the enlisted men of the schooner. I beg of you to address this breach of military and naval etiquette, so that the officers of this Regiment will see that the honor of the nation's Navy is quite as high as that of her Army.

I look forward, as ever, to sharing your thoughts as to the direction of the conflict in this region and our mutual efforts at contributing to the glory of our cause. I shall be in Key West soon to inspect the companies of the 52nd that are manning the guns of Fort Taylor, and would be honored by your presence for dinner at my quarters there.

Your most humble servant,
Col'nl J'nthn Grosland, Cmdg.
52nd New Jersey Art'lry
United States Army
Fortresses Jefferson & Taylor
Florida

His hands were shaking in rage as Wake looked up from the letter to see Bluefield's face staring at him. Morris, still sitting at the chart table, spoke for the first time.

"Admiral, I see by the clock that we . . ."

"Wait just a moment here, Morris! I want to know what Wake has to say about this mess he has gotten us into."

The vehemence of Bluefield's outburst shocked Rork and Wake, but their glance at Morris found that he was not reacting to the admiral's insult. Wake knew he was in a very dangerous situation. Bluefield appeared out of control. And over a perceived discourtesy. Wake's rage subsided and he struggled to maintain his composure.

"Admiral, we captured the deserters over at the Marquesas for the colonel, shooting one to death when he resisted. Then we returned them all to the colonel's regiment at Jefferson. It *was* a disagreeable task, sir, but we did it.

"Upon our arrival with the prisoners at the fortress, I had to decline an invitation to dine with Colonel Grosland due to wanting to get under way prior to the dark setting in and making the channel unsafe. I meant no disrespect to the man or his regiment, Admiral."

"Well, Wake, it certainly was taken that way. What do you intend to do about this?"

Rork gently nudged Wake's boot again.

"Admiral, I intend to write a memorandum to the colonel apologizing for any offense I may have given and assure him that it was not intentional. It will be delivered this afternoon to Fort Taylor for his review."

Wake gazed over the admiral's shoulder to the harbor through the window. Bluefield stared at the two junior men as Morris got up from his chair at the table and removed his glasses. Morris punctuated the silence, speaking to Bluefield but looking at Wake.

"Admiral, I believe the colonel will be satisfied by that letter and that Wake here has an understanding of his transgression of etiquette. I would suggest, sir, that we concentrate on the matter of the ship disposition plan now that this minor issue is resolved. By your leave, sir, I will dismiss these two men."

"Very well, Morris, let's get back to the damn war."

Morris replied as Bluefield returned to the chart table. "Very good, Admiral. Mr. Wake, Rork, you are both dismissed. Mr. Wake, send a copy of that letter to me. And Wake, provision your schooner and be ready to get under way in forty-eight hours' time. You'll be making a run up the peninsula's west coast to the ships there."

Wake and Rork saluted and fled the room as quietly and quickly as they could. Once outside in the anteroom, Rork stopped and was about to say something to his commander but was preempted by Wake's raised hand.

"Not here, Rork. Later we'll talk."

"Aye, sir. Just a damned shame, sir. Thought you'd be a hero, sir."

"That's enough Rork, we need to get back to the ship. There're many things to accomplish and little time to do it."

They strode out of the outer offices past several astonished yeomen, who apparently had heard much, if not all, of the dialogue in the admiral's office. The clerks were more than a little wary of the look on the faces of Wake and Rork as the two men left the building.

Four hours later Rork joined Wake at the stern of the *St. James* The sun was outdoing its usual evening splendor. Rork didn't like the look on his captain's face—indeed, had been concerned about him the entire afternoon. Wake had left to Rork the details of getting the captured weapons to the armory and dealing with the *St. James*'s provisioning. Wake had concentrated on his letter of apology to Colonel Grosland and had finally sent it off to the fort. Neither had made further mention of the meeting with the admiral.

Standing at the stern of the schooner, looking at the sun descending amidst the clouds, Wake looked as melancholy as Rork had ever seen him.

"A volcano. A volcano for sure, sir."

Wake slightly shook his head and looked at Rork. "What are you talking about, man?"

"That sunset, sir. The sun looks to be a volcano boiling up out of the mountain of that cloud. Pretty as the one in Tenerife, sir. Funny, what a' image the clouds and a sunset can put together, Captain. Never get a tired o' lookin' at what sunsets they have down here. Better than even ol' Ireland."

"That they do have, Rork. These waters have some pretty aspects, to be sure. But they also have their terrors."

"Hells abound, sir. There's terrors everywhere that this ol' son o' Eire's been. Nothin' a wee bit o' rum ashore can't cure or cancel, sir. No sense in your bein' aboard this night, sir. We've got two nights ashore. I'll take the morrow's an' you take tonight's, sir. Head on over to the other officers at the Rum and Randy Tavern there and spill some rum down your gullet. Hold a one o' their comely wenches and dance a jig. Victory—*an' we've had a victory, sir*—demands its spoils. A sailorman can do no less, Captain!"

"Rork, you'll be the corruption of me yet. But perhaps a night ashore and a taste of rum would be welcome." The Rum and Randy Tavern, a forlorn structure located on a dirt lane along the edge of "Bahama Town," where the black Bahamian immigrants of the island lived, was not visited by the elite of Key West. That genteel class, now much impoverished by the war, tended to gather in parlors like the Russell Hotel along Duval Street in the main part of town. The walk out to the Bahamian quarter would be enough to deter them, but the rowdy behavior of the sailors on liberty ashore, even the officers who gathered at the Rum and Randy, scared away even the more adventuresome of the upper class civilians. And even the army provost troops were circumspect in their dealings with the establishments frequented by the enlisted sailors and commissioned officers on their liberty ashore after weeks on the blockade.

The Rum and Randy had its counterparts for the seamen and the petty officers. The lower ratings frequented the notorious Precious Pub, nicknamed the "Poxy Pub," which was located in the center of the black quarters. A dilapidated structure which appeared as if it would collapse at any moment, it had the worst reputation for violence, which was enhanced by the fact they never removed the bloodstains from the walls and floor, lending a slaughterhouse look and smell to the place.

The deck petty officers—boatswains, sailmakers, coxswains and quartermasters—patronized the Anchor Inn just down the lane from the Rum and Randy Tavern. The Anchor featured rooms to let by the hour in the back. Many of the petty officers had their own "shore wives," each of whom was perfectly prepared to swear that she was the wedded bride of whichever man she was with at the moment, should the authorities be rash enough to try to establish some type of law enforcement over the situation. Ropework decorated the walls of the Anchor Inn, which established it as a place of relative refinement, especially compared to the Poxy Pub.

The "black gang" petty officers—coalers, boilermen, enginemen and mechanics—bought their pleasures at the Steam Room, located just outside the gate of the naval repair yard. The customers of this shop were always obvious from their greasy, coal-covered appearance, the dirt *imbedded* in them from their daily work on the newfangled steam engines. Despised by the sailing ship sailors, who were normally fastidious in their habits about keeping a ship clean, the black gang looked down on all others as fools who were at the mercy of the men who kept the modern-powered ships functioning.

Sometimes these various groups, whose gathering places were spaced relatively far apart, would collide in intentional or accidental conflict. At those moments the provost guard would not even attempt to intervene until the companies of Fort Taylor could be roused and the force of a battalion could be applied to subjugate and reoccupy the area in turmoil. Only rarely did it happen, but when it did, the results could be far reaching.

It was two hours past sunset when Wake wandered along the lane toward the officers' tavern. Monthly pay had been distributed that morning to the squadron and the rum was flowing freely in Key West. The sounds of laughter from men and women were heard all along the waterfront and town. Thoughts of the gaiety around him turned Wake's mind to his own life, which had become devoid of that luxury. As he walked on, images of the time when he had known love, in this very town, filled his reflection with images of Linda and the stolen hours they had had together, laughing and crying, making love, but most of all he missed having someone to live for.

Now he had none of that. Linda had rejected him out of the stress of their impossible situation—she was a Southerner in an occupied town, and he one of the Yankee occupiers. And the war was far from over, judging from the newspaper reports coming in from the main battlefields of Tennessee and Virginia. This lack of feminine love, combined with the obvious hostility of his new squadron commander presaging a dismal professional future, made a mockery of the sounds greeting Wake along his path. By the time he reached the Rum and Randy he was in a decidedly foul mood, which the crowded and noisy parlor did nothing to dispel.

"A double shot of your best rum," he said to the burly older man, known as Old Tom, who stood behind the plank bar.

"Aye, then Cuban Toro it is, sir. That'll be ten and five o' them coppers in your pocket, sir."

Though it was twice the going rate of seven cents a shot, it also might be less destructive of his head the next morning. He had a month of pay money in a large wad in his pocket, which showed when he dug out the coins for the barkeep.

"Old Tom, slide the bottle over. I feel like letting my tired mind go on liberty too. No need to be sober till the morrow. I'll pay now for that bottle."

"Aye, Cap. The bottle's yours now. It'll be a good friend."

In the dim far corner a man started playing a fiddle, a plaintive tune that Wake didn't recognize at first but then realized was "Lorena." A sadder song hadn't been heard in this sad war. Wake sat on a barstool and listened as the fiddler was now supported by an officer who sang the lyrics. Half the room was listening, and the other was talking even louder over the music. On his second swig of the bottle with the gaily colored label proclaiming in Spanish it was the rum with the strength of a bull, a dark-haired girl came over and stood next to him.

Leaning over into his face she slyly whispered. "Cap'n Wake, ain't it? Remember me, Annie? Never seen ya take the whole bottle afore. Celebratin' something I can tell. Can I help ya celebrate there, Cap'n? I'm real good at celebratin', Cap'n."

Annie rubbed a thin torso against Wake's arm as her hair brushed his face. She was somewhere around thirty years but had seen a rough life and looked older. Her body may have been impressive at one time, but it now appeared sickly and slumped in a faded gingham dress that did nothing to assist her femininity. Her eyes held a shrewdness manifested in a continual evaluation of the worth and vulnerability of the man in front of her. Their blank gaze was surrounded by wrinkles set into her face by sadness—they were turned down at her eyes and mouth. Annie's voice was low and hoarse with a bit of a middle Atlantic state accent to it, projecting a sour odor that penetrated even the heavy perfume she emanated. That she was the best of the Rum and Randy's girls was not a large statement but did show a relative merit. And she did know men, and what to do and when to do it.

He had seen her many times but never spoken more than "hello" and "no thank you" to her. For some reason he couldn't fathom, her presence was reassuring now, and he didn't want her to leave him. In fact, he was almost desperate that she should stay next to him and share the evening in the tavern. He was tired of being alone, in command and here ashore on liberty.

"Annie, I'm not celebrating anything but that freedom a man has when he's got nothing but money and no one to spend it on. Can I spend it on you? I've got to spend it on somebody, and nobody else wants me."

"Deary, that sounds like a cause for celebratin' to me! The night is jus' startin' and we've got to spend that money in the proper'est way. Let's start out with some o' Old Tom's pork sausage to go with the rum. An' I'll need a glass, deary, 'cause a lady don't drink none outta the bottle now, do she?"

The bottle lasted only another fifteen minutes or so, by Wake's slow-minded calculations, and he knew at that point that his money would be completely gone by sunrise and there was nothing he could do about it now. He let Old Tom and Annie take over his evening and see that he financed what was turning into a major celebration in the tavern. When asked by a lieutenant commander what the occasion was, Wake replied that it was the occasion of his glorious victory over the *Wendy* and the possible engagement to his new sweetheart, Annie. Even as he said it, he knew it sounded stupid, but he didn't care. The rum had lifted the restrictions of what was proper and what was stupid. The lieutenant commander just smiled and walked away to a table of other officers from the *Itasca*, a steam gunboat just arrived at Key West that day for a port call on their way from New York to the Mobile squadron under the famous Farragut. Wake wondered what they thought of the East Gulf Blockading Squadron and its admiral.

The third bottle lasted even less time than the previous ones, and the band of musicians had grown with the addition of a guitar and a banjo. Soon, lively tunes played by the band were subsidized by a laughing Wake and his growing entourage, which now included Annie's friend Liza and a lieutenant named Carter from the harbor ordnance ship. As the evening went on, the frivolity of the tavern was increasing with the amount of money spent. The noise prevented Wake from hearing the comment made by the ensign at the *Itasca* table at first. But when Carter repeated the words and pointed at the steam gunboat ensign, Wake slowly registered them. Carter, a drunken twenty-one year-old who had not seen much of life or war, felt the need to repeat the comment once again, this time louder so that everyone in the tavern could hear.

"That man there says we don't fight in this squadron, we only play transport for the army when they get bored and need a *yachting* excursion."

Carter's attempt to sound offended was mitigated by his inability to stand and glare at the culprit, and the issue would have been dropped then and there if the lieutenant commander from the *Itasca* had not pressed the matter with his own pronouncement to his shipmates.

"Not true, Sidington, not true at all. It seems that the navy at Key West does face an enemy occasionally. I heard today at the squadron offices that some of our gallant sailors actually shot some of their soldier brethren that were trying to take French leave from Jefferson. Heard that it took twenty shots at twenty feet—but they bagged their man! I wonder what they'd do if they ever faced an enemy who shot back?"

Wake stood up from the barstool and faced the officer sitting ten feet away. The lieutenant commander felt Wake's presence and turned around, standing as Wake spoke. "Commander, that remark is a slur against the officers of this squadron, many of whom are in this room tonight. If it was a miscommunication, sir, then say it and we'll take it as an apology and drink on."

"Me, apologize to the likes of you? Go back and suckle on your dolly, boy. Or is she your mamma?"

It amazed Wake how fast the noise level dropped away. Silence was dominating the space between the two men as Wake sized up the man he knew that he now had to fight. The other officer was perhaps five years Wake's senior and had around twenty pounds of weight advantage, but Wake felt that the other's arrogance would lead to his demise in personal combat. The itch of his scar started up and his hand went to scratch the side of his head, an action that implied to others an uncertainty.

Carter said, "Damnation," and Old Tom was coming around the bar with a belaying pin. Annie began tugging on Wake's arm as disdain showed on the lieutenant commander's face. Her voice raised an octave as she tried to salvage her pay for the evening.

"Come on ol' Peter Wake. He's not to spoil our time. Not him, not anybody. Forget the bastard and let's have another tip o' the bottle."

"I haven't heard the commander's apology yet, my dear. Upon a suitable one, we'll all drink on my money to the glory of the squadron."

The movement was fast. Wake barely saw the initial twitch as the lieutenant commander grasped and slung the chair his hand was resting on. Wake's duck was too late to avoid the chair entirely and his shoulder caught part of the impact. It was followed by the lieutenant commander's shoe into Wake's face as he rose from his crouch. The instant pain cleared Wake's head of any rum-sodden fog and he roared out in anger.

"God damn you, sir! Now I'll show you how it is we fight!"

The belaying pin in Old Tom's hands was close by and Wake's eyes fastened onto it for a moment. Suddenly, and without conscious effort, his own hands snatched it as Old Tom was about to crack the *Itasca* officer over the head. The weight in his hands felt good as he shifted it between them. He used enough judgment not to use it overhand but instead to stab forward for the middle of the lieutenant commander's chest as the man lurched toward him. That blow stunned the larger man and Wake delivered his next to his target's mouth.

"Suckle this, you piece of pompous ass. And mind your mouth about the men of this squadron, sir!" This was followed by a knee to the side of the now doubled-over opponent.

Annie was screaming in his ear to go, and go now, with her. Wake felt some sort of slime covering his face, and the pain was starting to arrive in throbbing waves. He let Annie drag him along and out the back door, but not before he cast a glance at the lieutenant commander lying on the floor with his hands holding the bloody gash that had been his mouth. Blood was splashing out of the gash as he tried to speak. Then the door closed behind them as Annie dragged him down a back alley and across another lane to a path that led through the scrub brush.

After a hundred yards they came to a shed, and without knocking Annie entered and lit a candle. In the dim glow of the flame she sat Wake down on a straw tick mattress over a plank frame and looked at his wounds.

"Cap'n, I've got some salve to apply on those scrapes, but you'll have to part with a dollar, deary. Nothin's for free on this here island, 'specially if'n it's a medicine for the sick."

Wake assented and she laid him back on the thin burlap mattress while she salved his cuts and bruises and took away his ripped shirt. He agreed to pay her another dollar to repair the rents on his coat and shirt. Half naked and unable to stand or even sit, he lay back and let her touch him while dressing his wounds. He knew that come morning he would have to pay far more than money for this evening, but he didn't care. Reaching into his trouser pocket he pulled out the rest of his pay money and handed it to her.

"Annie, take all of this and charge me no more tonight. Just pretend you care for me. That's all I ask."

Disappearing outside with the money for a moment, Annie returned, blew out the candle and slid out of her dress, which dropped to the palm weave floor mat as she crawled onto the mattress beside Wake. Despite her hardened demeanor, her body felt soft. He was glad she couldn't see the tears in his eyes in the darkness. Her fingers caressed his chest and arms lightly, and in a surprisingly soft voice she whispered to him.

"'Tis all right now, Peter Wake. Tonight you're safe and soun' with ol' Annie, deary. I'll make that war and those fools of the navy seem far away. Mornin's a long way off, deary."

The events of the long day played in his mind as Wake drifted off to semi-sleep. *Was it really this morning that we sailed into the harbor in our foolish triumph? And just today that my pompous new admiral showed his opinion of me, and the course of my future career. And just tonight that I showed an ass of myself? Oh God, what will tomorrow bring? Will I need witnesses? Who was that lieutenant commander I hurt?*

And then Annie, with the consummate skill of a veteran in her profession, tenderly removed all thoughts of his depressing day from Wake's mind. Until the morning sun showed itself, he was a man and she was a woman, and that was all that mattered.

4
Weighing Anchor

A shaft of sunlight through the unglassed window bored into his eyes like a hot poker. Wake tried to move away from the dazzling light and suddenly dropped off the edge of the mattress frame onto the woven mat with a thud. An oath came forth immediately, followed by a cackle from the woman still in bed.

"Capsized, did ya, Cap'n?"

The humor was lost on Wake as he tried to sit up, shielding his eyes from the glare that seemed to follow him around whichever way he turned his head. His temples throbbed and his mind reeled from the visions passing through it. *Did I really assault a lieutenant commander in front of other officers? Oh God, what have I done?*

Annie had no such reservations regarding the previous night and was mildly perturbed at being awakened at such an early hour, far earlier than she was used to rising. Usually her sailor customers left quietly, but she knew this one would be different. He had been different all night long. No pity clung to her survey of the man on the floor next to her, but a certain curiosity picked at her as she tried to categorize Wake among her men. He just didn't fit in, and she knew that the money she had gained from him the previous evening would probably be the last. But one never knew for sure, and it always paid to be nice to an officer.

"Deary, let me help you up and get you dressed. I'll sew them rips up in a wink and brush off your coat. Then you can look presentable like for the town on the way to your ship."

"Thank you. I'm afraid the rum hurts worse than the wounds do this morning. You'll have to help me find my way back to the tavern."

"Aye, well, Cap'n Wake, but I think the less you're seen 'round the tavern today the better. I'd say that makin' your way back to the *St. James* as quick as a priest from the Protestants would be the smart thing today, sir. That row there last night will be remembered this morn."

The following hour was spent in munching a few biscuits and water while Annie sewed up the shirt and coat of Wake's uniform. The bloodstain on the shirt was mostly hidden by the coat, and the one on the blue sleeve of the jacket was dark enough by now to be less noticeable. One of his sleeve laces had to be resewed also. He had heard that new regulations were going to be made regarding officers' rank insignia, but he had no idea what they would be. Undoubtedly they would require more expenditure on his part. At sea he wore what was comfortable and expected his crew to do likewise. In port under the eyes of the admiral and the populace he had to conform to the uncomfortable regulations.

Wake stood at the door as she brushed him off. He was confused and slightly embarrassed by his relationship with the prostitute and didn't know quite what to say.

"Annie, thank you for getting me out of there last night. I seem to remember you managed to get me away before I could do more damage. I remember us together last night also. Thank you."

The prostitute stood back and looked up into the eyes of the young officer. She had heard it all before and never allowed herself to believe any of it. Her sense of order in the world was absolute, and she didn't need or want any fool disrupting it. It only led to greater hurt, and she was past all that now in her life.

"Peter, you paid me well and I delivered. And I will again with pleasure, deary, as often as the money's real. Now let's get you along to the town and your ship."

Annie started walking away from the shack down the path. For a moment Wake stood watching her, then finally followed when she didn't slow or turn. He had to stride to keep up with her on the pathway through the scrub bush, realizing that she was far more energetic than he this morning.

The path seemed much shorter than it had the previous evening, and before five minutes had passed they were back amongst the houses of the town of Key West and well away from the area of the Rum and Randy Tavern. Annie turned to him and said good-bye. With a light-hearted laugh that made her appear to be years younger, she told him that she would see him again at the tavern—to be sure to bring as much money as he had last night. And then she walked away, leaving Wake to make his way toward Duval Street and the harbor.

As he walked, Wake noticed that something was different this morning in Key West but could not determine what. Then he placed it. There were no sailors or officers in the streets. A few townfolk were about but no navy men. He also noticed that he was getting stares from the civilians walking nearby. A provost marshal patrol was marching away from him down a side street, not with their usual relaxed and indifferent manner but with an agitation plainly visible. It all made Wake uncomfortable and he hurried his gait toward that which was familiar and safe for him—the harbor and his ship.

The familiar voice from the alley to his left halted him in mid-stride.

"Good morning, Peter. I heard about last night. Are you all right?"

Linda Donahue. Standing there in the morning shadows

beside a bakery shop and looking like she had stepped out of one of his daily dreams of her.

She walked toward him, stopping a few feet away. He closed the distance until he could almost touch her. He desperately wanted to but dared not after their farewell six months ago. His eyes said more than his startled words.

"Linda, what are you doing here? Your goods shop doesn't open for an hour. What do you mean, am I 'all right'?"

"Peter, I came this way hoping to see you and make sure you were safe. I thought you might be walking this way back to the navy docks after being ashore last night."

Though plainly dressed in her working smock, she was radiant to him. Mist started to cloud his eyes and his throat felt constricted. He stared at her and stumbled through the words forming in his mind.

"Linda, I'm fine. Linda, you look so beautiful this morning. It's been so long. I've missed you more than I can say. Darling, Linda, I still love you."

"I know that Peter. I've missed you horribly too. I think of you all the time and worry about you. I saw you sail in yesterday with a prize. Then this morning I heard about last night."

Suddenly he realized she had mentioned the night before three times now. Was she aware of Annie? Of the fight at the Rum and Randy? "Linda, last night was something I want to forget. A moment of melancholy that generated a stupid decision. Please forgive me, darling. I'm not like that, and you know that."

"Peter, that fight was something men sometimes do, even men like you. I understand that. But I was worried that you were hurt worse from the stories I heard about the riot."

Wake's mind took in her words and their meaning. She was referring to the fight, not Annie. But a riot?

"Dear, what riot? I had words and then blows with an officer just arrived in port. He insulted my men. But I saw no riot. I left after the officer and I exchanged knocks. What are you talking about, a riot?"

"Peter, the story is all over town that a Lieutenant Wake started a riot at the Rum and Randy Tavern last night that spread to the other navy pubs. They're saying that sailors from the local ships were fighting sailors from visiting ships, or something like that. Dear, it got so bad they called out the troops from Fort Taylor to put down the fighting.

"Where were you last night? You didn't know about the riot? All sailors are confined to their ships or the yard today. The town leaders are upset and everyone is talking about how terrible and undisciplined the Yankee sailors are!"

Everything he had seen so far in his walk through the town now made sense: the absence of sailors, the looks of the civilians, the nervousness of the soldiers. He couldn't believe it. His altercation with that lieutenant commander had just taken a few seconds and he had left. He also realized that he couldn't tell Linda where he had disappeared to after leaving the tavern.

"Linda, darling, I drank too much rum from loneliness last night. I felt insulted and fought that arrogant fool of an officer from a visiting ship. Then I ran from the tavern and passed out from the drink and woke this morn. I know nothing of a riot. This sounds serious."

"Peter, it certainly does. Your name is being used as the instigator. I am so relieved to see you're all right. I was terrified that you were badly wounded or arrested, or both."

"Darling, thank you for telling me this. I've got to get back to the *St. James* right away, but I've got to see you again. Linda, I love you and need you. I need you forever. I've got to see you again and hold you. I *will* see you again, Linda, and nothing can stop me. Even your fear of others seeing us together."

Wake put his arms around her and kissed her, lingering for a long while and savoring the taste and feel and smell of her. Her body gave no resistance and wrapped around his as if no time had passed since their last embrace. Neither let go.

The voices on the street returned Wake and Linda to the world around them. Two women, chattering about the news of the day—the riot last night—walked on without seeing the pair embraced in the dark shadows ten feet away. As the lovers let go of each other Wake saw that Linda was crying.

"I'm sorry to make you cry, dear. I'll make you happy, I promise I will. Just please don't send me away again."

"I know we will be happy, Peter. I was wrong to send you away. I can't live in this crazed world without you. I can't stand it around here. I hate this place and what it has done to us!"

"I'll see you when I get back after this run up the coast. Probably in a week or two. Stay strong, darling. I'll be back soon, then we'll think of a way to lead a normal life."

Another kiss and an emotional good-bye left Wake drained of strength, and he turned to go north to the naval yard. He never looked back for fear his courage would evaporate, marching on toward the inevitable collision with the consequences of the prior evening.

Passing the O'Hara building, one of the highest in the town and a landmark for ships coming in from sea, he spotted another provost patrol by the gate to the naval yard. The patrol of soldiers was questioning a sailor on the street. They were obviously upset. Wake walked by them to the portico and was just about inside when he heard a man calling from behind.

"Lieutenant, may I speak with you for a moment, sir?"

The sergeant of the patrol was speaking to him in a respectful but firm voice. It was clear from his manner that he expected the naval officer to comply. The pit of Wake's stomach cramped, just like it did when in physical danger. Then he remembered that he was an officer and should have nothing to fear from a mere sergeant on guard duty.

"Sergeant, I have just a brief moment. I'm expected aboard my ship. What can I help you with this morning?"

"Sir, we are stopping all sailors who are coming into the yard this morning to ascertain what ship they are from and where they were last night. There was an altercation between some of the sailors and the men of the fort who were called out to quell a riot last night."

"Well, Sergeant, I am not a common sailor, and I know nothing about any riot. Good luck with your endeavors. I am busy."

"Lieutenant, beggin' your pardon, sir. But I see that your uniform is a bit torn and you look to have a bruise on your face, sir. Were you in a fight last night? Were you assaulted?"

Wake was on very dangerous ground. His reply would be remembered and repeated. His wording must be calculated. He mustered an arrogant mien and spoke deliberately, attempting to mimic Admiral Bluefield and the obnoxious lieutenant commander from yesterday.

"Sergeant, I am busy on important business. I do not have time to dawdle on your problems, and I do not like the impertinent tone of your voice! Your disrespect is noted, Sergeant. I command a ship destined for a hot reception by the enemy, and my concentration and effort are upon that. I would suggest that you spend your time more appropriately assisting those of us who are fighting the real enemy. Now, good day and good luck on your assignment!"

The sergeant's face displayed no fear or anger, only the traditional neutral gaze of the noncommissioned officer who has offended his superior's ego and must now deal with that fact.

"Sir, I meant no disrespect, sir. Please take none, sir. I was only inquiring for your safety to see if the ruffians had accosted you. I am surely sorry for offending the lieutenant."

Wake made no reply to that but walked on to the gate, leaving the sergeant standing at the salute while the rest of the soldiers stood open-mouthed. The naval yard gate was ostensibly guarded by an older petty officer detailed from the guardship in the harbor. All morning he had watched the soldiers question sailors outside of the gate. The petty officer, who had been watching the drama play out just twenty feet from his post, straightened up from his bemused slouch against the wall bordering the entrance and knuckled his forehead in an approximate salute as Wake marched past.

"Well said, Lieutenant! Them soldier bastards've had the sore ass agin' us for a long time, an' *we're* the ones doin' the war work 'round this place! They jus' march around an' look pretty."

Wake couldn't help but smile at the predictable comment by the petty officer. But he had to maintain his composure, especially since he had an unknown adversity to face yet this morning.

"Enough said, man. Do your duty."

When he reached the officer's landing and waved over a boat, relief flooded through him. At last he was back where he could breathe and think. He had to find out exactly what had happened last night and what his role was thought to be. There was only one man he could trust now, and he was on the *St. James* waiting for him. The row out to the schooner amidst the crowded harbor seemed to take forever. Rork stood smiling on the main deck when Wake came alongside and climbed up the main chains and shrouds. Rork almost hugged him as he got to the deck.

"Captain! Very good to see you, sir! Was a bit worried, I was. Stories're floating 'round the harbor this mornin' like a wee turd in a chamber pot, they are, sir. An' nary a one of 'em would make the admiral a happy man!"

"Rork, I am more than pleased to be aboard *St. James* myself. Now, tell me what you've heard."

Both men went below to Wake's cabin and settled down in chairs by the chart table. Rork's smile had changed to a grimace as he began.

"Captain, the guard boat rowed round the anchorage at dawn as usual, but this morn they came here straight away and asked for you. Said you was in a bad row at the Rum an' Randy last night that spread to the Poxy Pub an' the ol' Anchor Inn, even to the black gang mechanics over at the Steam Room! 'Course the lads of the Anchor Inn was the most ferocious they say, as you'd expect from the bosuns o' the fleet! Said that some twit of a commander from that steamer gunboat that came in yesterday an' insulted the honor o' us men of the squadron, and *St. James* most particular, an' that you, sir, had made him eat his words quite forceful like. The coxswain said that word went round about it, an' the lads in the other pubs from the yard an' the squadron rose up and defended their honor too from those arrogant steamer bluejackets what just arrived here. That's the word the coxswain had, sir."

"Any word of the commander's condition, Rork?"

"He'll walk an' talk, they say, sir. No bad harm done to 'im 'cept to his pride an' his scupper hole, but that'll heal soon enough, Captain. Seen it enough in me own self, I have, sir. Reminds me o' a time in Waterford town. Now that was a proper row!"

"What of our men ashore? Are they all right?"

"Now that is a bit o' humor, sir. The drinkers of 'em was ashore in the afternoon but came aboard in the evenin' at the end o' their liberty, just after yourself departed. They were getting' liberty today again, but it was tonight, sir. The only ones ashore in the evenin' hours last night was the teetotaler temperance boys, sir, an' they came back on the guard boat afore the big row. See, they wasn't at a pub, but at a dinner room at the ol' church on Duval, sir. Singin' the praises, they was, sir. No, the only lad ashore in a pub last night from this ship was *you*, sir! Made up in spirit for what lacked in numbers, from what we hear, Captain!"

Wake had forgotten that the main liberty party was going to be today and this evening. Now his crew would miss that, and surely would not be pleased.

"I'm afraid the liberty today will not come about, Rork. The men will no doubt blame me."

"Now the men o' this ship, an' the whole lovin' squadron, thinks it's just fine what you did, sir, accordin' to what ol' McDougall heard ashore at the repair dock this morn. But the coxswain of the guard boat says the admiral ain't too pleased. Said the yeomen from the offices said ol' Bluefield was ragin' with fury, sir. Shoutin' and swearin' this mornin', he was, they say. That's why we was so glad to see ya, sir. Thought ya just might be imprisoned for rebellion or such, the way the gossip is flowin' round here."

Wake was stunned. All of this must have happened after he and Annie had crawled into her bed. He had heard nothing of the sort all night. This was serious trouble. Rork had more, and continued.

"Captain, last evenin' orders from the squadron office came aboard for us. Addressed to you, sir, so they're not opened. On the table."

Rork pointed to the familiar blue official envelope that orders were sent in, which lay on the table atop a pile of charts of the Cuban and Mexican coasts. *Was that only yesterday that we brought in the* Wendy *from Mexico?* Wake suddenly felt incredibly tired as he reached for the weighted envelope and tore it open. A small shot weight rolled out and two pages unfolded that proved to be the formal orders to Wake and his command. The naval schooner *St. James* was to proceed as soon as possible to the western coast of Florida with mail, dispatches, sundries, and small arms ammunition, to resupply several named ships from Sanibel Island to Tampa Bay. And to receive from those ships intelligence of the enemy, mail, dispatches, and sundry items for return to the squadron, no later than two weeks hence. Wake, his mind working rapidly, looked up at Rork.

"Anything else come yesterday?"

"Aye, sir. The yard victuallers provisioned us, the squadron yeoman's office delivered some mail an' such, an' several crates came aboard for ships up the west coast. I deducted that we'd be sailin' that way soon."

This was excellent news. The admiral in his wrath to prevent Wake and his crew from enjoying the pleasures of Key West for too long had provided for an excellent reason not to be here any longer. Duty, that burden that frequently ruined pleasure, now called to offer an escape from the ire of an enraged admiral. A crucial factor now crossed Wake's mind.

"Did the coxswain say anything about an arrest or orders for me?"

"Nary any such thing, Captain. Just wanted to know if you were aboard. Looked as if he wanted to give his congratulations!"

That was the most important fact—no order to arrest. Wake permitted himself a slight smile.

"Are we ready to sail?"

Rork's grin showed that his mind was one with his captain's.

"Aye, sir. I got her watered from the lighter this morn early, an' we got food and supplies yesterday to last a couple weeks. Wind is piping up to the east this morn, an' I can get her underway in two shakes o' a bishop's hat!"

"Well then, Rork, that bishop's hat is shaking now. Let's get her out of this harbor right away! We've got orders to carry out. And the sooner the better!"

They emerged on deck a moment later and the crew was called to stations for weighing anchor and making sail. The sun was already two hours into the sky as they hauled with enthusiasm on the rode and the halyards, the sailors walking away with the lines faster than Wake had ever seen them before. A general air of light-hearted fun showed from the crew as they participated in the escape of the most famous man in the squadron, their very own captain.

The east wind provided a perfect beam to quarter reach, the best point of sail for the *St. James*, as they glided out of the harbor in the smooth water behind the reefs and up the Northwest Channel. All hands were watching aft to see if some vessel would come charging along with orders to stop and return, but none came. Still, the crew peered at the southern horizon, until the town and fortress of Key West receded into the distance, looking like a child's toy model of a town.

Nervous as he was, Wake also felt a thrill and pride as they sailed away from the harbor. His pride in his men was never higher. They were willingly forfeiting their liberty, one certainly due them after the dangers and deprivations of the chase to Mexico. Their eagerness to help their captain was heartwarming to him. Even old McDougall was smiling at him from the foremast, where he was cleaning firing strikers.

But it was more than that. His interception by Linda had turned his attitude and outlook around completely. Her words and her eyes and her embrace had filled him with a hope that his future could have meaning. Not even the dire consequences of the previous night's riot—for even he was thinking of it as that now—could diminish his elation.

Wake stood by the main shrouds and breathed in the full-bodied salty air of the Gulf of Mexico. He stretched his limbs and sat on the gunwale, relaxing for the first time in what seemed to be ages. Even the pain from the wounds on his head and shoulder were fading away as he thought of all that had happened in the last twenty-four hours. He had gone from arriving hero of the *Wendy* chase, to undisciplined subordinate to the admiral, to drunken fighter with a visiting superior officer, to tender lover of Annie the whore at the officers' pub. And now this morning he had Linda back, albeit at a distance, and was some sort of roguish champion to the sailors of the squadron. It was all too much, too fast, and as relaxed as he felt, there was a gnawing question within him of what the future would bring.

His next interview with Admiral Bluefield would no doubt make the last one look like a Sunday picnic. And prior to the next meeting with Bluefield, he had to fulfill his apparently routine assignment on the Florida west coast, a place where he had known many tough times in this war. The threatening potential of his mission and his future invaded his soul and displaced the euphoria of his temporary fame and good fortune.

Wake returned to his cabin to begin the navigation plot of his course to the coast, over a hundred miles away. He was at sea again, in command of a ship of war, and there was no room for whimsy. In the dim light of the cabin he struggled to stay awake long enough to complete his initial course entries, finally succumbing to the exhaustion that had taken over his body. An hour later Rork found Wake slumped across the chart table and did not disturb him. He knew the captain of the *St. James* might well need that rest in the days to come.

5
The Jungle Coast

Sanibel Island appeared low on the horizon, sinister in the moonlight, like the hump of a great black monster rising out of the sea in response to this interloper who dared to intrude upon the desolate coast of Florida. Wake had spent quite a lot of time here in the last year, but he had never become used to how he felt when he arrived here after the bustle of Key West. It wasn't just the beauty of the land and sea, the sparseness of habitation, nor even the incredible danger from disease, shoals, and Rebel bullets. Perhaps it was the mystery left behind by the ancient empire of the Calusa that had once governed this coast.

The broad reach was producing a quick passage, and Wake estimated his arrival at Boca Grande to be sometime just before the coming noon. His watch on deck would end just after sunrise, and then he could plunge into the mundane duties he hated: review the provisions list, update the pay list, inspect the stowage of the storeroom, inspect the magazine, check the cash account safe, and write up the monthly report. He sorely wished he had a paymaster or even just a yeoman aboard to help with the clerical duties, but a small schooner with a complement of only twenty-five did not rate either. He remembered that the captains of his family's schooners in New England also had to do their own paperwork, but there was so much less in the merchant service than the naval service. He frequently wondered who actually read all the reports he was required to submit to the squadron office. He suspected few were actually perused, but the failure to turn them in on time was always quickly noted.

Faber was the petty officer of the deck when the call came down from the lookout an hour before the meridian that a large rigged ship was several miles ahead and sailing close-hauled south toward them. Faber's report to Wake down in his cabin included the opinion that it was most certainly the *Gem of the Sea*, the ship they were to meet with first on their passage along the coast. The *Gem of the Sea* was a bark-rigged sailing ship with the duty of guarding the coast from Boca Grande Pass down to Marco Island, a coast with many deserted islands and bays—perfectly suited for the Confederate blockade runners that operated there. The *Gem*, as she was known in the squadron, had the almost impossible task of trying to plug all these holes. She had some smaller sloops and schooners to assist, one of which had been Wake's first naval command. This section of Florida held many recent memories for Wake, some of which were most unpleasant. As he stood on the deck after hearing Faber's report, Wake looked from the ship approaching to the coast of Captiva Island a few miles off to windward, and his hand reached to touch the scar on the side of his face. The battle that produced that scar took place just two score miles from these islands, at a place misnamed the Peace River. Some of the crew from the *Gem* were also at that battle. Wake shook his head at the memories.

Rork came up to him from behind.

"She's left her station at Boca Grande Pass, sir. I wonder what the lads on *Gem* are up to? Perhaps they've gotten word ol' Johnville is back with another runner at Punta Rassa."

Wake smiled at the suggestion. Robert Johnville had a reputation among the Rebels as a blockade runner with a charmed life. He ran cotton and turpentine out to Cuba and the Bahamas, and rum and manufactured goods back into Florida. Occasionally, in a bow to his state's cause, he even brought in munitions for the war effort. Whatever he brought in, he sold it for enormous profits. Captured a couple of times earlier in the war, he had been released repeatedly, but the charm had left him and he was back as a prisoner in Key West, having been caught the latest time on the Caloosahatchee River. One of his schooners, the *Director*, had been destroyed at Punta Rassa several months earlier. Wake remembered that the battle up the Peace River had been with two other vessels of Johnville's flotilla.

"I think not, Rork. Robert Johnville is still our guest at Fort Taylor."

"Maybe another then, sir. There's so many of the devils about on this coast. I'd wager a guinea to a penny she's after one of 'em."

"Well, we'll find out soon enough. When *Gem* gets closer, get *St. James* around on their tack. I want to speak with Captain Baxter, and we can at least send over their mail by heaving line even if they can't stop."

The distance narrowed rapidly and soon Rork had the *St. James* brought around heading south alongside the larger bark. Wake leaned out while hanging onto the port main shrouds and yelled across the agitated water between the two ships to his senior counterpart on the *Gem.*

"Captain Baxter, sir! We are two days out from Key West with mail and provisions for you. Do you wish to heave to and transfer them?"

"No, Mr. Wake! We are after a runner thought to be coming out of the islands by Punta Rassa. I have the ship's boats searching the inside passage and we are bound to rendezvous in several hours. I dare not delay. Send over the mail and return later to transfer the provisions on your way back south."

Wake told Rork to get the mail ready for sending over on a messenger line, then continued his loud conversation with Baxter. The wind and waves created a background noise that made any attempt to speak sound like a scream.

"Captain Baxter, sir! What runner? I thought Johnville was a prisoner at Key West."

"Mr. Wake, evidently some of his men are still operating in these islands. A small sloop was seen there yesterday."

A line was thrown over to the *Gem* by Rork and secured by a bosun's mate there. Next an oilcloth-wrapped package, lashed to a larger line, was hauled across the chasm but not before it dipped into the waves momentarily. Taunting and critiquing by both crews accompanied the procedure as the package finally made it over the gunwale of the bark. Another package similarly dressed came across to the St. James. Seconds later the two ships were unleashed from each other and Wake shouted a farewell.

"Good luck, Captain Baxter! We'll be back this way in a few days."

Baxter waved his good-bye and turned to an officer who was standing there holding a bundle of letters. For the hundredth time Wake was thankful he did not have to stay on the coast at one spot for months at a stretch like the captain and crew of the *Gem of the Sea.*

"Very well, Rork. Get her turned back to the north, and we will set course for Tampa Bay."

A turn through the wind around to port laid the schooner over on a broad starboard reach. *St. James* headed northward, her bowsprit touching on the horizon, as her crew settled into the routine of watch keeping and deck and sail chores. Wake returned to his documentary duties in his cabin while Faber eyed the set of the sails and Rork went forward to inspect the ground tackle.

Faber's watch had ended and Rork had the deck when the next cry came from the lookout in the crosstrees. In his cabin

Wake could hear it all above him as he struggled with the proper format of the ledger book on pay dispersion and pay deduction.

"Deck there! Sail broad on the starboard bow. Sloop or cutter rig. By the large island, behind that point, an' headin' nor'wes' sorta."

Rork's bellow in reply was loud even for Wake below decks.

"An' what does she look to you, Thatcher?"

"Don' know her, Bosun! Don't look right to me though. She's jus' luffed up and worn 'round to go back behind the island. No refugee boat would do that."

Seconds later Rork was in Wake's cabin.

"I heard the lookout, Rork. We're off Lacosta Island, aren't we?"

"Aye, that we are, sir. Twarn't one o' the *Gem*'s boats and probably not one o' the Useppa refugee boats. Sounds a bit daft, sir, but I'm awondering if it's the runner Captain Baxter was talking of. Maybe she somehow got past the *Gem*'s boat amongst those islands in there and is coming out Boca Grande Passage thinkin' ol' *Gem*'s agone away."

"The wind will still serve to get us in there after her, right?"

"Right as rain, sir! We'll have a good run inshore after 'em and catch the nippers just when they think they're as safe as a fox in a henhouse."

"Very good, let's get *St. James* close-hauled and get in there before she has a chance to get too far away from us. Get the boat ready in case we have to go into the shallows after her."

Rork bounded up the ladder and issued the expected orders to the crew who were already at their stations preparing to bring the schooner closer to the wind. As she came around to the east, the *St. James* picked up speed and heeled over, the wash along her lee port railing making a loud and constant swish of apparent satisfaction. The increased apparent wind in her rigging started to hum in concert with the flapping of the mainsail's leech. Wake felt she was communicating to him, happy that she was able to move on a close reach bounding through the small seas. Even the sailors' manner changed as they replaced the routine of a coastal supply run with the prospect of a chase and capture. Everything and everyone seemed to come alive at the notion.

The island was three miles off to the east with the wind from the southeast. Wake and Rork knew the Boca Grande Passage very well, and the bars and shoals that had led many a vessel to its demise posed no threat to them in this good breeze with clear visibility. The crew started to go about the business of readying for a possible fight. McDougall oversaw the readying of the two twelve-pounders, and his mate passed out the small arms. Faber went about the task of making sure all equipment was secured on deck and aloft, and White prepared the schooner's boat for launching a boarding party. At the end of ten minutes the island was two miles away and Rork was reporting all was ready for whatever might come.

The top of the gaff on the mainsail of the sloop was just visible over the sabal palms at the northern end of Lacosta Island. The sloop was now heading southerly away from the passage. Moving slowly behind the island and tacking into the wind, it was obvious she was aware of *St. James* and was attempting to escape, something no refugee vessel would do. Wake was now convinced that she was a blockade runner.

"Keep a good eye on her, Rork. We've got a flood tide, which should help us get up behind the island quickly, but then we've got to get her before she can lose us in the small islands."

"Aye, sir. She may try to sail down by Useppa to escape. White will have to go after her through those shoals."

Just as they rounded the point of Lacosta, the lookout lost sight of the suspect craft's sail over the trees. *St. James* came roaring up close alongside the point, heading as far up into the wind as possible behind the island to maintain speed. The sloop was a mile away, beached on the island with her sails down and crew scrambling ashore into the thick jungle.

"Bloody buggers have done it now! We'll have to go in and get them, sir."

"Yes, you're right, Rork. Get all hands ready to go ashore except for Faber and four men. I want this done quickly. I'll take the right wing and you take the left. Four men to guard the sloop and eight each to follow us. Load them all into the boat for one trip."

An acknowledgment of the orders from Rork was the prelude to frenzied activity on the schooner's deck as she came up into the wind and luffed to a point right off the beached sloop. The crew turned to with a will as they fairly threw the schooner's boat into the water alongside as the schooner's sails came tumbling down and the anchor slid into the water. Within moments, the boat, which usually carried ten men but now carried twenty with all of their accouterments, was heading the fifty yards ashore.

The three details immediately went to their areas upon splashing ashore, having been told of their tasks while in the boat. Four men went to the beached sloop and searched it, finding no prisoners but five bales of cotton and ten kegs of turpentine. Wake's party ran north along the beach for a hundred yards then turned inland. Rork's group did likewise to the south.

The run decreased to a slog as Wake's men slashed their way through the tangled vines and thick undergrowth. Any attempt to be stealthy was lost as the sailors cursed and stumbled in their unaccustomed mission. Inside the jungle it was dark, and Wake realized suddenly that the late afternoon was arriving and that this thing had to be done quickly, before nightfall. He did not want his crew scattered through the island in the dark. Too many disasters could and would befall them.

"All right now, men. Spread out with fifteen paces between us into a line, then we'll head south. The bosun is doing the same and heading north, so we should find the Rebels between us. Make sure of who you are looking at in front of you. It could be our own crew. Everyone understand that?"

A chorus of "aye's" replied. The men spread out so that each was only barely visible to the next, such was the extent of the forest around them. They slashed and staggered and cursed their way in a ragged line south. Wake knew the line was not straight but hoped he could cover around five hundred feet of frontage with his small group.

The shadows were growing longer and Wake's worries were escalating when they heard voices to their front. Curses and laughs coming at them indicated it was not the enemy but their own shipmates slogging toward them. Soon the distinctive sound of Rork could be heard above the rest.

"By the power of God above, I will cut your throat me own-self if you don't stop that caterwauling Goldston! Bloody fool. I've seen whores in church better behaved than you."

Wake couldn't repress a smile at the sound of his friend. Looking over at the next man in his line he saw a similar reaction as Goldston replied.

"Damnation, Bosun. I jes' never seen anything like this place. Even the damned plants in here are trying to kill me, what with 'em tripping my feet and cutting my arms and all. And these flying critters are in my hair, Bosun. They're drivin' me mad. We need to go back to the ship."

Wake called out to the other group. It was time to gather and go back to the beach. At least they had the sloop.

"Rork, can you hear me?"

"Aye, sir. Ye're right in front of me. Yes, I can see you now, Captain."

"Gather the men together and head back to the beach, Rork."

Several comments from throughout the forest relayed enthusiastic support of that idea, and the men started to gather in from the western ends of the two lines as Rork and Wake met under a giant gumbo limbo tree. Rork, normally unflappable and humorous, was covered with sweat and greenish-brown stains from the swampy undergrowth. A serious sound in his voice alerted Wake.

"Captain, they could be right next to us in this mess and

we'd never see the devils. We're a fish out of the water, sure as hell, sir."

"Yes, I know. Night is coming and we'd better get back and secure the prize. Leave the Rebs to their own reward in this place. Let's go."

The sound was definite but muffled by the trees. Rork responded first.

"Sweet Jesus, Captain. That's a gunshot from the beach. They're attacking the boat crew!"

More shots came through the jungle. The sailors were yelling and running toward the beach, hoping their loud approach would scare off the attackers of their comrades on the beach. Hurtling over vines and bushes, wildly swinging their cutlasses, the disheveled men held their muskets high in the air as they sometimes ran, sometimes fell forward, toward the beach. Wake was running and yelling like the rest, all semblance of commanding manner lost as all of them scrambled their way back to the eastern shoreline of the island. Wake's mind played images of what he would find at the sloop as he struggled to keep calm enough to determine what he would do when he got there.

They suddenly emerged from the darkness onto the beach. To their right, fifty yards south along the sand, was the beached sloop and ship's boat. Two men in blue were lying doubled over by the water's edge, a third kneeling and using a musket as a crutch as he tied a bandage around his thigh. Two others were kneeling with muskets pointed at the woods to their front, with four other bodies sprawled in unnatural poses at the line of the jungle behind the sand. Two shotguns and a pistol were visible close by them. One of the enemy bodies moved an arm slowly, not the jerking movements of a man in pain but the lethargic motion of one who is beyond pain and near death. Then it stopped moving, its arm still outstretched and looking for all the world like it was beckoning others to follow him into death.

Yelling that two more of the Rebels had gone into the woods that way, the two sailors pointing muskets let off their shots in the direction of the Confederates' flight. Rork immediately told his party to follow him and plunged into the bush in pursuit. Wake told four of his party to stand picket guard at the tree line and the rest to tend to the wounded. Coxswain White was one of those, Wake saw as he arrived panting at the sloop. White was clutching his left side tightly, his arm trembling uncontrollably.

"White, what happened? Can you speak?"

"I'm sorry, sir. I'm damned sorry they got us, Captain. Came outta the woods while Mason an' I were below in the sloop looking for any Reb papers for ya. Berger was pushing off the ship's boat. They musta' crept quiet-like up to Jackson and Scarbond who were out on picket. Scarbond's gut shot, Captain. Jackson took one in the leg but kept on firing. I think Mason and Berger are unhurt.

"Them Rebs didn't run off that far from the boat, Captain. Jus' laid down and let us run past 'em. Then they jumped us. Never thought they'd have guns, most o' them runners don't. Figured they'd give up easy when we ran 'em down. Thank God for McDougall and his men on the ol' *Saint*, Captain. Cut loose and knocked down a couple of 'em with musket shots. Damned sorry on all this, Captain."

"What about you, White? How is your wound?"

"Caught one that went in my side and out my back, sir. Here 'tis."

White rolled over to show Wake the wound, which showed a ragged small gash in his left side by the lower rib where the bullet had tumbled as it entered. Eight inches further around on his back another gash showed the exit. Both were bleeding steadily, but not gushing, so no artery was severed. With pressure to close the holes, the bleeding should stop eventually. Wake thought that perhaps White would live, the bullet apparently having not penetrated into the region of the most important organs, but it couldn't have missed them by more than an inch or so.

"We'll get you some good medicines for the pain, White. It looks to me that you'll get a passage to Key West. You'll be a naval hero there. Free rum at the Anchor Inn to a man with a good-looking wound."

White groaned and grimaced a smile. Wake was glad to see it.

"You did well, Coxswain. You did just fine. Don't worry about anything. You did your duty just fine."

As he spoke, Wake held White's arm to try to steady it from shaking. He realized that White was fighting to retain his self-control. He also realized that the pain of his wounded men was more than the laudanum aboard *St. James* could handle. He would need help from the *Gem of the Sea* quickly to treat these men. It was crucial to get them medical treatment and keep their wounds as clean as possible until then.

Scarbond had two sailors trying to bandage his wound as Wake knelt down beside him. The bandage was not securing well due to the location of the wound in the front of the lower abdomen. A four-inch-wide crater showed in Scarbond's torso. The sailors were cursing at him to stop moving and let them pull the bandage tighter. Scarbond was sobbing and swearing loudly back at the sailors as he gripped his stomach and doubled over from the waves of pain that radiated out from the wound. The sailors had to pry his arms away from his body to reapply the dressing. Wake helped to hold the arms as he looked into the face of the nineteen-year-old from Ohio who had been in the Navy for only four months.

"Arthur, let them help you. We've got to get a dressing on this wound. We'll get you something for the pain quickly, but this bleeding needs to be stopped. Arthur, listen to me."

Scarbond made no reply or acknowledgment of recognizing his captain. His agony transcended any normal communication as his screaming got louder. A cursory examination of his wound showed that it was probably from one of the shotguns lying by the Rebels. It was massive and the intestines were visible as they partially emerged from the crater. Blood was everywhere, and the sailors who were trying to help had terrified expressions. Wake helped them manhandle Scarbond's bandage onto the wound and cinch it down around his middle, and then he assisted in carrying him to the boat. White, already in the boat by then, grabbed Scarbond's arms and dragged him over the gunwale with the assistance of two other men, all three gritting their teeth against the screams of the youngster. Jackson, limping along in the shallow water, came up last to the boat and Wake helped him aboard.

"How's your leg, Jackson?"

Jackson smiled through clenched teeth.

"Not bad, Captain. Hurts like hell an' they'll have to dig the lead out, but it don't feel like it's in too far. Just don't let that fool Mason mess about with it, please, sir."

Mason, Jackson's friend and messmate, was organizing sailors to row the wounded out to the schooner. He turned to look down at Wake standing waist deep in the water.

"I'll get 'em all out to McDougall, sir. That ol' salter'll know what do to for 'em, Captain. Just please get the two that's run off. And be careful like, sir."

"Very good, Mason. Tell McDougall to give them all the laudanum we've got aboard. He knows the medicine chest."

Turning back toward the beach, Wake heard noises coming from off in the woods as he waded ashore. The men on picket stared into the gloom of the forest trying to make out what was happening as the noises became discernible as voices in anger. Nervous fingers loudly cocked muskets. Wake saw the look in the eyes of the pickets.

"Mark your targets, men. Make sure they're not our own coming back. Let's not have *that* happen."

The four sailors acknowledged the reminder and eased up a bit but still watched the jungle darkness in front of them intently.

Two seamen were shoving the sloop into deeper water before the tide turned to ebb. Wake assisted them with an eye and an ear turned to the bushes for intelligence of how Rork's party was faring. Straining with all their might, the three men finally succeeded in budging the heavily loaded sloop into floating on her own with an anchor holding the vessel to the current, as Wake observed that the wind from the south was now starting to diminish in strength. Looking at the flood tide line on the beach, Wake saw that they were at the top of the tide now, and the ebb would soon start.

That greatly complicated his situation with the wounded men. The *Gem* was off twenty miles to the south, the wind was dying, the daylight was ending, and the nearest help lay on Useppa Island, which was two miles against the ebb current in the bay. The wounded needed help right now.

Words became distinguishable from the woods now and it was obvious the sailors were returning to the beach. Rork himself could be heard as he bellowed at some bluejacket.

"I want them alive and talking, you fool! I'll not tell ye agin without some pain attached, Connelly. Lord above, deliver me from fools such as these!"

The crashing sounds grew louder and eventually manifested in a column of sweating cursing sailors emerging from the shadows, dragging two trussed up wretches who were bleeding from a dozen cuts. Some of the cuts were large. Rork came up to Wake and reported. He looked exhausted.

"Captain, we got the Rebs. They're cut up a bit from being uncooperative at first in marchin' back here, but they'll survive. They jes' needed to have a little encouragement, not too much though, sir. I'll wager they'll be singin' like birds for food in a hour. No one of ours is hurt. How're our men from the beach party?"

Wake relayed the condition of the wounded and the need for medical assistance. Rork nodded his understanding of the situation then jerked his head up to the right and stared over Wake's left shoulder.

"By the Saints above and all around us, Captain. Methinks help may be here!"

Wake spun around and saw a small craft under sail and oar

approaching from the south. An older man standing by the tabernacled mast shouted out.

"Captain Wake, sir! Is that you?"

Wake didn't recognize the boat or the man. He hoped they would be some sort of help—he had all the adversity he could handle just then. Several of the seamen standing on the beach watched the boat approach and had their muskets held in readiness. Rork stood next to Wake as the latter replied to the stranger.

"Yes, I am Captain Peter Wake of the United States Naval schooner *St. James.* Who are you and what is your business about here?"

"I am Hervey Newton of Useppa Island, sir. We heard the shooting and saw you had wounded through our long glass. With the wind dropping, we thought you would need assistance, Captain."

Wake did not have his telescope with him on the beach, but he now started to recognize the voice and stature of the man in the boat. Hervey Newton was an old man in his seventies, father of one of the women refugees on the island whose husband was away at war with the refugee militia that was now called the 2nd U.S. Florida Cavalry. Wake had met him the year before at a gathering on the island when he had been supporting efforts to form the militia made up of pro-Union refugees on Useppa hiding out from the Confederates on the mainland. Newton was a trustworthy man who had fought in the Seminole wars in the 40s and 50s. He was too old to fight for his country anymore, but he was doing what he could to help with what he had available. The boat was only a hundred yards away and the sailors on the beach were making a commotion and pointing to the crew of the boat. They were women. They had sailed and rowed two miles to get there.

"Thank you, Mr. Newton. Yes, we can use your help. Come ashore, please."

Newton nodded, turned, and relayed something to his female crew. The sail, limp from lack of wind, came down the mast and the oars came inboard as the vessel slid into the shallows off the beach. Two of the four women rowing jumped overboard and pulled the bow up as a couple of surprised seamen ran to help. Newton stepped off when the boat stopped and strode over to Wake and Rork.

"Captain, good to meet you again, sir. Did you get 'em all? We saw 'em traitorous vermin hide behind the Barras Islands as the *Gem*'s boats sailed by going south, but we couldn't get to the sailors in time. Then the rascal Rebels came out and made for Boca Grande, and we thought they had made their ill-gotten profit since the *Gem* had left too. That's when your welcome arrival put paid to their notions, Captain. Well done, sir!"

Newton looked over at the captured sloop piled with cotton bales on her deck and surveyed the situation ashore and afloat. He was excited and acting years younger than age. Wake liked the man and his spirit.

"It was no plan, Mr. Newton. Just luck that we saw them while sailing up the coast."

"Luck, Captain Wake? Luck is not given, sir—it is made! And you made it today. We hear that that sloop is the last of Johnville's vessels, and good riddance to all his kith and kin.

"Now, what about your wounded? Can we help? We have not much, but we can make them comfortable until Baxter can return with his surgeon. One of my women here is part Seminole and knows their medicine herb ways."

Rork glanced quizzically at Wake. Newton's women were approaching closely. Wake sighed.

"Mr. Newton, we'll be very appreciative of any help you can give, sir. I have two badly wounded and one less so. All need help. Their wounds need to be cleaned and bandaged again, and they need to rest easy. Do you have anything for great pain, sir?" Wake went on to describe the wounds.

Newton's expression was hardening as he heard the description. His reply started but was interrupted by a dark-haired woman in a faded brown smock who had walked up as Wake was talking.

"Yes, we can help. My name is Sofira Thomaston. I have earth medicines at Useppa that can help. Mr. Newton, we need to get those men back where we can tend them. We should do that now, sir."

With that simple statement the woman reversed her steps and spoke quietly to the other ladies who waited twenty feet away, whose demeanors deferred to the Indian woman as their apparent leader. They all started to wade back out to their boat as Newton spoke to the astonished Wake and Rork.

"Sofira is half Seminole. She and her husband and baby arrived at Useppa six months ago. Her husband is a sergeant now with the refugee troops who're up the river at Fort Myers. She knows herb medicine. She'll take care of your men fine, Captain."

Rork spoke first.

"A real Indian maiden, sir? I've heard o' them but never thought I'd meet one in the person. She looks as like any other lass."

Newton gave Rork a curious stare and spoke to him directly. There was no mistaking the message.

"She's a good girl, sir. I knew her grandfather's family before the last war here just a few years ago. Unfortunately they were on the other side in that sad affair. Her husband's white and a good man and friend too, and he's on our side in this sad affair."

As Rork protested his innocence of intent, Wake decided to change the subject and implement the plan immediately.

"He meant no harm, Mr. Newton. Bosun Rork is from Ireland, as you can readily tell, and has heard of Indians but never seen one. Actually, I haven't either. Now, let us take you and Mrs. Williams up on your kind offer. Rork, get six seamen to row Mr. Newton's boat. Our boat will carry the wounded and return our men back to the *St. James.* I want them under way in ten minutes. And I want to sail north tonight as soon as our men return and the evening land breeze pipes up."

Wake's order meant the wounded had to be transferred from the *St. James,* where McDougall was doing his best for them, to the schooner's boat again. Rork said "Aye, sir," then spun on his heel and walked off bellowing orders.

Newton stood looking at the Irishman's figure recede and shook his head.

"We are a little sensitive about our women, Captain. I am one of two old men left on the island, and am more than a bit protective out of necessity, sir. The bosun appears to be a good man, though, and perhaps I misunderstood his comment."

"You certainly did, Mr. Newton. Sean Rork is as good as they come. He is my friend as well as my senior petty officer. But I completely understand your concerns and appreciate your protective attitude regarding the ladies of the island."

Neither of the men said that which was on their minds. The year before, a naval petty officer had gotten drunk at an celebration in honor of the navy's role in protecting the refugees, and in a animal rage attempted to sexually assault one of the girls on the island. That man had been the bosun of the sloop Wake had commanded at the time. The man had gone insane and subsequently committed suicide before standing trial. Both Wake and Newton remembered the horror of the ordeal well. Rork had been the man's replacement a month later.

"Well, Captain Wake, we'll be going. We'll tend your men as well as we can. They'll be far more comfortable on Useppa than in the small confines of your schooner."

"Thank you, sir. I'll bring the *St. James* to the island on my way back south to Key West in a week or so. *Gem* should be back on station here by then, I'm sure, and their surgeon can give some medicinal help if needed. Thank you again, Mr. Newton. You have been a great help to me and my men, sir."

"Our patriotic duty and honor, sir. Even if they won't let me fight anymore, I still can do something to help out."

Newton waded out to his crude island boat and his ragged but proud feminine crew, who helped him over the side despite his fussing that ladies should not have to do that kind of thing—that he wasn't *that old* yet. Watching him go off in the descending gloom of the dusk, Wake was impressed by the behavior of Newton and the women. In order to arrive at Lacosta when they did, they must have shoved off from Useppa while the skirmish was still ongoing. Not knowing what they would find, they still made their way toward the battle sounds in order to assist. He was also impressed by the attitude of Newton toward the women under his care at the island.

If Wake had been Sergeant Williams, off fighting the Confederates in the interior of Florida, he would have been at least comforted by the fact his wife was as safe as could be expected because of the company of a gentleman who displayed such a protective nature. The thought made him think of Linda and the fact that she had no real protector when he was away from her. An idea started to form within his mind, but it was interrupted by Rork's calling to him that all was ready to shove away from the beach.

Moments later the *St. James's* boat got under way, headed south after the islanders. A myriad of duties devolved upon Wake in the half-light of dusk: an armed anchor watch was set, the prize crew of the sloop under Faber was detailed, a cursory report of the action written and given to Faber for transmittal to the squadron commander, the prisoners were securely lashed to the sloop's mast, and the schooner's arms and ammunition were stowed.

Wake told Faber to try to make Key West if he could or to report to any naval vessel they might intercept along the way. He was admonished to make sure the prisoners made it in good condition to the squadron. So far, they had not been forthcoming with information but just sat in a daze looking at the mounds of sand where their recent compatriots lay underground on the beach. The nature of their endeavor and its outcome was becoming quite clear to them. Wake suspected that one of the surviving pair was the leader of the blockade running effort. He had better clothes than the others in the Confederate crew, and just might be related to Robert Johnville himself. If so, he would be of great interest to the interrogators in Key West. Faber received his orders without comment and proceeded to make ready his vessel and small crew of four. A serious countenance clouded his face as he oversaw his preparations. There was no room for error in his mission.

An hour after his return to the schooner from the beach, Wake watched the total darkness of the tropical night fill the air around the islands where *St. James* lay anchored on the calm waters of the bay. Physically and emotionally exhausted, he sat down at the stern of his ship and looked off at a faint glow on the eastern horizon. He had just registered it in his mind as the moon rising when Rork sat down next to him with a sigh.

"A day to remember, Captain. A hard day, sir."

"Aye, that it is, Rork. And I'll see Scarbond in my mind's eye for many a year. That's a sight I could do without."

"'Tis the nature of the work, Captain. By the by, sir. I meant no disrespect to the lady Indian. I said nothing that I know of that would infer that, Captain."

"I know that Rork, and so does Mr. Newton now. It's just that much has happened in these islands and among these people. They are more than a bit protective here, even of one who is not originally of their own, like that Indian woman. I like that in a people and respect them for it. This is an odd place, but the more I'm here, the more I like it. If only this damned war would stop so that men wouldn't have to get shot over six bales of cotton and some turpentine. What a waste for all of us."

Rork had seen Wake in this mood after battles over the last year, when the bloody consequences of his decisions would haunt him. Rork was a man of the world far beyond this civil conflict in America. His understanding of people and war came from a wider perspective.

"Aye, sir. But that devil McDougall has already figured the adjudication price of the sloop in admiralty court and totaled it at five hundred dollars, maybe more. The fo'c'sle's not angry about what happened today or philosophizing upon it at all. It's a war, like any other, an' they're all bad. But ye've gotta get what ye can, when ye can, Captain."

Wake looked up at Rork, knowing that a story was coming, and finding a smile in his heart for the man next to him. Rork went on undaunted.

" I knew a wench in New York who taught me that, she did. Took no money from me, sir, not a single coin. But she taught me more than most o' the sailors' girls about how to look at life and the bad times. More than any other lass in any other place in the world this ol' son o' Eire has washed up at. 'Bad times are the spaces between the good times,' she taught me, Captain Wake. 'Sometimes they're long spaces an' sometimes they're little wee ones. Ye've jus' got to weather 'em for a bit, an' then things'll be looking up.'"

Wake shook his head and laughed out loud, startling the watch on deck.

"Rork, you should have been a priest."

The bosun joined him laughing.

"Oh, Captain, me dear mother would want to hear ye say that sentiment, sir! That she most certainly would. 'Twas her most heartfelt desire for her second son Sean to be a man o' the cloth. Did all she could to make it true, but failed in the end, sir. Pleasures o' the flesh held too much sway o'er this lad, to be made into saintly stuff. Still, she's smilin' down upon us both from heaven above, Captain, for what you say in humor was a serious quest for her."

"Well, you do sound like a priest at times, Rork. But you'd disappoint the saints if you were, for you surely don't act like one!"

Rork was clutching his side in mirth at that image. He spoke while trying to catch his breath between chuckles.

"The saints up there are alaughin' with us down here at the idea o' Sean David Rork, o' County Wexford in the Isle o' Eire, being a priestly man!"

Laughter subsided and strength started to leave Wake's mind and body. He made his way slowly forward and down the ladder to his cabin below. As Wake descended, McDougall, the petty officer of the watch, called for the lookouts to pay mind to the jungle island that lay close by in case there were any other Rebs ashore that wanted to shoot a schooner sailor. The comment had its intended effect upon the alertness of the watch, but it brought Wake's mind back to the deathly seriousness of his position and the image of young Scarbond screaming in pain. As exhausted as he was, it took a long time for Lieutenant Wake to finally fall asleep.

6
Random Opportunities

The storm was apparently pursuing them. Typical of the summer weather, monstrous thunderheads were building rapidly over Tampa Bay, expanding outward in all directions. It would not be long before the *St. James* would have to deal with the effects, if not the full brunt, of the storm. Out along the coast, the daily sea breeze was piping up. Wake was tacking his ship out the northernmost entrance channel of the bay, having just left the supply depot at Egmont Key. He estimated that they should have some sea room before the storm could reach them.

The *St. James* was bound north to the Cedar Keys station to unload some supplies for the naval vessels in the area and take on mail and prisoners or passengers for Key West. Cedar Key was the end of their run, and a place Wake had only sailed to once, the year before when he had been stationed on the lower west coast. When he was done there they would sail back to Boca Grande and check on the progress of their wounded, who he hoped had benefited from the attentions of the surgeon aboard the *Gem of the Sea* as well as the kind women of Useppa. Perhaps they had even been transported to the Key West hospital aboard another ship bound there, but Wake doubted that was the case. Few ships put in at Boca Grande, most were in transit and didn't stop there unless ordered. Wake himself was desperately anxious to return to Key West. The prize sloop should be there by now—it had been a week since Faber had left—but the primary reason was Linda. Wake was now certain about their future together. The idea that had germinated that night at Lacosta Island when the boat from Useppa came to their aid had culminated into a definite plan. He knew that some who might hear of his plan would not agree with it, but the time for pondering was over. He was impatient to get on with it, but first he had to complete his mission.

The coastal terrain of Florida changed as Wake sailed north. No longer did he see the mangrove jungle crowd close down to the water's edge. From Tampa Bay northward the topography showed more height and fewer tropical features. The coconut palms of the Sanibel Island area were gone, and more marsh was visible. As they sailed northwest with Egmont Key receding behind them, Wake remembered hearing about the ship captures made by the squadron along the next hundred miles of coastline. Clearwater, Bayport, Cedar Keys, Suwannee River—they were all places the squadron had encountered the Confederates afloat and ashore. With any luck, *St. James* might pick up another small blockade runner that thought she'd slipped past the regular patrol vessels. That would make for some more pleasant prize money arithmetic for MacDougall.

The storm cloud behind them looked like a volcano erupting, the main head was climbing so fast. An angry dark gray line was hardening on the eastern horizon below the giant anvil of cloud. Jagged lines of bright white javelined out from the squall lines below the monster as if they were thrown at potential prey in its path. Wake had never seen thunderstorms like this in New England. The Florida summer storms were like miniature hurricanes and could often reach that force of wind. Every summer day sailors had to plan around the building and onslaught of the storms. The morning land breeze was followed by a noonday calm, which was followed by several hours of sea breeze, like that in which they were now sailing. Each day the weather was the same, little wind then a full gale. The lightning was something Wake had never gotten accustomed to in Florida. It made the summer storms even more deadly and added an almost intentional evilness to them.

The squall line on their side of the storm was just about to Egmont and gaining speed. Soon the wind would shift. Wake could see the wall of rain in the distance underneath the line of clouds rolling toward him. Above the rain, clouds the color of blue-gray gunmetal were swirling and tumbling horizontally in an intimidating show of power. Wake knew this was going to be a bad one.

"Rork, get her sail reduced now. That storm looks to be particularly unpleasant. Down to the jib, if you please, and we'll run to the northwest out to sea with it."

Rork, standing by the starboard foreshrouds, grinned aft and nodded toward the thing heading for them.

"Aye, sir. 'Tis them Rebs ashore that cooked that one up!"

By the time the wind shifted, the main and fore sails were lowered and *St. James* was wallowing in her slackened speed. Rork took the tiller himself and all hands braced themselves as first the rain came and then the blast of the wind. The wind blew the waves down at first with tremendous gusts that came one after another, getting stronger with each successive attack. The schooner had little canvas showing but she heeled over until her leeward beam was awash. Hanging onto a windward shroud as the other side of the deck dropped, Wake looked aft and saw that two other men were helping Rork fight the tiller around to prevent the schooner from broaching.

The attack of wind increased to a constant roar, accompanied by the shriek of the rigging and the crackling sounds of wooden spars and decks reacting to the sudden strains thrust upon them. The jib flogged a staccato percussion to the cacophony, which sounded as if gunshots were going off. Then the storm's heavy artillery struck. Lightning rent the atmosphere very close by, the ripping sound so clear above everything else that Wake almost expected to see God Himself gashing the cloud apart in an effort to fling a bolt of electricity into the schooner. It was a profoundly personal conflict between the storm and each man aboard. The fact that it happened almost every summer day made it no less terrifying, for all hands knew that any vessel could succumb to such an onslaught if not handled properly, and sometimes even then. Yelling could not overcome the wall of sound that had descended upon them, but no orders had to be given, for most of the men had been through this kind of maelstrom and knew what to do.

Visibility decreased until the helmsmen could barely see the bow. They steered by feel, for the binnacle compass was spinning with the skewing of the ship in the building seas. By aligning the schooner with the wind-driven seas they steered her out to the northwest, away from the dangers of the land behind them. Sea room was safety.

Wake had heard stories that the Rebels would wait until these summer storms appeared and then sail out of their harbors into them, knowing that the naval vessels on blockade would be preoccupied with self-preservation and blown off station. The runners would then slip through and make their way to Cuba or the Bahamas. Good luck to them, he thought. If they were desperate enough to enter these storms intentionally, then the strangulation of the blockade must be working.

It seemed like longer, it always did, but after an hour and a half of surging along out to sea under jib alone, the lower sky cleared enough for Wake to see his immediate surroundings. No ships were in sight. The soundings of the lead and their dead reckoning indicated they were about ten miles to the west of Egmont. Wake ordered the ship turned northward on a broad starboard tack and set more sail as the wind began to diminish slowly.

Within another hour the wind had lain down enough so that

all plain sail was set and the ship's complement started to repair the damage done by the storm. The jib that had flown during the high winds was doused and resewn along the leech where it had flailed the edge to tatters. Why it did not part was a cause for some conjecture among the men. Rork himself examined the canvas and oversaw the repair, while others went aloft to see about the running and standing rigging. As the sun descended through the haze of the remaining cloud cover, the sailors of the *St. James* got ready for their supper, talking of the hazards of blockading this coast and wondering what they would find at Cedar Keys, seventy miles distant and due north.

They never found out. The next morning, when still twenty miles south of the Cedar Keys, they caught a glimpse of a sail to the northeast, just off the coast. Wake was on deck when the yell first came from the foremast crosstrees. The coast in this area trended back to the east so that *St. James* was out of sight of land. Wake informed MacDougall, who had the deck, to sharpen up into the wind some more and close with the sail. The slight morning land breeze barely reached out this far and was only providing for three knots of speed, so Wake knew the chase, if it turned out to be that, would be a long one. Still, the prospects for some excitement, and possibly some prize money, invigorated the crew of the schooner so that they turned to the trimming of the sails with a will. Constant supposition about the suspect vessel, her cargo, and her destination was heard in voices from the deck and aloft.

Then they saw a second sail, south of the first and apparently further into shore. Now the speculation changed. After another half hour they saw more details in the distant canvas and deduced that there were two schooners over there, within a mile of each other, and both heading north northwest on a broad reach in the wind from shore.

"This is getting more interesting, Rork."

"Aye, that it is, Captain. Is it a courtship or a rape? That's the question from this perspective as I see it, sir."

MacDougall's usually silent manner loosened a bit as he joined in the conversation at the windward rail.

"You'll know soon enough when the range betwixt 'em closes. Then, if it ain't love with those two over there, you'll hear a growl from a twelve-pounder, sure as God made bosuns to carry gunners around the oceans."

Wake put down his glass and looked at the two petty officers standing to his left, the gaunt older gunner looking grim in spite of his humor and the younger giant of a bosun grinning at his friend's homily. Wake, not for the first time, felt a kinship with these two men.

"MacDougall, I do believe that on occasion you can be profound, even if it is at the expense of the bosuns of the world!"

Rork, who could not pass up such an opportunity as this, added his opinion of the gunner's mate's theorizing. "Captain, my friend the esteemed gunner has made some trifle bit o' humor and I, for one aboard this here schooner ship, am glad that he recognizes that without the bosuns to bring 'em into range, the gunners o' the world would be useless as an Irishman in a whiskey vat."

"No gunners, no navy, sir. Simple as Rork's brains."

Even taciturn MacDougall couldn't help but smile with his last comment, and all three shared a laugh as Rork put paid to the debate.

"By the Lord above and around us, he's got me there, Captain. MacDougall, you are truly an evil old man!"

A shout from aloft interrupted them.

"Deck there! Land ho! Behind the sails to the east."

The horizon began to change into faint irregularity as low marshy islands off the mainland of Florida grew into focus. The coast was now about eight miles away, the sails of the two schooners half that distance. The report of water depth below them came next from the leeward foreshrouds.

"Two fathom! Two fathom!"

It was an odd coast indeed where a ship could be this far offshore and still be in only twelve feet of water. The morning sight had indicated they were somewhere off the Crystal River area. From that point the coastline of Florida started to curve back to the north northwest, before making almost a right angle and trending about due west for a dozen miles or so at Waccasassa Bay. Cedar and Seahorse Keys should be ahead of them somewhere. The bottom here was notorious for shoals and rocky reefs. Wake was not comfortable with their position and wondered what the captains of the vessels further inshore were thinking of at this moment. The camaraderie of the moment before was gone as he turned to Rork.

"I want the lookouts doubled. There are reefs quite far offshore on this coast, and the chart is very vague. Have them look for reefs especially. The Cedar Keys should be dead ahead or a point off the port bow."

"Aye, sir. Decisions to be made soon enough."

Rork walked forward to a group of men working on pitching the foredeck seams and sent two of them up the masts to observe for dangers. MacDougall returned to the helmsman and made the hourly log entry. Wake remained at the rail, feeling the light wind coming over the water from Florida with the scent of forest and beach upon it. It was at times like this, when decisions were about to be made, that a ship's captain was the most alone, set apart by his responsibility, and the authority given him to carry it out.

"Deck there! Land ho, two points on the port bow! An island, I think sir. No, two islands. Now more, sir. A bunch o' islands ahead of us."

MacDougall came back to Wake holding a chart. He pointed to a smudge to the left of the forestay.

"Appears to be Snake and Seahorse Keys, sir, by my reckoning."

"Yes, I agree MacDougall, and it appears the flood is setting us to the east more than I had thought. Now, I wonder what is going to happen over there with those two?"

"According to this chart we should know soon enough,

Captain. They're running out o' water over there. Hold course, sir?"

"Yes, gunner, we'll hold course a little further. If they can sail through, we can. If the one ahead bears off to go out further, we can head her off."

The two vessels were to windward and forward of the *St. James*, and both were showing no sign of altering course to get into deeper water farther offshore. By now the common opinion was that the second vessel was the naval schooner *Annie*, trying to catch up to a blockade-runner. The chase between them had narrowed to a mile. Soon something would happen, but what exactly could not be known yet.

The puff of smoke came as the striped ensign soared up to the main gaff peak of the second schooner. The lookout then provided additional information.

"Deck there! Gun from the schooner behind, sir. No splash. Musta been unshotted. American ensign flying now and some signals too. Starboard main spreader. Can't read 'em, sir."

Rork came up behind Wake and MacDougall with a signal book in his hand. He asked for the telescope glass from MacDougall and stared at the other naval ship. The lead vessel was not stopping. Rork was now looking in the squadron signal book each ship carried and glancing back up at the other schooner.

"I am almost certain that those are the numbers for the *Annie*, sir. One, Three, Nine. Schooner *Annie*, sir. Shall I acknowledge? Any other message?"

"Very well, Rork. No other message. It's pretty obvious what is happening. We'll stand by with them until this is done. Let's just watch our depth around here."

Rork went to the signals locker below and returned to the quarterdeck, where he had a seaman send up the signal and an ensign.

The sound of the second gunshot was louder, with the resultant splash ahead of the chase and to leeward. MacDougall was conversing with some of his gun crews, explaining the aspects involved in the shooting of a moving target from a rolling deck. His professorial tone altered slightly when the third shot came close aboard the chase.

"An excellent shot, by God! Mind ya now, we wouldn't want to come closer than that. The point is to scare the buggers into giving up without damaging the hull or cargo! Remember that, lads. Close, but do not hit. That's prize money they're shootin' towards over there."

Wake at first thought that some part of the shot had hit something aboard the runner, for she slowed and swung around to the west rapidly. But then she stopped completely, sails askew and sheets flogging. Men could be seen looking overboard at the water. The *Annie* immediately bore off to the port and slacked her sheets. She was now running almost wing and wing dead downwind.

Rork was the first to speak.

"Aground! They ran her aground, God bless 'em!"

"Rork, ye've got a fine sense o' the obvious, my friend. I just hope that—"

MacDougall stopped in mid-sentence. A chorus of groans and epithets rose from the men of the *St. James.* Their sister ship's bow had dipped down suddenly and now the schooner halted, a quarter mile behind their prey, sails and rigging protesting.

Wake tried to sound calm as he gave his orders.

"We go after the runner. Bear up for her, Rork. Get the boat ready with a boarding party. You'll lead it. I want to anchor as far away from her as *Annie* is. The boat will take you the rest of the way. No sense in going in further."

Activity commenced with each hand fulfilling a task that had to be accomplished quickly. *St. James* was shorthanded because of her wounded and men on the prize crew. That left fewer men and another boarding party would mean even fewer still aboard the schooner.

It wasn't long before *St. James* luffed up into the wind and lowered her sails, the anchor sliding over and holding her head toward the coastline. Signals from *Annie* said they did not need assistance, but Wake saw that no boat was being lowered from the other ship to capture the runner. Rork came over from the railing and saw Wake surveying the *Annie* with the glass.

"The jolt must've parted the fall tackle for the boat. They'll be needin' their boat to kedge off afore they do anythin' else anyway, Captain. Do we capture the runner under our name or *Annie*'s?"

MacDougall was trying not to be too obvious in his attempt to hear the answer, which would mean the difference between the primary share or a secondary share of prize money.

"*Annie*'s. It was their chase."

As he replied, Rork smiled over at the gunner's mate and strode to the port railing where *St. James*'s own boat was now lowered and alongside.

"*Annie*'s it is, Captain. Honorable choice, sir. Right, gunner?"

"Just make sure the Rebs don't scuttle the bitch on ya while ya're bein' so noble over there, Rork."

The boat was heading off as Wake swung his glass between the *Annie* and the unknown vessel. The naval schooner was teeming with men getting the kedge anchor into the gig while others tried to get the larger ship's cutter up off the deck and over into the water. Others were climbing into the rigging to repair damage done by the strain of the abrupt collision with the rocky reef. With each wave, the masts and decks jerked wildly as the hull crunched into the rocks. Wake could see Lieutenant James Williams, her captain, holding on through each shudder of the hull and issuing directions from the afterdeck.

The Rebel schooner had her sails still set and was heeled over, crashing further ahead onto the reef with each wave. The men aboard were standing and staring at the approaching boat from the *St. James.* No action stirred them and no attempt to save their vessel could be seen. Their war was ending, the schooner wasn't important anymore.

Still, as the crew of the *St. James* had discovered to their pain just a week earlier, this was no time to take chances or assume the blockade runners would meekly surrender. Wake watched as Rork led half the boarding party up and over the gunwales of the schooner with cutlasses and pistols drawn, as the other half of the party stayed down in the boat with muskets leveled at the men on the deck.

The rest of the bluejackets then ascended to the deck, some herding the Rebel crew forward while others disappeared from view as they went below to complete the search of the vessel. It certainly looked as if all was going well, but Wake was worried about the *Annie.* It might be the top of the flood tide and getting her off the rocks could prove difficult, if not impossible. Not knowing the tidal times and sequences on this section of the coast made gauging the situation more of a guess than an appraisal.

"MacDougall, get me two men and the dinghy. I want to go to Rork and then over to *Annie* to ascertain precisely their plight. It appears that the boarding party is safe. You stay here."

MacDougall affirmed the order, and soon two of the younger seamen were rowing Wake to the Rebel schooner. The air was warming and the noonday calm was approaching as the wind started to lighten. That much was a help to getting the ships off the rocks, thought Wake as he surveyed the situation aboard the schooner ahead of him. He could see Rork speaking to a person aft, who appeared to be a leader of some sort, probably the captain. The man did not look cowed and was animated in his gestures.

After one of the sailors helped him up the main chains to the deck, Wake looked around to examine the state of the prize vessel. The sails were now down and the crew lashed together forward by the sampson post. The rhythmic crunch of wood on rock with each low swell caused Wake to wince, but the bluejackets getting an anchor off to deep water in the *St. James's* boat reassured him that all was being done to get her free as soon as possible. Rork came up and saluted.

"Sir, she is the *Random* of Nassau. Hundred tonner with

Captain Young, a limey, commanding. He says they were in Clearwater hiding until yesterday's storm. Then they slipped out and thought they were past our ships until dawn when they saw *Annie*. I'm afraid that Captain Young is not a happy man, Captain Wake. Not a happy man atall, sir."

"Is he claiming not to be running the blockade?"

Rork smiled as he continued.

"No sir. He's a bit embarrassed about hittin' the reef when he only had another day till he got to his destination. Mad as a hornet, he is, Captain. Said that the money he would've made on this run would allow him to leave Nassau and return to England. Says he hates the Bahamas and the Americans and their war. Just wants to go back and live in the old country. Says he was on his last run. Carryin' bits and pieces o' things that'd bring a good price. Haven't had time to look myself yet, but the manifest says tools and medicines.

"Trades southern turpentine and cotton for 'em, then sells that for a fortune in Nassau. Young says they're all astarvin' an' desperate on this coast cause o' the blockade an' the war. A bit disillusioned with the grand cause an' all evidently. No glory when you're slowly starvin', Captain. Saw that in my own day, back home. Ain't a pretty sight."

"Where precisely was he bound for?"

"Some place with the evil soundin' name of Deadman's Bay, Captain. Has run into there six times in the last two years from Nassau. Do you know of it?"

"Yes, I saw it on the chart. The squadron caught some runners there last year. *Annie* got some there earlier this year. The channel into there appears tricky. I believe we'll need some local knowledge, and he sounds like he knows it."

"That he does, sir."

Rork was watching him closely as Wake went on.

"They're disaffected with the Confederacy there?"

Wake's hand went up to absently rub the scar on his face. Rork knew what that mannerism meant. Wake was thinking up an idea, and the immediate future would become interesting.

"That's what he says, Captain. Your mind is workin' again, I can tell."

"Bring him here, Rork."

"Aye, Captain. But he's madder than a bishop caught in an Orangeman's pub!"

Wake stayed aft as the British captain was brought to him, the rest of the captured crew of five watching the proceedings intently. Captain Vincent Young was a disheveled man in his late forties, heavy set with a florid face that betrayed a fondness for liquor. His demeanor was anything but submissive as he started in right away without the usual courtesies.

"Well, you've got me now. This Irish idiot says you're the captain commanding this rabble. Are you the fool who ran aground after us or the one from the anchored schooner?"

Wake's germinating idea had not included an obnoxious blockade-runner captain. He was amazed by the man's attitude. The smell of rum and the slur of the words provided a partial explanation for the bravado. But that would be gone by the next morning. The plan could still work. It would mean a delay in returning to Key West, but opportunities often entailed an investment of time and effort. This opportunity was unique. The profit in terms of the navy's war efforts in Florida would be worth the chances taken.

Wake regarded the man before him and spoke in a low monotone.

"I am Lieutenant Peter Wake of the naval schooner *St. James,* anchored over there. You are a prisoner of the United States Navy and will be taken to Fort Taylor in Key West for adjudication prior to being sent to Fort Warren, up north."

Young made an indignant clucking sound and tried to interrupt, but Rork ground a boot on the top of the merchant captain's foot, leaned close to his ear, and said something quietly that Wake couldn't hear entirely. Young's eyes showed that he could hear the bosun's words clearly as Rork spoke a little louder.

"This here Irish idiot is tellin' your lordship to shut your hatch while my captain is speakin' to ya. You're not endearin' yourself to me, ya limey bastard. In fact, you're remindin' me o' some o' your countrymen in Eire that have done things that need to be revenged. An' it's a long way to Key West. Do ye understand me plain?"

Young squirmed his foot but Rork ground down harder, with one hand, to anyone watching, resting apparently innocently on the Englishman's neck. Wake knew it was anything but innocent. Young looked up at Rork and nodded his head as Wake spoke again.

"It is obvious to me, and will be to the government authorities in Key West, that you have openly and repeatedly been part of the operations of the enemies of the United States in a time of war. No protest of neutrality can be supported nor will be entertained. This is war and you are the enemy. We put our prisoners of war in special camps until they can be exchanged or the war ends. In your case there is no reciprocal for exchange. Your past actions speak to the matter, *Mister* Young, and mere words on your part will not change that past. . . ."

Wake stopped and let his words sink in. He hoped the man was not too drunk and could understand the import of what was just said. Young stood staring at his captor. He looked up at Rork again and back at Wake, shaking his head.

"I want to go home to England. Just let me go and I'll not return. I hate this country and your squalid little war. I hate this damned heat. Why in the devil's name did I ever leave England for this forsaken place, just to be with you people!"

Wake stayed silent. The creaking and smashing of the hull on the reef went on as men worked ceaselessly on the deck pumps to keep up with the leaks below. The heat built palpably with the sun high overhead as the wind died away and the sea glassed over. Men around them yelled and cursed and grunted as they went about the task of trying to save the vessel and her cargo, which until a hour earlier had been Young's financial assurance of a return to the cool green hills of his homeland. Still Wake did not speak, he let the intent of his words permeate Young's mind: the heat, the din, the years in a prison. Young glanced around, slumped, and looked down at the deck.

"You're saying that there is something I could do to show I am not an enemy of the Federal government and navy?"

Wake kept up the somniferous drone. He would show Young no sympathy. The dislike in his voice was no act.

"If you are sincere in your desire to show the United States that you are not our enemy, and that this was an accidental situation that you have been mired in, then there is something you can do. It will require action on your part."

"And if I do whatever this is, then what?"

"Then you are not an enemy. Just an unfortunate neutral British subject caught in our war. We turn you over to Mr. Howell, at the British Consulate in Key West, and you are forbidden to ever come into our country again. Perception, Mister Young, is based upon actions. It is time for your actions to give us a better perception of you."

"I'll do what you want. Just get me back to Nassau so I can make passage back to England. God help me."

"God will help you, Mister Young. And so will we. Rork, escort Mister Young to his cabin and get all of his charts and papers, then bring him to the *Annie*. There will be a conference in Captain Williams' cabin in fifteen minutes."

"Aye, Captain. Me an' Mister Young're making fast friends now, aren't we now Mister *English* man?" Rork glanced over at Wake and winked.

With that said the bosun led Young off below as Wake went forward. The work was progressing aboard the *Random* and Wake's plan depended upon her being ready to sail soon. The carpenter's mate from *St. James* was boarding up the cracked planking inside the hull after a sail had been fothered over the ripped planks outside to reduce the flow of water into her. A shouted answer from down in the hold to Wake's question yielded the hoped for answer—an hour or two more would be sufficient to make her seaworthy, with planks boarded and caulked inboard and outboard of the hull.

That left the reef. The schooner was floating easier now, and the sailors were about to haul away on the hawser of the kedge anchor to pull her off the rocks. With no wind to push her further into shallow water, they should have her floating in deeper water by the time the carpenter finished his work.

Ten minutes later Wake was aboard the *Annie*, greeting his old friend, and senior in the grade of lieutenant, James Williams.

"James, how is she? Bad?"

"Touched a bit hard but nothing we haven't done before, or will again. Should be off any moment. It was good to see you sailing up, Peter. In the proverbial nick of time. I understand you have captured her in our name. Thank you for that. Greatly appreciated. Gates went over and received the particulars on your boarding and her cargo and crew. He will be her prize master and take her down to Key West tomorrow. You and your men will of course get the 'in sight share' of the adjudicated amount."

"Our honor to assist, James. But about that Key West business. Perhaps you could delay *Random*'s departure for a few days. I have an idea that will assist us both and enhance our operations on this coast. Rork is bringing the runner's master over to *Annie* in a moment. Could we have a conference in your cabin prior to their arrival?"

"Oh Lord, Peter Wake. I have seen that look in your eyes before. You've a notion in that head of yours that will be the grief or the glory of the both of us, don't you?"

"Tons, James. Just tons of grief, or maybe even glory!"

Wake grinned and followed his friend down the ladder to the cabin that was as cramped as its counterpart on the *St. James.* Once in his cabin, Williams related how he had been at the very southern end of his patrol station by Clearwater and saw the *Random* coming north out of a squall line. The chase had taken all evening, concluding just as the *St. James* had come upon them.

Williams had known he was playing a dangerous game in those shallow waters but felt that it was worth it.

Wake narrated his own adventures along the coast on this mission. Then he explained the plan that had come to him on the deck of the *Random.* Williams enthusiastically added his own refinements to the scheme and both prepared for the coming interview with Young. For the first time in quite a while, Wake was pleased with how events were unfolding. The initial steps of the plan had already come together. Key West, and even Linda, could wait a few days more.

After Wake and Williams had completed their talk, Rork was told to bring Young into the cabin. The chart of the coast of Florida from the Cedar Keys to the Saint Marks River was unfolded on the table before them as the four men gathered around it. Wake spoke directly to the Englishman.

"Young, show us the channel leading into Deadman's Bay." Young said nothing, but began to sullenly trace the channel on the chart with a tobacco-stained finger. Afterward he looked up at Wake, who continued.

"Now tell us the following: controlling depth at low tide, tacking width, and the location of stakes or marks."

Young did as he was told, with Williams taking notes of the information gained.

Wake went on to inquire about the depths in the Steinhatchee River, which flowed into the bay and had the docks at which ships were loaded and offloaded. They also learned the type and number of ships that might be there, Confederate militia forces in the area, and names of prominent persons who were disaffected with the Confederacy. Young answered all the questions, starting out with some hesitation but gaining in assertiveness as he went along. When he had finished, the Englishman got quiet and sat down in the one chair of the cabin without permission. A barely perceptible question came out of him, like air from a deflating balloon.

"You're going to make me take *Random* in there with your

men aboard, aren't you?"

Wake smiled at Young for the first time since they had met.

"Mister Young, I think you have failed to comprehend the scope of this operation. Of course, we are going to have you take us through Deadman's Bay and into the river on the *Random.* But then we will capture the ships there, capture any cotton and turpentine on the docks, burn the depot, and rescue off any loyal United States refugees. And you, Mister Young, are going to demonstrate to one and all your affinity for our cause and thus the indisputable reason for our not putting you in a prison as an enemy of our country. And furthermore, we will ensure that our Southern cousins know of your services to the United States, so that they will never again try to tempt you to become mired in our affairs of conflict."

Young made no verbal response. He just hung his head, staring at the chart.

"And one more thing, Mister Young."

The head came up, flaccid eyes gazing at Wake.

"Bosun Rork here will be right by you every step of the way to ensure your wholehearted participation in the operation. Do not give him the impression that you are doing otherwise. Are you clear on all this?"

The mumbling was close enough to an affirmative that Wake nodded to Rork to take the man away to the *St. James.* The two naval captains had some other decisions to make, and time was of the essence as they talked over exactly how they were going to accomplish all that they wanted. Williams laughed as Wake climbed down the side into his dinghy for the short row back to the *St. James.*

"Well, Peter, in for a penny, in for a pound. If all goes well in two days time, you and I will have redeemed ourselves with that admiral down in Key West. He couldn't think any worse of *me*, anyway."

"James, I am afraid it will take more than a victory to convert the man's opinion of me. Something of more biblical proportions might be needed for that miracle!"

The two men, both volunteer officers who had been former merchant mates and now found themselves in the deadly serious business of naval war, shared a final grin and good-bye. They knew they would not meet again until after the attack.

Seven hours later the sun set in a resplendent display following a rare afternoon with no storm. The three vessels sailed out to the west, and seemingly into the cosmic work of art, as darkness enveloped the eastern horizon behind them. Wake hoped that word of the capture was not spread on the coast. In fact, it was crucial to the success of his plan since surprise equaled safety, and any forewarning of the Confederates would enable them to bring up elements of the 11th Infantry Regiment, stationed at Madison, to the Steinhatchee River.

Sailing close-hauled, the schooners would turn slowly to the north northwest in four hours time. Twenty hours of transit northward, far enough offshore to preclude observation from land, would take them to the entry point of the channel among the shoals and reefs of Deadman's Bay. It would be a finely balanced thing, equally dependent upon weather and upon navigating skill.

Williams and Wake decided that Young would lead them all in the *Random*, with Rork standing by him constantly, and a crew of naval seaman to work the captured ship. The ships' boats of the *Annie* and *St. James* would be towed alongside those vessels for the final approach, and each would be filled with well-armed sailors ready to board and capture anything in their path.

Williams, as the senior officer present, was in command of the operation, but he delegated the command of the actual landing party to Wake. The *Random* would lead the flotilla and go alongside the dock at the depot. *St. James* would follow closely, mooring alongside *Random* at the dock. Any vessels anchored in the river or at the dock would be instantly overwhelmed and captured by the boats' crews. The sailors filling the decks on the two schooners would be used as the landing party and would capture the depot and gather any refugees found ashore. *Annie*, with a shorthanded crew, would remain at the entrance of the river and cover the others with her guns. In the event of disaster, she was their hope of escape.

7
Deadman's Bay

The night went easy for the ships broad reaching to the north with a light land breeze. Morning showed no land to the east. As they sailed onward, the petty officers and bluejackets aboard the three schooners readied themselves and their weapons. Orders and signals were repeated among all the men so that each understood what would be required of him.

Wake studied the chart, noting that the channel into Deadman's Bay started about two and a half miles off the entrance to the river and wound its way through two lines of reefs that paralleled the shoreline. Only at the high water of a summer lunar tide could larger schooners such as these get into the river, Young had explained. The channel was usually only marked with stakes if the Rebels knew a blockade runner was coming in, otherwise they would pull them out or deliberately misplace them to trap a blockading ship on the reefs. The Rebels knew the *Random* would be coming in sometime in the next week or two, so the stakes might be there, and the tides were conducive for the schooners to enter. Everything was as thought out and ready as Wake could make it.

An afternoon storm appeared later that day, repeating the chaos of two days earlier. The ships separated in the hour-long fury of the storm and only came back together in the half-light after the sun had disappeared into the gray mass to the west. No flamboyant show of good luck came from the sun that evening. Instead, it was a depressingly indistinct dusk that, with a falling wind and rising humidity, gave the impression the heavens were not optimistic about the outcome of this very risky enterprise.

Sailors on each vessel, superstitious by and large, engaged in speculations of what they would find, how Young would carry out his part, and how many would stay on that coming shoreline for eternity. The discussions were not apprehensive but simply reflected the seaman's constant appreciation for the statistical odds of things. Mere life at sea was dangerous, adding warfare to the equation made the odds unfailingly longer.

The night was covered with hazy clouds, making the dead reckoning more of an educated guess than usual. At the appointed hour of midnight, the three schooners closed up abreast and luffed up into the wind coming out of the southeast. Rork, Wake, and Williams conferred over final preparations.

Williams announced that his position put them approximately ten miles west of Bowlegs Point, which was on the coast around eight miles south of the Steinhatchee River. This meant that a course to the northeast for three hours in the present wind should place them at the entrance to the channel into Deadman's Bay and the Steinhatchee River. Wake concurred and Rork acknowledged. Williams gave the order to proceed onward, and Rork got *Random* close-hauled on the starboard tack, followed by the other ships. No rousing speech of glory or victory was given. The men were too tired or too anxious, and in any event were not in that mood. It was time to go forward and get the task accomplished. They had already passed the point of no return.

Two hours and thirty-seven minutes later Wake saw the *Random*'s sails luff, and then she turned to starboard abruptly, settling down on a course even closer to the wind. At the same time, the leadsman aboard *St. James* called out that they now had two fathoms under her. *St. James* luffed to windward and settled on the new course, the crew as quiet as Wake had ever seen them. Not even whispers were exchanged as the men stared off to the east where they knew land, and the enemy, waited for them. Glancing aft, Wake saw *Annie* alter course to follow them. By his calculations, they should now be in the channel, but he saw no stakes marking the course. Indeed, he could see nothing around them, though there should have been land two or three miles away. The tide, wind, and clouds were cooperating. But was Vincent Young?

Suddenly ahead a commotion filled the night air. The *Random* was luffing her sails even further upwind now. She continued around and settled on a port tack, heading southerly. Wake quietly gave orders to follow, but MacDougall was ahead of him and had already eased the sheets. *St. James* came around smoothly with the *Annie* imitating them a moment later.

Four short minutes later—Wake was timing each tack and course for his dead reckoning plot on the chart—the lead schooner tacked again, now heading northeast again on the starboard tack. This time the maneuver was quieter, and each schooner behind followed through silently. The leadsman now whispered that they had a fathom and half: three feet under the keel.

Wake could feel every muscle in his body tensing and the blood pounding through the veins in his head. For the tenth time that hour, Wake thought about the fact that all of this was his idea. But for that glimmer of inspiration on the deck of a blockade-runner two days earlier, he and his crew would be sailing south by now on a course for Boca Grande and eventually Key West. The ownership of the plan did nothing to mitigate his uneasiness.

The leadsman's muffled shout brought him out of his interior thoughts.

"By the mark, one. One fathom . . ."

Wake looked ahead quickly and saw that the *Random*, which drew as much water as *St. James*, was still sailing well. They must be plowing over a silt bottom. Sailors around him were staring at their captain until MacDougall roused them to return to their duties. According to James Williams, who knew the tides on this coast, they should have another four hours of flood tide, which would translate to two more feet. The leadsman announced his results again.

"One and a half fathom. Deep two."

Another swing of the lead followed as all hands strained to hear the words.

"Deep two. By the mark, two fathom."

They were past the outer reef. Sighs could be heard from everyone. Young had brought them this far, and without any markers that Wake could see. Possibly Young was going to be true to his word. Wake had no doubt that Rork was doing his best to see to it.

A movement among the men forward, and some sort of communication coming aft along the deck, told Wake that something had been sighted. MacDougall leaned close and passed it along.

"Captain, shoreline seen dead ahead 'bout a mile or less."

Peering through the gloom Wake could see a darker form on the edge of his visibility. Now the form was spreading to the left and right ahead of him. He heard the clatter of sails from ahead and saw the mainsail coming down on *Random*. They must get theirs down too and reduce speed or risk collision.

"We're very close, MacDougall. Bring the mainsail down."

Three men loosed the halliards and eased the gaff and sail down as quietly as they could, putting an easy furl on it and returning to their positions along the deck. Without turning around, Wake could hear Williams doing the same. The three ships were now only fifty yards apart from each other, with little room to maneuver should one ahead take the ground.

The leadsman spoke again.

"One fathom. Hard mud."

The keel was now bumping the bottom as the *St. James* slowed down. *Random* was still moving though, and Wake nodded to continue to follow when MacDougall glanced at him with a questioning look.

"Deep two. Silt bottom again."

They were over the inner bar now. A little over twelve feet of water. The river mouth should be close ahead. Around them Wake could see the dark land closing in toward them, with the water reflecting the few stars starting to penetrate the haze. To the port he saw marsh grasses. There were almost no beaches on this coast. Even the smell was different, more earthy and sweet.

The current was providing most of the motive power since the land breeze was diminished by the trees they could make out ahead. The man on the helm said the steering was getting sluggish. Then they stopped just as the leadsman called out urgently in his low voice.

"One fathom! One fathom now."

Glancing ahead, Wake registered that the *Random* was stopped too, at a different heading than *St. James.* Studying the situation, he stared forward to the shoreline but soon saw a look of alarm on the faces of his men who were looking aft past him. Wake turned around as the *Annie* smashed into the port quarter of the *St. James.* The blow came on the hull just aft of *Annie*'s bow on the starboard side, sparing her bowsprit, but splitting the bulwarks of both vessels with a rendering crash.

MacDougall instantly told everyone to stay quiet and get spars to push off the other schooner's bow. He addressed Wake in his gravelly tone.

"Captain, I can get her off with the dinghy and kedge, if'n you want to take the lads ashore an' get those bastards. Let's not make all this for nothing. The river mouth is right over there. Captain Williams and I can handle the schooners, sir."

"Very well, MacDougall. Put the landing party in the boats. We'll row to the docks. Should be a quarter mile at most."

MacDougall loudly whispered his encouragement.

"Good luck, sir. An' bring back a fair load. I could use a bit a money in my pocket for my pleasures!"

The three ships' boats gathered at the stern of the *Annie*, where Williams approved the modification of the planned approach to the docks. On the schooners, efforts quickened to free them from the mud and wait for the returning crews. Spars to push off and kedge anchors to pull off were hauled out and by the skeleton details remaining aboard. All knew that there was but a short time to accomplish the mission. If they were still there at low tide, the ships would be a stationary target for Confederate field artillery at point-blank range. And the field artillery could arrive at any moment.

The boats had their oars muffled with rags to diminish the sound of their approach. Even though he knew it was not possible, it seemed to Wake that they could be heard for a mile. The creak of the oar, the whispered curse of a sailor, the swish of the bow wave, all seemed to cry out in the night. No sound came from the land except for the raucous squawk of a heron, which startled many of the anxious men.

The three boats, one from each schooner, each loaded with a dozen men, made their way swiftly on the flood tide into the river mouth, around the first curve to starboard and up the narrowing stream. Rork and Young stood in the bows of the first boat, the Englishman still guiding the operation with his local knowledge.

The men in the boats were silent; even those grunting and gasping at the oars tried to be as quiet as possible. Ears straining to hear any alarm on shore, the sailors brought the boats past some crudely built houses that jutted out of the scrub oaks and palms. Some of the homes had thatched roofs, and none had any refinements such as glass or ornamental trim. A few rickety docks, undulating in height from several feet to more than ten feet off the water leaned out from the shoreline. Small sailing punts bobbed on lines to the docks. The smell of fish and seaweed came from nets hung over tree limbs between the houses. Obviously the place was a poor frontier village that had been thrust into prominence during recent years by its ability to assist in the Confederate war effort.

It was two hours until dawn, and there was no sign of sentry or fisherman or passerby. Wake couldn't believe their luck. Except for the grounding off the mouth of the river, everything had gone according to plan.

Then the dog started barking.

At first it was a startled bark, transforming into a low growl, then frenzied barking. In the misty gloom the precise location of the animal was not at first apparent. Then on the left bank a large dog could be seen running on a dock close by. Soon a half dozen other dogs were barking, awakening their owners, who could be heard yelling into the night with questioning tones.

In an effort to lesson the noise of their approach, Rork had his men rest easy on the oars as his boat glided forward on the flood tide. Wake's craft and the last boat did the same. They slowed and let the current take them up around a bend to the left, a trail of cacophony rising from the bank twenty feet away. Wake saw Rork, standing tall in the bow of the lead boat, point to something further around the bend. His gestures seemed to indicate two ships just ahead. Soon Wake's boat came up to that spot, and he could see the objective of the entire endeavor looming up out of the darkness.

As he surveyed the sight ahead of him, angry yells from downriver behind him gave notice that the inhabitants of the village had paid heed to their dogs and were aware that boats were in their river. The one distinguishable word from them was "Yankees!"

No shots had been fired, but Wake knew that was only a matter of minutes, if not seconds, away. It was no longer time for stealth. Hesitation now could be fatal to them all. Wake spoke loudly into the still night air to the men in the three ships' boats.

"Forward, Saints! Forward, Annies! Pull to the ships at the dock!"

All three boats gained speed rapidly toward the dock a hundred feet away. With muskets and pistols cocked and cutlasses drawn, the men in the bows clambered up and perched on the gunwales ready to leap. At the last minute the oarsmen tossed their blades up and then folded them aft as the boats came up to the two sailing vessels moored to the dock.

Rork's boat arrived first, careening into the stern quarter of a schooner on the right side of a frail dock built thirty feet perpendicular out from the shore. At the base of the dock on the shore stood a large open-sided pole barn with a thatched roof, stacks of cotton bales and barrels of turpentine piled underneath. Wake's boat came alongside the large sloop on the opposite side of the dock, as the *Annie's* boat landed at the head of the dock.

Barely controlled mass chaos burst out on the boats as the sailors rushed up and over the Rebel vessels like ants, yelling curses and waving their cutlasses and bayonets. Confused locals on shore responded with their own yells, while the crews of the Rebel ships came up from below to find cold steel aimed closely at their throats. It was all over in seconds, and Wake put a petty officer in charge of each captured vessel with orders to get them ready to get under way immediately.

Eight seamen were put out as a picket guard around the depot as Wake and Rork formed up a dozen other sailors to march back down the riverbank and into the village they had just passed by. Young, shaking with terror, was propelled along by Rork. The miniature column started out on the hundred-yard march with Wake leading, followed by Rork and Young and the other bluejackets.

Moving over the land was far more difficult in the night for, unlike at sea, there was no starlight reflection from the ground. Stumbling along, with curses issued whenever someone lost his footing, was taking far too long for Wake. He could hear men talking in angry voices up ahead where the dogs were still barking incessantly. Words became more understandable as they got closer.

"Bastard thievin' Yankees've got our cotton an' turp'. We gotta take it back afore they get away!"

"That gunboat out there will blow us all to hell if we try to fight 'em."

"How many a 'em are there? Can we run 'em off?"

Wake could hear no indications of pro-Union sentiments and wondered about Young's earlier presentations. Judging by Young's information and the size of the village they had passed, there might be around two dozen men in the place. It was time to use an overwhelming show of force.

"Bayonets and cutlasses, men. Forward at a trot and follow me!"

The column broke into a run behind their lieutenant, accouterments jangling and making a racket worth far more than twelve men. Wake turned while trotting and spoke to Rork.

"I want Young up here in front with me, Rork."

The bosun eagerly responded with a hard slap to the back of the English merchant captain, who found himself in a very dangerous situation. Rork was laughing as he cajoled his charge.

"With pleasure, sir! Mind the captain, your lordship, and double quick now!"

Another fifty feet found them around a bend in the pathway and facing a crowd of fifteen armed men of varying ages dressed in an assortment of filthy rags. The villagers raised their shotguns and pistols as Wake stopped three feet from the man he picked out as the leader. Wake pointed his cutlass to the large man's chest. The sailors spread out to either side of their lieutenant and leveled pistols and muskets at the ragtag group in front of them. Rork pushed Young up to stand next to Wake. Two lanterns held by what appeared to be boys provided enough light for both groups to see the other.

"I am Lieutenant Peter Wake of the United States Navy. Put down those arms immediately and stand easy."

Rork, standing to the rear of his commander, quietly gave the order to the sailors to cock their weapons. The sound of the clicking punctuated the scene and several of the local men laid their firearms on the ground. Others, including the big man in front of Wake, stood fast, holding their guns. Wake was correct in picking him out as the leader, for the man spoke next.

"Jes' who the hell are you, mister high and mighty, ta come on in here in the middle o' the night an' steal our boats an' cotton an' such! We ain't part o' your country no more, an' we doan' wanna have none o' y'all down here. Just get back in yer boats an' go off back on up north an' leave us be. Jes' leave us be!"

Wake stared at the man, who was a head taller, forty pounds heavier, and twenty years older. The man pointed his shotgun at Wake's abdomen. No one else in the group spoke. The man started up again, this time in a louder voice, the muzzle of the shotgun waving around as his emotions got stronger.

"I said git outta here! Take yer Yankee ways an' go home. This is our land an' our homes, an' I'll die afore you steal my work!"

Wake stared into the man's eyes in the loom of the lantern light. The man was not threatening so much as pleading. The war had come to this little place in the middle of the backcountry, and this man was going to lose all that he had spent a lifetime building. Behind his right arm, Wake could feel Rork moving slightly. He felt the hard barrel of a pistol sliding along his side, now under his armpit. Events were deteriorating quickly and the planned rescue of refugees was unraveling. One more try at diplomacy was worth it.

"No one has to die. No one has to be hurt. We are here to see if any of you want to come to the safety of the Federal areas of Florida. We are not here to hurt you or take your small fishing punts. You know my name. What is yours?"

"Y'all a pack o' lying Yankee dogs, an' we shoot dogs that doan' mind down here. Y'all er here ta take our cotton an' turp an' the ships that carry 'em. Those are our lives now. Ain't nothin' else left, 'cept fishing ta eat.

"We heard all that about the Union places in Florida. Been

hearin' that for two years now, an' saw my own kin uncle go down the coast ta y'all. But it's all lies an' we know it. None o' them folks ever come back."

The man's facial muscles flexed and his eyes grew larger. Like a snake about to strike, the shotgun muzzle swung up toward Wake's face. Tears were coming out of the man's eyes even as he grimaced, as if he were trying to steel himself against the flood of emotional pain. Seconds were taking hours. Wake became aware that he was about to be shot and that many would die in the reaction of the sailors, but he had no idea of what to do other than keep talking.

An older man in the back of the group, one who had already put his own shotgun down, calmly spoke.

"John Newton, I think we can think an' speak for our own selves here. Ain't nothin' we can do ta stop these Yankees an' we all know it. Only thing we can do is maybe ta not have a person hurt doin' somethin' that won't mean nothin' in the long run o' things. If'n ya shoot this man, a lot them and us're gonna get shot too. Your uncle Hervey'd be mighty disappointed at you if he heard o' all this carryin' on. Maybe this here Yankee man is right after all, an' it's time to go where ya don' have ta worry 'bout such things as this. Ol' Hervey did it more 'n a year ago, an' I'm a thinkin' now he was right."

Several other older men grumbled agreement and the sound of metal thudding onto the sand path was noted with relief by the sailors. But the distraught man holding the shotgun on the lieutenant stood his ground, even as some of those in his group turned and walked away. His eyes were locked onto Wake's. Something in the words just said was bothering Wake. Then he made the connection.

"You are John Newton and your uncle is Hervey Newton?"

"Never you mind who my uncle is or ain't."

"I know your uncle and was with him a few days ago. He and many others are doing very well at Useppa Island by Boca Grande. He is a good man and well respected by all. I know for a fact he would want to see you and your friends come to safety. This is no way to live, in fear and tension. Do you want your family to live like this? Come away with me to your uncle Hervey until this war is over."

"Ol' Hervey is doin' right? We ain't seen him in two year abouts. He was a landowner down Suwannee way an' lived a might different than our part o' the family. Always was a good man, though. Folks all 'round these parts knew 'im, but some talk poorly 'bout 'im now, 'cause he went off with the Yankees."

"The folks that spoke badly of him aren't doing so well now though, are they, John? This war is going to reach everywhere in Florida soon. We hear what the Confederate conscription and tax men do to you. It's worse than when the navy comes to your places. This war is bleeding all of you from both sides. It's time for it to end for you people now."

Only four men were left standing near Newton, and all had dropped their guns. One of them walked up to Wake and put out his hand.

"Lieutenant Yankee, I guess y'all er right. It ain't makin' no difference for Florida for us ta stay here. This war is jus' a draggin' on an' bleedin' us down. It's time. My family will go with ya."

Wake tried to smile and look relaxed as he shook the man's hand. The fisherman went on.

"My name's Ramsey. Jake Ramsey. They said I was too old at first ta join up the Reb army, but now they're getting' so desperate the conscript man tol' me I go next month. Gotta send so many and don' got many left ta send."

Ramsey turned to his friend and put a hand on the shotgun's barrel, lowering it away from Wake's face.

"John, got to for our families. You do too, an' you know it. It's over now for us."

Newton's body sagged as he let the gun drop to the ground and looked again at Wake, this time with sad eyes that betrayed the inner turmoil of a man who's world would never be the same. Newton looked as if he would cry openly as he croaked out a quiet acquiescence.

"We'll go with ya, sailorman. We'll all go with ya."

Making an effort not to show the release of tension in his body, Wake slowly exhaled as he felt the pistol barrel ease back away from under his arm. Rork's other hand came up and rested on his shoulder. Newton's hands were trembling when Wake reached out and shook one with his own.

"Thank you, Mr. Newton. Your uncle and his friends will be very glad to see you. Life for your family will be much better now. Why don't you all go and tell your friends to get their things and meet back here at this spot in half an hour."

Newton and the other men nodded their agreement and walked back to their log and thatch homes. No more angry voices came through the darkness, but words of confusion and despair could be heard as the men explained to their wives and families that they were going to have to leave with only what they could carry. Wake turned to his men.

"Well now, let's all uncock our arms. I do not want anyone getting hurt through foolishness. You all did very well in a rather tense circumstance and I congratulate you. Now let's have Rork and three men stay here to help the people back to the boats. We have room for all who want to go. Those that don't should stay away. Any that get in the way of those leaving will be arrested. Young and I and the rest of this party will return to the dock. We will see you there in a few minutes, Rork."

"Mary, Joseph and Jesus, sir! I never have seen such a thing as the thing I just did see. You had me more nervous than a trollop in the front pew o' a Sunday mass, Captain. Thought for sure we all were dead, but most especially your sainted self, sir."

"Well, Sean Rork, I must admit to being a little concerned myself there for a moment. Not only about the shotgun in front of me, but about a certain pistol from behind!"

One of the seamen walking next to Wake added his words with a chuckle.

"Captain, you'd a been more than concerned if you'd seen how it was a shakin' in his hand!"

The sailors spoke with humorous relief as they recounted the events while walking back to the depot dock, except for Young, whose apoplectic state had not altered with the ending of the standoff. He stayed silent and staring as he was led by the arm along the path by a burly sailor who didn't care about the foreigner's former status.

Calling out the password "Michigan" as they came back through the picket lines, Wake examined the scene around the depot. Lanterns were casting a dim glow as men in dark blue loaded the last of the gray cotton bales and reddish brown turpentine barrels on the ships at the dock. Sullen prisoners from the ships were sitting on the ground under guard in the pole barn. Some of the pitiful refugees, crying children in tow, were already arriving at the depot, carrying a few bundles and boxes. The scene was one of purposeful energy, and all hands were engaged in accomplishing the many tasks needed to get the ships and people under way in time to have a high enough water level to cross the shoals and reefs outside the river.

One of the Floridians came up to Wake, followed by a disheveled woman and two dirty youngsters. The man looked distraught.

"Sir, we have a small punt boat. I need that boat. Can we take it away with us, tow it behind? We all need our boats to fish wherever we go. They only 'bout ten ta fifteen feet. No problem for ya ta tow."

Wake saw the need instantly and agreed, speaking to the man and a petty officer standing next to him.

"Yes, of course. This petty officer will arrange for your boats to be towed."

Wake sighed and looked at his pocket watch, surprised to see they had less than an hour before dawn. The tide was now past slack high with no current showing in the river, but that would soon change. They had to get out quickly. The refugees, confused and not certain this was the right choice, were milling about at the dock. Rork could be heard coming down the path with more of them.

A sudden disturbance close by shifted Wake's attention to a refugee man cursing and assaulting someone. The attacker called out to the men around him.

"That's the bastard, right there, that led them inta our river! That limey bastard gave us away ta the Yankees an' caused all o' this. I'll kill ya for bringin' the war to my family here. We came here last year to get away from it, ya greedy bastard."

Two sailors pulled the fisherman off Young, who cowered on the ground after receiving several blows from the man. The fisherman's family looked on with blank faces in the lantern glow as he was led away to where the other prisoners sat. When Young saw Wake, he got up and stood in front of him.

"You've got to protect me from these people, Lieutenant. These evil miscreants want to kill me."

"Young, you stay with the sailors on the ships over there. Just remember the danger you felt here tonight and don't come back."

Wake got Rork to herd the refugees onto the ships at the docks. While he was doing so, Rork explained that of the forty-two people that lived at the mouth of the river, thirty-five had elected to leave with the navy. The other seven fled up the road to the interior on horses taken from the other homes. Rork said the refugees advised him that there was a militia company stationed ten miles away up the road and that the refugees were now afraid they would be captured as traitors by the militia before they could escape.

Wake's voice came out grim. "It's time to depart right now. If they left when we had our first confrontation, then it won't be long until that militia arrives. All refugees go in the ships' boats. They can get out then even if the schooners are hard aground. Cast off the vessels at the dock and get ready to fire the depot."

"Aye aye, sir. We better be quicker than an Anglican through Derry, 'cause I see the first light acomin' now!"

Dawn was beginning to be seen and heard as the sky took on a grayish tint and the marsh day birds started their calls. The ebb tide could now be identified by the swirling eddies around the pilings of the dock and the small boats trailing off downstream. Cursing rose to the dominant sound as the sailors pushed the sloop and the schooner off from the main structure of the dock, while other bluejackets torched a trail of gunpowder leading to some turpentine and lantern oil that had been splashed over the dock and barn.

A flame rushed up the pine column of the depot barn and ignited the thatch of the roof. The fire spread in all directions, producing billows of black smoke that rolled up and away from the scene. The glare of light reached far out into the river, illuminating the civilians and sailors in a momentary tableau before the light flickered down. The seamen and refugees grew pensive as they watched the crackling of the flames. The sounds of the fire roaring ever louder scared the morning birds into silence. Patches of flaming thatch soared above the flotilla as it drifted down toward the first bend in the river.

The ships' boats, even though overloaded with the Floridians and their most valued personal belongings, moved faster than the larger vessels as their oars bit into the water and propelled them with the current. The refugees' small fishing boats were towed three and four in line astern of the ships, like adolescents following their elders away from danger. Sailors aboard the sloop and schooner readied spars to push off the upcoming shoals. Sails were hoisted in an effort to catch the faint zephyrs coming off the swampy shoreline. Everyone in the flotilla watched the northern bank, where the settlement's dwellings clung along the river—the refugees taking a last look at their homes and the sailors looking out for any signs of the Confederate militia's arrival.

A boom from the mouth of the river startled the atmosphere. A second boom was followed by gun shots and a yell from around the bend. A staccato rash of pops and bangs came resounding upriver, echoing between the banks as the flotilla of the sloop, the schooner, and the three small boats made their way around the bend. There they saw the gauntlet that lay ahead of them. Wake, on the schooner, took a deep breath and pointed toward the musket flashes among the homes on the bank, yelling to Rork over on the sloop.

"Rebel militia! Get everyone behind cover of some sort. Lay your fire into the Rebels on the bank as soon as you can. We must protect the refugees in the boats! Get the boats on our port sides."

"Aye, Captain! We'll be firing now, but the boats are too far ahead!"

A fusillade of musket shots came from the deck of the schooner as another blasted out from the sloop. Sporadic shots came from the boats as sailors and refugees fired over the gunwales to protect the men rowing. Small clouds of gun smoke hung above the vessels in the strengthening light. From close by a hut on shore a volley of shots whizzed around Wake, some of the lead missiles thudding into the wood deck house and mast near him. Then the militiamen fired again and continued without respite. The volume of shots was more than any other time Wake had been under enemy fire, and he was immediately impressed with the ability of these Confederates to maintain it.

Return fire from the sailors was now individual and carefully aimed, but the enemy had more to barricade and conceal him than did the navy men. War hoops and yells could be heard with shouted insults to the Floridians fleeing in the boats. Simultaneous blasts of the muskets and shotguns from groups of Confederate militia sent a wall of bullets and pellets across the water from the river bank into the crowded ships. Soon screams could be heard, some of them female. Wake started to feel his legs weaken and gripped a shroud for support as he urged the men to fire as fast as they could.

"Fire at them, damn you. Keep shooting. Shoot them down now!"

Finally the mouth of the river was in sight, with the *Annie, Random* and *St. James* visible, anchored off the village. There was enough open space in the river now for the morning land breeze to speed up the flotilla. It also enabled them to edge further away from the settlement dwellings that were sending flaming death out over the water toward the terrified women and children in the boats.

Boom . . . boom . . . boom, boom. The twelve-pounder guns of the *Annie* and *St. James,* two on each ship, blasted lethal flashes out over their sides with clouds of smoke billowing up into the rigging. Wake glanced over to the shoreline and saw what the wave of grapeshot had wrought. Everything in a line fifty feet across had been sheared off at the ground or waterline. No tree, bush, dock, boat, or dwelling was left standing untouched. Several men could be seen dragging others away into the woods beyond. Moans mixed with curses rose from the land along the river bank. No more shots came out from the settlement, but the sailors kept up a steady fire into it as they slowly floated farther from the Confederates.

The armed schooners again fired a volley of grapeshot, literally mowing down another section of the refugees' former village. Wake looked around the decks of the schooner and saw that two of the sailors aboard had been hit by the Rebel fire, one in the arm and the other in the shoulder. Both were being tended by their shipmates, and neither wound appeared mortal. Looking over at the sloop, he saw that several there were wounded but was relieved to see Rork standing tall by the helmsman. His survey of the ships' boats revealed a sadder result, however.

A woman was crying while she held a civilian man, presumably her husband, in her arms as she sat in the stern of the *Annie*'s boat. Two sailors on that boat were lying in the bottom, bent over in pain and cursing in rage as they clutched their left sides. Both had been rowing when a volley came into the boat. Exposed as they were while rowing, they took the brunt of the fire. Wake couldn't tell for sure at that distance, but by the writhing of the men, they both appeared to have very serious wounds. Two Floridian men had taken their places at the thwarts and were rowing. Others were bailing out water as quickly as they could.

The *St. James*'s boat held wounded also, two or three by the looks of it, with no way to tell the severity. Both it and the

Random's boat were closing in on the naval schooners and preparing to go alongside. Rork's sloop, ahead of the captured schooner by twenty yards, had picked up speed and was heading out the channel without stopping. As he got closer to the anchored schooners, Wake could see them hauling in their anchors and setting sail. Soon all of them would be heading out the channel and away from this place—if the water was still high enough.

Several isolated shots popped along the shoreline but were silenced permanently by a last massive blast from the *Annie*'s guns as she turned to the west. The two naval schooners' sails started to fill and move the ships. The *Random* was behind them and turning westward, followed by the ships' boats, the prize sloop, and Wake's prize schooner. Wake wanted to have Young lead them out the channel again but could not afford to have the flotilla wait while the sloop gained the lead. Time was precious due to the tide and the Confederates behind them. They would have to trust to luck.

The leadsman's cry did its best to discourage any hope as they crossed the first shoal off the river's mouth where they had grounded—was it only three-and-a-half hours earlier?

"Deep one! Now one fathom!"

The ships ahead were still sailing forward, albeit slowly, so Wake was reasonably certain his captured schooner would make it through this shoal. Then, just as he was reassuring himself of this fact, the *Annie*, in the lead, stopped.

Next the *St. James* slowed but kept sailing. The sloop, with a lighter draft, had no problem and glided up to the stranded naval schooner. Rork called out to James Williams.

"Captain! Send us a line and we'll put a strain on it as you heel her!"

A line flew through the air and landed on the deck of the sloop, to be secured to the mast and led out over the stern. As Wake's schooner approached, with all hands on the leeward rail to increase her heel and diminish her draft, the towing line from the sloop to *Annie* jerked out of the water between the two vessels. The sloop suddenly slowed while the schooner, heeling over as far as she could, bumped ahead a few feet.

The *Random*, sailing by *Annie* to leeward, also took a line and put her weight on it, producing another forward gain of twenty feet. But it was all taking far too much time. They were now past the time and water level of when they sailed into the channel. The ebb was flowing fast, draining the bay and threatening to strand all of them. The decision properly belonged to Williams, but Wake could not support the idea of leaving *Annie* there, at the mercy of a field artillery battery that at this very moment was probably arriving in the settlement.

St. James was farther out the channel, scouting for deep water, and thus was safe. It was up to Wake and the prize schooner to try their effort to get *Annie* off, in conjunction with the sloop and *Random*. An exhausted Wake realized the sun was climbing over the horizon and heating the air. He yelled over to Williams.

"Take our line, James! We'll try too."

Turning to the petty officer beside him, Wake struggled to keep his voice calm.

"Set everything she's got. Every rag aloft and all hands to leeward."

The jerk on the line as the schooner took the strain startled Wake and he felt her slow and stop. But he heard a chorus of hurrahs from *Annie* as that vessel slid forward, slowly but inexorably out over the shoal. Once released from the tether of the *Annie*, all the other ships eased forward toward the *St. James* a quarter mile further offshore. The report of the leadsman in the port shrouds now sounded more positive.

"By the deep two. Two fathoms."

"Oh Lordy! Not now."

Wake turned around at the seaman's comment and looked astern. At first he could see nothing due to the glare of the rising sun over the trees. Then he was slowly able to follow the pointed arm of the sailor and focus on some movements at the shoreline of the settlement half a mile away. He saw horses and a wagon of some sort. Then he understood. It was the field battery. He had no idea what type of gun it was or its effective range. If it was anything like a navy twelve-pounder then the flotilla was within its destructive power.

Wake shouted over to Rork and Williams on their vessels and pointed at the battery, then up to the sails, gesturing to set more sail and speed up. They instantly understood and followed suit, the risk being that if they grounded at a greater speed the chances of floating off decreased considerably. The hope of getting the ships out the channel now rested on MacDougall in the *St. James*, who was exploring the waters ahead of the rest to find the deep route. As that thought formed in Wake's mind he heard a sailor say the same thing to another bluejacket, and he smiled, proud of these men he served with. Whatever would happen, they would stay together.

A faint pop brought his attention back to the shore. There was no telescope glass on the deck and his eyes could not tell what kind of gun it was. A small skipping splash astern was followed by another larger one, a hundred feet ahead and to starboard. The seaman who had just spoken offered another opinion to his shipmate.

"Brass six-pounder, by the sound of it, Roger. Just a toy gun unless you're close an' they're shootin' grape at ya. Saw 'em when I was a soldierin' down here in '56. Useless against the Indians, but the officers insisted we haul 'em damned things about."

Grateful for the unsolicited information, Wake decided to ignore the Confederate artillery since there really was nothing he could do about it. It was time to concentrate on getting away and finding a naval surgeon for the wounded.

The second shallow area was a rocky reef that was easier to see in the daylight with the sun from astern. A few more desultory shots came from shore, but none came close and the Confederates soon stopped wasting their ammunition. Heeling over with all sail set, the ships and boats kept on sailing until they were in two and a half fathoms and the shoreline of Deadman's Bay lay four miles to the northeast.

At that point Williams called all the vessels together, hove to under jibs and foresails, with the senior men gathered aboard *Annie* for individual reports of the situation.

After receiving reports from various people on the status of the flotilla, Williams and Wake conferred alone. Then, looking exhausted but relieved, Williams called the petty officers to the afterdeck, there being too many men for a meeting in his cabin below. A chart of the coast was spread on the deck and the men sat down around it, the first time off their feet since the operation had begun last night. Williams was quick to the point.

"Here is our situation, men. We have two men mortally wounded who will probably die by tonight. Another seven are shot with moderate to minor wounds, all of which require a surgeon's care immediately to prevent a gangrenous infection. One man, a Unionist refugee, is dead and will have to be buried at sea as soon as possible this morning.

"We also have eleven prisoners in our custody from the settlement and the blockade runner vessels. Finally, we have thirty-four Unionist refugees who we have to get to safety as quickly as is possible. So much for the human factors.

"Now for the ships. The naval schooners are seaworthy, but the *Random* is leaking considerably from the strain of the groundings. The Rebel schooner, the *Princess*, and the sloop, *Hermosa*, are in good shape in spite of a great many bullet holes. Twenty-three bales of cotton and thirty barrels of turpentine were seized, along with a dozen shotguns and pistols. The firearms will be returned to the refugees who owned them."

Williams smoothed out the chart as he pointed to a place on the coast and continued.

"Our position is about fifty miles from the steamer *Clyde* off the Suwannee River. She has a surgeon aboard, and with the wind as it is, will be the closest help for us on a close reach to the south. Any disagreements on the status of our situation?"

The grim recital and question produced no comments. The men were experienced and knew what had to be done. Williams went on.

"All right then, here is what we will do now. I will take the wounded to the steamer at Suwannee. Then I will return to this area and see what more will develop. Captain Wake will take the refugees to Egmont Key for transshipment to wherever the navy wants 'em, which will probably be Useppa or Boca Grande. Then he will proceed to Key West with that Britisher, Young, where he will make the report of what has happened here.

"Rork, you will take the *Random* to Key West for adjudication. Nyland, you take the sloop *Hermosa* to Key West. Parton, you'll have the *Princess* and go to Key West also. *Hermosa* and *Princess* will accompany *Random* closely while sailing to Key West, with Bosun Rork, of course, the man in command of the group.

"I understand that all vessels have enough provisions to reach their destinations. We will get under way as soon as the wounded and refugee people are transferred between the ships, which means twenty minutes. Any questions?"

The strain of constant tension was showing on the faces of the men circled around the chart. Williams looked at each in turn, receiving a nod of understanding from each. As the men pushed themselves up off the deck, Williams paused and then said a last word to them.

"I am very proud of how you handled yourselves in the face of adversity and uncertainty, men. You did a difficult duty very well, and will be recognized for it by the authorities in Key West."

Saying their thank-yous and good-byes, the petty officers went forward and down into the waiting boats to be rowed to their vessels. Wake lingered for a moment and spoke to Williams.

"Your grapeshot saved us, James. They were cutting us up from the riverbank. It was bad and getting worse. When I heard the women screaming, I almost lost my self control."

"But Peter, you didn't lose control. I watched you coming

down the river. You brought them all out. Many people are alive because of you. Your plan worked, and even Admiral Bluefield will have to recognize that, no matter what antics you've done in Key West to annoy him. Good luck, my friend."

The two friends laughed at the thought of the pompous admiral, then shook hands and parted. Each was bound on his own course, away from a place they would never be able to forget.

8
Decisions and Consequences

It took all of the two days' sail from Egmont Key south to Boca Grande for the sailors of the *St. James* to rid the ship of the dirt and rubbish from the thirty-four refugees that had been transferred aboard off Deadman's Bay. The maxim that a clean ship is a happy ship had its reciprocal truth apply during that passage to Egmont Key. The crew did what they could for the dazed Floridians but could do nothing to lessen the overcrowding and meager rations that were spread so thinly among the fifty souls aboard the schooner, twice her normal naval complement.

During the daily afternoon thunderstorms women and children were sent down into the hot and humid decks below in the well-intentioned but mistaken belief they would feel more secure. The sloshing, stinking bilge water, groaning frames, and screaming children in the dark berthing deck did anything but make them feel better. The refugee men, many of whom were sailors experienced on small craft, assisted on deck when they could but usually felt useless and humiliated in front of their families. Until the sudden uprooting from their homes in the middle of the night, these people had been living a subsistence life with little cleanliness or organization and so did not, indeed could not, understand and obey the iron-bound rules of discipline for life aboard a naval vessel. The sheer number of people aboard resulted in an accumulation of debris and frayed nerves from both sides. By the time the schooner had anchored off the Egmont Key naval depot, the displaced civilians were miserable and wondering if the decision to cast their lot with the Federal navy and government was the correct one.

Leaving most of the refugees ashore at Egmont, Wake set sail for Boca Grande, hoping to receive his men convalescing there. John Newton and his family of two young boys and timid wife were the only refugees still aboard, for Wake was honor-bound to fulfill his promise made at that tense moment of confrontation four nights earlier, and also because he knew it would be better to separate Newton from the others. His history of emotionally antagonistic leadership of the people of Deadman's Bay was such that the other naval officers at the Egmont anchorage concurred with Wake that the best policy was to isolate Newton where he could not cause any problems. The other refugees would take passage to Key West on the next steamer bound there.

Fumigating below decks and holystoning the main deck, the sailors restored their ship and returned to their routine—and were glad of it. As they sailed up Boca Grande Pass, with the *Gem of the Sea* in sight anchored off Gasparilla Island, all hands in the crew prepared their ship and themselves for a reunion with their friends aboard the larger ship. Tales would be told of their exploits, and no small boasting would ensue about their captures and the resultant prize money to be shared with the men of the *Gem.* But most of all they looked forward, though with some apprehension, to seeing the wounded shipmates they left behind for treatment.

"Faber, we will go alongside *Gem* instead of anchoring. Starboard side to. We won't be there very long."

Faber turned to the watch and passed the word to lay mooring lines fore and aft on the starboard side. This was greeted with enthusiasm as it allowed more of the crew to visit with the men of the *Gem* than would anchoring and sending one boat's crew. The tide was flooding against the easterly morning breeze as the schooner, under plain sail, short tacked up the channel. Wake could see Baxter standing on the stern of the other ship waving to him and returned the courtesy.

Men on the decks of both ships were now yelling over to each other with ribald wit and reminders of past promises of debts or deeds. The only people on the deck of the *St. James* not in a positive spirit were the Newtons. They stood together by the port twelve-pounder with blank expressions as they watched the proceedings. To Wake's mind they appeared more like prisoners of war watching their captors than refugees beholding their liberators.

Soon the fenders were over and the distance between the ships was diminished enough to send lines across. The sails on the schooner were doused as she coasted forward and was secured against her big sister.

"Secured alongside, Captain. Orders, sir?"

"First, get our wounded men back aboard, then, receive the *Gem*'s mail and items bound for Key West, Faber. Be quick about it. I want to be under way to ride this flood over to Useppa Island as soon as we can. I will be aboard the *Gem* with Captain Baxter."

Baxter met him at the quarterdeck when he crossed over.

"Peter. Good to see you. From the shouts of your men I gather you had a stimulating time north of here. You must tell me what you have been about. I hope that at least one of us has been successful in the war effort."

"Stimulating is an interesting word, John. I would say more than stimulating. But yes, we have been successful, I think. First, how are my men who were wounded?"

Baxter did not answer but led Wake down into his cabin where they could talk. Baxter's cabin was larger than his but still cramped. In the light of a brass oil lamp Baxter cleared away some space for them and called for his steward and drinks. Wake repeated his question when they were each seated with a glass of lemonade in hand.

"Let me tell you, Reeder, our surgeon, did all he could. We got back here two days after you left, and we took all three of them aboard for care. The Useppa Islanders did their best but had not enough medicines for wounds like those. One of your men did not make it, Peter. Seaman Scarbond died just after we returned here. Reeder was surprised he lasted that long with that wound and the infection that was raging. We buried him at sea offshore."

"And the others?"

"Coxswain White is coming along well. Reeder says that the wound has kept clean and shows no suppuration. He evidently will require several more weeks of convalescence. The hospital at Key West can accomplish that better than we here.

"Able Seaman Jackson's leg is not doing so well. There has been inflammation from an infection and some atrophy as well. Reeder has done the things he could here, but doubts if Jackson will be able to serve in the navy any longer. I understand he is a regular?"

"Yes, he has ten years of service and was considered for a bosun's mate promotion. He's a good man and seaman. The navy is his life."

"I am sorry, my friend, but I fear that Jackson will be invalided out of the navy with that wound."

Wake understood the burdens and consequences of command by this point in the war. He accepted the fate of his men with a deep breath and expression of gratitude for the care they had received from the *Gem*'s captain and surgeon. He asked for the immediate transfer of the wounded to his schooner and begged the pardon of his senior for a prompt departure for Useppa Island. He wanted to deposit John Newton and his family there as soon as possible and return to Key West.

Wake and Baxter said good-bye ten minutes later, and the *St. James* caught the last of the flood tide to sail through the small islands in the bay around to Useppa. Anchoring off the island, a wave of memories, both enjoyable and horrible, from previous visits came over Wake as he looked at the tiny settlement of huts. It had been a while since Wake had set foot on Useppa's hills, originally the temple mounds of the Indians of the powerful Calusa Empire. The island held a strange air about it, almost mystical, even to a pragmatic man like Wake. He didn't believe in the superstitions of sailors, but there was something in the very smell of this island that gave him pause.

He didn't want to take too much time, but there were three important issues he needed to discuss with Hervey Newton before his sailing for Key West. Wake went ashore in his dinghy as the Newton clan and their meager belongings were rowed in the larger boat.

Hervey Newton greeted him at the beach.

"Captain Wake! An unexpected pleasure, sir. Please come and rest a moment and let me hear of your recent action against the enemies of our nation. I heard some of the boys just say you had been in a fight at Deadman's Bay."

"Mr. Newton, thank you, sir. Let me pass along the news directly, for I must be on my way before the day ends, sir."

"As you will and must, sir. Pray sit and tell me your news."

They sat under a seagrape tree on the beach, the heat and humidity of the summer afternoon making the slight shade ineffective in providing any comfort.

"Mr. Newton, yes, we had a fight at Deadman's Bay. Captured several vessels and burned the depot there. We also took aboard refugees for Egmont Key and this island. Your nephew John and his family are among them. They're being brought ashore as we speak."

Newton looked around at the boat grounding on the beach, instantly recognizing his nephew's family, a smile beginning on his face. Wake went on.

"We left the others at Egmont. They will be taken to Key West, but I thought John would be better here, with you. He is confused and very unhappy. I believe your advice to him would be welcome, sir. They need more help than just the material type, if you understand my meaning, sir."

"Yes, Captain, I do. It is a hard time for Floridians, and especially the men. Old ways die hard here. I will do what I can. He may want to enlist in the Second Florida Union Cavalry Regiment. To salvage his self honor."

"Precisely what I thought. But he has to be sure of that decision. And now two more matters, if I may, before you go to see your family."

"Yes, of course, Captain."

"I want to profoundly thank you for helping my wounded men. It was a Godsend to me, and we are all very grateful for all you and the other islanders did for them."

The old man raised his hands in protest.

"We did what we could, Captain. I'm afraid it wasn't enough for your man Scarbond though. We are sorry for his death. The two others we hear are doing better."

"Much better, Mr. Newton. We are taking them to Key West with us. Which brings up my last point—a request actually."

The elder listened as Wake spoke from the heart on an issue quite different from the others. Newton nodded gently as the lieutenant explained his situation and the plan for rectifying it. For Wake, it was like speaking with a grandfather who understood exactly what his intent was and how it could be realized. The two men, from such different backgrounds and generations, had been thrust together by the momentum of the war and fate. Wake showed his huge relief when Newton said he would be honored to help.

The shadows had lengthened to the east of the seagrape tree when they stood up and shook hands. The mosquitoes were starting to be felt and both men absentmindedly swatted them away as they spoke.

"Good-bye, Mr. Newton. I hope things work out for John and his family. I don't know exactly when I will see you next, but hope it will be soon. And thank you again, sir, for all of your help. Now, and in the future."

"Good-bye, Captain. God bless you and your men. I will be here waiting."

Wake thought about saying farewell to John Newton, but the beach was crowded with well-wishers greeting the family and helping them ashore. Instead he waded out to the dinghy and was rowed to the *St. James*.

As the sun began its descent the schooner rode the ebb around Patricio Island and toward Boca Grande, short tacking in the westerly sea breeze as another afternoon storm rose along the eastern sky. It was hard work maneuvering the ship through the shoals and out the channel, but finally they were free of the land. Turning due south, they sailed on her best point of sail, a broad reach, and slid down the coast of islands toward the squadron's headquarters.

Wake knew that whatever his reception might be from the admiral in Key West, the plan first conceived upon meeting Hervey Newton a week and a half earlier was at last well on its way to fruition. All he had to do now would be to convince the main participant. And deal with the admiral.

Boca Grande to Key West in the light summer winds was usually a two-day voyage. The *St. James* sailed it overnight, enjoying a rousing sail with fresh westerlies uninterrupted by the storms brewing inland along the coast. The spirits of the crew, already high in anticipation of the delights of Key West, soared even higher with this confirmation of their luck. Even the morning easterly was strong enough to move them fast, six knots and frequently more, toward their destination. The sunrise was clear and clean and invigorating.

None of these signs of celestial approval eased Wake's mind, however. He knew that he faced probable discipline for his part in the riot. Was it really only three weeks earlier? So much had happened since that night. He tried to prepare himself for the interview with Admiral Bluefield but found himself lacking any plausible explanation for his behavior that night at the fight. The obvious excuse of defending the honor of the men of the squadron sounded hollow in his mind, especially when placed against the undoubted reaction of Bluefield.

The buildings of Key West came over the horizon at the same time that Fort Taylor loomed up in its malevolent way. They were an odd sight, the structures of man built for commerce and society and that built for war and death. The fort dominated the harbor vista, forming the main point of referral for everything else as a ship approached the docks and anchorage. The massive authoritarian walls reminded Wake of his upcoming meeting with the man who had power over every aspect of his life in the navy.

St. James anchored just to the northeast of the naval wharf as the heat of the day increased. Wake searched the harbor for Rork's vessels, finally spotting them a quarter mile away nested together. He saw no sign of Rork.

"Faber, get the wounded to the hospital straight away. MacDougall, water and provisions immediately. No liberty for anyone until I return. I will be at the squadron offices."

With those terse instructions Wake descended to the dinghy without looking back. Acknowledgments were mumbled as the petty officers and men watched their captain rowed to the officers' landing at the wharf. The men knew what was awaiting him. All knew he would have to face it alone, but that the outcome would affect them too. They knew not to call out and wish him luck. That would be a breach of discipline and an embarrassment to him. But they nodded their heads a moment later as they watched him get out of the dinghy and climb the steps toward his fate.

The guard came to attention at the front door and the yeoman stood up in the outer office. Was it Wake's imagination or were they both staring at him? He was past caring and determined to get it over with.

A young flag lieutenant newly attached to the staff, smooth

and unruffled in an immaculate uniform, came out from a side office and greeted him politely. Extending his hand and speaking with more grace than Wake had seen in quite a time, the lieutenant explained that the admiral was occupied with some rather weighty matters but that he would be available to see the captain in half an hour, if the captain would be so gracious as to kindly wait. The man had the air of a social affair about him. With all the tension that had built within him, ready for an immediate confrontation with the imperious admiral, it was all Wake could do not to burst into laughter at the preposterous demeanor of the lieutenant. The man looked the very image of a stage actor playing at what he thought a naval officer should act like.

Wake sat down and waited. The half hour went by with no additional sign of the flag lieutenant. At one hour Wake told the yeoman to see what the situation was. The youngster returned with no definitive information except to say that the flag lieutenant said to please wait further.

At eleven o'clock, an hour and fifteen minutes since Wake's arrival, the flag lieutenant emerged again and profusely apologized to him for the delay. It seemed that the admiral had been dealing with the colonel of the Fort Taylor garrison on a matter of urgency. This mention of Colonel Grosland caused Wake to remember that he had enemies in that quarter also, even though he had sent his promised letter of apology. He set his jaw, took a deep breath, assumed his most professional manner and strode into the office of the admiral commanding the East Gulf Blockading Squadron. But Bluefield wasn't there.

Instead, as the yeoman called out his name to the men in the room, Lieutenant Wake found himself facing Commander Morris, the Chief of Staff of the squadron, and another man who was a stranger. Morris left his position by the window overlooking the harbor and approached Wake, shaking his hand and demonstrating far more hospitality than during Wake's previous visit. Morris's voice was actually pleasant as he introduced Wake to the other man, seated at the chart table without uniform coat and therefor devoid of visible rank.

"Admiral, this is the young man I spoke of earlier, Lieutenant Peter Wake of the *St. James.* He's just returned from Deadman's Bay."

Morris paused and looked at Wake, who spoke the expected words but still did not know whom he was addressing.

"Sir, Lieutenant Wake reporting in from patrol."

Morris finally understood and smiled.

"Ah . . . Lieutenant Wake has been gone from Key West for over three weeks, Admiral Loethen. He doesn't know of the change in command. Lieutenant, Admiral Bluefield was sent to Washington a week ago and has been relieved by Admiral Loethen."

Wake tried not to show the confusion he felt. The situation was now different, still dangerous, but changed. He had never heard of Loethen and wondered what his previous service had been.

"I see, sir. Welcome to the squadron, Admiral."

Loethen got up from his chair and crossed the room. His stature was impressive, with a large-framed body that stood over six feet tall and an intelligent face with expressive eyes. He was somewhere around fifty-five years old, Wake gauged, so about forty years of service in the regular navy. The man spoke slowly, with a Southern accent.

"Thank you, Lieutenant. I am anticipating an interesting assignment here. It certainly has been thus far, hasn't it, Commander Morris?"

Loethen eyed Wake intently. It was obvious that he was examining a man he had been briefed on earlier.

Morris replied to the question with a laugh. "Admiral, it has been quite a week, sir. In fact, Mr. Wake here was a subject of some of your interaction with the army authorities this week."

There it was. Wake waited for the onslaught of anger. But Morris was still smiling, and Loethen joined him in a chuckle. The admiral turned his face to Wake.

"Young Mr. Wake, I have never met you and yet I have had to deal with you in this last week. It would seem that one of the matters that I inherited from Bluefield was one involving a certain riotous affair that you, sir, evidently initiated after drinking too much Cuban rum in some little hell hole around here."

Morris wasn't smiling now and also spoke to Wake. "I would imagine that you recall that incident, Lieutenant, do you not?"

"Ah, yes sir."

Morris went on, with Loethen listening closely. "And the officer that disparaged the honor of this squadron, do you remember him?"

"Yes, sir, vaguely."

"And the ensuing riot that required the garrison to be called out of Fort Taylor?"

"No, sir. I do not recall that. I was in a bed and asleep by that point, sir."

Morris didn't react to the answer and his manner stayed serious. Loethen wasn't smiling anymore either as Morris asked further. "And then you left the harbor at sunrise in the *St. James* and haven't been seen here since for three weeks or more. Correct?"

"Yes, sir. I departed upon my mission up the coast and have just returned."

Loethen sat in the chair, sighing as he dropped a heavy hand onto a chart of the Caribbean Sea lying atop the table. Morris shook his head and walked away from Wake, going to his spot by the window as the admiral quietly spoke.

"So, Lieutenant Wake, you understand what happened and acknowledge your role in starting this commotion?"

The moment had arrived. Wake braced himself as he replied.

"Sir. I do acknowledge that I fought with that officer over the honor of this squadron and that I am given to understand that subsequently there was a large disturbance that required the use of the soldiers of Fort Taylor to restore order. I acknowledge that the next morning I departed pursuant to my orders and fulfilled my mission, which culminated in my return today, sir."

Loethen's eyes grew as cold as his voice. "And Colonel Grosland, what about him? Do you know of his complaint about your behavior and what he recommends be done with you?"

"No, sir."

"He says that three of his soldiers were injured by our sailors and that you, sir, were the instigator of it all and should be reduced in ranks to seaman and sent to Portsmouth Naval Prison for mutiny! What say you to that, young Lieutenant Wake?"

A flush of heat filled his face as Wake struggled to remain calm. These men could do just what Grosland had suggested. Confusion gave way to the raw fear of prison but then was replaced by emotion of another kind. Anger swept over Wake, the same cold anger he had when under enemy fire. His entire body tensed, and he knew that he should control the words that were coming as he confronted the admiral's gray eyes.

"Admiral Loethen, I did as I saw my honor and duty would require of me. I apologize for nothing, sir, and if the army thinks I would not defend the honor of this squadron again then they are very sadly mistaken. Furthermore, sir, I was not present at any riot or disturbance that may have occurred after my fisticuffs with that naval officer, but I can say with certainty, Admiral, that if they had used bluejackets to calm the situation there would have been no more serious bloodshed and all hands would have returned to their ships and barracks without further incident. It is a well-known fact that the soldiers use no common sense in dealing with the sailors and, in fact, look for opportunities to injure and humiliate them."

Loethen stared at Wake and said nothing, finally glancing over at Morris.

"Well, Morris, you're right. This young man is a fire-eater. Glad he is on our side. A few more like him and Florida would've been ours a couple of years ago. Why don't you advise Mr. Wake of the outcome of Colonel Grosland's complaint."

Morris's smile reappeared as he sat down with his arm on the windowsill.

"Aye aye, sir. Lieutenant Wake, the colonel commanding the Fifty-second New Jersey Artillery Regiment, Colonel Grosland, did make the complaint against you to Admiral Bluefield. Admiral Bluefield concurred and was pleasantly anticipating your return to his control in order to have a court martial go through its proceedings and endorse his opinion and impose his sentence."

Morris paused for effect in the quiet room. Wake was suddenly aware of the stifling heat in the room.

"However, unforeseen events in Washington intervened and he was recalled before he could implement his desires. In fact, Lieutenant Wake, his recall was so immediate that he had no time to even write orders to set formal disciplinary proceedings into motion. He left the same day Admiral Loethen here brought the orders of his relief. Do you comprehend thus far?"

Wake had no idea what had occurred "thus far," but answered in the affirmative. Morris eyed him sharply and went on.

"Very good. To continue, when Admiral Loethen took command he had already received some background on the situation from sources in Washington. It seems that Colonel Grosland had written to the War Department and General Hunter in Carolina that he was going to rid Florida of a particular young pup of a naval lieutenant who had no idea of how to conduct himself as an officer and a gentleman. What do you think of that, Mr. Wake?"

Wake didn't know how to answer that question so replied as neutrally as he could.

"I am concerned over that opinion, sir."

Loethen laughed hard and pounded the table.

"Good Lord, Morris! Young Wake is 'concerned.' He has an army full colonel with connections in Washington trying to ram and sink him and he is 'concerned.' Do you have any others like him I've not met yet?"

Morris grinned again. "A few, Admiral, a few."

"Well tell him the rest then, Morris."

"Aye, sir. A long story very short, Mr. Wake. Admiral Loethen here reviewed the matter and found that you should be counseled against a public, repeat public, display of violence with a brother, not to mention superior, officer in the future. Consider yourself counseled. As for the rest, he believes that the complaint of Colonel Grosland against you is unfounded. No further action is necessary. There will be no other discipline."

Morris stopped abruptly. Wake, thinking a reply was expected, was about to speak but noticed Loethen was getting up from his chair and putting on his uniform coat. The admiral's tone was angry, his face in a grimace.

"Damn them all to hell and back! In all my years of duty in ships at sea and even in the snake pits of Washington, I have never seen such an accumulation of bilge scum as I did in those memoranda of Grosland and Bluefield. I've known poxy trollops with more sense of perspective than those two. And I will not take one of the few men who have exhibited leadership and innovation in this squadron and subject him to the small-minded petty revenge of some bureaucratic nitwits who've not the least idea of which end the shot comes out."

Loethen stood there, an imposing figure in the gold braid of his uniform, with his hands held open in the fervor of his comments. Wake was very appreciative the admiral was not against him. He would be a dangerous and unrelenting enemy to have.

"Wake, continue to fight the war! That is what we are about, not some social fawning and promenading around to make old men feel important and secure. Fight the war, sir! Do what you do best. Now do you understand?"

Wake was stunned and could say nothing. Was it possible that this man, whom he did not know and who had never met him, had really decided to ignore that entire matter of the riot? Wake had never heard any superior speak of an even higher superior in this way. It all made him very nervous. Loethen was now gathering up some papers and heading for the door, speaking to Wake as he walked.

"I said, do you understand, Lieutenant? You have *enemies,* sir. One of them is this Colonel Grosland, who can do you damage on this island. But as long as you continue to fight against the damned Confederates as you have, I'll not participate in the cheap assaults of parade ground puppets upon you. Now get out there and do your duty, and God speed to you."

There was only one answer Wake could make to that kind of statement. "Aye aye, sir."

Loethen slapped Wake on the arm and turned to his chief of staff.

"Morris, I am off to meet with the U.S. Attorney on that seizure the Spanish are acting so vexed about. Makes you wonder what the deuce *they* are really all about too. Damned Spanish grandees. As if we don't have enough to worry about with the Rebels."

Without waiting for a reply he swept out of the room, leaving Morris sitting at the chart table with a bemused look on his face and Wake standing in the middle of the room with thoughts swirling in his mind.

"Not what you were prepared for, I'm guessing, Mr. Wake. Am I correct?"

"Quite correct, Commander. I am a bit dazed, sir. Pleased but dazed."

"Don't be too pleased, Wake. The subject of your lady friend is well known to Colonel Grosland. He hates you, and she and her Rebel family are tools for him to use against you. There is blood in the water and he is a shark on the prowl. You are the prey. The admiral knows about Linda Donahue. He can only do so much, and he can't protect you against yourself. Understood?"

"Yes, sir. But I am still confused about Admiral Bluefield and the disturbance and all of that."

"Admiral Loethen heard about your exploits when the prizes came in from Deadman's Bay last week. Was impressed by your initiative. Later he read the letters from Grosland and Bluefield. They arrived after he learned of your victory. A matter of timing,

Wake. Pure luck, which this time was on your side. Next time you might not be so lucky. Think about that."

"The prizes, sir. Did a bosun named—"

Nodding his head in agreement, Morris interrupted Wake.

"Rork was his name. Came in and made quite a report about your leadership. Admiral Loethen was not only impressed by what you did, he was impressed about the way the bosun spoke so highly of you. The admiral is an admirer of loyalty and those that inspire it. Remember that."

"Thank you, sir. I will do just that."

"All right then, you will receive your orders tomorrow noon. Reprovision, supply and water your ship. You will have three days personal liberty here, with permission to stay ashore, and then go back to the coast again. Possibly up to where you just were. I don't know yet exactly where."

"Aye, sir."

"And Wake . . ."

"Sir?"

"I know what you probably thought of Admiral Bluefield. And me, for that matter. Just know this. Someday, since you have decided to make this a career, you will change from a volunteer to a regular officer and may very well rise to the position where you direct and are responsible for the lives of hundreds or thousands of men."

Morris stood a few feet from Wake, fixing his eyes upon him with a sadness that was disarming. His tone echoed the look in his eyes.

"Loyalty to one's commander can be trying, but it is the honorable thing to do. You spoke of honor this morning in regard to that drunken brawl you engaged in. I can assure you it is much harder when you're sober and have to do it day in and day out for a man whose company you might not personally enjoy."

Morris put his hand out and Wake clasped it, bowing his head gently toward the commander.

"Yes, sir, I understand that. I understand it even more now.

Thank you, Commander Morris, and I am sorry for any problems I may have inadvertently caused."

"Onward and upward, Lieutenant Wake. You have things to do. Remember what was said here—there are men, and not just army officers, who view you as an enemy or an obstruction. Don't forget to keep a keen lookout astern. Now go, son."

"Aye aye, sir."

Wake made his way out of the admiral's office, through the anteroom, and into the outer waiting room of the building. His ears were ringing and his head aching from the multitude of worries and hopes racing through it. The sun was blinding when he stepped outside, the heat radiating off the whitewashed stucco walls with ovenlike intensity. He moved over to the shade of a coconut tree and leaned one hand against it, pausing to think out what he had just heard and seen.

Bluefield, his obvious antagonist, was gone from the scene. Gone in a very odd way, too, suddenly, without recourse or delay. To Washington, where he would be among his own kind, secure in some staff position of rank and respect but without the command consequences of life and death decisions. A parlor admiral, Wake had heard someone say one night over a drink of rum at the Rum and Randy. The kind that can tell a good story to the ladies.

Morris, the man he had thought a lackey to Bluefield, was still here and not the person Wake had previously gauged him to be. Evidently not an antagonist, but maybe not a proponent either. Still, a man to be reckoned with.

Grosland was the one constant. His minor annoyance with Wake had escalated into a serious dislike, based on the perceived infraction of his ego. The fact that his opinion of Wake had gotten to Washington and been circulated enough that Loethen over in the Navy Department had heard of it was troubling. The additional fact that Grosland was in command of the army operations in this part of Florida, and thus the martial law, made him extremely dangerous to Linda. He was the kind who would stop at nothing to harass her as long as she was on the island of Key West.

And Loethen. What of him? He sounded and looked the part of an old sea officer, but Wake was not familiar with his name. That was not surprising since Wake was relatively new to the navy, but it would have to be corrected soon. It was imperative to know about how Loethen would react to the plan that Wake was soon to implement.

Two things must be done before the plan could unfold. First find Rork and ascertain the situation in the squadron and particularly in Key West. Then find Linda and determine her willingness to do what Wake would ask. By the look of the clouds toward the east, Wake judged he had about three hours to accomplish both those things before a storm would be unleashed on the town.

Finding Rork wasn't difficult. The Anchor Inn, shoreside home of the bosuns and other deck petty officers, was dark inside after the white glare of the sun out on the street. Closing one eye before going in, an old trick sailors used before going below decks on sunny days, Wake was able to see a little when he got inside and made his way to the plank bar. That an officer was in the Anchor was unusual, but that he ordered a beer as if he belonged there was exceptional. Wake saw the eyes watch him as he moved to the darkest corner, where Rork was seated with one of the women who worked there. Rork waved him over.

"Afternoon, Captain. I saw that ye'd gotten to port. Tried to get o'er ta the *Saint* afore ye went to see that new admiral we've landed, but was a bit astern of ya. Ol' Mac said you'd set off already. Please, sir, sit down and rest your oars. This little darlin' is called Louisa, an' she's a wee bit thirsty, aren't ya, dear?"

Looking at his bosun and the dark-haired girl, Wake raised his mug in simulated salute.

"Thank you, Rork, I will."

He sat on a crude stool and smiled at Louisa, who smiled

back as she tossed down a glass of evil-looking rum in one try. Wake shook his head at the memory of drinking rum. Rork saw his look and laughed. His eyes were glassy and words came out thickly.

"Rememberin' the excitement of your last liberty, Captain?"

"No, Rork, just the misery of the morning after the rum-soaked night before. I do not want to repeat that episode . . . ever."

"Aye, been on that reef my ownself, Captain. Many a sailor has made that vow. An' I bet Louisa here has made them forget it the next time they came to the Anchor with a jingle in their pockets, didn't ya, my sweet darlin'?"

The fact that Louisa seemed not to reply didn't faze Rork. It was appearing that soon not much would faze him. Wake realized that he would have to broach the subject he had come to discuss while Rork was still in a condition to speak. Meanwhile, Louisa was staring at Wake, evaluating him with wide, frank brown eyes.

"Louisa, my dear. Would you please excuse Rork and myself for just a moment? Perhaps you would be kind enough to get us all a glass of your finest rum?"

Louisa kissed Rork on the cheek and smiled at Wake, then got up and sauntered seductively over to the barman. Wake still had not heard her speak. Like many of the women in the bars, she was of an age difficult to determine, but her experience in manipulating customers was obvious.

Wake turned to his bosun. "Rork, listen carefully, for I have a serious question."

Rork brought himself upright on his stool and faced his lieutenant.

"Aye, sir. Ye look more troubled than a soldier in a shipwreck."

"Rork, first, thank you for the kind words you gave the admiral about me when you reported in a few days ago. They did much to smooth out the turmoil I had expected to be plunged into upon my return."

"Jus' tol' the God's honest truth, Captain."

"Secondly, what do you know of this Admiral Loethen?"

"Only what I've picked up from the others, mainly in here. He arrived one day without warnin'. Down from the Navy Department he came, an' took over the same day. Admiral Bluefield was out of here like harlot from a church, sir. Same ship, same day. Gone like magic, they said.

"Heard that Loethen went into an early retirement at the start of the war. Man is from South Carolina and many in Washington worried about his loyalty, so he up and left the navy, after thirty years. They got him to come back a month ago as an acting rear admiral to run the blockade of Florida."

Wake looked down at his mug of beer. His hands formed an arch with his chin resting atop. His words emerged pensively.

"I see. A Southerner, who probably understands other Southerners well. But a man loyal to the United States."

Rork leaned forward.

"No doubt on that, sir. A real fighter. He was with Foote at the battle of the Chinese forts in fifty-six. A proper dustup that was, I hear. An' served in the Med an' Africa aginst the corsairs an' slavers too. A filthy duty that. A sailor's man, by all accounts, Captain. Nary a bad word by the salts that drink here."

Wake smiled. It was good news. Loethen was the kind of man who might understand what Wake was planning to do.

"Thank you, Rork. Now, one last question before your Louisa returns."

"Ah, my little darlin', Louisa. A girl that was made for a man, if ever there was one made. What's your last question, Captain?"

"I only ask because you seem to know so many things, Rork. But you might not know this answer. Do you know of a minister that will marry a Yankee navy officer and a local girl, quietly and quickly?"

Louisa was approaching the table with the glasses of rum Wake requested, but Rork half stood and waved her away gruffly. Frowning, he sat back down and eyed his captain. His tone was approaching that which he used at sea on deck with an ignorant new seaman.

"Sweet Jesus, Captain. What, in the name of Saint Michael, do you have boiling in that steam engine mind of yours? I may be more than a wee bit drunk right now, but even so I've more sense than to even think about marrying the daughter of a well-known Reb in a town where the army hates me and her family hates me. Have you taken leave of your senses, Lieutenant Peter Wake, of the United blessed States Navy?"

Wake met Rork's stare.

"I just might have, Sean Rork. I just might have. But I know what I must do, and I will do it and that's that. Now, do you know a clergyman that would do this for me or not?"

"Captain, the Catholic priests at St. Mary's won't because you're not of our beloved faith. That heretic Episcopalian priest is pro-Union—he's got 'em sayin' prayers there regular for the president and congress—but in his eyes the lady's a Reb, an' that'll bugger that. The old Baptist and Methodist preacher men won't because you're a Yankee. There's only one preacher that might, though I'm not sure his ceremony would be recognized as legal. And believe me, sir, it would be a highly irregular image of a wedding."

Rork's visage changed from grim to whimsical as he said this, intriguing Wake. He goaded the bosun on. "Out with it, Rork. What clergyman are you thinking of?"

The whimsy turned into laughter. "Why Captain, sir. A Bahamian preacher. A black African Baptist preacher man. They like the Yankees and would probably be glad splice you two in the eyes of the Lord."

Wake sat in silence and thought it over. An African Baptist wedding. Yes, why not? The important thing was the commitment, not the scenery. If it was the only way, then so be it.

Rork waved Louisa over to the table with the rum. She placed three chipped glasses filled with amber liquid in front of the two men and sat down on Rork's lap, stroking his head and trying to tickle his side. Rork's voice grew louder as he ignored the girl on his lap and slapped the table for emphasis.

"Captain, this is surely not a decision to make without the benefit of some rum to facilitate the mind, sir. Drink it down an' have another. My honor to purchase it. It's not every day I see a man toss a pile o' dung at a whole town, the United States Navy, an' a certain twit of a colonel, all at once. A brave sight it will make, Captain. A truly brave sight indeed!"

Wake took the offered glass and downed it in one gulp as the second one was placed in his other hand. He stood up and drank that one too, slamming the glass down on the table. He and Rork looked at each other, grins spreading over their faces.

"Rork, you'll not make me too drunk to stand. I know your ways by this time, Bosun. Now, I don't have too much time and I need your help. Go find the Bahamas preacher man and ask him to marry Linda and me with the words from the Lord. Ask him when and where, but it must be tonight, by sunset at half past eight. I've got three days of liberty ashore and I want every moment I can with Linda as my wife. I'll meet you back here at five. And I want the honor of having you be my best man. Can I count on you now like I do when there's death in the air? Yes or no, man?"

Rork caught the excitement in his lieutenant's voice and stood next to Wake, fairly shouting his answer. "By God, yes sir! I say *yes* to the man in love. We will make this happen and make it happen tonight! Come on, Louisa, there's no time for lollygaggin' in this here pub, we've got a wedding to make happen."

With that blast of words Rork slammed his own glass down on the table, sprinkled some coins on the scarred wood surface, and marched out of the room with a giggling Louisa in tow. Wake, still standing there, laughed at the scene just unfolded before him and then made his own way out as the few old salts sitting around in the darkness cheered him on. They had heard every word and thought it all great fun to see young hopeless fools trying the impossible.

The hibiscus bushes were thick with bright red flowers behind the house on Whitehead Street where Linda lived with her uncle. Wake managed to edge his way through them and stand beside some fragrant yellow frangipani as he threw a small shell from the alley pathway up to the window of her room. No response came from the interior and he tried again, whispering her name. She usually worked in the shop over by Duval Street until this time of afternoon, when many of the shops would close before the daily rains.

A third tossed shell got a response from a confused Linda, who stood in the window and glanced around outside before locating Wake in the far corner of the backyard. The smile that transformed her face warmed Wake's heart and he motioned for her to come out into the back yard to the cooking shed.

Wearing a red and white gingham dress, having just arrived home from the shop, Linda looked like some sort of dream girl as she walked quickly across the yard. Wake moved into the darkness of the cooking shed and took her into his arms when she crossed into the shadows. The smell of her hair was more intoxicating than the rum he had drunk, and it was all he could do to let her go and speak.

"Linda, I've missed you so much. I can't tell you how much or how often I thought of you. I love you, dear. More than you will ever know, I love you."

"Peter, I saw the *St. James* in port and came home early hoping you'd be able to come to the house. Rork came by the shop on Monday and told me about what you did up in Deadman's Bay. He said you'd probably be in later this week. He was very kind to take the time to let me know. But that battle and your wounded men. How awful it must've been for all of you. I worry so much for you, Peter. I love you too and worry so much when you're gone."

"It's all right now, I'm back. I'm glad Rork let you know too."

Wake could feel her tears on his cheek, and she clasped him again, clinging with desperation to him. His mind was starting to mist with emotion and he knew he had to regain self-control and get on with what he had to do.

"Linda, how is it here with your uncle?"

"He's still dreadful, Peter. Not physically hurtful, but he is constantly distressing me with his talk about the Yankee animals and how they have destroyed his town and family. He still blames them for mother's death from yellow fever last year."

"And your father, what of him?"

"No word since he was sent to the prisoner of war fortress up north. That aggravates my uncle's hatred too. Knowing that his brother is in a prison cell torments him every day. He feels he should do something for revenge."

"Does he speak of us?"

"Peter, he knows we are acquainted but not to what extent. He is outraged that I would even speak to a Yankee officer if I didn't have to in the course of my work at the shop. He would kill us both if he saw us here right now. The man is consumed, totally consumed. You can see it just in his eyes."

"And how do you feel about us, then?"

"The same. Peter, I love you with all my being. I don't care what the ladies of the town say about us. I am worried about the provost soldiers though. They come around and speak to my uncle and Mr. Carter, the shop owner, about being related to Confederates and loyalty to the Union. It just makes it worse with those two. One time they talked to me at the shop about what I knew of my father's activities. I don't know why they all can't let it go. The war is elsewhere, why can't we live in peace here?"

"Did any of them mention a colonel? A man named Grosland, who's the commander of the garrison."

"The man who talked to me was an officer, a young one, and he said to another soldier something about the colonel, but I can't remember what."

It was enough to confirm what Wake had speculated about

the motives of Colonel Grosland. With no combat command, the colonel had time to pursue other enemies far less able to hit back. Linda watched as Wake grew quiet and pensive.

"Why, Peter? Why all this about Key West and the family and the soldiers?"

He remained silent, sighing as he held her in the gloom of the dark shed. Thunder was detonating on the east side of the island, sounding like the guns of ships far away. It was time to ask, and he steeled himself for her answer. It all came down to that—what she said next.

"Linda, I have a plan that will take you away from here and this sad existence. It will not be an easy life, but it will be an honest one. It'll be a life where you can hold your head high among people who will respect you and respect us together. But most of all, it will be a life that you and I can build on, someday maybe having our own family."

Wake paused for a moment as Linda pushed her head away from his chest and looked into his eyes.

"Peter, I'm confused. What are you saying?"

"Linda Donahue, will you marry me tonight? Will you be my wife as of this evening? Will you trust me enough to leave this place of misery and go to another island far away where people are not as materially comfortable as this, but far more content and tranquil? It will be very difficult at first, being the wife of a sailor, and I can't promise you anything of a life of ease, but we will be free and no longer have to hide our feelings."

It was hard to hear her soft, simple reply through the sobbing, and he worried that he had frightened her from the prospect of a life away from all that she had known. She repeated herself in a clearer voice.

"Lieutenant Peter Wake, I love you and would be honored to be your wife. Physical and mental ease is something I have not known for so long that I won't miss it, but having the freedom to express my love for you will be a balm for my heart and mind. I will follow you wherever, Peter."

He smiled and then laughed as he kissed her again. Soon she was laughing too and they held each other, trying not to make noise that would attract her uncle or others. In their struggle to contain themselves they rolled from the bench by the fireplace to the floor, where Wake ran his hand over her soft auburn hair.

"Linda, I have sent Rork to find a clergyman to marry us tonight. I will meet him at the Anchor Inn at five o'clock to find out where and when our wedding will be."

"Peter, I don't know that any church will have us, especially without warning and because of who and what we are."

"Well, it might be a very unique wedding, my love. One we could delight in regaling our grandchildren about when we are old. But it will be a proper wedding and marriage in the eyes of the Lord, done by a real man of God."

"But who, dear?"

"A Bahamian preacher. A black preacher in the African Baptist Church from the Bahamian quarter. Does that upset you?"

Linda thought for a moment and smiled. "No darling, quite the contrary. I think it would be deliciously perfect for our situation, after all we are the black sheep to many people around us. Why not have a black preacher—the miserable people around us won't hate us any more or less for it."

Nodding his head and rejoicing in his mind, Wake kissed her again. It was a long lingering kiss. Finally he let go and stood up.

"I'll go find Rork, then return here around seven o'clock. Have a bag packed with what is dearest to you and be ready to leave. After the wedding we'll get a room here on the island for a few days and proceed onward from there. I'll get you passage on a ship bound up the coast to that island I've told you about before, where those kind refugee people live, Useppa Island it's called. You'll like them. Do you remember?"

"Yes. How long do you think I will live there among them?"

"Until the war and this chaos ends. Until we can settle into a proper home somewhere. Maybe a year, maybe more."

"Peter, my heart is pounding, can you hear it?"

"No more than mine. It won't be easy, Linda, but we'll handle what comes our way and make ourselves a life together. Until later, darling."

He straightened himself and walked out the back of the shed into the sunlight of the western sky. Behind him the eastern sky was a jumble of white billowing clouds sitting atop a line of dark blue-gray with lightning streaking through it. Thunder rumbled and the wind picked up. Excitement was in the air and Wake felt like he did after making the decision to take his ship and crew into a dangerous situation. Exhilaration filled him. The moments of doubt were gone.

The Anchor Inn was more crowded than earlier but Rork sat at the same table in the far corner. Louisa was on his lap and pouring a beer into his mouth when Wake sat down at the table. Rork, tipsy but not totally drunk, glanced over at his captain.

"Ah, sir. Good news for the lovebirds. The Reverend David Pinder of Andros Island will be more than delighted to perform the sacred deed. It would appear that the preacher is a supporter o' the recent proclamation o' his honor the president and views us in the navy as Lincoln's sword and shield, sir. Reverend Pinder did say that he believed that the marriage might not be recognized by the strictest legal interpretation of the Key West authorities, however. He said they can be quite dull about such things, sir, but that the important thing is that the marriage is a covenant before the Lord. The man was as elegant as a bishop on the matter, don't you agree, Louisa?"

Louisa said nothing but smiled at Wake, who was beginning to think she might be a mute for her apparent lack of speech so far in their acquaintance. Wake turned his eyes back to the bosun.

"Excellent, Rork. Now, where and when?"

"Well, Captain, when I suggested this should all take place somewhere other than his rather wee church where the congregation might suffer retribution from the army authorities, he agreed and suggested a place that will provide a most secluded dignity, sir. But I don't know if the lady o' your life would fancy the thought o' it."

A mocking grimness came to Rork's face as he raised his eyebrows and rubbed his chin with his hand. Wake could tell the bosun was enjoying it all and went along with the flavor of the moment.

"Well Rork, I think at this point she might very well appreciate any place, so long as there is a wedding with a real preacher. Where and when?"

Rork assumed an exaggerated look of decorum, with his back straightened, chest expanded, and his voice deepened.

"The African Cemetery on the south beach at sunset, sir. Secluded and dignified. An' a wee bit romantic with the sunset an' ocean an' all."

"The African Cemetery, Rork?"

"Aye, the African Cemetery, with all its grandeur, sir. A mighty statement if e'er there is one, sir."

Wake did not know what to say. None of this business about black Bahamian preachers and a wedding in an African cemetery had been in the plan he had imagined weeks earlier. He did not know much about the dreams of girls for their weddings but felt sure Linda had never dreamed of this situation. Rork was now grinning again, pleased that he had produced a positive, if somewhat unusual, solution for the seemingly impossible problem. Wake found the bosun's manner infectious and couldn't stop himself from grinning also.

"Rork, you are truly one of a kind. I am very glad you are on our side in this war. The African Cemetery it is then. At sunset on the south beach. God help us all."

"Well done, sir. 'Twill be a wedding that will be remembered for its love, Captain. What better could one say o' it?"

"Right, Rork. Remembered for its love and the solemnity of

its location. I will meet you there ten minutes before sunset. But now I need you to go to my cabin and get some clothes for me for three days. We have liberty in port for that long. Tell MacDougall he has the first night's duty, you will have the second, Faber will have the third. Our orders should arrive aboard tomorrow and I'll need you to get them to me. I want *St. James* ready for sailing on Monday at sunrise. Understood?"

"Aye, sir. All will be taken care of. I'll deliver the things you need when I see you at the wedding. Not to worry, Captain."

Easy for you to say, thought Wake as he imagined the wrath from all sides their escapade would stir up.

"Very well. Now I have to go tell Linda about her fairy tale wedding. Wish me luck on this mission."

"Aye, sir. May the luck o' the Irish be with you an' comfort you!"

Looking over at the door, Wake became aware of the general muttering of the sailors around him and the fact that he was the subject of much of it. As he rose to depart, several of the old petty officers raised their mugs and glasses to him. Calls of "good luck, sir" and "well done" followed him out the door.

Outside, the first strong gusts of wind were arriving, a wall of rain sweeping across the island as the trees shed their loosest leaves and fronds. Wake made his way down the lane and sheltered in the lee of a house as the heaviest of the cold rain poured from the sky and filled crevices in the hot sand and shell road, making steam rise. He always marveled at the volume of frigid water that came from these Florida afternoon thunderstorms. It was as if the weight of heaven was crashing down. The temperature would immediately drop ten or fifteen degrees. Afterward, the wind would lower and the humidity would become total, slowing even the most vigorous man.

Wake trudged along to Linda's house for the second time that day. He had walked several miles just that afternoon and knew that he would have to walk several more before he was able to rest later that night. Uniform soaked and clinging to him, he felt anything but the sterling image of a United States Naval officer as he made his way back into the nicer area of town.

By the time he arrived at the familiar house Wake looked and felt bedraggled. The weight of his planned endeavor was increasing upon his mind and the rain and wind were not lightening his mental outlook. He and Linda were courting danger, both bureaucratic and personal, and their life would be difficult at best.

His pocket watch said seven, but she was nowhere in sight. He waited in the cooking shed where the fireplace was still hot from the dinner that had been prepared there. The rain was starting to let up and the humidity was oppressive.

Mosquitoes were stirring, and their whining added to Wake's tension. There seemed to be even more of them this July than last year. That was another Florida phenomenon he had never gotten used to. The torture of the insects was constant in the summer months and drove him sometimes to the brink of insanity. Their attacks at the moment did not ease the time he was spending in the shed, waiting for Linda to appear.

He could hear voices inside the main house and thought that there were at least four or five. They seemed to be coming from the area of the dining room. A dinner party? It was becoming unbearable to just wait and wonder what was going on inside when their wedding would take place in an hour and a half. A feminine laugh came across the yard and he saw Linda waving to someone inside as she walked out to the shed and into the darkness where he stood.

"What happened, dear? I hear voices in there."

"Peter, my heart is pounding and my head is throbbing. It has been so tense since we last met this afternoon. You won't believe what has happened."

Wake's own heart felt weak and he sat on the bench.

"Tell me. What has happened?"

"My uncle invited over Mr. Carter and his wife and old man Selkirk. I had to make up a dinner for all of them and we are eat-ing it now. I came out here to get dessert and see you."

"Well, what about our wedding?"

"Peter, please. If I am to be your wife you'll have to be more trusting in my ability than that! My bag is packed and sitting behind you. I have also been to Ann Mary's house and asked her to be my bridesmaid. A bride has to have one of those, you know, and she is my best friend. She is thrilled to be part of this. Said it was more romantic than anything she has ever heard of, even if you are one of those Yankees!"

"Very well. It sounds like all is ready here then. You'll be prepared to leave here at eight o'clock?"

The moment he said it he realized he might have sounded bit dictatorial, so he smiled and shrugged his shoulders in apology.

"Peter, I am not in your crew and receiving orders, you know. Yes, I will leave here at eight, come what may, and get Ann Mary to walk with me to the place where we'll marry. But where will that be?"

Wake's smile vanished, replaced by a pained look. He hoped she would understand.

"The African Cemetery, down on the south beach of the island. Rork and the minister will meet us there. You know the way? Past Bahama town down that sandy pathway."

Linda stared at him and waited to see if it was a joke. When it was clearly not by the expression on his face, she put her arms around him and held him.

"Peter, that will be fine, dear. It *will* be a wedding to remember, won't it?"

"Yes, darling. Not elegant, but one from the heart. Our lives will get better from this night onward. Now, not to be rude but I must go and attend to some things. I will see you there at just before sunset. I love you, Linda. Thank you for all of this."

He walked back through the bushes as she whispered she loved him. Swatting an insect, he thought of the several things he had to do. First get a ring and a room, then at some point find a ship for her to go up the coast. He had only an hour to solve the first two problems.

As he walked to the Chambliss Boarding House to find the man he hoped could provide one thing he needed, Wake saw a provost army patrol marching from the regimental barracks on the east side of the island to Fort Taylor on the west. Their appearance reminded him of the dangerous situation for Linda in Key West and the need for him to get her away. He knew what he absolutely had to do and braced himself to do it.

It was after half past seven by the time he had made it to the Chambliss Boarding House on Fleming Street. He met with the manager and arranged to get the back room for three days. Privacy was mandatory, Wake told him, and meals would be taken in the room. There would be a lady in the room, but discretion was crucial and Wake did not want anyone knowing. The manager assured him that his stay would be quiet and private. He did not tell the manager, a Mr. Wakefield, the lady would be his wife. That would cause too much speculation. Better that he think she was just another prostitute with an officer on liberty.

Next Wake went to the chandlery store that officers of the squadron used. Uniforms, insignia, equipment, charts, and sundry other items were for sale. Most were used, having been sold by officers when they were transferred away and needed money. Occasionally jewelry was available and could be bought for wives or sweethearts.

The store was closed and Wake went around back, pounding on the door until the chandler opened it up with an angry growl. Pulling out his money pouch, Wake explained that he wanted a ring he had seen on his last liberty, if it was still available. Money transcending annoyance, the chandler brought Wake inside and said that ring was sold but another was for sale. It was a plain gold band but was all that Wake could afford. The story behind the ring was morbid, the officer who sold it dying later from typhoid, but Wake bought it and resolved not to pass the story along to Linda.

He thanked the chandler and dashed out the back door,

walking fast down the alley, across Eaton Street, then south along Whitehead Street to the path leading to the beach on the south side of the island. Confusion reigned in his mind as he went over the options of how to get Linda out of Key West to a place of safety and security. But it was all too much to think through right then and he resigned himself to take it as it came.

The clouds were gone from above the island, replaced by a deep grayish-blue sky. The storm that had swept through with such fury was off to the west northwest, heading in the general direction of the Marquesas Islands. A gentle breeze from the southwest, just enough to give steerage way on a schooner like the *St. James*, rustled the coconut palms that covered the island. The wind did its part to dispel the cloying humidity and waft the scents of the many types of flowers that grew everywhere and became even more fragrant after a rain. With the sun now descending through its final degrees of arc, the overbearing heat was gone and a softness enveloped the atmosphere. It was as if the violence of the daily storm drained all the malevolence from the island and even the very air around it. It was the most calming part of the day, and Wake finally felt at ease enough to enjoy the sensations of the evening surrounding him.

Reaching the beach, he turned left and walked past the startled sentry at the Martello fortification. Naval officers walking the beach in that area were rare, and the boy soldier stared at him while leaning on his rifle. Continuing on, he passed the Seymore Plantation's orange grove but saw no one. The beach was deserted. Wake had never been to the African Cemetery but knew it should be there somewhere close by. There was a point of land gently curving out just ahead of him and Wake resolved to go to that location and see if he could see anything from there. He heard people talking and searched eastward in the direction of the voices, finding the simple cemetery a few feet back from the beach. What he found at the cemetery was not what he expected, however.

Instead of the immediate wedding party and the preacher waiting for him, Wake found at least fifty people among the wooden crosses. Most of them wore blue naval uniforms. To his complete astonishment he saw half the crew of the *St. James*, several of the yeomen from the squadron offices and workshops, and many of the petty officers he had earlier observed at the Anchor Inn. Rork was there in his best uniform with Louisa in a gay yellow dress next to him. A tall dignified black-skinned man in a dark suit and white collar stood next to Rork, a Bible in his hand. Two other black men stood to one side, one holding a large conch shell and the other holding two crossed palm fronds in his arms. Though not as well dressed as their pastor, they wore their best clothes for the service. Everyone was smiling and laughing, several of the petty officers with glasses or mugs in their hands.

Suddenly Wake felt that old feeling of weakness that came over him whenever he went into physical danger. It was all too much. Too many people. He never thought this many people would be there. They saw him and called out to him. His pulse pounding, he slowly walked toward the crowd of smiles, abruptly struck with the incongruity of the scene: the beginning of a life together with Linda in the place that commemorated the ending of the miserable lives of the Africans on the island. Shaking the thought out of his head, he walked up to Rork, who was beaming as he introduced Reverend Pinder.

"The man of the hour! Captain, may I have the honor to introduce you to Reverend Pinder of the African Baptist Church, who has graciously agreed to perform the marriage ceremony this fine evenin.' A wonderful evenin' for it, sir."

Pinder spoke immediately, the lilting Bahamian drawl accentuating some of the words in a deep bass voice.

"Captain Wake, it is my honor to perform this marriage ceremony. I admire and appreciate your work, sir. And I respect your personal commitment to the covenant of marriage even with all the odds arrayed against you. This marriage will surely be blessed. I have done several funerals here. It will be a pleasure to do a marriage. We of the African community are honored by your presence here."

Wake was oddly calmed by the black man's demeanor. He had what the navy would call command presence. Wake responded to the man's sincerity in kind.

"Thank you, Reverend Pinder, for honoring Linda and me by doing this service. We shall always be indebted to you, sir."

The naval men out of habit formed several lines, seniormost in the front, and waited for the proceedings to begin, nodding their hellos to Wake. Linda and her friend were not visible, making Wake worry that they could not get away from the house in time. Rork, sensing his friend's worry, explained that Linda and Ann Mary were certainly there but behind a laurel tree and would soon emerge to take their places.

Reverend Pinder called for those congregated to gather around as he stood at the high point of the sandy ridge overlooking the ocean, gently lapping the shore fifty feet away. Directly behind him stood one of his assistants holding the crossed palm fronds over the reverend's head. The other assistant stood on the beach, head bowed, arms folded in front, holding the shell. In his sonorous voice Pinder thanked everyone for coming and showing their support. Then he began the ceremony.

To Wake it all seemed impossibly beautiful and profoundly emotional. Pastel colors among the scattered clouds above them formed a majestic backdrop to the scene framed by the white of the beach, the faded steel blue of the ocean, and the green of the grassy graves. The heavy air coming off the sea mixed with the smells of the jasmine and frangipani planted around the edges of the cemetery. The surf provided a solemn backbeat for the slow intonation of the preacher as he explained the coming together of man and wife and the solemnity of the covenant. Then he called for the bride to come forward.

From behind the tree at the rear of the cemetery, a tall man with gold braid on the sleeves of his dark uniform stepped out. He was in the shadow of the tree and Wake couldn't make out his face and identity. He held his left arm out as Linda came into view, wearing a white dress that must have been for church going.

She looked more beautiful than he had ever seen her as she accepted the officer's arm and they slowly walked forward to the sound of the waves landing on the beach. A shaft of sunlight, one of the last of the day, came through the laurel trees to illuminate the couple as they made their way between the lines of men. Then Wake was able to see who was escorting his bride. Lieutenant James Williams had come to show his friendship and respect.

It was almost too much for Wake to maintain his composure. He could feel the tears welling up, so proud to have these men attend his marriage ceremony, so proud to have a woman who would forgo the trappings of a society wedding to pledge herself to him in such humble surroundings. He knew that he would remember this moment for the rest of his life. Beside him Rork, struggling to stop the tears himself, put a hand on Wake's shoulder to steady them both as Williams and Linda arrived in front of the preacher.

James gave the needed reply to the required question, shook Wake's hand with a smile, and walked to the front line of sailors. Ann Mary took her place beside Linda and all turned to face Reverend Pinder, whose serious inflection now described the volition of the man and woman who were about to marry. When both Linda and Wake had given their assent, the preacher increased the pitch of his voice as he listed the requirements of a good marriage. The man's words boomed out in a measured cadence like a ship's gun salute, every person present listening to every word spoken.

And then the final assents were given, Linda in a frail voice filled with awe and Wake with a quiet simple genuineness. Wake looked into her green eyes and said he loved her as he slid the plain gold band on her finger. After she received her ring, Reverend Pinder's bearing changed from solemn to light-hearted as he gave permission to Wake to kiss his bride.

The sun made a last burst of luminescent colors on the western horizon as Wake held his new wife tightly to him, closing out the world as he touched her lips with his. Tears streamed down both their cheeks as they held each other, physically and symbolically, against all they knew would come their way. When they released themselves the misty-eyed sailors raised three cheers for the newly wedded couple, who laughed shyly with the nervous newness of it all.

The black man standing alone on the beach now came into his own, as he faced the final speck of molten red glowing far out at sea. Puffing out his face, he blew deeply into the seashell, producing an alternately rising and descending sound of joy that went on for many minutes. It was a wail of pure emotion from deep within his soul, strange and wonderful and ancient, as if Africa itself were saluting Wake and his new wife. All present stood there in silence as the man completed his primordial homage, diminishing the tone until it conveyed a soft farewell and good luck. When he was done no one spoke for a long time until Reverend Pinder grinned and shook Wake's hand, congratulating him and Linda on their marriage.

That started a general throng of well wishers presenting their respects and admiration for what they had witnessed. It was a sight that none of them would ever forget.

Someone broached a bottle of rum, which in turn produced sea stories from the assembled sailors, who had gathered around a growing fire of driftwood down on the beach. One of the reverend's assistants then produced a pair of small drums, which he played with surprising effect, and the other pulled out a bamboo flute. The drum man began singing the songs of his people, with Reverend Pinder and Rork joining in the harmony, and the flute player providing a lilting melody. Soon the sounds of singing and laughing came from the beach by the African Cemetery as the stars began to emerge in the darkening sky.

Heading away from the party, Peter and Linda Wake walked down the beach arm in arm, both silently drinking in the sensations of the sky and sea and sand around them. Linda stopped and stared out over the ocean, a tiny voice coming from her.

"Peter, we've made the right decision. I know it in my heart.

Whatever happens in the future, this was the right thing to do, and the right way to do it. Peter, I love you so much."

Wake could barely speak for the depth of feeling in his own heart.

"I love you too, dear, and I always will. It was and is the right decision and I am proud that we did it the way we did. And someday, we will tell our children and grandchildren about how and where we were married. And how fortunate we were to have such a special moment for our wedding."

9
An Officer's Duty

The manager of the boarding house was true to his word. With a minimum of intrusions, the couple stayed in room four, tucked away in the back of the building on the second story, overlooking the alley. Linda told Wake the story of the building as she traced the outline of his scar with her finger while they lay in bed the first morning.

"When I was a little girl this was one of the grandest homes in Key West. It was owned by a family that had shipping interests in Charleston who would come here in the winter. My parents knew them through business, and my mother would take me here for tea sometimes. They had a little girl I was supposed to play with, but she was a spoiled brat and I tried to ignore her as much as I could and be polite. My mother always insisted I be polite with everyone." Linda paused and gave a smile to her husband. "Have I been polite enough with you, Peter?"

He responded with a grin and kissed her. "*Deliciously* polite, my dear, as you should be. A wife should be as polite as possible, as often as possible, with her husband. Please remember that for the future."

Linda laughed. "Why Peter Wake, you make me want to be as *polite* as I can, all the time!"

He took her in his arms again. "I do believe Mrs. Wake, this would be an excellent moment to demonstrate some of that politeness."

An hour later, Linda went on to describe how the building had gone from beautiful home of a rich merchant family to wartime officers' boarding house. She explained that when the war came, the son of the owner had stayed loyal to his state and entered the Confederate Navy. He was assigned a staff position in at naval headquarters in Richmond with Stephen Mallory, the Secretary of the Navy for the Confederacy, and an old family friend from Key West. Linda had heard that he had survived the war so far, but he would never again see his family's home in Key West since the taxes had not been paid and it had been subsequently sold. By the time of the tax sale it was in disrepair and well past its glory. The new owner, residing in Philadelphia and operating it through the manager, felt no need to address the problems as he just wanted some income while he could get it. The home was divided into six apartments that were rented out to army or naval officers by the week. It was just another of the war's effects upon the town. Linda told the story without rancor, but with disappointment of how the once-grand home had come to be so faded and worn in such a short time.

Each day the scullery maid, a black girl of thirteen, brought a newspaper and breakfast into the room then withdrew until she brought lunch, and later, dinner. Wake wondered if she had heard about the wedding in the African Cemetery but did not ask, as she was very shy and he did not want to draw any extra attention.

Wake hadn't known the comfort of a soft bed for a long time. To lie there, holding his wife after making love, and spend the day talking about their future hopes and dreams seemed almost decadent after the privations he had recently endured. He wished they could live like this forever. But he knew that her family and his duty would continue to keep them from a normal life together for as long as the war lasted.

Linda's family and friends had discovered her deed by three hastily written letters. One she had left in the house for her uncle, and the others she had given to Ann Mary, sworn to secrecy, to deliver to her friends. These letters started out with the statement that she was a twenty-year-old woman who was used to making decisions for herself, as her mother had taught her. They continued with a description of her love for a decent man and their hopes for life together as husband and wife. She expressed her fervent desire for the horror of the war to end and peace to return to Florida, and she explained why she did all of this suddenly and without her family and friends in attendance. The letters did not contain the name of her new husband nor his profession. That most would soon guess his identity she took for granted, hoping to put off at least until they had left Key West any moves toward retribution against him. She knew it was the severance of a way of life, a serious one, but taken without hesitation beforehand or remorse afterward.

The second obstruction to their happiness was Wake's involvement in the war. The orders Rork brought him that week said he would take the *St. James* to the Cedar Keys to assist in army operations along that part of the coast. It would mean that he would be away for at least a month and probably far longer. When he would see Linda at Useppa Island he could not know.

Rork had brought other news, however. It seemed that he knew the third mate on the army steamer that took supplies up to Fort Myers on the Caloosahatchee River. Because many of the men in the Union militia regiment at Fort Myers had families and ties at Useppa, they usually stopped there for any supplies needed to go upriver. Linda could travel on the steamer, called the *Yucatan*, as a regular passenger and no one would bother her about her new identity. The ship would depart the commercial dock on Monday at noon, six hours after the *St. James* would sail at sunrise.

Linda had specific questions about life on Useppa. Over the last year, Wake had talked several times about the refugee community there, and in particular Hervey Newton. Her questions now concentrated on the details of life there and how she could be ready for it. She had lived in Key West all her life and had never known the kind of basic existence she would have on that little island.

Key West before the war had been prosperous, having in the 1830s the highest per capita income in the nation. All the amenities had come to the town through trade from around the South and the Caribbean, so that Linda Donahue had lived an easier life than many in similar sized towns of three thousand people on the mainland. Wake knew that Useppa Island, with its population of several dozen refugees living in palm frond huts on fish and fruit would be a considerable change for her. As he discussed the islanders' way of life with her, Wake had nervous visions of her not adjusting to it and being miserable. But she was adamantly willing to go, and her spirit bolstered his.

Included in the price of the bed and fare was a daily newspaper, the first Wake had seen for a month or more. It carried the news of the island's affairs as well as information passed along from other parts of the country about the war far to the north. The reports were of events four to six weeks old, from back in June and July. Wake pored over it each day, trying to obtain some sign the war was ending. He could find none. In fact, the Confederacy's armies appeared as strong as ever, as chronicled in the newspaper's litany of disasters.

Grant had been severely repulsed in a frontal assault at a place called Cold Harbor, Virginia, 7,000 soldiers dead in half an hour. The newspaper correspondent wrote that the despondent soldiers had known they would be killed in the battle and had pinned notes to their coats with their names and families' addresses. Many of the politicians from the states whose regiments were decimated were calling for inquiries into Grant's leadership.

The depressing news went on. In Mississippi, a Rebel general named Forrest defeated a Union force at Brice's Crossroads. The Rebels had also repulsed a Federal cavalry raid in the Shenandoah Valley of Virginia under a general named Sheridan. In Georgia, they had driven back U.S. General Sherman at a Kennesaw Mountain. They even had gone back up into Maryland and beaten the Union army at Monocacy. Washington was in a panic.

Wake read that the Republicans had nominated Lincoln again, this time with some politician from Tennessee named Johnson as his candidate for vice president. All in all, it looked like the hope from the previous winter that 1864 would be the last year of the war was not going to come true. In fact, 1864 was unfolding very badly. The men of the Confederacy had demonstrated that they still possessed plenty of skill and endurance to fight onward. They were far from beaten, and Wake marveled at their commitment.

The only good news he read about the war was the product of extraordinary efforts by the U.S. Navy. After months of searching, the U.S.S. *Kearsarge*, commanded by Captain John Winslow, had finally brought the C.S.S. *Alabama* to battle off the port of Cherbourg, France, in mid-June. The Northern papers reported that Raphael Semmes' *Alabama* had been sunk in a glorious manner but that the "pirate" Semmes, who was responsible for the destruction of fifty-eight Union ships, had escaped capture when a British yacht had picked him up out of the water. As he read the account of the battle, Wake wondered what Alexander Semmes would think of the news. Alexander was Raphael's pro-Union cousin who had stayed in the U.S. Navy and served on the west coast of Florida in command of the U.S.S. *Tahoma* until last December. He had an excellent reputation in the navy, but still it must have been difficult to see that a man of your own family was so successful against the cause you were fighting for. Well, he's not the first, Wake reasoned, and he probably won't be the last with family on the other side.

The Rebel cruisers had been one of the reasons Wake had been forced into the war. They had caused the Union merchant marine so much aggravation that insurance companies would not cover ships without exorbitant rates. Without coverage, the ships went idle and crews were subject to the conscription laws. But Semmes' ship was only one of many cruisers the Confederate Navy had on the oceans, so Wake knew the sea depredations would go on along with those on land.

Rork's visit to the newlyweds brought Wake more than orders and a report on the status of the *St. James*. He brought news from the squadron offices of another great naval victory at Mobile Bay. He heard from a yeoman that only a week earlier Admiral Farragut had pushed past the forts at the mouth of the bay and defeated the Confederates. Word had come from one of the ships involved that had put into Key West on her way up north for repairs. No longer would the port of Mobile be open to the blockade-runners.

Rork also brought word of the rumors going around the petty officers of the squadron, several of whom had actually attended the wedding, that Wake had married a "secesh" girl. Significantly, according to Rork, the talk was not barbed, but merely curious, as if it was one more odd thing "that danged Wake" had done. The bosun felt the talk had made it to the squadron's officers but of course could not inquire in that quarter. Wake had not seen James Williams and so had no idea of the reaction of the leadership to the talk of his wedding.

Rork also reported that yellow fever had been found on the island. Sporadic cases had made their appearance all summer, but in the last several days they were coming in steadily. The army and naval surgeons were worried. The hospital was starting to fill. Rork and Wake were both relieved that Linda was getting away from the unhealthy island of Key West in this deadliest part of the summer season.

All of this information from the outside world made Wake cling to his new wife even more, trying to make every second count. He memorized their times together for those future moments in his cabin at sea when the privacy of his rank might allow him the luxury of returning to Linda in his mind.

Monday morning arrived far too quickly. Wake remembered that first morning in May of the year before when he had to force himself to do his duty and leave Linda to go out to sea on the *Rosalie*, an armed sloop that was his first command in the squadron. Many times over the last year he had had to do the same thing. This time it was so much harder, for she had become part of him, the best part of him. She was his anchor to what was good and kind and decent in the world. He knew that when he walked out the door he would go back into the rough world of men on ships in the deadly business of war, and he dreaded it.

They ended up walking out the door together in the hours before dawn when, except for the army's guard patrols, the streets were deserted. Wake walked her to Ann Mary's home on Eaton Street, where she would stay in a back room until time to embark on the steamer. She only had what she could carry, and to Wake's misty eyes she looked very pitiful. Linda's attitude was the opposite of her appearance though, and she buoyed up his spirits once more by making the entire ordeal an adventurous lark. Laughing and with a wink of her eye, she told him she would be his South Sea girl on that island called Useppa, waiting for his arrival with various kinds of fruits and pleasures. They kissed good-bye as Ann Mary stood behind them, sighing with the romance of it all and watching out for any family member who might come awake at this odd hour and see them.

At last Wake set his jaw and turned away, trying not to show the tears welling up in his eyes. He marched off down the street without a glance back. He had many things to think about and needed a clear head to do it. As he walked toward the docks he went over again in his mind what he had talked about with Hervey Newton. The islanders would take care of Linda and treat her as one of their own until the war ended and he and

Linda could make a proper home somewhere. Newton had been honored that Wake would ask him to help and had assured him Linda would be made welcome.

Arriving at the *St. James* as the sky was beginning to lighten, Wake saw that the crew was up and at their stations. Rork greeted him in a cheerful manner, and as Wake responded likewise he felt his demeanor returning to the lonely manner of a captain of a warship. Ordering Rork to get her under way, he watched as the crew, many with smiles in his direction, went about their business with a minimum of fuss and noise. Observing the men on the foredeck haul away on the foresail halliard, he heard a voice that startled him because it shouldn't have been there.

It was White, the coxswain, moving slowly but still vigorously supervising the activity forward. Rork saw his expression and came over to Wake.

"Sorry, sir. I forgot to tell ya about the cox'n. The ol' boyo has some considerable charm, ya know, an' was able to talk his way out of the hospital and get back aboard. Had a paper sayin' he could, signed by the surgeon all proper like. Wound is clean an' he jus' needs to take it easy for a few more weeks. We can do that for him. The little fella says he's tired o' bein' cooped up ashore in a place where they're all sick. Wanted to come back home to the ol' *Saint*, sir, an' we can't fault him for that, now can we?"

For the first time since he left Linda that morning Wake felt good about something and he smiled.

"Fault him? No, if he wants to forgo the pleasures of Key West and the hospital, then we'll just have to take him along, Bosun. I just hope he doesn't regret his decision too soon."

"Well, Captain, I thought that you, who was also a guest at that establishment last year with your wound an' all, would understand his need to escape their clutches. Sometimes the sawbones do more harm than good."

"Aye on that, Rork. Pass along my compliments and tell

White he is welcome back by me. Now, let's shape a course for the Cedar Keys so we can help the army one more time get to where they are going."

"Aye aye, sir. Due north it will be, once we're out o' the channel."

Wake nodded his assent and stared astern at Key West. Rork relayed the orders to Faber, the petty officer of the deck, and returned to stand at the rail next to his friend.

"She'll be fine, Captain. She's a strong-minded woman who will do jus' fine. If they've used the brains God gave 'em, then most likely the good lady'll be voted the head o' the islanders by the time we see her next."

"I hope you're right, Rork. I can't stand to leave her like this. I feel like a cad who's fleeing adversity on a cheap excuse."

"You're doin' your duty as a naval officer, Captain. There's plenty that have done so, an' plenty that will. Grief an' glory are the lot o' an officer."

Realizing that some humor was needed to break the maudlin conversation, Rork turned the subject to himself. "Now, I'm a thinkin' it's time for some o' that glory. Without any attendin' gunfire, to be sure, but a wee bit o' glory an' some prize money for me pockets. Then me an' the girls o' the Anchor Inn will be happy!"

It did the trick, for Wake laughed and looked at his friend with mock surprise.

"The *girls* of the Anchor? As in many? Why, Rork, what happened to that one girl of the Anchor Inn? The one and only silent Louisa?"

Rork knew he had succeeded and responded in kind.

"Well now, Captain, that lass is a fine one, to be sure. A bit quiet, but she has her moments when she's louder than a banshee. You jus' ne'er witnessed 'em, bein' an officer an' all. Gets finer as the evenin' goes along. But she's a workin' girl an' me best friend only when she hears me pockets ajinglin' with what it takes to make her happy. Ol' Sean Rork is too old an' been in too many ports to get confounded on that issue!

"Besides, there's a few other girls that would fancy the chance to be happy with me on an evenin' ashore. I may be only an Irish peasant, but even I know it would be very impolite to deny them that pleasure, Captain, an' I am anything but impolite in the area of pleasure, sir. A petty officer's duty, so to speak, sir."

Wake smiled and shook his head at the image of Rork as a peasant in Ireland.

"Well said, my friend, but a peasant you're not. And I'll do my very best, subject to the whims of the soldiers we'll be with, to get you some real glory and the money that goes with it, so you can bring those poor lonely Key West girls some pleasure. One must do his duty, of course."

"Quite right. Thank you, sir."

"It does make me glad to see you're not getting too soft on the subject though. A firm mind will be always needed to keep all your women organized and under command."

"Command, Captain, as you're only too well aware, is a lonely burden, be it a ship or a port full o' girls. 'Tis only for the stout-hearted lads like us."

Faber, standing a few feet away, smiled as he listened to the bandying between the captain and the bosun. He, like many in the crew, attended the wedding and was happy that someone had found happiness in the ordeal they were all going through. But they were all worried for Wake and the revenge that might come his, and thus their, direction.

The egos and jealousies of officers were mysteries to most of the sailors. Faber, like most of the "saints," as the crew of the *St. James* called themselves, knew that Wake had alienated several of the regular veteran naval officers in the squadron with his unorthodox actions. The sailors knew that the regular officers resented him, a mere upstart volunteer officer commanding a schooner and producing tangible results in a backwater area of the war. There were other officers who simply did the minimum of what was expected and nothing further. The men in those crews had no respect for that type of officer.

The fact that Wake had married a Rebel girl was just another reason some of the career officers would hate him and aim to curtail his success. So Faber decided it was good to hear the light-hearted banter between the captain and the bosun and to know that all was back to normal on the *St. James*, whatever they were bound for.

The weather was unusual for the summer months, with three days of westerly winds bringing small gales and rains and no visibility for celestial sights. Dead reckoning their way up the Gulf of Mexico for three days on a broad port reach, they reached what they hoped would be the latitude of the Cedar Keys at twenty-nine degrees north of the equator. The schooner bore off before the wind, which was now from the southwest, and sailed east toward the peninsula of Florida, taking soundings as they went.

When it became apparent they wouldn't find the Keys during the daytime, Wake ordered the ship be tacked on and off through the night, staying well away from the shallow coast. Memories of Deadman's Bay and its reefs and shoals demanded caution.

On the fourth day they continued east as the sun finally emerged, allowing the lookouts to see almost six miles. At the end of the forenoon watch they saw a smudge of land on the horizon, but it took until the end of the first dogwatch to get close enough to tell the land was not the Cedar Keys but the Sweetwater Keys, south of the Withlacoochee River. There was nothing for it but to head back out to sea in the ensuing darkness and steer northwest. They were twenty miles south of their destination in some very dangerous waters.

On the fifth day the lookout spied the land they were looking for. In the morning sun the Cedar Keys showed as humps, darker than the coastline behind them, and soon the five-gun steamer *Nygaard* could be seen heading out for them fast. Before the *Nygaard* arrived, the details of the Keys came into better focus and Wake could see several vessels at anchor offshore of the islands. This was obviously more than a routine army transport assignment. Something important was happening, and he wondered what the role of the *St. James* would be in those events.

The captain of the *Nygaard*, a very tall thin lieutenant commander named William West, whom Wake had met at a conference at the squadron offices, hailed the captain of the *St. James* as they came alongside forty-five minutes later. He advised Wake that the *St. James* was to anchor with the rest of the ships off the islands and to wait there for the troops that would be embarked the following morning. No additional instructions were given, and the *Nygaard* reversed course back to the anchorage so quickly that no queries could be made.

The anchorage was in the deeper water four miles to the west of Seahorse Key, the southernmost of the Cedar Key islands. Surveying through his glass, Wake counted eight ships anchored there, which was a larger group than any other he had seen in Florida outside of Key West. Rork joined him at the rail.

"A grim scene, Captain."

"That it is, Bosun."

"Looks as if there's somethin' agoin' on here, Captain, but I heard nary a peep back at Key West about a big push up this way. Jes' some of the soldiers headin' north on the *Fort Brooklyn* there, but I thought they were bound for Tampa, maybe to set up a battery on Egmont Key."

"When did they leave port?"

"Saw 'em loadin' up some field howitzers last week, while you were living the life o' a English lord with her ladyship at the boardin' house. Must 'a been Sunday that they departed. Even that ol' barge got 'em up here fast. Surprised it made it, really."

"Rork, if they're bringing artillery, this is no routine run for us. This many ships mean a regiment possibly."

Both men assumed a grim face as each contemplated the possible scenarios they were getting involved in.

"Aye, Captain. Somebody's been getting' ideas inta their head about goin' ashore up on this coast in a big way. I jes' hope they knew what they're about when they planned this little excursion, so's those poor sods that has to do the doin' ashore don't get done in. This ain't a place for fools' ideas."

Wake didn't like the tone of the conversation and tried to present an air of confidence toward the upcoming mission, whatever it was and whoever had planned it in Key West.

"I think the word fool is a bit too drastic, Rork. In any event, we'll find out when we get up to the anchorage there."

Rork maintained his serious look as he turned to his captain. His eyes reflected a strange sadness even as his voice sounded neutral.

"Among the Irish, Captain, there is a sayin'. There's not a thing in the whole world as dangerous as a damned fool who is convinced he is right and who thinks he's got a strong punch."

Wake sighed as he turned back to eye the ships anchored ahead. More than Rork's words, his very manner bothered Wake. It was unlike the Irishman, who was always the man to buck up other men when events got difficult. It made Wake uneasy.

"Well, Rork, we'll soon find out one way or the other. Let's get that mains'l hauled in better. She's luffing a bit."

The steam gunboat, making nine knots, was back at the anchorage with her hook down long before the schooner arrived. When *St. James* finally arrived, Wake anchored near the other schooners that had been gathered from all over the squadron's area of operations. With no further instructions, Wake had the men set about their usual duties while he examined the small fleet they had joined.

The *Ariel,* under Master Russell, was there from Tampa Bay; the *Fox,* under Ensign Chase, came from the St. Marks River; Ensign Robbins' *Sea Bird* had arrived from Clearwater; and the *Two Sisters* under Master Partridge came from Suwannee. Only the *Annie* with James Williams was missing from the smaller schooners of the squadron, she being still assigned to the station around Key West. With her absence, Wake found himself the senior officer of the assembled schooner captains.

In addition to the schooners, there were several steamers anchored. The former ferry boat *Fort Brooklyn* was there from Key West. She was quite unseaworthy, being built for harbor work in New York, and had a bad reputation in the squadron. Wake had heard in Key West that she was going to be a station ship anchored at Tampa Bay and could not fathom the reason she was here at the Cedar Keys. Wake did not know her commander's name.

There was also the four-gun *Bonsall,* commanded by the well-known Lieutenant Thadeus Taylor, a large muscular man with an enormous mustache and hearty laugh whose very name was synonymous with aggressive action against the coastal Confederate enclaves. Wake had become friends with Taylor over several shared evenings at the Rum and Randy. Wake had learned that Taylor was a former merchant mariner too, but unlike Wake, who had sailed there in schooners, Taylor had sailed a coastal steamer in the Chesapeake.

The two-gun tug *David* was anchored astern of the *Bonsall.* Commanded by Lieutenant George Jonathan Erne of New York, she was one of the workhorses of the East Gulf Blockading Squadron and in demand all along the coast. Erne had a good reputation as a man who could overcome adversity.

On the far side of the anchored ships, Wake could see a merchant ship converted to a transport, her decks crowded with hundreds of men in army blue. Rork pointed to the soldiers' ship and nodded his head.

"Aye, Captain. An' there'd be the ones to make a little history ashore soon. I wonder what they told those poor beggars? Ya know, it could almost make a sailor feel sorry for a soldier."

A set of signal flags soared up the halliards of the *Nygaard* a few minutes later while Wake was below. It requested all captains to repair aboard the *Nygaard* at the end of the first dogwatch for dinner and a conference with Lieutenant Commander West.

Wake was advised of this by Rork, who also suggested with a wink of his eye that his captain wear something more formal than his usual seagoing rig of tan cotton trousers and white cotton shirt. That, of course, meant changing into his regular sea service uniform of heavy blue coat, trousers, and cap.

The new 1864 navy uniform regulations that had come out six months earlier had finally relaxed some of the old uniform rules and provided for more comfort in hot locations, but Wake did not have one of those new uniforms. Officers had to buy their own clothing and the chandlers in Key West had none of the new lighter weight shell half coats that were authorized. It didn't matter anyway to Wake, as he had no money to buy a new outfit—it had all gone for Linda's ring.

The regulations had changed several times during the last few years, and meetings of officers frequently displayed a conglomeration of the various types of allowed coats, hats, and insignia. In a squadron like the East Gulf most of the officers on the smaller ships, Wake included, ignored the uniform regulations anyway and dressed for comfort.

West's cabin on the *Nygaard* was magnificent compared to Wake's aboard the *St. James*, spacious even with six officers already standing there. It held a real desk and a large table with four chairs. Several oil lamps were stationed around the cabin, their glow making the stifling hot air even warmer. A bed that actually looked soft and pleasant was built into the bulkhead along one side. A skylight above brought the sun into the cabin, but by this time of day the rays were oblique and mercifully weakened.

Wake saw that the table had charts of the area spread on it and that the executive officer of the *Nygaard*, Lieutenant Partington, was quietly explaining something to the commanders of the others schooners and the tug. Nodding heads acknowledged Wake's presence as Partington continued his narration and Wake sidled over to the corner of the table. The gunboat captains and *Fort Brooklyn*'s commander had not arrived yet.

Abruptly, a burst of laughter came from the passageway outside the cabin and the door opened. West entered, followed by an army colonel and major as well as Taylor, the captain of the former ferryboat. Both the colonel, an older man with the smiling ease of a lawyer, and the quiet, almost shy major, wore New York infantry insignia. They had beads of sweat covering their faces, which were blanched and mottled. Wake thought they looked seasick and felt a slight sympathy for them. He hoped for their sake they did better on land.

Partington introduced everyone, Wake learning that the man commanding the ungainly ferryboat was a lieutenant named Charles McKinney. The army officers were Colonel Lucien Wherley and his adjutant, Major Robert Martin, of the 195th New York Volunteer Light Infantry Regiment. They had just arrived from Port Royal, South Carolina, where they had been on guard duty for six months.

West, Wherley, Martin, and Taylor, as the senior officers present, took their places in the chairs around the chart table as Partington gave preliminary information about why everyone was there.

"Gentlemen, all of you have been ordered to rendezvous here at the Cedar Keys in order to carry the war to an area of Florida that has hitherto been untouched. The Rebels in the area have been sending their beef and foodstuffs to the main Confederate armies in Tennessee and Georgia for two years now. We are all here to put a stop to that. In addition, we hear that many parts of the area are ripe with disaffection for the

Southern cause and would come over to the Federal side if they saw a credible force locally. Accordingly, the navy will land the army at the mouth of the Timucuahatchee River, one day's sail to our north."

Partington paused and looked around the cabin. No one broke the silence and he resumed talking in the direction of the darkened forward corner of the cabin.

"Major, would you care to continue on with the army's plans, sir?"

Major Martin came forward from his place in the shadows and stood before them, breathing deeply and placing a thin index finger on the chart's line showing the coast.

"The men of the One Hundred Ninety-fifth New York, supported by a battery of field six-pounders manned by men from the Fifty-second New Jersey Artillery at Key West, will land at the mouth of the river and march inland. The first day will be taken up with getting our supplies and baggage on the land. The next day we will march to and capture the crossroads at Claresville, where the coastal road intersects the road east to Collmerton and the railroad beyond."

Martin continued in his low monotone, breathing audibly and occasionally mopping his face with a scarf from his pocket. "At that point we either march the next day onward to Collmerton or make a left turn on the coastal road and proceed north toward Columbus or Jasper to sever the main east-west rail line in Florida. We anticipate hundreds if not thousands of loyal Unionists to rally to the colors as we go further inland. Any questions to this point, gentlemen?"

Martin stopped and waited for the men around him to speak. Most of them stared at the chart and moved their hands with nervous tapping or fumbling. The officers with experience on this coast, Wake included, knew that the water offshore of the Timucuahatchee River was shallow with many reefs. Getting over the bar at the mouth of the river to ascend the stream could only be done at the top of a high tide, and then only with the schooners and tug. The gunboats and ferryboat drew too much water.

And then there was the issue of the Floridians and if they would really rally to the United States colors. Wake had seen some that would but had never heard that thousands were waiting for the chance. And why only one regiment? This operation should take at least a brigade of three or four regiments. Of course, Martin, Colonel Wherley, and their regiment had no personal knowledge of Florida and her people. They were relying on information supplied to them.

Wake looked at the other naval officers who stood there silently. He could see they were thinking the same thing but not speaking up. He was about to talk when Taylor, with his customary bluntness, spoke first.

"Damnedest idea I ever heard of. The water's too damned thin at the mouth of that river, the march is too damned long in this heat for you New York boys, you don't have half the number of soldiers you need, and there ain't no thousands of folks around this coast willin' to give you anything but some lead in your belly. You might get a hundred refugees, and most of them will be women and children. Who gave you boys this idea, Major?"

Several of the other naval officers grunted out affirmations of Taylor's opinion as Martin stammered out that the plan had come from army officers in Key West already familiar with the situation in Florida and that his regiment had been sent down to make this assignment successful. His sweat now dripping onto the chart below him, Martin glanced over at his colonel for support. Wherley stood and faced Taylor while West leaned back in his chair and watched with a bemused glint in his eyes. Wherley's voice was loud and clear, like an actor on stage or a lawyer in a courtroom.

"Captain Taylor, I can appreciate your thoughts on this matter. *However*," he waited for a second and went on, "the time for debate as to whether the planners planned for any and all contingencies is over. We have been given a mission and we, that means we in the army and you in the navy, are going to carry it out. Will it be easy? No. Will it be successful? Yes."

West now waved his hand impatiently and spoke from his chair.

"Gentlemen, it is an officer's duty to follow his orders and to have his men follow those orders. The colonel is quite correct, the time for debate is gone. Let's continue and see how we can do this the best way with what we have here."

Taylor was getting angrier and replied with barely controlled emotion, his mustache twitching as he pronounced the words. "Captain West, an officer is also duty bound to point out when a plan is flawed, and that is precisely what I was doing, sir. I resent any implication from anyone that I had any other intention. Sir."

Wake noticed that Taylor's right hand was clenched in a fist and the look in his eyes was anything but respectful. West turned to the colonel. "Colonel, what opposition do you expect from the Rebels?"

Wherley's voice assumed its stentorian dimension as he described what he had been told. His confidence was loud, but it reminded Wake of what Rork had recently said about the old Irish saying about fools who are convinced they are right.

"Captain West, Colonel Grosland in Key West, who is quite familiar with the situation in Florida, has assured me that we might face a militia rabble at the most. They will probably have shotguns and pistols but no field pieces. They don't even know how to serve them if they had them. The militia will probably be somewhere around Claresville. After they are captured, we should have an unopposed march until we reach the main rail line."

Taylor greeted this information with a snort but said nothing. Wake didn't like the attitude displayed by the army officers and West. They were far too nonchalant about the difficulties to be faced. But Wherley wasn't finished yet.

"Captain Taylor, you expressed concern that our regiment would be too few men for this operation. That is not the case. What Major Martin did not get a chance to say was that the navy will be furnishing a landing force to assist us, and therefore we will have enough men. Colonel Grosland has planned all of this out very carefully and has assignments for naval officers and their detachments."

West smiled at Wherley, then around at the gathered officers. It was clear he and the army colonel shared an optimistic outlook on the operation, and that he was already counting on some of the reflected glory from it success. The other naval officers leaned forward and stared at Wherley.

"Ah, now I've got your undivided attention, don't I? The ships here will provide a portion of their crews to form a landing party under Lieutenant Peter Wake. He will be assisted by Ensign Chase and Ensign Robbins. Lieutenant Wake will command one hundred men who will hold the beachhead and the crossroads at Claresville after we capture it. Any questions, Lieutenant?"

All eyes swung to Wake, who had his own focused on West, whose smile never wavered. A sinister dread started to build within him as Wake replied with as much nonchalance as he could muster to match his superiors. "No questions at this time, sir. Of course, we will all do our duty. I must tell you, however, that a month ago I personally faced the militia on this section of the coast and found them to be well armed and persistent. They also had a field piece with which they shelled my ship, without success. Just so you know, sir."

Wherley and West seemed to be enjoying this. Wherley's reply had the character of repartee.

"Precisely, Lieutenant. You make my point for me, sir. They were no match for your sailor boys and you accomplished your goal, so they certainly won't be much of a contest for my New Yorkers."

"As I said, Colonel, the sailors will all do their duty. We've fought on this coast before and will again in this war."

Wherley now stood taller, beaming in his perceived rhetorical victory, and put a patronizing touch to Wake's shoulder. "Excellent, Lieutenant. Captain West here said you were the man for the job and that Colonel Grosland had made a wise choice. Now, let us return to the mechanics of this endeavor, so that all will know what is expected. This will be a great victory for all of us to share. I dare say, gentlemen, that our efforts in Florida will provide some much needed welcome news for the nation this week. Martin, my good man, would you be so kind as to continue in describing the assignments for these officers."

Martin stepped up as Wherley sat down. A triumphant grin spread across the colonel's face and he gave a smiling nod to West, who nodded back and then returned to gaze at Wake and the others.

Martin's narration of the details included the times of debarkation to the shoreline of the river, about a quarter mile in from the mouth, where the road met the water. The gunboats would provide fire if the militia showed up at the landing, and the ships would all furnish their boats for the troops to go ashore. The tug would tow the boats up the river to the landing while the schooners would remain just off the bar, their guns loaded with grapeshot. The whole period of the operation was put at a week, maybe more. By that time, success would be assured and more reinforcements could be requested from the Union forces in South Carolina or Louisiana to follow up and perhaps even take the state capitol at Tallahassee.

Just before sunset the *Fort Brooklyn* would steam south, with smoke bellowing profusely and all lights aboard lit, close along the coast in order to confuse any Rebel lookouts into thinking the intended target was Bayport or Clearwater. At midnight the ferryboat would reverse course and return to the anchorage. All ships would weigh anchor two hours before dawn and be gone from sight by the time the Confederates in the area could see the anchorage.

Argument against the idea was futile. The egos and personal stakes were too high to sway the senior officers involved. The smell of fame and promotion was in the air and the personal agendas of the army colonels were obvious. Wake resolved to make his part of the plan as efficient as possible and to protect the lives of the sailors entrusted to him to the best of his ability. He had no illusions of easy victory for the soldiers and hoped that any obstacles they would most certainly encounter would be overcome with a minimum of blood shed.

After the meeting, dinner was served for them in the wardroom of the *Nygaard*. For the schooner captains it was an unexpected pleasure to eat the much better fare available in a larger ship. They devoured a meal of fresh vegetables and somewhat fresh beef, followed by several pies with citrus fruit fillings. Wake was no culinary expert and had no idea the names of what he ate, but he appreciated the work of the cook and wondered if his aboard *St. James* could accomplish the same if the ingredients were available. He made a mental note to have his cook contact the *Nygaard*'s and find out how he did it.

As the evening wore on, the more senior officers expounded on the war and how it should have been fought from the beginning. West and Wherley were in agreement with each other on many of the issues, with Martin and McKinney remaining silent. The often boisterous Taylor was quieter than usual and sat with the junior officers at the other end of the table. The fine provisions of the meal helped make up for their apprehensions regarding their immediate future, and none of the food went to waste.

When Wake went down the side of the *Nygaard* to his boat the uneasy feeling in his mind had subsided somewhat, placated by good food and drink and the company of the other junior officers. The sunset had just finished and darkness was descending rapidly, the very distant shoreline already gone from sight.

Wake was very tired after a long day. When finally in his

bunk, his thoughts drifted to Linda and despite his exhaustion he started to feel some hope that the mission, or at least his part of it, could be pulled off without a major loss of life or equipment and that a night's sleep might make it all look better. There was nothing he could do for the 195th New York Infantry's part of the operation, and he decided not to worry about it. In any event, the morrow would not be dull.

The morning sun rose clear and hot with a light land breeze moving the schooners so slowly that West decided to use the steamers to tow them north. They were fifteen miles offshore and invisible to the occasional observer on that desolate coast as they plodded onward through the jade-colored Gulf of Mexico. The day progressed like a furnace being turned up, and by the afternoon watch the decks were so hot the pitch in the seams was sticky and metal surfaces too hot to touch for long. The breeze caused by the five-knot speed of the tow was a Godsend to the men, who tried to stay in what little shade there was as they readied the ship and themselves for the coming action.

Rork was not pleased that he was not in the landing party. Wake told him he was staying with the schooner and would keep ten men aboard. Fifteen would go with Wake, crowded into the *St. James's* long boat. Rork listened carefully as Wake outlined the plan for the initial landing, which would be made by the navy's landing party.

Wake's boat would join the four other schooners' boats, with ten men in each, and the steamers' boats with fifteen men in each. The tug would not furnish any men to the landing party since she would need all she had to tend to the towlines and man her guns and engine. That made a total of one hundred sailors going ashore under Wake's command. After the sailors were ashore just upriver from the mouth, the boats would all withdraw with their skeleton crews to be towed to the transport and anchored out in the deep water with the gunboats. There the boats would embark the 195th Infantry and carry the soldiers from the transport ship to the beachhead as fast as they could be towed. It would be a distance of three miles each way.

The tug *David* would be crucial to getting the men and their equipment and field guns ashore as quickly as possible. And all of this had to be done within two hours of the high tide. Timing and efficiency were of paramount importance. If one link in the chain of planned events broke, the entire endeavor would be doomed.

Rork was quiet as his captain presented the outline to him. Both of them knew their opinions of this operation were similar, and both knew there was nothing for it now but to try to make it work. As he was explaining the plan, Wake kept remembering what Rork had said the day before about fools' confidence. He was appreciative that Rork wasn't repeating it now.

They estimated high tide at the mouth of the Timucuahatchee River to be near eight o'clock in the morning, two hours after the sun would lighten the sky. Actually, no one was sure of when it would be since the tides on this coast tended to be somewhat erratic and few of the sailors knew this section of the coast well at all. The fleet was to anchor before the next day's dawn and supposed to be already landing the sailors when the sun rose, to get there just ahead of the top of the tide and use the flood and the ebb to beach. Wake knew that the navigation tonight by West and Partington would be the determining factor in the achievement of that timetable. If the speed was too slow they would arrive too late, too fast and they might arrive before the sunset glow had left the sky and be silhouetted against it to the west.

There was a sliver of a moon that night. Wake insisted that all off-watch men get as much sleep as possible so that only the men of the first watch saw its rising, a cold orange that turned to liquid silver, like some slow-motion signal rocket from the eastern horizon. The sailors who saw it were disturbed by the moon's appearance, for they knew that by the time they would be anchored it would shine a glow of light on the sea, just enough that a shore lookout might see the distant shapes of ships upon the Gulf. The beauty of that celestial display was lost in the ominous consequences of its splendor, and the men of the *St. James* turned their backs to it as they would an alluring whore who was known to rob a sailor.

Wake was unable to follow his own order to get rest and stayed on deck for the night. On the third bell of the first watch the *Nygaard*, in the van of the fleet, swung to the east. The gunboats, ferryboat, tug, and transport followed her around, each with a schooner under tow. Wake did the mathematics. It was now one-thirty in the morning and they were making about five knots and had seventeen miles to go to reach the anchoring point for the larger ships, that is if the navigation on the turn was correct. This would be a very close-run thing. They would have just enough time to anchor and launch the boats, load them and get them under the tug's tow to the shore before the sun came up in strength—if nothing went wrong between now and then.

Wake was in his cabin at the chart table when he heard the commotion on deck. The watch had just changed and at first he thought the men were bantering back and forth in the nervous prelude to action. Then he heard a man, he thought it was Cantrell in the starboard gun crew, loudly exclaim something about something looking like a volcano going up. Seconds later Wake reached the deck and saw Faber and the watch standers lining the starboard railing, pointing toward something ahead of the ship. Then he saw the object of their comments and made an oath himself.

The stack of the *Fort Brooklyn* did indeed look like a volcano. Sparks and cinders were shooting high into the air, followed by dense billows of smoke which were in turn followed by more flaming cinders. Groans could be heard from the men around him as they discussed the possibilities of even a blind man on shore seeing that a steamer was approaching.

Faber saw him there finally and told the men to shut up, the captain was on deck, whereupon they all looked at Wake for some comment about this unwelcome event. Wake did not know what to say. He shared their worry, their fear. But there was nothing they could do. They still had to go about their tasks until told otherwise.

"Well men, that's just another reason I still like sails on my ships. Go on now. Off watch, go below and get some rest if you can. We'll have plenty enough to do in just a short while, so don't worry about what you can't change."

Silently the off-watch men went forward and down the hatchway to the berthing deck. The duty men dispersed to their stations. No one said a word in reply or support of Wake's speech, but there was resignation to the inevitable in their deliberate movements.

After they had gone, Faber glanced past Wake's shoulder and nodded. "Mornin', Bosun. The ferryboat got her stack aflamin' for a while there. Nice little bonfire for the Johnny Rebs to see."

Rork stepped up beside Wake and nodded his acknowledgment without saying a word, signaling Faber with his eyes to go forward.

When they were alone Wake spoke in a low tone to his bosun. "It was pretty bright, Rork. Anyone on or near that shoreline would've been able to see it probably. Not a good omen for those who believe in signs. Damn. Well, we should be about five miles offshore right about now. The lead confirms that."

Rork set his jaw and looked over at the *Fort Brooklyn*, whose stack was now under control and no longer belching sparks.

"We'll do what we have to, Captain. We'll make it through

all this somehow."

Wake decided to lighten the mood. "Rork, you're right, of course we will. How can we not, my friend, with the luck of the Irish with us?"

"Aye, Captain. The luck o' Irish has stood me in good stead many a time. Did I ever tell o' the time in Wexford, with a wee bitty lass who had the temper o' a tigress? Crazier than Finnegan's cat, she was, an' that's no lie."

Wake held up his hand for Rork to stop. The ships ahead were slowing. They must be getting near the anchoring point for the gunboats. It seemed too early by Wake's timepiece—they must still be too far offshore, but Commander West had determined that here was where the gunboats and the ferryboat would stop. The tug would tow the schooners, two at a time, further in toward shore to the place where they would anchor. Then the final leg would come when the tug would tow the boats full of sailors ashore.

The gunboats *Bonsall* and *Nygaard* stopped and were anchoring abeam the shoreline with springs on their hawsers, the better to cover the landing with gunfire if needed. The *Fort Brooklyn* anchored to seaward of the gunboats to stay out of their line of fire. There was some confusion, with the men's whispers between ships becoming louder with frustration until they were shouts, as several of the schooners cast off their towlines to the other steamers and were taken by the tug two miles further east into the very shallow water. While all of this was going on with the schooners, the steamers were also lowering their boats and readying their portions of the landing party to make for the beach. It was chaos to Wake's orderly mind and he hoped it would soon resolve itself into an organized effort, but he doubted it.

The time taken to move the five schooners seemed interminable to Wake as he waited for the *David* to take *St. James* and the *Fox* forward. The wind at least was cooperating, a slight breeze coming out of the east off the land retarding the ability of anyone on shore to hear the commotion out in the Gulf.

Finally the tug came alongside and took *St. James* under tow, with the *Fox* towing astern of them. The tow lasted about a mile until they arrived where the other schooners were anchored and already disembarking their sailors into the boats.

Wake looked at his watch as they anchored *St. James*, noticing that it was now six o'clock in the morning. The eastern sky was changing from dark gray to light gray. A check of the horizon showed no sign of land and he started to wonder exactly how far offshore they had anchored the fleet. Had there been some giant miscalculation of position? The water depth was ten feet, which indicated that they should be around two miles west of the river entrance, but where was the shoreline? At two miles they should be able to see it.

Rork walked up to him with a puzzled mien. "Where would the mainland be, sir? I can't see it an' we're behind the schedule now."

"I don't know, Rork. We may be farther off than they think." Wake sighed but tried to keep a positive face. "Means a longer tow for the tug, Rork, but at least we're not having to row."

Rork was not amused and not positive. His tone was borderline sarcastic, a rare manner for him. "Aye, Captain, towing not rowing."

The sky was actually light now, with clouds visible to the east and a glow starting to be seen over the water. Details of waves coming toward them with the easterly wind could be seen easily and a smoke plume was in sight somewhere beyond the horizon where Florida lay waiting. But Wake could still see no land.

"Send your sharpest-eyed man aloft to the masthead and report, Rork."

Rork acknowledged the order, sending a youngster to the top of the mainmast with a stern warning not to drop the telescope he was given, the precious instrument not usually taken aloft. Moments later the boy yelled down.

"Deck there, land in sight way far off to the east, where the sun is risin', sir. Smoke column from the land, too, sir. Two points off the starboard bow. Big black smoke. There's another one, sir. Just startin'. Down further to the south."

Rork climbed up the starboard ratlines to the crosstrees, then ascended the upper shrouds to the head of the topmast. Once there he took the glass from the sailor and trained it on the two separate columns of smoke, the first of which was now dissipating.

"Captain, the first is goin' out, an' the second is goin' strong. Oh Mary an' Joseph, there's another o' the little devils further south now, sir. The Rebs have lit off their warnin' fires."

Wake yelled up to his bosun, keeping his voice as calm as he could. "Bosun, would you kindly estimate the distance to shore?"

As he spoke, Wake could hear the lookouts on the other ships around them report the smoke columns and the officers below opine on their meaning. Everyone was thinking the same thoughts. Rork's booming voice came down from above. "Captain! I would say it's all of five miles. Maybe six."

"Very well, Rork. You may come down."

Wake felt the familiar gnawing in his gut again. Men were about to die and he couldn't stop it. He looked around him at the men descending into *St. James*'s boat, led by old McDougall who would be their petty officer on this landing party.

The men were weighted down with the equipment of battle, making their descent more difficult: muskets and pistols with the accompanying cartridges and bullets in their pouches, cutlasses and axes, provision bags and water butts and canvas for tents. A box of medicines was carefully handed down into the uplifted hands of silent men who had no illusions about what was to come. The schooners around the *St. James* had their own boats loading men and equipment in corresponding scenes. All were strangely quiet. There was no yelling of the sailors, no loud thuds or creaks of boxes or tackle, just the muted efforts of a hundred men getting ready for the inevitable.

The boats from the steamers farther offshore were approaching under oars. They were ready after a hard row to accept a tow from the tug *David*, which was even now readying lines for towing two separate lines of four long boats each, to the river somewhere along the shore to the east. *David* took several boats in tow, making a wide circle back to the anchored schooners where the other boats secured themselves to the towline astern of those already on it.

Wake stood at the main shrouds surveying the scene around him as Rork came up with his hand extended.

"Captain, good luck. We'll be here a waitin' for you an' the other Saints to come home. As much as some o' them may complain about the navy life, methinks they'll fancy it kindly, after some time ashore with those doggo soldiers!"

The statement his father made to him when he decided to join the navy a year and a half earlier came to Wake on hearing Rork's comment. Wake's father, an old sea captain, had gently told his son with misty eyes to go into the navy and not wait to be conscripted into the army. "Soldiers live and die in the mud. At least a sailor lives and dies clean, son." Wake sighed, shook Rork's hand and locked his eyes with the bosun's.

"Well, I guess there's nothing for it but to go now, Rork."

The bosun smiled down at his friend who had started climbing down the ship's side.

"Aye, sir, show them elegant New York soldiers how real men do their duty, then come on home, Captain."

Wake smiled up at Rork from the sternsheets of the boat as she shoved off, then he faced the bow and whatever was in front of them.

10
The Elephant's Breath

The *David* had the boats in tow at four or five knots, according to Wake's best estimate. He could see Erne scowling as he stood on the stern of the tug, arms akimbo, checking on the lines of boats being dragged to the distant shore. It was obvious he was angry.

Wake wiped away the cool spray that occasionally flew back into his face and thought about the speed that was making the spray. Fortunately the waves were small, making only the occasional splash but not big enough to slosh solid water aboard. It was an odd feeling, moving effortlessly through the water. Wake had never been towed in a ship's boat by a steamer like this before. He was very appreciative they didn't have to row or sail the five or six miles to the landing place. It would have been exhausting in the heat and humidity.

Trying to determine their position, Wake had a seaman swing the small lead stowed in the boat. At first it was almost two fathoms, but soon it became one, with a rocky bottom. That meant they were nearing the first of the reefs that paralleled the coast and that they should be two miles offshore. But that was impossible, as he could see with his own eye, and that meant the charts were wrong. If the charts were wrong this far out, the depths inshore might be completely different from those expected also. Worry about the depths then logically progressed to thoughts of the tides.

With the incoming flood tide believed by West and Wherley to crest at around eight o'clock in the morning, the operation had little time to get the naval landing party ashore, then go back out the seven miles or so to the steamers to start to bring in the soldiers. Originally, based on the charts they had and the estimation of the tides, the plan had been to get as many of the soldiers as possible ashore on the first high tide of the day. It was hoped they could land four or five of the infantry companies, approximately five hundred men of the eight companies of the regiment, ashore in that period. Then, at the second high tide of the day, around sunset, they would bring the remaining infantry, with the artillery battery. The critical factor for the boats bringing them in was the draft of the steamers. Drawing eight feet, they had to anchor far offshore, beyond the outer reef. The inner reef only had enough water for the tug, which drew five feet, a depth available for a couple of hours, at the most, on either side of high tide.

Wake could see that the planned timetable was falling apart. If the chart was wrong on the depths over the inner reefs, their situation could get even worse. It was frustrating having to follow orders without the authority to change them as the circumstances shifted. Too many factors in the plan were interdependent, and Wake knew he could not unilaterally alter the chain of events that were already under way without large consequences. Colonel Wherley and Lieutenant Commander West had made it abundantly clear to all the officers that this attack would go forward in spite of any particular officer's reservations. He would continue onward, Wake decided, until some definitive obstruction made it obvious they should stop the attack.

Gradually a dark line made itself known on the horizon. Straight and without detail at first, it grew into an undulating smudge and then into individual treetops and blurs of sand and marsh. The lead still showed a fathom or more as they approached, but mud was being brought up astern of the tug.

The smoke from the two signal fires had vanished. No other fires were lit and no other signs of life could be seen ashore. However, the smoke from the tug was filling the air for all to see. It was obvious that the element of surprise was lost and the Rebels would know they were here. Wake wondered how the Confederates would respond. He knew from his latest landing experience that they could muster militia to this part of the Florida coast within two or three hours. He figured the fate of this operation depended upon how far away the militia was coming from.

Could the sailors get established ashore, set up a defensive work and hold it until the New Yorkers arrived? When the militia attacked—for Wake no longed permitted himself the luxury of wondering *if* they would attack—what would their force be comprised of? Would they have artillery or cavalry? The sailors had muskets and pistols. The request to carry a boat howitzer to the beach had been denied by West as taking up too much weight, which he said would be better used transporting more sailors.

The thought of a boat howitzer reminded Wake of the range of the gunboats' weapons. They had anchored so far offshore that they were out of range and useless to help.

McDougall, seated next to Wake, had the same thought at the same time. He saw his captain look back at the distant gunboats and sagely wagged his head. "Aye, Captain. They're of no use in this fight. We're on our own here, for they're too far away. The largest gun on both the *Nygaard* and the *Bonsall* is a hundred-pound Parrot rifled cannon. It can fire a six-point-four-inch shell five miles at thirty-five degree elevation and a ten-pound powder charge. But that means nary a thing 'cause those bastard-s'll be watchin' the fight, not partakin' of it."

Wake looked at the unruffled gunner and bobbed his head

in return. "Then I presume that upon our return they'll have to endure our tales of victory, right, Gunner McDougall?"

McDougall caught Wake's tone and smiled. "Aye, Captain. There's them that do, an' them that watch others do the doin'. A shame there's no prize money on this little dustup. Would make it a wee bit more enticin' for a lad like me."

"Good Lord, McDougall, you sound like Rork. Are all Irishmen as mad about money as you two?"

McDougall showed a rare laugh at his captain's question. "Nay, Captain, many are worse!"

The bowman suddenly pointed ahead and yelled out a warning. "The tug's slowing. Look at the mud!"

The water around them had turned into coffee, swirling about with seaweed and bottom mud everywhere. The tug slowed to a crawl with the boats in tow surging forward into her and each other. Shouts to fend off and steer away came from the small craft as the men on the stern of the *David* tried to keep the lines from fouling the propeller. The bowman called back to Wake that they were in a bit less than a fathom and that the tug ahead was plowing up the bottom.

As abruptly as they slowed, the tug crept faster again and the man with the lead told Wake they were past some sort of reef or bar and in a fathom and half. The shoreline in front of them was now coming into sharp detail and the beach could be seen to be a narrow strip of brown muddy sand between the water and tall marsh grass. The smell of the swamps drifted out to them, reeking of rotting plants and sulfur. All eyes on each boat searched for any indication of the enemy but found absolutely nothing. Not even the entrance to the Timucuahatchee River could be seen.

Wake wished he had insisted upon riding on the *David* so that he could confer with Erne as they approached the coast. Being a passive passenger irritated him and having to wonder what would be done next was infuriating. Wake tried to will the tug to turn to the north and go along the beach until they could find the river mouth. Minutes later, at seven-thirty-three by

Wake's pocket watch, the *David* turned to the south, swinging the boats behind her in a wild curve.

A half-mile down the beach they found it, proving Wake's estimation wrong, and turned inland to ride the sluicing flood tide up the river. It was a narrow river, not more than a hundred yards wide. The lead showed just a fathom at the entrance, but once inside it got deeper as they went further up between the marsh and palm-covered banks.

Wake shuddered as he thought of the last river he had entered—just a month earlier. This one had the opposite appearance of that one though. Here no sign of human habitation could be seen, not even the small dock that was supposed to be a quarter mile inside the entrance, according to the plan. Instead they found a curve of rocky beach below a six-foot-high sand bluff on a bend of the river. The area behind the bluff was the only open land around, maybe an acre, surrounded by a tree line of oak and palm. Apparently that was the landing place. The river had narrowed to fifty yards at the most, the jungle-covered banks offering concealment to any Rebels who might be watching.

Erne returned to the stern of the tug and shouted to Wake that he was casting off the tows and they could row ashore here. The boats' crews broke out their oars and rowed the few yards to the beach where they grounded and leaped out, moving through the shallow water, up the bluff and out into the open area behind it. The sailors went about their business quietly, with an unusual lack of noise or show. Usually when they were called upon to act like soldiers there was some cajolery, but not this time. This time it was as if they were trying not to disturb the area and awaken some malevolent force. Their faces showed more than concern—they showed fear.

With the boats back undertow again, the tug tried several times to back astern and turn in the current-swept narrow river, but Erne was clearly having difficulty with the maneuver. Wake saw his blond head moving from one side window to the opposite in the pilothouse of the tug, his arm gesturing to the bosun on the afterdeck who was overseeing the sailors trying to keep the towed boats from being damaged or fouling the propeller with their lines. Finally, when it seemed the bow of the *David* would not come around, she turned abruptly into the current and made speed against the flood tide, heading out to the ships far out to sea. The sailors in the boats and ashore watched as the tug left them and moved out the entrance of the river. No one said a word.

Wake walked ashore and climbed the bluff to survey his new domain. Out to sea he could see the anchored schooners and on the horizon the masts of the larger ships. They seemed impossibly far away. He shook his head slowly as his right hand absent-mindedly traced the scar over his right ear. Turning inland, Wake walked over to where McDougall stood motioning for some men to bring the supplies up the bluff.

"McDougall, present my compliments, and I would like to see the ensigns and the senior petty officers in five minutes for a conference, right here."

McDougall acknowledged the order and went off to notify the others. The open field was crowded with sailors now, some at the tree line facing outward with their muskets in a picket line and others busy hauling provisions and setting up canvas awnings for shelter. It all looked quite organized and efficient, but Wake didn't like the current disposition of the defenses. It was too close, too confined. It reminded him of a similar navy beach camp at the Myakka River the year before, where the Rebs had quickly overrun the defense line and the camp. Only the guns of Wake's armed sloop had prevented a massacre and saved many sailors' lives that night. He didn't want to be in that position again if he could help it. And this time there were no ship's guns to save them.

McDougall came up to him and advised that the officers and senior petty officers were gathered for him, pointing to a group of men seated in a circle on packs and boxes under a sail awning by the edge of the bluff. Wake nodded to the gunner and walked over to his subordinate leaders.

"Well, gentlemen, we are here and I want to go over a few of the necessary things immediately so that there is not, and will not be in the future, any confusion."

Wake stopped and looked around the group to ensure that he had their attention. The older men, the senior petty officers, wore the neutral expressions of veterans. They were waiting for orders and showed no emotion. Their confidence was such that they figured they could probably get through anything, even such an obviously misguided endeavor as the one they found themselves in. The younger ones, the ensigns, had rapt countenances. They knew they were unprepared for what was about to unfold and hoped Wake would dispense some profound plan of action that would give them the self-assurance they lacked.

"All right then. First we organize the men. Ensign Chase, you are the senior and will take the men from your vessel, the men from the *Ariel*, and the men from the *Two Sisters*. Bosun Ford, Coxswain Stanforth, and Gunner Simmons from the *Ariel* will assist you. I want you to take those thirty men and form a picket line out into the woods at least fifty feet. I want the picket line to have a breastwork cut from saplings and bushes, with the area in front of it cut down for at least thirty to forty feet. I want that accomplished before you have your noon meal. Understood?"

Chase and the petty officers voiced their understanding.

"Now, Ensign Robbins, you will take Bosun Kingston and the ten men from your schooner and form a reconnaissance to go up the road four miles toward Claresville. I want you to go and see what's about in that area, but do not go into the town or engage any Floridians anywhere. If you see any, only observe and report back what you see. I want that done immediately and I want a report back from you in person within two hours. We need to have intelligence of what we face here in our immediate vicinity. You will provide it. Understood?"

Though Robbins and Kingston nodded their heads, it wasn't good enough for Wake. Robbins did not appear to be very assertive and Wake worried that he might not control his men as needed.

"I could not hear your answer, Ensign Robbins. Repeat my instructions."

Embarrassed, Robbins repeated the orders in a halting fashion but included everything Wake had told him. Wake was still not confident in the man but his point was taken and could not be belabored.

"Now, I will have Gunner's Mate McDougall, Bosun Faber, Quartermaster Hilderbrandt of the *Nygaard*, and Bosun Meade of the *Bonsall* with me. We will have about sixty men in all. The petty officers will command the men from their own ships, and all will be under McDougall and me. Until the army arrives, my unit will form the main defense line here at the beach camp. Our line will be just inside the picket line, among the trees, with packs and boxes for positions of defense. If attacked before the New Yorkers arrive, we will all defend from within the trees, and if needed, we will withdraw to below the bluff and fire over the top and across the open ground. Understood?"

All the officers and petty officers spoke up and said they did.

"Very good, men. Once the army is here, they will push inland. My unit will follow along and guard Claresville once they capture it and move onward. Ensign Robbins' unit will patrol the road between the camp here and Claresville to ensure our route of . . . departure. Ensign Chase's unit will guard this camp. As the army is moving around the interior, the navy landing party will keep this area secure. Any questions?"

Kingston looked at the others and raised his hand. Wake nodded for him to go ahead.

"Sir, what do we do with any refugees that come up to us?"

It was a good question, one which Wake had overlooked.

"Excellent question, Kingston. All refugees will be sent back here, but, and this is very important men, they are to stay outside our defense lines. There are some among them who are treacherous. Have all of them over the age of sixteen swear the oath of national allegiance and document when they made it. Help them if you can, but do not trust them. Once we can arrange evacuation we will allow them to pass through our lines. Any refugee men who wish to join us and bear arms against the Rebs will be given the opportunity to enlist in the loyalist Florida militia later."

Chase now had a question.

"Sir, what about the water side of our camp here. What do we defend it with? I don't have enough men to cover everywhere."

It was a sensible point. Wake thought that out and replied in an assertive voice. "The tug will guard that flank. We'll have them anchor in the stream fore and aft. Good question, Mr. Chase."

The men were asking good questions on issues that pointed out the vulnerability of the landing party without army support. Wake could see that each man was making the same mental assessment of their situation. None of them appeared encouraged at their prospects. Wake bid them to go on about their duties and stood up, signaling that the meeting was over. As the men walked back to their respective commands, Kingston stopped at Wake's side. His thin body was tanned and weathered, with ropy muscles. The man was a veteran of at least ten years in the navy by his tattoos, rank, and demeanor. He looked into Wake's eyes for a moment, then cast his gaze downward.

"Sir, Ensign Robbins just arrived in the squadron. Took the *Fox* the day we left St. Marks for here. He was in the North Atlantic Squadron off Virginia before. Ain't used to the heat and the bugs down here, but he'll get the hang of it. No disrespect intended, sir, but I just wanted to let you know that."

Wake regarded the man in front of him. Not many would have said what he did. Not many would have had the self-confidence to say it. Wake remembered Kingston's question about the refugees. He was a man to be remembered.

"No disrespect observed, Kingston. Thank you for that information. That reconnaissance must be well done, remember that."

"Aye aye, sir. We'll find out what the Rebs are up to out there."

Two hours later—three hours after the sailors had first arrived at the landing—several reports reached Wake, who was seated with McDougall at their position within the main defense line in the trees. First, Faber reported that the ships' boats could be seen coming up the river, without the tug and under oars. The tug could be seen anchored offshore of the inner reef. Evidently the tide had not served well enough to provide water for Erne to cross the reef and the soldiers had had to row their way to the landing. They were still near the mouth of the river and would take another hour to stem the flowing ebb tide that had commenced. That meant that it would be another eleven hours, somewhere around sunset, before they could get more reinforcements on the next tide.

The second report came to Wake moments after the first. Ensign Robbins and Bosun Kingston arrived in the camp, soaked with sweat and filthy from muck. Robbins made his report in a halting voice that hadn't improved since the commanders' meeting.

"Sir, we proceeded easterly up the road. It's sandy and winds around a lot with bends but ends up at the town of Claresville. Well, town is too strong a word really. It's just a crossroads with nine buildings—six dwellings, two barns and what looks to be some sort of trader's hut."

Wake watched Robbins' Adam's apple bob up and down in his throat as he talked. He found himself wondering about the young man's background and how he came to be here in this inhospitable place.

Robbins was wilting under the eye of his commander but continued his narration. "The odd thing is we didn't see anybody anywhere. Nobody on the road and no one at the crossroads. Couldn't see any sign of anyone living there. Even the horses and farm animals are gone. A bit disconcerting, sir."

Wake considered this information and posed a question to clarify the report.

"Ensign, did it appear they had all left suddenly and recently?"

"Well, sir, I sent Kingston here up to one of the homes to see about that. Tell him, Kingston."

The bosun stepped forward and told his part of the story in even tones. "The ensign, sir, he told me to go see about where the folks were and when they'd left. So I went into this one home, a hut actually, and found the cook hearth still warm, clothes still hung, some food still stored in the larder. Later I found some fresh tracks of horses and wagons in the road leading inland to Collmerton. Saw one other track going north along the coastal road from Claresville. The tracks have been there since the rain yesterday evening. They'd only been gone about a couple hours, I'd say, sir."

Wake was silent for a few seconds. "Thank you Mr. Robbins, Kingston. Rest your men for the next half hour. Ensign Robbins, I want you to return here for a conference in five minutes."

Wake stood and turned to McDougall, who was still lethargically reclining against a rock. The lieutenant spoke quickly as his mind was busy formulating a plan. "McDougall, present my compliments to Ensign Chase and have him visit me here in five minutes. Then go to the bluff and gauge the progress of the soldiers in the boats. Return here and tell me when you think they will arrive."

The energetic tone of Wake's voice spurred McDougall to rise off the ground as quickly as his old frame would allow. He strode across the clearing while Wake contemplated the breastworks around the camp. Part of Chase's men were slashing bushes and small trees, piling them in makeshift fence lines around the perimeter. Others were cutting down the areas in front of those lines. Still others walked sentry posts, staring off into the gloom of the forest trying to see any enemy before they could attack the as-yet-unfinished barricades.

Behind the outer line, Wake's men were doing the same for the main defense perimeter line. The few who were not working to improve their chances against the attack they knew would come were setting up the provisions, medicines and supplies under the canvas awnings by the tree line. The open area by the bluff was left unoccupied by men or equipment.

The heat and humidity competed with the insects for the enmity of the sailors as they worked in the junglelike surroundings. The seamen were no longer quiet as they sweated at their tasks with oaths and shouts. Wake was worried about exhaustion, but the absolute necessity of having strong lines had overcome his concern and he had driven his petty officers to make their men accomplish the work without letup.

Now he had an idea. It was risky, but he thought it was an acceptable risk for a considerable gain. He sat down on the rock and waited for the McDougall and the ensigns. When they arrived he was blunt with them as they sat or knelt down.

"McDougall, what did you see?"

"Looks like the first o' them will be to the bluff in ten minutes or so, sir. But the poor sods are heavin' an' hollerin' like they's damn near dead, an' the line o' them boats is stretched out for what looks like half a mile down the river and off the beach, sir. They'll be a hurtin' for certain sure when they finally get here."

Wake's mouth twitched as he nodded in response to the gunner's mate's report. "All right. Then here is what we will do, gentlemen. We are going to seize an opportunity that has been presented to us. It won't last long. Listen carefully."

Each man leaned forward with attention. There was no mistaking the tone of Wake's voice. "In half an hour my unit will depart, march up the road and occupy Claresville. Ensign Robbins' detail will patrol the road between this camp and my unit. Ensign Chase will maintain the perimeter here. The soldiers will be here soon but will probably take two hours for all of them to arrive and form up. They can then follow us up to Claresville. There is no need for them to wait for tomorrow. We need to establish defensive works as far forward of this camp as possible. I do not want to wait until the Rebels come in force to move down that road against us here. Thirty minutes, gentlemen. Questions?"

Chase bobbed his head in affirmation. McDougall had a glint of glee in his eye and smiled. Robbins replied that he understood and turned to leave but was stopped by Wake.

"Mr. Robbins. The road is bordered by dense swamp on either side, is it not?"

"Yes, sir. It's very thick with plants and vines and things. The water looks to be at least chest high."

Wake locked his eyes on Robbins'. "We are dealing with Floridians who dwell in these swamps, Mr. Robbins. They are not intimidated by them. Make *sure* you place pickets out in the swamps away from the road so that you, and by extension me, don't get flanked. They need to listen for the enemy moving around you. Understood?"

Robbins stared back at Wake. His words were uttered slowly. "Yes, sir."

"Mr. Robbins. A naval officer says 'aye aye, sir,' when given a command. You and your detail are the lifeline for sixty sailors and many more soldiers. Make sure your duty is done, sir. You may go."

"Aye aye, sir."

As Robbins walked away, Chase went to find his petty officers and give them the word. McDougall glanced at Wake but said nothing. The old gunner went off to get Faber and see about getting their men ready. Wake was left alone, sitting under the oak tree on a limestone rock, thinking about the consequences of the decision he had just made. He knew it was the right decision. He just hoped that it was going to be a successful operation.

Thirty minutes later they were formed up into a double line on the road leading out of the camp. Faber, Hilderbrandt, and Wake were at the head of the column with McDougall and Meade in the rear. Robbins' men had moved out ahead of the main body. In addition to a cutlass and pouch belt, each of the sailors had a .69-caliber muzzle-loading Plymouth musket on his shoulder. There was some grumbling from seamen who had served with other squadrons that had been issued breech-loading carbines and rifles, many of which were repeaters. Finally the petty officers told them all to pipe down, they would all get the chance to shoot a Reb soon enough and it didn't matter how many holes they put in him.

The first of the 195th Infantry had arrived a quarter hour before the sailors formed up. The young lieutenant in charge of the first boatload of soldiers was amazed to find the camp's defenses as well prepared as they were. He also was taken aback by the navy's willingness to go ahead and move inland without all the troops, baggage, equipment, and artillery. Wake explained to him that the navy was used to traveling fast and light, and that they were going to take advantage of the time given them.

Wake also told him that a detail of soldiers needed to remain at the camp to guard the riverbank portion of the perimeter since the tug was not going to be able to perform that important function. Once the tug could stay in the river, the detail could move up to the rest of the regiment.

The army officer smiled and advised Wake that upon Major Martin's arrival he would recommend that the regiment should send up a company to augment the sailors occupying Claresville and also assign some men to the camp perimeter. He explained that two companies were arriving by boat currently and three more would come on the next tide. The artillery and the last three infantry companies would come on the tide after that. It seemed that Colonel Wherley was still aboard the *Nygaard* and would be coming ashore with the second contingent of the regiment. The lieutenant pleasantly assured Wake that the army would be delighted to take over all of the offensive operations from the naval landing party once it had established itself ashore properly and in good order. He was sure that Major Martin would take the recommendations into consideration.

Wake recognized the bureaucratic inertia of the army lieutenant and realized that he would have to present Major Martin with a fait accompli by the time of his arrival. Bidding the smiling lieutenant good-bye, Wake quickly walked over to the column of sailors and told the petty officers to get them under way and follow Robbins' men who were already far out ahead. There wasn't time for the army to get established in good order, for Wake had an uncomfortable feeling that the enemy already was.

The road was as sandy and winding as Robbins had reported. The four miles seemed much longer, primarily because of the clouds of mosquitoes. Back at the camp a sea breeze had penetrated that far inland and moved through the shadows of the trees, keeping most of the sand gnats and mosquitoes at bay. But there was no movement to the air on the road and the trees overhung it to form a dark murkiness, even in the height of day. Swarms of the biting, torturing insects descended upon the bluejackets as the column trudged along the track that was little more than a pathway. It was worse than anywhere else in Florida Wake had been, and he wondered how and why the Floridians lived here.

From either side of the roadway the swamp reached out for them with barbed vines and branches. Occasionally their feet sank into what looked like solid ground but was in reality a calf-deep mush that stranded several men until they were pulled out, bringing with them an underground odor redolent of decay and death. The hot, humid air combined with the smells and insects to assault every sense of the miserable sailors.

It was an inauspicious start to their mission, and the sailors began complaining about ever leaving the sea and coast, in spite of dire threats from the petty officers to remain silent lest they warn the enemy of their approach. To the slogging, swatting, sweating sailors the primary enemy was the place itself, and they were losing that contest rapidly.

Halfway there, by Wake's calculation, the column came upon Robbins standing in the road. He gestured to Wake to come to him.

"Sir, we are about a mile and a half or so from Claresville. I have placed five men off in the swamp on either side of the road, about two hundred feet out. I'll leave three here and keep the others patrolling up and down the road to keep it secure."

"Very good, Mr. Robbins. We'll go forward now and leave you to your duties."

"Sir, it's horrible in that swamp. We're trying to keep them quiet, but they've never seen anything like it and are scared out of their wits about snakes and alligators. The mosquitoes are driving them mad in there."

Wake sympathized. He didn't think he could handle the horrors of the swamp. But someone had to be there. The Floridians wouldn't have had any hesitations. He wished he had a few men with their experience with him now.

"Mr. Robbins, I understand that. If they can't hear the Rebels approach then they will die and then many other soldiers and sailors will die. They are our insurance against a flanking movement against our avenue of escape. Rotate the swamp duty among all your men. It will make it slightly more tolerable. Good luck, Ensign."

Wake turned away from the man and marched forward, motioning his column to follow him. Faber took five sailors a hundred yards ahead to scout in advance of the main party.

By the time Wake and the column arrived at Faber's position at the edge of the little settlement, the detail was already distributed among the structures at the crossroads. Quietly entering each of the buildings, they confirmed Kingston's earlier assessment that the inhabitants had hurriedly departed in the early morning hours. The confirmation supported what Wake felt when he had first heard that report. The alarm had been sounded on the coast for sometime. There were probably troops moving toward them now.

Assembling the petty officers, Wake explained his plan for holding the crossroads. "We will keep it simple. The swamp road we've come up continues on inland to Collmerton and beyond that to the railroad that crosses Florida to our north. The coastal road that intersects it goes northwesterly along the curve of the coast. I think the enemy will come down the Collmerton road or down the coast road from the northwest. From what I have been told, most of their main units, both regulars and militia, stay in the area to our north. I do not think they will come from the south, but they might.

"So, I want all of us to stay inside the buildings. No one outside. I want to surprise anyone coming into the town. We will wait until they are close, then fire into them. Gunner McDougall and the Saints will cover the northeast approach of the Collmerton road. Bosun Meade and the Bonsalls will cover the northwest approach of the coastal road. Quartermaster Hilderbrandt will divide his men between the southerly approach of the coastal road and the westerly approach of the swamp road we just came up.

"Remember, stay in the houses and buildings. You may eat their food, but do not, and I repeat that, *do not*, allow any stealing from these people's property. Keep your men quiet and under control. Any questions?"

Hilderbrandt spoke up quietly, the German accent still quite apparent even after fifteen years in the American navy.

"Zir, how long till zee soldiers comes to zis place?"

Wake exhaled slowly. "I don't know precisely. Probably tomorrow. Maybe tonight. They will move through us either to Collmerton or up the coast road."

Hilderbrandt nodded thoughtfully at that information and asked another question.

"Und zee Rebels, how long till zay come here, zir?"

Wake looked hard at the quartermaster to gauge his intent with that question. The man's face revealed no emotion.

"Hilderbrandt, I do not know. Maybe today or tonight. Maybe tomorrow. I am a bit surprised they haven't already."

Hilderbrandt ignored the glares of the other petty officers and nodded again at Wake. The petty officer stood and stretched his considerable muscles, speaking directly at Wake. "Ve vill be ready for zem, Captain Vake."

The petty officers took their men around to the various

buildings as Wake examined each of the structures to look for any intelligence of the enemy's intentions. As he walked through the deserted town he felt a little like a criminal, disrupting these peoples' way of life and violating their privacy. He knew it was war, but it was hard to think of the families whose crude homes he inspected as people he could hate enough to hurt. And just being here and occupying their homes would hurt them.

The enormity of the danger he was in returned his concentration to his task, however, and he went through everything he could in each place—boxes and shelves, food bins, barrels, trash—trying to deduce the immediate risks to the sailors in Claresville. After looking at everything, he found absolutely nothing of intelligence value and was convinced that this collection of huts and hovels was only a gathering place for poor farmers and hunters who had nothing of monetary value nor any real involvement in the Confederacy. After the search, a message relating a description of the town and their defenses was sent by courier to Major Martin at the beach camp, with an acknowledgment requested.

Next he made a tour of their defensive positions. None of the windows had the luxury of glass but each now had a sailor with musket, hidden within and pointed outside. The sailors appeared to be well dispersed with half on watch and the others resting. By the time Wake completed his inspection of Claresville and its new inhabitants, the sun had passed its zenith. It was getting perceptibly darker under the clouds of the afternoon thunderstorm shielding the earth from the sun's glare. The bugs were less oppressive in the town, but could be felt increasingly as the afternoon lengthened. He swatted a mosquito and wondered how Robbins and his men were doing back in the fetid misery of the swamp.

McDougall looked tired. He sat down with a thump in the chair by a table in the traders' hut. Across the table Wake sat studying a chart of the coast—they had no land maps, other than the diagram he was making of the area. Grunting with the effort,

McDougall turned in the chair and put his legs out, massaging his thighs. He was in a strangely pleasant mood.

"Well, Captain, I've put more miles on me legs this morn than in many a day. Reminds me o' back in the sainted old country. Why, we walked for dozens o' miles there, with nary a notice. Been too long for these old sticks, an' I fear they're out o' practice."

Wake looked up from his chart. He had never heard McDougall speak such pleasant length. It made him ponder why the gunner was in such a mood, especially considering the unpleasant situation in which they found themselves, but he laughed out a reply to continue the light-hearted spirit. "McDougall, six months from now you'll be at the Anchor Inn regaling the ladies about your romp among the Rebels in the middle of darkest Florida. But I'll wager now that you'll not include the part about how you were exhausted after only four miles!"

"Aye, sir. 'Twill be a glorious story to be told, an' the lasses will be spellbound as they pour the rum down me throat to facilitate the telling. About time that rogue Rork had a spectator's part an' let a veteran such as meself have some o' the fun."

Wake grinned at the image of the storytelling of this adventure at the Anchor Inn.

"Get some sleep, gunner. Your story may get very exciting, indeed, very soon."

"Aye aye, sir. Shut-eye it is for this old sailor."

They waited the afternoon. No messenger came from the camp or Robbins' detail. No movement stirred the landscape around them. The huts were mostly of thatch, with a few that were partially wood—coarse-sawn logs without finished boards. The air inside them grew hotter, forcing the men inside to strip to their waists. Everything about the place and the atmosphere debilitated the sailors, and Wake occasionally went from building to building to make sure they were alert. The far-off rumbling of thunder did nothing to alleviate the feeling.

As the sun's descent started to make shadows lengthen, Wake worried about the lack of an acknowledgment communication from the rear, or even the return of the original messengers, and sent two more men with a message to Major Martin, advising him again of their dispositions and inquiring about the time of arrival of the 195th Infantry. His worry transcended concern and was evolving into a fear that they had been cut off from the beach camp.

His unease was aggravated by the storm building to the south of them. It was growing into a gigantic mountain of energy rolling outward in all directions. The top of the storm was rapidly ascending in a column through the sky until it appeared to be hovering over all of Florida. The color of the clouds grew darker as one looked lower, until the squall lines at the bottom were a swirling blue-black over the dark gray of the waterfalls of rain that poured out of the clouds. The closest edge of the storm looked about five miles distant, which meant around half or three quarters of an hour away to Wake's practiced eye. He thought of Rork and the *St. James* anchored offshore but was not unduly concerned. Rork could handle it. He knew Robbins and his men would be miserable patrolling the road and swamp and the men at the beach camp would have to continue to unload the boats and improve the breastworks in the storm. That the crude structures of Claresville would at least provide some protection from the elements gave Wake a reason to smile. It was the first good thing he had to think about since they had left the schooner in what seemed an eternity ago but actually was only ten hours.

The thunder reminded Wake of the naval gunfire he had heard during this war. The continuous background of far-off reverberations was interrupted more frequently by sharp explosions of lightning and thunder cracking nearby. The storm's impending onslaught was now robbing the air of any movement at all, the barometric pressure suddenly lowering to a degree that was apparent to the ears.

The time just before a storm struck was that time when men would stand mesmerized on a ship's deck, staring at nature's violence coming to them on a scale they could not comprehend or adequately describe to those who had never seen it. The sailors in this little town reacted the same way, gazing out their rudimentary windows and thinking that they should do something to get ready, but on land they had nothing to do but wait.

Wake was eyeing the nearest squall line a mile away when he heard a sailor yelling for him. McDougall woke up at the sound and stood next to Wake as a young seaman rushed in the door of the trader's hut, breathlessly trying to tell his information.

"Sir! That army lieutenant is here. They ain't coming!"

Wake and McDougall glanced at each other. McDougall spoke first. "Sailor, compose yourself man, an' give a proper report to the captain."

"Sorry, Gunner. Sorry, Captain. I ran all the way here from the west side of the village. Quartermaster Hilderbrandt sent me as fast as I could go, sir. That army lieutenant should be here any second now, but Hilderbrandt knew you'd want to know as fast as you could. Sorry for being shortwinded, sir."

At that point the doorway was filled by the trim young lieutenant of the 195th New York Infantry. He immediately spoke to the men staring at him. "Lieutenant Wake, I must apologize, for I believe we were never properly introduced before. Let me rectify that oversight now. I am Lieutenant Stansfield Hammersley, staff lieutenant to the adjutant to Colonel Wherley, the commanding officer of the 195th New York Volunteer Light Infantry Regiment."

Wake was stunned. The man was in an incongruously clean and pressed full dress uniform. He must have changed into it at the camp when the regimental staff baggage came ashore. He had the manner of a gallant young officer at a society ball, not a professional soldier deep in enemy territory who might be attacked at any minute. Wake didn't understand how the man could be so clean and neat after walking four miles through the swamp road. Wake did not say a word, but waited for the man to continue speaking since Hammersley had obviously paused for theatrical effect.

"Yes, . . . well, . . . I am here to assess the situation and report back to Major Martin. He is most curious. Are there many volunteers rallying to the national colors? Have you found anything of military value here?"

Wake was further stunned. The man obviously didn't have the faintest idea of the situation and neither did his major.

"No volunteers and we haven't found anything of military value. Other than the crossroads."

"I see, no volunteers. Hhmm. Your defensive dispositions are completed? I didn't see any as I walked into the town."

"The men are using the buildings for fighting positions. A full perimeter is set up. Didn't you get my messages? I sent men back to you twice today with a report of our situation and asking for the time of your advance here. I've been waiting for a reply."

"No messages arrived from you at any time. I would know, of course, as the staff lieutenant to the adjutant. And, of course, there will be no advance today. Possibly the day after tomorrow, which would make it Wednesday, if we can get all of our equipment and men ashore tomorrow in your navy boats. We will need a day, once everything is ashore, to get organized properly for a march into the interior. And, it goes without saying, if the equipment and baggage are not on land and organized by Wednesday, then it will be unfortunately delayed until the following day.

"I must say the transport from the ships to the shore has been somewhat less efficient than we had hoped for. Some problem about tides and shallow water has stopped your colleagues, Lieutenant. The major is most distressed about how the colonel will view this disruption."

Wake was no longer stunned. Now he was angry. Staring at Hammersley, he heard the wind outside arrive with an abrupt whooshing sound, bending the trees and rustling the hut's roof and walls. Sand and loose sticks blew past the open window as the sky outside grew even darker, making the inside of the trader's hut sinister and gloomy. The force of the wind rose and lowered and then rose even higher in strength. The malevolence of the gusts matched the outrage in Wake's mind at the pomposity of Hammersley. The gust gained even more velocity until the sound of it in the trees was a constant wail and rain started to pelt the building and the ground, thudding like bullets as a piece of thatch flew by the window from a nearby dwelling.

Lightning struck very near, sending a jolt through the crossroads as the ground itself vibrated. Thunder, no longer a distant rumble but now a constant barrage of massive noise, surrounded them, making speaking in conversational tones impossible.

Wake raised his voice above the din. "Hammersley, have you ever seen battle? Are you and your regiment *completely* new at this?"

The superior mien on the mask of Hammersley's face cracked at that comment, but he recovered in quick order and replied with an even tone. "I and the 195th have not yet had the honor of *seeing the elephant*, as they say in the great newspapers. Our sister New York regiments have known that moment in Virginia, but we have only been in service for four months. We were hoping to get a taste of it at Port Royal but were only in South Carolina for a week when the army called for our help in Florida. Needed our regiment down here to assist in the various invasions the army is conducting right now on the peninsula. I feel certain that we will conduct ourselves with honor if that elephant, as they say, does appear, Lieutenant."

Again Wake didn't know what to say in response to the attitude of the man, who was a supposed leader of men about to go into battle. But Hammersley wasn't done.

"Don't you worry, the army is here close by in force for your support. But I really doubt if the Rebel renegade militia is anywhere around here. There won't be any enemy force in strength. No elephant for any of us, sailor or soldier, to see I fear, Lieutenant Wake."

McDougall touched Wake's elbow and leaned over to say something. "Our lads, Captain. If the lieutenant here knows nothing of them, they must not have made it to the camp. The

Rebs might have got 'em, sir."

Wake's mind was swirling with possibilities, made all the more chaotic by the incessant crashing of thunder around them. He struggled to remain calm with the man in front of him.

"Lieutenant Hammersley, did you see the sailors patrolling the road and swamp as you walked here?"

"Why yes, I did meet a young naval officer and some sailors on the road. Have you lost some of your men, Lieutenant Wake?"

Wake sat down on the chair again as McDougall remembered the seaman standing in the corner watching the exchange in wide-eyed wonder and dismissed him back to his post.

"Yes, Hammersley. The men I sent to you are missing and I can only deduce the Rebs have got them." McDougall looked at Wake but said nothing. Wake registered the expression on the petty officer's face and sighed. "And they may have captured our plan of dispositions from the message I sent to you."

Hammersley pouted his mouth and rubbed his chin. "I see. This is most distressing. The major and colonel will not take kindly to this development, at all."

Standing up again, Wake directed McDougall to send four men and a petty officer to escort Lieutenant Hammersley to the beach camp. Enroute he was to find Robbins and tell him to bring his detail to Claresville immediately. McDougall, looking grim, strode out of the hut shouting for Hilderbrandt. Wake turned back to the army lieutenant.

"Hammersley, you don't have the faintest notion of what we have here. The sailors have done your job for you and secured an inland position when the soldiers were sitting around trying to unpack their dress uniforms. If we hadn't done that, your regiment would have been bottled up at that camp at the far end of that swamp road and never gotten further than a hundred feet from the beach."

Hammersley started to speak, a perturbed sneer on his face. Wake's courtesy had left him though and his anger finally burst out.

"Shut the hell up, Hammersley, and listen to me. These Floridians are much tougher than your soft city boys, especially in this country. These boys down here kill things *to live*. This is all *their land*, and they know it well and will defend it viciously. Only a fool would think there'll be no opposition here. I am tired of fools. There will be opposition. Strong opposition. There may very well be far more than militia here too."

Wake walked to within two feet of Hammersley's face. "So get back there and tell Major Martin that if he wants to make this invasion of his work, he had better put his baggage down and get his courage up. Move forward toward the enemy, and that means come right here. Now! Not three days from now when we are surrounded by five times our number while he's having a full dress parade of the regiment. Now. Today! Do you understand that message, Lieutenant Hammersley?"

Terror replaced hauteur on Hammersley's face. He suddenly looked much younger. He stammered out a reply. "Ah, yes, sir. Come now. There are enemy around the area."

Wake returned to the crude map spread on the table. "Good, now go and find the petty officer who will escort you back. I want some army blue coats coming up that road in two hours at the most. I just hope it isn't too late."

Hammersley mumbled a reply, saluted, and turned on his heel, fleeing the room.

Wake sat down again at the table and stared at the sketch map he had drawn. The anger had drained him, but he had to think this through. Overpowering sounds of the storm filled the dim room. The sweet smell of rain-laden air mixed with the caustic odor of lightning and the foul stench of the nearby swamps. Outside he could hear petty officers and sailors yelling to each other above the din. McDougall plodded back inside the hut, stamping the mud off his brogans and advising that he had formed the escort detail to go the beach, before he collapsed with fatigue in the other chair. Wake was too tired to reply.

The crack of another lightning strike smashed through the

air. Men were shouting something outside. Wake was temporarily dazed as one more lightning bolt detonated close to them. The rain must have turned into hail now for he could hear a constant shower of it hitting the building—thudding hard into the thin walls, some of it coming through the cracks. Then he heard men screaming—screaming in pain. Wake went to the window with McDougall to see if lightning had struck some of his sailors.

Both men stood staring, mute with shock, at the scene outside. Wake felt sick.

The attack had come. The Confederates had timed their assault on the crossroads to coincide with the overwhelming noise of the storm's onslaught. In the seconds since the attack started two Rebel field pieces had blasted open several of the thatch huts and their infantry was now charging into the hamlet. Hilderbrandt and Hammersley and the escort detail were just leaving the village for the beach, but ran back into the buildings when the first volleys swept through the air. Hammersley stumbled back into the trader's hut, tripping over the threshold. He finally stood against the wall and clung to a log post. Wide-eyed, he screamed at Wake.

"Oh dear God, they're attacking us! They're attacking now!"

McDougall glanced at Wake and shook his head as he dashed out of the hut to his defensive position on the perimeter, yelling at the army lieutenant as he shouldered Hammersley out of the way. "Aye, ye've got the grand honor o' seein' that elephant now, young Lieutenant. Hell, you'll probably be close enough to smell the bastard's breath!"

Hammersley stood motionless, sword askew, full dress uniform soaked and disheveled, looking around for someone to give him guidance, to give an order. Wake rushed out also and left him there. There was no time for instructions on what to do.

As McDougall ran to a dwelling on the Collmerton road approach, Wake ran to the other side of the perimeter to get an idea of how big an attack it was. He got only to the northerly coastal road approach when he saw that it was a large-scale attack—by regulars in tan and gray uniforms, with regimental and battle flags. The enemy musket fire was coming in massive volleys, unlike Wake's previous experience with Rebel militia. The artillery was evidently firing grapeshot from somewhere in the trees on the north side, the blasts cutting through the dwellings and barns as well as the open areas. Wounded sailors, some with gaping laceration wounds from the artillery, stumbled back to the center of the crossroads as others, led by Bosun Meade, withdrew slowly as they fired at the enemy. Meade rushed up to Wake and shouted to be heard over the rain, wind, and shooting.

"Sweet Jesus, Lieutenant, but they got us! Blasted us with grape when the lightning an' thunder was striking. Then they charged. Before we knew it they was in among us."

Wake tried to think rapidly. The sheer pandemonium of noise and motion around him made simple concentration difficult. The noise would not stop. His fights with the Florida irregular companies in the last year were nothing like this. These Confederate regulars were overwhelming in their ferocity and discipline. The sailors would have to hold here to give everyone else time to withdraw. Otherwise it would be a massacre.

Wake gestured at a dwelling nearby. "Can you hold at this second or third house?"

"We can try, sir."

"Good man. Try to hold here while I check the rest of the perimeter."

Meade turned and rallied the rest of the *Bonsall* sailors, calling them to stop and shoot from behind the dwellings next to him. Of the fifteen original sailors in his detail, only ten answered his call. Wake ran the hundred fifty feet to the western side of the defenses where Hilderbrandt was calming his men. So far this side and the southern coastal road approach had not been attacked. The Rebels had concentrated on the north and east.

"Doan waste zee ammunition, men. Vait til you zee the Rebels, zen shoot zem down!"

Wake slowed down his run to a walk and spoke to the quartermaster. "Hilderbrandt, pick five men and send them to Meade. Let me know immediately if the enemy attacks this side."

"Ya vol, zir!"

The sounds of musketry increased now from McDougall and Faber's area on the northeastern approaches, as the wind and rain subsided to a slower but constant rate. Sloshing in his soaked uniform, Wake quickly walked toward the trader's hut only to stop one building away. The Confederates had already taken most of the structures on this side of the crossroads. Several sailors still lay in unnatural poses on the ground.

Wake recognized one of them, lying face down with his right arm and leg strangely out of position from his torso. The flesh was shredded, like meat emerged from a grinder. It was young Beasley, the apprentice seaman from Kent Island on Maryland's eastern shore who told Wake a month earlier that he had family fighting for the Confederacy in one of their regiments. Beasley's father had told him the proper thing to do was to be loyal to the Union, even if the rest of the family wasn't. Beasley didn't look very proper now, Wake thought, listening to a drum roll from the enemy. After the drum sounded he noticed something had changed.

A lull in the noise around him jarred Wake from the sight of the boy, unnerving him by the relative silence. He glanced around nervously to ascertain why the volume of sound had decreased. Soon it was obvious.

The firing had slacked as the enemy soldiers advanced in twos and threes from cover to cover, no longer pouring shots at the sailors from massed volleys. Artillery fire had stopped altogether since their own infantrymen were now in the target area. The sailors were firing as best they could at the darting shapes coming toward them. Wake could hear McDougall in his gun deck voice admonishing his men.

"Mark your targets before you fire! Mark them and shoot them down, steady like, lads."

Faber came around the corner of the barn next to Wake and

ran over to him. "Sir, we've taken some casualties. Down to somewhere's around nine or ten men. Don't know how long we can hold. Those are real soldiers out there! They ain't some militia boys from the neighborhood."

Wake walked quickly with Faber over to another corner of the building where Foley, the seaman who had run to tell him of Hammersley's arrival, was lying on the ground calmly shooting at the men in tan who were moving across a field in front of him. Faber crawled up behind Foley to get a look at what was on that side.

"Foley, I'm coming up behind ya, keep on shootin'."

As he finished the statement Faber and Wake heard a crack, louder than the other noises around them, and they saw Foley's head snap impossibly backward over his neck, then roll to the right. The front of his face had a huge hole where his nose had been and the back half of his head was gone, showing the interior cavities of his skull. Wake had never seen such a sight and stared until he heard a moan growing into a wail from the man beside him. Bloody brain matter was splattered all over Faber.

"Oh God! Oh Jesus! Captain! Foley's dead. Look at his brains on me!"

Wake dragged Faber away, pushing him down behind the opposite corner of the barn. Then he returned and grabbed Foley's musket out of his limp hands. It was still loaded and he knelt on one knee, leaning around the corner to fire at anything he could. He saw a figure in the window of a home across the way and tried to determine if it was a sailor or a soldier. Then he saw a kepi hat, the sign of a soldier, and fired the musket. The soldier wasn't hit. He didn't even duck. He just looked around to see where the shot had come from. His steadiness impressed Wake. It was obvious that these were not only regulars, but unshakable veterans of battle.

Another drum beat a tattoo and the shooting decreased. Wake could hear Southern accents yelling.

"Hold your fire, now. Fifteenth, hold your fire now!"

Soon the shooting to the north tapered off. All around the crossroads village the sounds of guns firing had stopped. Only the rain continued, in a slow, steady drip from the low clouds overhead. It was a relief from the cacophony that had heralded the death of so many, just moments earlier.

Faber was still distraught, refusing to look in the direction of Foley and staring at his bloodied uniform. The bosun's mate sat with his back to the barn wall, trying to keep the tremble out of his voice. "They's a stopped shootin', sir. What's happenin', sir?"

"I'm not quite sure, Faber, but I'd better find out. I need your help."

Faber calmed his breathing and nodded to his captain.

"I want you to tell Hilderbrandt to send three more men from his area to this side of the crossroads."

Faber acknowledged the order and brought himself up from the ground, running at full speed across the open space where the two roads intersected. Wake dashed over to where McDougall was standing by the wall of a thatch house.

"McDougall, what do you make of the lull?"

"Don't rightly know, sir. They'd pushed our lads back but then didn't follow through. They had us, Captain. Had us dead to rights."

Again a drum sounded, a plaintive long roll that was prolonged by the musician playing it. From behind one of the dwellings on the Collmerton road, Wake heard a man shout something indecipherable, then shout it again. He understood it the second time.

"Yanks! Can y'all heah me? Sendin' in a parley flag of truce. Doan y'all shoot. White flag of truce, Yanks. Come out an' us meet halfway!"

McDougall shook his head.

"Trick, Captain. It's a trick."

Wake stood there trying to think about what had happened. The Rebels had all but overrun them. Could do so at any minute, in fact, or even stand off and continue to blast the crossroads with grapeshot. Why didn't they? Why stop when they were so close?

As he asked the questions to himself, the answer became clear. It was so simple and clear it astounded him.

As McDougall grimaced beside him, Wake called out to the enemy. "Fine, Reb. This is Lieutenant Peter Wake of the United States Navy. I'm in command here and I'll meet you halfway. I'm coming out with a white flag too. I want to talk to your commanding officer."

The voice called back, Wake registering that it contained no bravado or timidity. It was a calm voice, one that had done this before.

"We know who y'all are, Yank! Our colonel says he will meet ya' halfway. No tricks now. Any tricks an' y'all're dead first."

McDougall grasped Wake's arm, locking his eyes into his captain's. "Captain, we've been through more than jus' a wee bit together. Don't do this. I'll go. I'll carry back any message they might be havin'."

"No, it's my decision and I will go. You will have command here if I fall. Now, what can I use for a white rag?"

McDougall exhaled a deep breath with a sigh, then stripped out of his blue jumper and handed over his grimy undershirt.

"Could use a bit o' washin', sir, but it's close enough ta' white for them Rebs. Come back in one damn piece, Captain. If I don't return to the *St. James* with you aboard, I'll have the hell ta pay with that young Irish fool Rork."

Wake smiled at the older man, bare-chested now and appearing even more gaunt and aged than usual. After shaking hands, he left the gunner and walked out into the open, holding the rag high and telling all around him to hold their fire. He noticed that the rain and breeze had stopped too but couldn't remember when. Above the stillness of the air, Wake could hear the men of both sides talking. He knew they were talking about him, but couldn't make out the words.

In front of him, standing maybe seventy feet away, by the side of a crudely built log home beside the road, stood a tall middle-aged man in a tattered gray uniform, officer's gold cuff lacing faded, with a slouch hat flattened on one side. The man was holding a white rag of some sort also, a bed sheet perhaps, as he walked forward toward Wake, a limp apparent in his left leg. They met halfway between the positions of the two forces, each man surveying the other's posture and eyes, trying to determine the measure of his opponent. The man in gray spoke first. His face displayed no emotion even as his voice gave a pleasant greeting.

"Good afternoon, Lieutenant Wake, allow me to introduce myself. Colonel Daniel Bates Holland, commanding officer of the Fifteenth Florida Infantry Regiment, at your service, sir."

Wake took a moment and considered this Colonel Holland and the Fifteenth Florida before replying. He remembered reading a captured Tallahassee newspaper in Key West three months earlier that had given a detailed and glorious account of this regiment. The Fifteenth Florida, the "Fightin' Fifteenth" they had called it, had fought in Tennessee with General Sims at Bloody Ridge and Byrus Mountain and Detarville. They had been at the battle of Schmidt's Mill in Georgia the previous February. The Fifteenth, the last infantry regiment formed from Florida, was down to half its strength, replacements being nonexistent anymore since the eligible men of Florida were already fighting, dead, invalided, or gone over to the enemy. The men of the Florida Fifteenth had "seen the elephant," as Hammersley had put it, a dozen times in the last year. Now they had been sent to defend their home state against the increasing Yankee coastal raids, for Florida was the last remaining breadbasket area of the South.

"Colonel Holland, it is an honor to meet you, sir. The fame of your regiment has preceded your arrival here. How is it that you know of me, might I ask?"

Colonel Holland permitted a smile to cross his face. "Lieutenant Wake, you seem to have been, shall we say, active, on this coast. The people at Deadman's Bay advised us of a naval officer named Wake who faced down a group of very angry citizenry there. Those types of situations can erupt in tragedy. That one did not. It impressed many people. Unfortunately, of course, you are also the enemy, so one's appreciation can only go so far. But still, it appears by all accounts you're at least an honorable enemy, which I've found to be distressingly rare is this sad conflict between our peoples."

Flattery notwithstanding, Wake found himself liking this man's sense of style. It was a relic of another era, a gentler time that seemed long ago, before the obscene insanity of this war. "Thank you, sir."

"Some of my artillerymen who are local militia, the Gulf Guardians they style themselves, remembered you from that morning at Deadman's Bay and called your identity to my attention. Thought you might be prevailed upon to stop this useless bloodshed. This is, after all, not much of a place for you to die for, Lieutenant. It's not even anywhere near your home state, which by your accent I would place somewhere in New England, probably Massachusetts."

Wake nodded his head. The suave colonel with the dry humor was certainly correct in that statement. Wake decided to play this game of raconteur and smiled at his enemy.

"Well, you certainly have me there, Colonel. Massachusetts it is. That this place isn't much to die for, I'll be the first to admit, but then glory or fame is no prerequisite for a man to do his duty, is it? And it appears that my unfortunate duty as an officer in the United States Navy requires me to stand and fight right here, at this sad place someone has called Claresville. Colonel, believe me, for my family's sake I wish it was someplace more impressive."

"Ah, but young Lieutenant Wake, this fight's not for you and your sailors. You're men of the sea, as useless as fish on the land. We have you outnumbered and outgunned. You and your men will all die here. And why? For what? You can't beat us. That infantry regiment down the road at the beach can't help you. You have done your duty already, sir. Retire from the field with an honorable surrender now and spare your sailors' lives. We in the Fifteenth have seen too much bloodshed in this war and are heartily sick of it. I ask you to stop it now."

That *was* it! In the midst of the chaos earlier, Wake thought that might be the case. The colonel's comments, meant to be facetious and then sympathetic, had proven the point. The Confederates had been warned of the Yankee landing but hadn't known of the quick occupation of Claresville by the sailors. If Wake and his landing force had not been at the crossroads, the 195th New York would have been bottled up along that swamp road to the beach camp. Colonel Holland and the Fightin' Fifteenth Florida wanted to get past Claresville and cork up that bottle with the New Yorkers inside. If they could do that, then the Union forces couldn't go inland and the foodstuffs of Florida could continue to feed the vast armies to the north.

And Wake couldn't believe that Holland had just made the ridiculous suggestion of surrendering to him. He must have known Wake would laughingly decline. So why did he do it?

"Well, Lieutenant Wake, I'm afraid my pleasure at our meeting cannot delay the exigencies of the situation. I must demand a reply to my admittedly very kind offer."

Wake examined Holland's eyes a few seconds more before answering. It was a bluff. It was all a bluff. A gigantic bluff. He absolutely knew it. They wouldn't have stopped if they didn't have to, and they didn't have to for lack of men or guns. It was ammunition. That was the reason. They were low on ammunition. Wake realized that if he was wrong, they would all probably die in battle or a prison camp, but there was no other choice.

"Colonel Holland, I must express my admiration for your tactics thus far employed. The attack in the storm was quite impressive. Very innovative and educational for a landlocked sailor such as myself. I must remember to return the favor should we meet again like this. However, regarding your kind offer, you know I cannot surrender. You know I will not surrender. You also know that the forces of the Federal government in this area are far stronger than your gallant, but under-strength regiment. Sir, the needless shedding of blood will be your decision."

Colonel Holland smiled again, a slight curve of one corner of his mouth, a sadly knowing smile eroding Wake's confidence that he was right. Maybe the colonel was playing bluff poker on a grand scale.

"Very well, Lieutenant Wake. I know you understand that I had to at least offer the chance of surrender. It has been an honor to meet you, young man. Your country should be proud of you. Your death really will be a pity. Good-bye, sir."

"My honor also, Colonel. May we meet in better times someday, sir. Good-bye."

Wake saluted the colonel smartly and spun around. He walked away at as slow a pace as he could discipline himself to make. He tried to appear with as much nonchalance as he knew the colonel was displaying behind him. Wake kept an unconcerned look as he reached his men's lines among the damaged buildings of Claresville. McDougall met him at the side of the barn where Foley's body still lay where he died, a graphic reminder of the end for them all if Wake was wrong.

"Well, sir? What was the parley by that Reb colonel?"

"It appears that they want us to surrender, McDougall. Ridiculous, of course. I believe they are getting quite desperate now. What is happening around our perimeter?"

McDougall's jaw dropped open and his shoulders slumped. A moment later he spoke, shaking his head in disbelief as the words came out. "Sweet Jesus, but I wish that damned rascal Rork were here to see this! The captain himself says the Rebs are desperate now. They've shot down a third o' our men and are fancying to blast the rest, an' the captain says *they're* desperate now! Captain, I'm a hatin' to piss on this little celebration o' yours, but we're about done in, an' those Rebs over there've got a whole lot more to throw our way, sir. Maybe the time has come to go back to the beach. Back to the water where sailors belong proper, sir. We can't fight these regular soldiers, sir."

Wake understood McDougall's plea. He was reluctant to let the gunner know his hypothesis but felt the peril of the scenario they found themselves in demanded it be given.

"Think McDougall. Not emotion, but logic. Think this through. What is the first thing you tell your men when they start shooting?"

"Mark their targets. Make every shot count. Don't waste ammunition."

"Correct, Gunner. Now, how much do we have left?"

"A fair amount, Captain. Forty rounds per man. They fired off about ten a man. I just checked. The lads didn't get much time to fire off what they had, what with the surprise an' all. The Rebs broke out of ranks and charged us in small groups soon after they fired off all o' those volleys, so's the lads didn't have no big target groups to shoot at."

"Precisely. Now, remember the Rebel barrage of artillery and musket fire? How many rounds do you think *they* fired?"

"Oh Lord, Captain. Hundreds of musket rounds and a dozen at least of the cannon grape . . ."

Wake could see the mind of the old gunner turning the information over. McDougall started to shake his head again and smile.

"Now, Gunner, think some more. The Fifteenth is a used-up regiment that came back from the main fighting areas to do guard duty in Florida. How many rounds do you think they even have with them?"

McDougall was grinning now and nodding his head. He understood.

"Sweet Jesus, Mary, and Joseph. If you aren't one for the books, Captain. I do believe you're right as rain. Most o' the soldiers are probably carrying twenty or thirty rounds with maybe ten or twenty left an' some cannon shot. The buggers're low on powder an' shot, aren't they Captain. An' the Rebs are bluffin' us into lettin' them by."

"Exactly, Gunner! And they don't want to waste all of what they have on us when they've got to deal with a fresh large New York regiment that's a few miles away down the road. We call their bluff. We stay."

"Well, I'll be a pagan at Christmas! They had me fooled, but not you, Captain. Well done, sir. Well done."

McDougall came out with a rare laugh and went on to advise Wake that Ensign Robbins and his men had come into Claresville from the swamp road when they heard the fighting, bolstering the east and north sides of the lines. As the gunner's mate was speaking, Wake heard shouts coming from the west side of the crossroads where Hilderbrandt's men were. At first startled and concerned, he soon realized they were humorous shouts of welcome to the men of Ensign Chase's detail who were walking into the perimeter from the swamp road. McDougall got his captain's attention.

"Sir, they's taken down that white flag over there. I think the parley truce is over."

"Yes, well, of course that was to be expected. Now, McDougall, I want all of the officers and petty officers to meet me at that house over there by Hilderbrandt's side in five minutes. And please hurry, I don't know how much time we have."

The gunner's mate went off to locate the men required as Wake made his way around his little command, running between the cover of the walls when out in the open, and walking when out of sight of the Confederates. He was concerned about the lack of medical care for the wounded, who were gathered in the dwelling hut on the unengaged south side of Claresville. There were a dozen men in there, tended by well-meaning but untrained sailors who had already used up the few basic medicines and bandages in the medical box brought ashore from the schooner.

As Wake walked among the wounded, seeing men of his own ship and those of others, he was struck by how old they looked, even those he knew to be only eighteen or nineteen. Their contorted, powder-blackened faces were aging fast with the agony of untreated punctures and gashes. He should have insisted that the one assistant surgeon in the flotilla, Tate of the *Bonsall*, accompany them ashore. But he had forgotten that factor, thinking their role would be a minor one behind the army's position. They would simply be guarding the rear, he had thought, when all of this was initially proposed. How wrong he had been—on so many things.

Saying words of encouragement to the sailors lying there, he tried to convey an air of confidence, even when they asked about how the enemy had surprised them and how they would hold the place. For the questions about where the army was, and when would they come, he had no answers. Those were questions in his mind also, and he would make sure to get the answers—if they lived through the next hour or so.

The sun was low behind the storm clouds that had moved off to the western sky when Wake trudged over to the house where the others were waiting for him. He walked into the darkened one-room dwelling and greeted the men with whom he had been through so much in the last fourteen hours. It seemed like so much longer. Someone lit a lantern as Wake started to speak.

"Evening, gentlemen. Well, we're still here, and we may very well have a difficult night of it, so I want this gathering to be short and to the point. First I want an updated report on your commands, starting with Ensign Chase."

Chase had been leaning against a wall and now stood straight. His voice was clear and strong. "Sir, I have all of my men, ten from my ship the *Fox* and four more who arrived back at the camp today as messengers from you. They are with all of their ammunition and are in good condition, ready to fight. We are currently in the center of this town, or whatever it is, awaiting your disposition of our force. I apologize for our late arrival. We were ordered to stand fast at the beach camp by Colonel Wherley, who is now ashore and in command there."

Wake was concerned and regarded the ensign closely. This was very important information he was giving. At first, Wake thought to interrupt the man and have him narrate the rest of it in private. Then he thought that witnesses to the report might be prudent—given the import of its contents. He nodded at Chase to continue. Surrounded by men staring at him, the ensign took a breath and went on.

"Ah, yes, sir. Well, we heard the shooting coming from here and prepared our arms and equipment to march up the road. We were formed up and about to move when Colonel Wherley himself came up to me, in front of my men, sir, and said to stand fast. He said you would be falling back soon and coming back within the perimeter of the camp. I said that we would go out and meet you and he ordered me point blank to dismiss the column and take our positions in the breastworks. Said that we would all go out against the Rebs together tomorrow or the next day when all of the army's artillery and baggage was ashore."

The silence in the room was accentuated by the humidity clinging to everything. Wake didn't understand what Chase was saying. It didn't make sense. There must be more.

"All right, Mr. Chase, what about my messengers?"

"They came in and Major Martin and later Colonel Wherley heard their reports, sir. When I asked about following up on them and sending troops to you, the colonel said it was unnecessary, that you and the rest of the landing party would be coming back. He was, well, he seemed . . . "

Chase paused, obviously uncertain of how to proceed. Wake waved him onward with his hand. "Say what you have to say, Mr. Chase. The men in this room have no time for politeness. Be blunt. We all owe that to each other."

"Aye aye, sir. Well, the colonel seemed to be pleased that you would have to retreat back to his lines at the beach. Seemed to gloat over it, sir. Wanted you to have to retreat from the enemy, sir. Was that your impression, Ford?"

A burly bosun's mate in the dark corner in back of the hut spoke quietly. "Aye, sir. The man looked like he enjoyed the thought o' Captain Wake havin' failure with the Rebs, sir. I think he hates us sailormen, sir."

Wake knew the information was potentially explosive. The man had withheld help from a naval landing force under attack.

This testimony could result in Wherley's court-martial.

"I see. And then how did you come to take your men up to us then, Mr. Chase?"

"We heard the firing stop and couldn't stand it any longer, sir. Order from the army or not, we had to find our mates and help. Simple as that, sir. I disobeyed a direct order from Colonel Wherley."

A commotion erupted at the doorway as a petty officer swore at a man just walking in who stepped on his feet. The oaths stopped and Ford muttered as the other man pushed his way to the center of the group. "It's that army lieutenant, Captain Wake. He wants to join the meeting."

Hammersley stood in the middle of the gathering, looking around at the men who made no disguise of their disgust for him. Wake shook his head and sighed.

"Lieutenant Hammersley, you seem to have an uncanny knack for arrivals at the wrong time. Where have you been?"

Hammersley's condescending demeanor had returned. Wake was amazed he could still summon it up after his experiences that day.

"Well, Captain Wake, as I presume I evidently should call you, since you are the captain of a ship even though you are but a lieutenant, I have been right where you left me. With no orders, no support, and no help. The Rebs got into that trader's hut and I had to wait against the wall of some decrepit hovel next door until you decided to have your visit with that scum Reb colonel. Then I waited around for the report you should have given me of your conversation with the Reb, but you left for somewhere. I have been waiting for quite some time, Captain Wake, and Colonel Wherley will not be impressed by what I will have to report to him."

Wake rotated and stretched his neck muscles. They were tense and hurting. He did not need this army officer and his attitude.

"Lieutenant Hammersley, the message is still the same as the others I have sent. We hold the crossroads. Send the regiment now, and especially the surgeon for our wounded. We have held off the enemy and it is safe for the army to come up here now. Go tell your colonel that. Tell him now, Hammersley."

The army officer's chest began to expand, his jaw jutted out and his voice deepened.

"The effrontery of those remarks will not be forgotten, sir. You will answer for them! We have heard of your lack of decorum when in company of army officers before this, Captain Wake."

"You must have misunderstood me, Hammersley, this interview is over. You are incapable of assisting here. You are only capable of hindering us. Now go to your precious colonel and his parade ground regiment and get the surgeon here for the men wounded in the battle. *I said get out! Now!*"

Hammersley did not deflate his stature. Instead he stood there in the soundless room and spoke back to Wake in a sullen hiss. "Yes, . . . yes I'll go now. I'll need four armed men and a petty officer for an escort. I will leave right now."

Wake smiled for the first time since seeing Hammersley at the meeting. "No men to spare to protect you, Hammersley. We may be attacked again and I need every *sailor* on our defenses. Now that you have had the honor of seeing that famous elephant, I'm sure you are man enough to protect yourself. You can't get lost, just follow the road. Now get the hell out of here or take a musket and stand in the lines with the men for the next attack."

Hammersley stepped backward slowly, the men around him clearing away from the soldier. His mouth opened, but no words came out. When he had backed his way to the doorway they finally came out, petulant and high-pitched.

"You'll regret this, Wake. You'll regret this."

After he'd left, everyone looked at Wake for a response to Hammersley's bizarre behavior, but there was too much to be decided and no time to be distracted.

"So much for the pride of the army, men. Now, let's go over our dispositions of men and then I will tell you of my impressions of my meeting with the enemy commander."

Each detail gave a report on their casualties, as well as their remaining ammunition, food, and water supplies. Then officers and petty officers closed in around Wake as he went over how they would deal with the next attack that was sure to come, and what they would do afterward. He told them not to expect the army to relieve them that night, but the next day they would be heading back to the beach after the 195th's arrival. When he was greeted with looks of disbelief, Wake assured them that Colonel Wherley and his regiment would be coming to Claresville the next day no later than by the noonday meal, that he was absolutely sure of it. Of all the men listening to his confident assertion, only McDougall nodded in agreement, a touch of a smile showing as his eyes met Wake's.

All they had to do was hold the crossroads until then, Wake thought, and that possibility was dependent on the accuracy of his assessment of Colonel Daniel Griner Holland.

11

Perceptions

The men returned to their positions on the decreased perimeter in the village. As the darkness closed over Claresville, the sailors hurriedly ate what scraps of food they had been able to find as they scanned the enemy locations, alert for another attack. The seamen were allowed, a few at a time, to go back to the water butts at Hilderbrandt's position and quench their thirst with two cups of water, not nearly enough to replace that lost during the day. All were exhausted and nervous.

A strange quiet descended, the men speaking in whispers and moving noiselessly around the dwellings. The loudest sounds were the slaps for the mosquitoes that rose in swarms at dusk, plaguing everyone. The sand fleas and biting gnats, called by the locals no-see-ums, were even worse than the mosquitoes. Wake could not remember ever experiencing worse insects. They crawled inside clothing and hair, biting and buzzing until men shouted in despair. Wake wondered how the locals on this coast coped with them. He knew they lived with smoke pots constantly smoldering in their homes at night and covered themselves with animal grease to repel the bugs, but he couldn't allow fires and had no grease. He didn't think they would help much anyway.

All lanterns on both sides were extinguished, making the slight moonlight through the thin overcast clouds the only illumination. From the hut where the wounded waited came moans but no more screams. The most badly wounded had died by then, others were trying to stifle their fear and stay still in order not to open wounds that had congealed. The dead that could be reached were removed from where they fell to the western side of the crossroads and covered in blankets found in the homes. The line of shapes on the ground made Wake stop and bow his head, asking God for the strength to endure whatever was coming.

Wake circled the defensive lines again and found them as well as could be expected. His sailors were unaccustomed to this type of duty and totally untrained, but they were holding up well. Hilderbrandt advised him that Hammersley had left the crossroads and gone west along the road toward the army camp at the beach on the river, muttering something as he walked. Wake nodded his reply and walked on to the next position. By the time he returned to his own position on the northern approaches to the crossroads, he was sweating profusely, whether from fear or the numbing humidity and heat he could not tell. He just knew he felt miserable and exhausted and that his men must be enduring the same. Getting some rest was essential he knew, and after searching unsuccessfully for a real bed he lay down on the plank floor of a settler's home.

The moon's glow could barely make it through the clouds. It had traveled across the night sky until it was just above the western horizon, but still enough of it came through the open window to illuminate the interior of the crude home where Wake slept on the floor when old McDougall came tromping into the room. Wake blinked his eyes open as McDougall shook him and whispered close to his ear.

"Movement in front of Meade's men, sir. Sounds like men forming up."

"Very well, wake up everyone. But quietly."

McDougall went out to warn the others as Wake made his way to where Meade was standing by a rickety woodshed. The bosun pointed to a clearing just beyond the buildings.

"Over there, sir, at the tree line. Heard men moving around. Sounds like a bunch of 'em."

"Did they stop after you first heard them, or is it continuing?"

"Continuing, sir. There. Hear it?"

A faint voice sounded in the still air. Two other voices responded. Then the squeal of a wheel that needed lubricating could be heard. It was followed by the jangle of metal on metal. Wake put his hand on the bosun's shoulder.

"Meade, I think that's a gun they are moving into position. Get your men behind the most solid things you can find. They'll probably start with cannon fire, most likely grape or canister, then run in with their infantry. Wait until you actually see their men—then open fire. Don't waste your shots. Understood?"

Meade gripped Wake's arm and nodded. The man's strength was reassuring. "Yes, sir. Understood."

Another voice came out of the dark line of trees on the far side of the clearing. It was an admonishing voice, low and stern. Actual words could not be made out, but the serious tone was obvious. Somewhere among the Confederates an officer was giving orders, thought Wake, and probably the final orders for the attack.

He glanced over his left shoulder at the weakening glow of the moon as it descended in the west. The clouds filtered it even more as it got lower in the sky. Wake thought about the timing. It was still an hour before dawn. With the moon down low now, the attackers would be hard to see. He knew it would start soon, but how would it end?

McDougall's arrival was heralded with a groan as he sat down, followed by a sigh.

"Maybe that old dog Rork should've been here. My old

bones aren't used to this. Give me a deck, Captain. An' a good gun to serve an' fire."

Wake smiled at the image. He shared the fervent desire to get away from this place and back out to sea. When he joined the navy he never thought he would be lying in the mud in the dark at a dreary collection of huts on a forgotten backwater coast, waiting for the enemy to attack and try to kill him. Colonel Holland's last words came to him and a chill went through his body as he wondered if that prophesy that he would die here would come true. Would his family in far away New England ever understand what he tried to do here, and why?

"McDougall, I wish we had one for you to fire right about now. I truly do, gunner."

Meade held up a hand and interrupted the banter. "They're coming—"

Boom! A flash blasted out of the tree line and canister shot swept into the buildings. Boom! Another gun over to the right erupted with flame and more shredding sounds ripped through the night. Cheering rose from all along the Confederate side of the field as yet another blast came from the first gun position.

McDougall, tired bones forgotten, called out to the sailors in the slow baritone deck voice of a petty officer going through the drill of firing small arms. "Hold your fire until you hear the order, lads. Mark your targets. Wait for the order. Make every shot count."

The flashes were blinding, and Wake hoped that his men could actually see the enemy when they came forward. He tried blinking his eyes rapidly to no avail and finally closed them for several seconds. By that time several more blasts had come, but thankfully without any accompanying screams of sailors hit. Then the blasts stopped and Wake could hear a brief drum staccato followed by screams and war hoops as the veterans of the Florida Fifteenth Infantry Regiment came forward at a run. Meade turned to look at him.

"I can hear 'em, sir, but I can't see 'em."

Wake tried to sound calm, even as he thought his heart was going to pound open his chest.

"That's all right, Meade. They're doing us a favor by all that yelling. When they get close just fire at the sounds, but on the command. Pass the word."

As the bosun went along the positions of his men scattered among the huts, Wake told McDougall to check the other sides of their defenses and send more men here to bolster Meade's men. McDougall left at a trot as Wake stared out at the mass of men almost upon them. The Rebels were running fast. They were almost there. Meade ran up and slid in the mud as he fell beside Wake. Meade's voice betrayed his anxiety as he stared out at the approaching mass of noise.

"All ready, sir."

Wake nodded his head and stood, shouting as loud as he could over the screaming of the Rebel soldiers only yards away. "Navy men! Fire *now*!"

The sailors' muskets shot out into the advancing Confederates, flames illuminating them in a tableau that showed the ferocity on their faces. The momentum of the infantry charge carried the surviving Floridians through the blast of naval musketry and forward the last few yards in front of the defenders. The sailors had time possibly to reload and shoot one more time. Scattered shots flashed where faster seamen had gotten off a second shot before falling back.

Wake now called for his men to retreat to the back walls of the dwellings. Meade knelt to fire again but suddenly clutched his stomach and fell writhing to the ground. Wake picked up the musket and shot blindly into the dark, hearing a curse thirty feet in front of him as a shape lit by the gun's flash fell.

Now the Rebels were firing their muskets, but targets for them were harder to locate since the sailors were hidden behind the buildings and hastily constructed walls of boxes and hay bales. Wake looked around him and found that no sailors were near—they had all fallen back to the second line, reloading and firing.

He knelt down by Meade and tried to feel for the wound, but the bosun was clutching it so tightly he couldn't determine anything but that it was a "gut shot," the worst kind of wound. Meade was cursing in a steady low voice and his body was curled up, rolling back and forth in his agony. Wake then ran his hands around the bosun's back and felt an exit hole. Liquid was pouring out in spurts.

"Meade, it's bad, but you can make it. We'll get the holes plugged and the army surgeon will take care of you when he gets here."

A Rebel soldier with a bayonetted musket ran by, tripping on Wake and cursing at him as he charged toward the sailors. Another ran up and stopped close by, taking aim at the nearest building and firing. Wake flattened himself on the ground next to Meade's ear.

"Meade, I've got to go now but I'll be back. Stay low and stay quiet. I'll be back."

Meade made no response, and Wake noticed that the bosun wasn't moving anymore. Wake stood up and ran to the center of the crossroads. Collapsing behind a bale of hay, he realized that the firing from the Confederates was diminishing.

A yell went up close by and several sailors fired into the area that Wake had just vacated. Several others fired from another building behind him and he heard McDougall and Hilderbrandt urging the men forward, the high Irish brogue competing with guttural German for the attention of the sailors. Thirty sailors, brandishing their cutlasses in one hand, for they had no bayonets, and their muskets in the other, rose en masse and followed Ensign Robbins as he ran into the darkness where the Rebels had taken over the original defensive positions. Wake stood as they charged by him, McDougall stopping to catch his breath.

"Good God, sir, you gave us a fright! Thought you were dead an' gone out there."

"No, not yet, gunner, but I surely do appreciate the help. Aren't the Rebs running now? Seems like they are turning back."

The sound of the muskets from the opposing forces was different enough to discern that the louder reports from the naval muskets, with a higher caliber and powder load, were more numerous than those of the enemy.

"Their shootin's slowed down, Captain. I think you're right about their powder an' shot. They're runnin' out o' cartridges an' slowin' down for sure. We're holding the village." Wake nodded and told McDougall of Meade's wound and to seek help for him. He then turned and followed the men with Robbins as they reclaimed the ground initially lost to the Rebel charge. They had made it to the original defensive line and stopped advancing by the time he caught up with them.

Stepping carefully in the darkness, Wake made his way up to where Robbins stood looking down at a group of men sitting close together on the ground. As other sailors manned the defensive line, six seamen guarded fifteen Confederate soldiers who sat with their hands on their heads. Robbins reported the situation as Wake looked at the prisoners.

"They just laid down their arms and surrendered, sir. Just gave up. Rest of 'em ran off back to their lines. They're all gone now."

No shooting could be heard now by either side. Only the moans and occasional screams of the wounded were disturbing the night. Wake stood over a Rebel sergeant, then knelt down beside him.

"That was a brave charge, sergeant. You ran out of ammunition though, didn't you?"

The sergeant had a lined face with many days' stubble apparent even in the dim light. He might have been twenty years old. He shook his head and looked at Wake.

"They said y'all're navy sailors and would give in quick-like. Said we could get more rounds off'n y'all, like we used to up in the mountains. Hell, we'd get 'em all the time off'n dead Yanks up there. But tonight we jus' ran out of shots an' couldn't use yores. Yore bullets 're too damned big for our barrels. Jist don't fit.

Guess they didn't think on that."

McDougall came up, heard the sergeant's comments and spoke to him. "Our army uses fifty-eights, but we don't. You can't use our rounds without recastin' 'em."

The sergeant nodded.

"Damned fools. I been from Tennessee to Georgia an' back home to Florida, jus' to get caught 'cause some fool didn't know that. Fought all that way jus' to get caught back home here. Brings a man down, it does, sir."

Wake shook his head. "Rest easy, sergeant. No more fighting for you. You can sit out the rest of this war, but we've got to go on with it. Just rest easy knowing someday you can go home to your family."

Wake turned away and peered out toward the Confederate lines. McDougall and Robbins stood next to him as Chase walked up. The gunner's mate broke the silence. "I hate to have to tell you, Captain. Meade's dead. Never had a chance with that wound."

Wake nodded and waited as Chase began his report.

"Captain Wake, it appears the attack is broken and over. Our losses are three men killed and eight wounded. Our lines are reestablished and secure. We have fifteen Rebs captured here and another five over where Faber is. He's bringing them here. Included in the prisoners are two sergeants and a wounded lieutenant. We've also got around twenty other Reb wounded and about a dozen dead, from what we can tell. We're putting their wounded over here with the prisoners so they can try to take care of them themselves. Easier to guard them, sir."

"Very well, Mr. Chase. Did any of them say anything about their plan tonight?"

Chase nodded his head. "Said they thought we'd run. They ran out of ammunition and had to stop. Those that didn't run fast enough back to their regimental lines got caught by our sailors. Ridiculous idea, sir. Charging us with almost empty cartridge and bullet bags. What the hell were they thinking, sir?"

Wake saw the eastern horizon was getting lighter as he responded. "Mr. Chase, they were thinking just what they told you. We would run. It's all perception. They perceived that we would run because they were convinced we believed they had us outgunned and outnumbered, that it would be hopeless to stay here. But we saw through it and didn't run. They paid a terrible price for their bluff."

Wake didn't want to discuss it further and walked away from the gathered men, calling for McDougall to gather the officers and petty officers together for another meeting. He found himself walking toward the line of blanketed bodies on the other side of the crossroads. He was angry and needed to be alone for a few minutes. He watched as the sailors brought the recently killed men, both Union and Confederate, to the place now being called the "morgue" by the seamen. The enemies were placed in two separate lines, as if even in death they were not allowed to mingle and must maintain their political animosity. But they'll all stink the same when the sun comes up, Wake thought as he watched the bodies being laid out.

McDougall roused him from his morbid thoughts and told him everyone was waiting at the house where they had had the other meeting. Trudging slowly across the muddy road, Wake entered the still dark room and looked around at the faces showing in the faint glimmer from the relit lantern.

"Gentlemen, I have received the casualty report from Mr. Chase. Now I want to know about your ammunition supplies. Give your reports."

Each man advised how much the men of his detail had left, most reporting ten rounds or more. Wake waited for them all to report and spoke again.

"Well, the enemy has done what we thought they might. We'll wait with all hands alert and ready to fight until an hour after sunrise. Then you can let half of them sleep at their guns for an hour, then switch the duty watch. Any questions on that?"

Nodding heads provided the tired response.

"Very well then. Let us return to our positions. Hilderbrant, pick a detail and get our dead buried, with markers. Have the Reb prisoners bury their own. I want a strong guard put on those prisoners. They are dangerous veterans. McDougall, see to that. Chase, you'll have the first officer's watch once we let the men sleep."

Hilderbrandt and McDougall acknowledged their orders. Wake stepped outside and looked around at the sky. It was cloudless in the east and a land breeze was beginning to stir. The light was increasing but was still not strong enough to allow Wake to see over to the tree line where the Fifteenth Florida was deployed. He was curious whether his hunch would be correct, but he would have to wait longer for the sun to make the woods visible.

He headed to the hut where he had slept earlier. Once inside he sat down and ate a piece of salt pork he found in his trouser pocket. Gnawing through the tough hunk of meat, he thought of what he would say to Wherley later in the morning. It would be a confrontation, he knew, but Wake was past the point of being patient. Too many men had been killed and wounded for politeness to be much of an influence on what was to come.

Claresville was a shambles. The battle, particularly the artillery, had destroyed what little structural strength there was in the buildings. Many were leaning precariously, others shorn of their thatch. The contents had been ransacked and anything of defensive value used by the sailors to build low walls between the homes. Many of the belongings of the former inhabitants were strewn over the ground. The ground itself had changed. Where once wild grass had provided at least a modicum of pleasant pastoral effect around the rough dwellings, there was now mud. The grass had been trampled by the feet of hundreds of men as they desperately tried to take or defend the collection of huts whose only value lay in the intersection of the two roads. The rains had completed the transformation and turned the pummeled earth into a sticky morass. As he walked out of the defensive works on the west side of the village, Wake observed that Claresville appeared even more depressing now than when he first had laid eyes on it.

Wake observed something else once the sun rose high enough to see better—no sign of the Florida Fifteenth Infantry in the tree line between the coastal road and the Collmerton road. It was not definitive—the Rebs could be hiding further back in the woods—but it was encouraging. Without more men Wake could not send a patrol to search the forest, but at least the Confederates were not close enough to attack without warning. The fact eased his mind a bit and allowed him to concentrate on the test of wills that was coming.

Walking alone along the road through the swamp back to the army's encampment, Wake was relieved to see no signs of activity along the way. The rains had blotted out the road so that any tracks would be easily visible, but there were none. The Confederate commander had evidently not tried to completely encircle and cut off the sailors, Wake figured. He had been worried about that possibility, but now he surmised that probably Colonel Holland's regiment was not strong enough to accomplish both the attack and a siege. The realization strengthened his resolve as he approached the army picket line across the road up ahead.

A tall sergeant came out from the trees on the side of the road and bellowed toward Wake. "Halt, who goes there!"

Wake was tired and kept walking forward. "Lieutenant Peter Wake, commanding officer of the naval landing party."

A younger soldier leveled his rifle, bayonet fixed, at Wake and called out in a higher voice. "The sergeant said to stop, mister."

The sergeant now recognized Wake's uniform and told the youngster to put down his rifle as Wake walked up to and past them both without a word. The sergeant saw the look in Wake's eyes and said nothing.

A hundred yards further on Wake came to the line of breastworks his sailors had started. The soldiers of the 195th New York Infantry had greatly enhanced them, putting equipment boxes and large limbs and logs across to make a formidable barrier to attack. It was not a temporary wall, but one made to protect a unit that was there to stay.

Wake walked through a second guard post without speaking when he was challenged. He felt it was apparent that he was a lone naval officer and he didn't trust his self-discipline to keep quiet when he saw the encampment within the breastworks.

The 195th New York had done much in twenty-four hours. They hadn't sallied out of their works to reinforce the sailors under attack, but they had made the river-bend beach camp as defensible and comfortable as they could. Tents sprouted in neat company rows, cooks tended cauldrons down by the water, and ammunition and supply boxes were arranged by unit in groupings around the perimeter. Several units were drilling in the open area between the tents and the breastworks. Hundreds of men sat, lay, or walked around. Wake could feel his anger growing, his jaw working tensely as his teeth ground and his eyes burned. Men turned to watch him as he walked through the encampment.

Then he saw what he was looking for. Regimental and American flags flew on posts in front of a large tent in the center of the camp. As Wake approached he saw a contingent of sailors by the bluff, not there for a work party, but armed with cutlasses and muskets and looking around them with disgust at the display of army organization.

He almost shifted his course over to them but heard a familiar voice rising from within the large tent. It was the enraged voice of Lieutenant Thadeus Taylor of the United States Navy. Taylor's words became distinct as Wake neared the opening in the canvas.

"Colonel, my sailors and I are going up to where they are. If we'd only known that the army was sitting here waiting, we would've come ashore to help those sailors and get the job done last night when we heard the fighting."

Wherley's indignant voice rose to match Taylor's. "What are you accusing this regiment of, Lieutenant Taylor? Cowardice? Let me tell you something, young man. If Wake had done what he was supposed to do and stayed here at this camp, we could've built up our strength slowly and overwhelmingly. Then we could have marched up the road and into the interior and liberated the state. We still can, in spite of what your damned sailors have bungled up at the crossroads. As for waiting, it was obvious that he would have to fall back, and I didn't want to add to the confusion. Of course, I don't expect a sailor to understand land tactics and strategy, Lieutenant. I just expect them to do their job and transport us ashore. Which, by the way, has taken far longer than I expected."

At that moment Wake entered the tent. The terrified aide to the colonel tried to announce his presence.

"Ah, . . . another naval officer, sir!"

Wherley paused only briefly, his lawyer's training coming through as he surveyed Wake's demeanor upon entry into the hot musty tent. "Well, as I was saying, Lieutenant Taylor, Wake will most certainly have to fall back, and here he most certainly is!"

Wake's struggled to control his voice and turned to Taylor, ignoring the colonel for the moment. "Would you please excuse us for a moment. Colonel Wherley and I have a personal matter to discuss. I want to thank you for coming ashore to reinforce us. I'll explain the situation to you later."

Taylor immediately sized up the situation, nodded to Wake and exited the tent with the aide, leaving Wake alone inside with Wherley. The colonel raised his right hand as if in admonishment, but Wake spoke first.

"Colonel, I would advise you to listen to what I am about to say. Carefully. Your personal future depends on your understanding the situation completely. Please acknowledge that, sir."

Wherley stood there in shock, hand still raised. He registered the anger in Wake's voice and knew that the younger man had the emotional and moral advantage. When he spoke, it was without the superior mien he usually adopted to intimidate others.

"Yes, of course, Mr. Wake. Go right on ahead. You obviously have something troubling you. I'm a reasonable man and would like to hear what it is you have to say."

Wake moved closer to the colonel and kept his voice low, so that only Wherley could hear him. "Very well, Colonel Wherley. Here is the situation. Your regiment has been sitting here literally parading around and making themselves comfortable while a small under-equipped naval landing party has been prohibiting the enemy, a force of enemy regulars I might add, from bottling this invasion up by blocking the swamp road to Claresville. In fact, the naval landing party, originally planned to be a rearguard, has been doing all of the fighting here and has defeated the Fifteenth Florida Infantry by itself. Even after we sent for help. Even after we almost lost the crossroads to overwhelming odds. While your regiment sat here waiting for us to retreat back to you. That is the situation. Now I will tell you the perceptions of this situation from various views."

Wherley showed no anger but did exhibit a curious look, as if he were waiting for a trial opponent to show his hand in court. He started to speak but stopped when Wake shook his head slightly.

"Colonel Wherley, this is vitally important and I need to continue."

Wherley narrowed his eyes but waved for Wake to continue.

"The perception among the hundred sailors at Claresville is that you and your regiment are either incompetent or cowards. More to the point, the perception among the Floridians of that infantry regiment is that they could've beat you if we weren't there to block them. That word will spread through Florida, and any of the citizens who might be disposed to come to our side will think twice. Making that switch in allegiance is very dangerous for them and they'll only do it if they feel they will be protected by Federal forces in the area. They won't have that feeling about your regiment. These perceptions are facts. They're already established. And they spell the end of your personal reputation. But there is a solution."

Wherley sat down in a camp chair, slumping over the folding table where a map of Florida was spread out. He suddenly appeared tired. He stared at Wake then said weakly, "Go ahead."

Wake sat down in the chair across the table and tried to look sincere.

"Your reputation can be salvaged. This operation can go forward. The Floridians loyal to the Federal government can be made to feel safe under our protection."

Wherley nodded his head briefly. Wake thought the man was coming undone and realized he must now proceed gently. Wherley looked as if he might start to cry at any moment.

"Turn the command of the regiment over to Major Martin. He is competent and can handle it. He can march forward and do what is needed here on this coast. You are sick with a fever. Order Martin to relieve you. Leave with the other sick and go to Key West, then go north on convalescent leave. Help the war effort by being a loyal supporter of the army and the president in New York. You can tell people what is needed because you have been to the front lines. You'll be respected, listened to by the people there. Do what you do best, and be an advocate for the president's efforts."

It was almost pathetic how Wherley's face showed a glimmer of hope upon hearing Wake's suggestion.

"Colonel Wherley, this will salvage your reputation and solve the other problems. But, Colonel Wherley, this has to be done right now. Right here. If you don't, I cannot stop your inevitable court-martial for cowardice. I can't help the operation here to succeed. And I can't get the loyal Floridians to come over to us. Only you can make this decision, but you must make it now."

Wherley cast his eyes down at the ground, his lips pursed, his hands clasped. "Who besides you will know I'm not really sick, Wake?"

"No one. If you make the decision to leave this regiment in competent hands, then no one will know. My men will hear from me that you were disabled by sickness, which caused you to make a mistake in judgment."

Wake stood up and half-turned toward the tent opening. "Well Colonel, I'm walking out of here now. What do I tell the men who fought their hearts out and want to know why you and your men did not come to help?"

Wherley could barely be heard as he tried to stand up also. His hands were shaking and tears filled his eyes. "Tell them I am sick, Wake. The fever has gotten me. I can't take this climate and I'm going home. Tell them that."

Wake could feel no sympathy for the man in front of him. His inaction, borne of pomposity and ego, had caused many deaths. He had offered a way out only to salvage the operation and the morale of all those involved. To have a court-martial and publicly expose such incompetence would only undermine the citizens' and the soldiers' confidence in their army. It was better this way. Colonel Wherley would never command and waste lives again.

"Very well, Colonel. I'll pass the word for Major Martin to come here to you."

For a brief moment, Wherley's eyes narrowed and his voice grew cold as he stood by the table trying to regain his composure. "One more thing, Wake."

"What's that, Colonel?"

"I never want to see you again. Ever."

"That would be my pleasure far more than yours, Colonel."

Wake shook his head, turned, and left the tent. Outside, the guard looked at him oddly then glanced at the aide standing twenty feet away with some other officers in front of another tent. The aide-de-camp came striding over with Major Martin. Behind them was Lieutenant Hammersley. Martin walked up to Wake, held out his hand, and smiled.

"Hammersley here tells me that you're not retreating back to our camp. Says you're crazy to stay up there at that crossroads. A lunatic is actually what he called you. Congratulations Mr. Wake, if a fool like Hammersley thinks you're a lunatic then you're pretty much my kind of man!"

Hammersley grimaced on hearing his major's remark but continued to glare at Wake. The aide-de-camp disappeared behind the tent. Wake regarded Major Martin, finally deciding that he was not being falsely amicable, and shook his hand.

"Why thank you, Major. A rather unorthodox compliment, but I'll take it."

Hammersley interrupted the two, almost getting between Wake and the major.

"Lieutenant Wake has maligned our regiment and our colonel, Major Martin. We cannot stand for that. He did it in front of others. He's done it before against the colonel of the Fifty-second New Jersey Artillery."

Wake's smile disappeared. He ignored the army lieutenant's whining remark and asked Martin the important question on his mind. "Major, we needed help and asked for it. Why was it not sent?"

Martin also became serious, setting his jaw and sighing.

"Mr. Wake, the colonel was convinced that you would fall back to our camp when the Rebs pressed you. He wanted to have all of our men and equipment ashore before moving forward. We still don't have it all ashore and probably won't go forward for days. He ordered us to stay put and receive your men through our lines."

Hammersley opened his mouth but didn't get a word out before Martin cut him short to continue. "Lieutenant Hammersley, I have heard your complaint about Lieutenant Wake several times. It was boring before and now it is annoying. I am sure you must have some urgent duties. Please accomplish them and leave us alone."

Hammersley walked away without a word. Wake saw that he was heading for Wherley's tent. It was time to get Martin aboard and on course.

"Major Martin, did you know that your colonel has been very ill with some sort of fever? I just saw him and he said he was quite sick and sent word for you. He wants you to take over the regiment while he evacuates to Key West to convalesce."

Martin's face showed his surprise. "I was just with him an hour ago. He was in very good spirits. Didn't look sick in any way."

"All I can say is that he looked extremely sick when I just saw him, sir. Evidently he had been sick for some time. Wanted you to take over immediately. Once you do, I would be honored to give you a tour of our lines and to turn them over to your regiment. Can we make a time for that, say half past eleven o'clock?"

"Well, all this is quite sudden, Wake. I'll have to see about all of that, once I get with the colonel."

Martin, clearly confused, went into Wherley's tent, Wake following behind. Hammersley was emerging and looking dazed as Martin entered. As the colonel and major spoke, Wake stood in front of the opening, visible to those inside. Wake could hear no details, but Martin's manner told of his continuing confusion when he came outside a few minutes later.

"Lieutenant Wake, you were correct. The man is ill with a bad fever. Damned strange. Never saw it hit that fast. Says he wished he had sent the regiment up earlier but the fever had dimmed his mind a bit. Wants me to take over the regiment and send it forward now. I'll send a company up to you in a couple of hours. They'll be there by half past eleven to relieve your position. Your men can come back to the camp and return to their ships at that time. I'll send the surgeon and his assistants now and get the wounded brought back."

Wake nodded his acknowledgment and left Martin shaking his head and staring at the departing naval officer. He called back over his shoulder. "Thank you, Major. I'll go see about getting the regimental surgeon and his mates going right now, if you don't mind. I'll see you later."

As he walked out of the encampment he stopped by Taylor,

who was standing with his men near the small bluff by the beach. Wake explained that the colonel had rescinded his orders and the regiment was moving forward to let the sailors go back to their ships. He also informed Taylor that Martin was now in command of the army troops and that Wherley was very ill and would need transport back to Key West. Taylor reacted with the same incredulity as Martin, gauging Wake and his information carefully.

"Didn't look sick to me, Peter. Looked like a pompous fool, but not sick."

"Well Thadeus, he was sick as a dog when I talked to him. Looked sad, physically weak. Been building up for some time probably. Got Martin to relieve him. Now Martin's got the regiment going forward and we sailors can get out of here."

"Yes, Lord let us all get out of this place and back where we belong. This has smelled bad since that planning session with Captain West and Wherley. Didn't think this one through very well."

"That's quite an understatement, Thadeus. But it might turn out well now. Thanks for taking the chance and coming ashore to help us. I know what that took. It's greatly appreciated, my friend."

"Hell, Peter! Your Bosun Rork was about to put the whole rest of your crew ashore, leave your schooner empty, and fight his way to you, through Yankee soldiers or Reb enemy! I had to order him directly to stay aboard and then convince him that I would personally bring you out. Man is a bit dangerous, Peter. Glad he is on our side."

They shared a laugh and Wake shook hands with Taylor, his parting words spoken quietly. "Thadeus, I don't want to make much of Wherley's decision not to reinforce us at Claresville. It'll only bring discredit upon all of us on this operation and bring down morale. He was sick and made a mistake. I don't want the Rebs to see us in discord and gain advantage in the newspapers. Agreed?"

Taylor hesitated and looked closely into Wake's eyes, then nodded. Wake left the encampment, surgeon and assistants trailing along with their instruments and supplies, on the road through the swamp to Claresville.

The sun was climbing and the heat was rising. Wake felt filthy and his thighs and armpits rubbed raw as he walked. The sweat aggravated his misery and the insects in the swamp completed the torture. The mosquitoes were all over them, so dense that the air was black with them.

The surgeon and his men were not enthusiastic about their journey and kept asking how much further up the road Claresville would be found. All in all, it was an ordeal for Wake, who kept his mind on the positive fact that Wherley would never again be in a position to get any more men killed and that the enemy would not profit by a public exposure of the colonel's behavior. And best of all, his sailors would be relieved shortly and back out at sea, where they belonged.

Things could still go far wrong, he reminded himself, but Wake smiled at the thought of returning to the *St. James* and Rork. He wanted to get away from political colonels and senseless battles and ridiculous schemes to liberate this horrible place. Tramping along in the breathless heat, his thoughts went on to the other colonel, the one from the "Fightin' Fifteenth," who had misjudged the tenacity of Wake and his sailors. Misperceptions of the situation by a commanding officer were more than mere mistakes in judgment—in war they frequently resulted in death. Wake felt the sad irony that Colonel Wherley would not face scrutiny for his incompetence, but Colonel Holland would live after the war in this state where he would be forever known as the man who gambled with his men's lives, and lost.

Wake picked up the pace, as if trying to run away from the fear inside him that perhaps one day it would be *St. James*'s sailors paying the ultimate price for one of *his* misperceptions.

12
Casualties of War

Wake noted the time as eleven twenty-one when the first men of the regiment came into sight from the crossroads. Major Martin had been true to his word. The regimental surgeon and his assistants had been busy for an hour by that time, administering medicines for pain and cleaning wounds. New dressings replaced the older ones that had become congealed with blood and filth. One of the wounded who had died was buried. Some of the others had grown worse due to the infection of their wounds. Wake felt anger at the waste whenever he looked over at the groaning men grouped under the shade in the ruins of a pole barn once used to store cotton and hay.

Several of the sailors jeered as two companies of the New Yorkers marched in parade formation into Claresville, until Wake put a stop to it. He didn't want any more animosity. He just wanted to get his men out of there and back to the sea where they belonged. The soldiers stared at the carnage around them as they broke ranks to take up the positions in the perimeter vacated by the sailors. The stench of death made the newly arrived young men grimace and feel uneasy in their clean uniforms, glancing nervously around. They stared at the wounded as stretcher bearers carried their moaning loads past the soldiers and down the road to the regiment's camp.

The grimy, disheveled navy bluejackets nodded at the soldiers relieving the perimeter defenses and then wordlessly trudged away over to the swamp road, ignoring the questions the soldiers called out to them. They were too tired to explain what had happened there. Wake sympathized with his sailors. The soldiers would have to figure it out themselves. After all, they were soldiers, and this was what they trained for and were supposed to understand.

A young army captain broke away from the formation and marched toward Wake, still in perfect unison with the company behind him. He was a strongly built man of around Wake's age and exuded confidence as he stood at attention three feet away.

"Captain Wake? Captain Palanson reporting to relieve your force, sir. Major Martin presents his compliments and has ordered me to assist you in every way."

"Welcome to Claresville, Captain Palanson. Thank you for relieving us. As you can see, we've been a bit busy since our own arrival. You may go right into our lines and we'll be out of your way immediately. The Fifteenth Florida Infantry has apparently departed to an unknown location with the main force of the regiment, but there is a rear guard in those trees over there. The enemy main force still has somewhere around four or five hundred men and two or three pieces of field artillery, but I believe they are very low on ammunition. They may reprovision, however, and return. I would suggest you maintain utmost vigilance. Good luck, sir."

Palanson eased his manner enough to look around at what was left of Claresville, then nodded at Wake.

"Very good, sir. And good luck to you." Palanson saluted and turned on his heel. Walking over to his noncommissioned officers he began issuing orders, frequently pointing to the spot beyond the perimeter where the enemy rear guard was positioned, and then around the village.

Off in the distance, a small group of Confederates could be seen standing in the line of oaks on the other side of the fields. It was a much smaller group than the previous day when the Rebel line had stretched completely along the tree line with flags flying their defiance. The rear guard detail was there to act as watchers only and warn of the inevitable Federal advance, Wake thought as McDougall approached him. The old gunner was even more gaunt than usual and his voice was without its normal force.

"Soldiers are in the perimeter, sir, an' I've got our men formed for the walk to the beach. Boys are tired, but they'll make *that* walk, for certain, Captain. Wounded have already left with the surgeon. Officers are all there waitin' for you, sir."

"Very well, McDougall. And how are you? You don't look well."

"Aye, Captain, I'm feeling a bit poorly this mornin'. Missin' the sea air in me lungs. Even that ol' Gulf o' Meheeco air is better than this foul place. I'll be better when I smell a little salt around me."

"Very well, gunner, present my compliments to the officers and pass on to them to get all hands moving off to the beach. Don't wait for me. I'll be along directly."

With that Wake went over to the place where the Confederates had made their main attack on his sailors. He walked along the sand street, now littered with the detritus of battle. Everything of use, such as weapons, ammunition and packs, had been picked up by the sailors. What was left was the depressing evidence that men had desperately killed other men in that spot: dirty bandages and dark stains in the sand, torn butternut-colored uniform tunics and blue navy caps, several family letters torn from pockets while searching for something of value, ripped paper cartridges and mangled muskets, and many expended bullets flattened from impact on something or someone.

Wake walked slowly, kicking through the trash littering the ground, and wondered again if his solution with Wherley was worth it, whether it was fair to the men, from both sides, who had died at this place.

He realized his aimless course had taken him fifty feet beyond the defensive lines and looked back at the village filled with dark blue forms gazing at the naval officer wandering around looking at the ground. Watching them watch him, he knew his decision and the gamble had been the right one. Those boys would need all the confidence and strength they could muster in this difficult land. Behind them, Wake saw the last of the sailors moving away from the wreckage of Claresville down the swamp road. A sudden odd thought intruded on his pensive mood. He wondered who was the Clare that someone had loved enough to name a village after? What was she like? And what would she think of the destruction that had been done at her namesake?

The sailors breathed deeply and stared at their floating homes getting closer as the tug towed them westward in their ships' boats. There was no refreshing breeze to energize the flat brown water, but that didn't diminish their relief. The air had salt in it and their lungs finally felt full. The horizon was limitless, and they felt free after the confines of the land. Smiles and laughter showed on their faces for the first time in days, as if they were now awake after a nightmare. Wake glanced over at the officers and petty officers in the other boats and saw that they too were looking better. The effect on the sailors of just *seeing* the Gulf of Mexico as they emerged from the Timucuahatchee River made Wake smile. The farther they got from the shore the more alive they all felt.

However, McDougall, who sat next to Wake in the stern sheets of the boat, was still looking ill. Wake saw that the movement of the swaying boat was making him tense up from obvious pain. Something was wrong with the gunner, and Wake made a mental note to have the surgeon over on the *Bonsall* examine him.

In contrast to the New Yorkers arriving at Claresville, as the sailors in the boats grew close to the anchored flotilla they heard cheering. The crews aboard the ships lined the decks and swarmed up the rigging, yelling a raucous welcome that made Wake laugh out loud. And there stood Rork, taller than most, in the foreshrouds of the *St. James*, hollering along with the rest.

Safely over the last of the shallow bars off the beach, Lieutenant Erne came aft and stood at the stern of the tug with his arms akimbo, smiling broadly at the sight of the boats tethered in lines astern. He slowly came to attention and raised his hand in salute while looking directly at Wake. Just then each anchored ship fired a blank charge to celebrate the return of the men of the naval landing party. Wake returned Erne's salute and struggled to maintain his composure, seeing that others around him were doing the same. It was the moment they all needed. They were back where they belonged.

Captain West of the U.S.S. *Bonsall*, looked concerned as Wake stood before him to give his verbal report, the written one having been delivered thirty minutes earlier. West invited him to sit at the chart table and have some tea, which Wake accepted.

"Mr. Wake, it was a close run thing, I see."

"Yes, sir. But we made it, and the operation can continue."

West changed his expression from smiling to a frown. "I am hearing grumbling though, Lieutenant Wake. Grumbling from Colonel Wherley's people that you precipitously went further inland earlier than originally planned and did not fall back to the camp when attacked. Other grumbling from naval officers that the army did nothing but sit at the camp and let the sailors fight their battle for them. Which was it, Lieutenant Wake? Your report does not indicate any major problems at all."

Wake took a moment to arrange his thoughts, for he had

anticipated this line of questioning from West and knew there would be no right answer. West wasn't interested in what happened, only how the events on shore would affect his career.

"Sir, the mission was accomplished. I did move forward earlier than planned because the situation unfolded differently than expected. It was taking longer to get the soldiers ashore and the crossroads needed to be secured. Once we were there, we found that the enemy was approaching for an attack. The enemy would've bottled up the Federal forces if they could have made it down that road through the swamp to the beach camp, and so we fought them at Claresville to stop that from happening."

"And the army's participation in all this, Lieutenant Wake?"

"They relieved us this morning at Claresville, sir."

West shook his head and looked at Wake closely. "I do not understand how it is that you constantly seem to antagonize senior army officers, Wake. First at Tortugas, then Key West, and now here. You're getting known for that. This operation was a simple one in concept and yet became convoluted when you became involved in its execution."

"There has been absolutely no intent of antagonism on my part toward any army officer anywhere, sir."

"Yes, well, I further understand that now Colonel Wherley is mysteriously sick and wants to go back to Key West immediately to convalesce, so I guess I'll have to put him aboard the *Nygaard*. Word is that he has a fever and regrets not taking quicker action to reinforce the sailors. Says the fever debilitated him."

"Yes, sir. I saw that he was feeling sick myself, sir. Appeared very ill just this morning when I saw him last."

West kept eyeing Wake. "From what I heard he was feeling quite well, and angry about you, until this morning. Then he told people he had been sick and put Martin in command. Is there anything else about this I should know?"

"No sir, that about sums it up. I believe the operation can go forward with some chance of success. Major Martin appears to be a competent leader and the New Yorkers have enough strength ashore to deal with the most likely opposition."

West shook his head again and picked up some papers lying on the chart table. A waft of breeze came down the companionway into the cabin and Wake watched the wind ruffling the water through the ports behind West. He struggled to remain calm and sip his tea as his superior spoke again.

"Well, on another matter, I have dispatches and orders from the squadron at Key West. It seems that yellow fever has broken out in Key West and at Tampa. Several ships' crews have been affected so much that they cannot work their vessels. Many people at Key West are down with it. Of course, it *is* the damned season for yellow jack, and so I guess we must expect it to come aboard our ships."

West paused in thought, then continued. "Now, *Bonsall*, the tug, and a schooner, are ordered to stay here and support the army operations. The other vessels will depart for other assignments. *Nygaard* and *St. James* are to report to Key West for further orders. *Nygaard* will stop at Tampa, and you will stop at Boca Grande to see about conditions at those places and report them to the admiral. You will depart immediately upon the wind serving. Questions on that?"

"No, sir."

"There was some mail delivered to your ship yesterday from the steamer that dropped off the dispatches and orders. Bosun Rork has done well in your absence and I have no complaints about him."

"He is a good man, sir."

"All right, Lieutenant Wake, you may go. *Nygaard* will be faster and will carry my official reports of the actions undertaken here. I hope for your sake that there will be no animosity amongst the army officers about the situation here. I tried to plan and implement a sound mission. I just wish the execution of it had been done with as much diligence and cooperation. My report will, of course, reflect that."

Wake took a deep breath, letting the air out slowly. "The

action was successful, sir. I am sure that the admiral will appreciate that, as well as your command of the naval forces in this area."

"Yes . . . well, we'll see about that. You may go."

Wake stood at attention but was ignored by West, who had turned around and was studying some papers on his desk. After a moment of waiting, Wake left the cabin and went up to the main deck where he had the officer of the deck summon his boat.

The mailbag initially revealed no letter for Wake, so he read the newspapers that had been sent aboard via the transiting steamer. Then a letter that had fallen out of the bag was found and brought to him. He recognized it right away as not being the hoped for one from Linda, but one almost as welcome from his family in New England. The envelope was postmarked July 23, only six weeks prior, written in his father's handwriting. That was not unusual. Of his parents, his father was the letter writer, though his mother occasionally would tuck a small note in the envelope. His father's letters arrived every month, with a concise summary of the news in Massachusetts, the family's schooner business, who was doing what in the family, and his opinion of how the war was going. Forty years of writing reports to and from ship owners had conditioned the elder Wake to be brief and informative, if not affectionate.

Four months ago Captain Wake the Elder, as he was widely known in New England to distinguish the man from his sons who were also captains in their own right, wrote that Peter's brother James had joined the navy also. James was quickly assigned to the Charleston blockade on an ironclad monitor and had been active in operations among the coastal islands there. The old man had expressed disapproval of a navy that would assign an experienced schooner man to one of those iron contraptions that didn't even have a mast. Wake, however, was glad that his older brother was at least on a vessel that could provide some protection from gunfire, even if it didn't have the beauty of a sailing ship.

As he tore open the envelope while sitting on his berth in the small cabin that was his sanctuary, Wake wondered about the war and when it would end. It had been predicted that by September the rebels would be suing for peace and Lincoln would win the November election hands down, but the newspaper accounts Wake had just finished reading told of a different future.

Wake heard a thud as Rork rapped on the bulkhead and requested permission to enter. The bosun wore a serious look as he came in and sat on the edge of the proffered chair. Wake put down the letter after removing it from the wrinkled envelope and regarded his second in command.

"What's the matter, Rork? You look like you have bad news to tell."

Rork's jaw was set and Wake knew from experience that was a sign of problems. Rork nodded and spoke in a low tone that Wake could barely hear.

"Aye, sir. 'Twas a good day indeed until I heard what I heard just now, Captain."

"All right, tell me. And speak up, man."

"By your leave, I'll keep it down, sir. Just got word on McDougall and those other lads I sent over to the surgeon on the *Bonsall*, sir."

Wake felt a sudden flush of sickness. "Go ahead, Bosun."

"McDougall's got the yellow jack. So's the others, sir. Five all told. Surgeon's mates told me themselves that the other ships have men down with it too. All from the landing party. Word'll be out soon, if not already."

Wake's sigh was audible. "How bad is he?"

Rork's eyes moistened as he replied. "He's bringin' up the black vomit now, sir. Must'a been sick for a couple o' days ashore."

"The others?"

"O' the four others I sent over, two's down in the sick bay an' can't move, the other two is feeling poorly but not as bad. Surgeon says since they're young they may have a chance, but the ol' gunner is too far gone. Delirious he is now, sir. Screamin' an' moanin' in Gaelic. Surgeon says he'll be dead by tomorrow's sunset the way he's emptying himself out."

Wake's head dropped. "The wind seems to be piping up with a sea breeze. I want to be under way in half an hour. Meanwhile I will go to see McDougall."

"Captain, the surgeon's not allowin' that. Quarantined. The old lad is gone out o' his head, Captain. He wouldn't know ya'. Time to let him go, sir, an' pray it'll be quick and merciful."

"Yes. You're right. Any more showing signs aboard our ship?"

"No others yet, sir."

"Very well, get under way immediately and set a course south for Boca Grande. We'll see how Lieutenant Baxter and the *Gem of the Sea* are doing, look in at Useppa Island, and then sail for Key West."

"Aye aye, sir."

"I'm sorry, Rork. I know how close you and McDougall are."

"Close as brothers, sir. But I know how you feel about the ol' boy too. The lads told me how you both together came through ashore with the Rebs. A damnable loss for us all. After all those years he's leavin' like this. Makes a man need a dram just to think about it."

Rork stood up and left the cabin without another word to Wake, who looked at the unread letter before him in a daze. It was hard to concentrate, and yet his mind registered that the schooner was starting to sway gently in the growing sea breeze and had swung on her anchor until the coastline was now astern and her bow pointed west. He stood up and stretched his tired arms and legs, then picked up the letter.

Above his head he heard the thumping of feet on the deck as the sailors went to their stations to weigh anchor and haul away on the halliards. Petty officers' voices rose to give the orders that all hands knew by heart. Next came the thundering of heavy canvas as it rose on its clattering parrels up the masts, and the clanking of the windless as the anchor rode came in over the bow. It was a familiar and systematic cacophony that Wake had heard so many times in his life. But now, as he read the second sentence of his father's typically brief letter, it faded away until there was only a beating sound in his ears from the blood pounding through his head.

His brother James was dead. Shot by a Rebel sharpshooter from a tree along a river in South Carolina. His father didn't even know the name of the place where it had happened, just that his son had been shot as they steamed up a river unaware that any danger was close by. James had been standing on the open deck speaking with the monitor's captain when the shot hit him in the chest and he fell dead. Wake's father reported that the captain had sent a letter saying that James Wake had died instantly and without any pain.

Peter Wake knew better than that. He had seen men writhe in horrible pain from chest wounds as they drowned in their own blood and begged for help. Only an improbable shot directly through the heart would kill quickly, and even then it would take several seconds. Wake hated knowing these things. He wished he could have been ignorant of how men died of wounds. The war had taken that away. He now knew too much about that subject.

Wake's chin quivered as he sat down at the chart table and said a prayer aloud for his brother James and his parents. The Wake family had gone to church for the celebrations of the major feasts over the years. They were religious but not pious. Their faith was not a pillar of their lives, but rather a backdrop. The brothers had occasionally spoken together on the subject and mainly reflected the attitude of their father—that it was the proper thing to be a Christian and show allegiance but it need not dominate the everyday actions of a man.

The ship heeled over suddenly and Wake realized they were under way, broad reaching south with a westerly sea breeze. His hands were shaking as they clutched the letter. He felt nauseous as the cabin seemed to close in around him, but his logical mind knew it wasn't seasickness. Taking the letter with him, he made his way through the cabin and climbed up to the deck, devoid of any sea legs and wondering if it was due to the time ashore or the shock of his father's message. Lurching on deck, he swayed aft to where Rork stood near the helmsman. At the stern rail he motioned for the bosun to come over to him.

Rork could see something was very wrong and strode quickly to the rail as Wake stared out to the endless horizon to windward, wishing he could appreciate the sight before him. It was a sailor's kind of day, with a good sailing breeze coming up, a few puffy clouds building over the coast, the schooner dashing along on her best point of sailing, and a course ahead free of dangers. The men on deck were performing their tasks with the confidence of sailors who knew their work, and were glad to be at sea again.

As Wake wordlessly handed Rork the letter, he thought of old times with his brothers, times at sea and other times at home when they were all much younger. Of how James was the one who was quieter than the others, sometimes enduring teasing about it, and how he had a talent for drawing seascapes and landscapes. As Rork read the letter beside him, Wake thought of how James had always sailed in New England's cold gray waters and never seen the beauty of the tropical seas.

When he finished reading it, Rork dropped the letter to his side and looked at his captain, but Wake didn't notice. He was thinking of how much James would have loved to be sailing with them at that moment. That quietest of the Wake brothers would have truly appreciated the wonder of it all.

The humidity was oppressive as Wake jumped out of the schooner's boat and waded onto the crushed shell beach at

Useppa Island. Old Hervey Newton was there to meet him and could tell that the naval officer had heard the news.

Wake was terse as he stood in front of the elderly man. "Where is she, Mr. Newton?"

Newton replied in a fatherly tone. "Son, she's at the last home up there on the hill. She's past the danger time and she's recovering now. She'll be fine in a while."

Wake didn't wait to hear the last of Newton's explanation—he was already running up the path to the top of the hill. The terror inside his heart and the heat in the air around him soaked his shirt with sweat until beads of perspiration flung off him in sheets as he ran by two startled women coming down the path. Yards before he had made the home at the top he called out in a voice choked with emotion.

"Linda! I'm here! I'm here, darling."

A young dark-skinned woman wearing a simple faded frock came out of the palm-thatched home and stood silently as Wake rushed past her and through the doorway. He stopped, adjusting his eyes from the searing glare of the sun outside to the black gloom of the interior.

"Linda? Are you here, dear?"

The voice seemed to come from far away. "Oh, Peter!"

A figure leaned forward in the crude cot in the corner. With his eyesight adjusted to the dim room, Wake could see her hand reaching out to him and he went into her arms.

"Linda, are you all right? What happened?"

"Peter, I'm sorry to be like this. Don't worry, dear, I'm getting better."

"I found out you were sick when we came alongside the *Gem of the Sea* at Boca Grande. Baxter said you were very ill and he was worried. Linda, he said you have yellow fever."

Her voice was finding strength now, but the pain in her bones made her lay back down, still holding his hand tightly.

"Yes, it's the fever. Had it for two weeks, but it's leaving now. I'm better."

His words were lost in his throat. He fought back the tears he felt welling up as he held her closely. "Linda, I love you. I need you. Don't leave me."

She managed a thin smile and stroked the scar on the side of his face. "I'll be fine in a few days, Peter. I love you and I won't die, dear."

He winced when she said that word.

"Peter, I'm acclimated and young and strong. I've made it through and will recover my strength. It will all be better, dear."

He lifted his head and looked into her green eyes. Nodding, Wake let out a sigh. "When I heard, it scared me, Linda. It scared me till I thought my heart would stop."

At that she actually laughed. It was weak, but still a laugh. "Well, Peter Wake, I was a bit interested in the outcome myself!"

Shaking his head, he joined in her quiet laugh and sat up beside her. Linda eased herself onto a canvas pillow and pointed to the woman outside the doorway. "Sofira there was the one who nursed me back to relative health. She moved here a little while ago. Her husband's fighting with the pro-Union militia with Captain Cornell. Sofira is a half-Seminole and knows things about healing. She gave me some teas and roots and things and stood by me when it was worst."

Wake looked at the woman standing out in the sun and could see the strong Indian features in her face. A little toddler girl ran up to the woman and hugged her legs.

"She looks familiar to me, but I can't place her."

"You met her after the fight on Lacosta Island. She was one of the women who came with Mr. Newton to help you. She told me she had met you. Sofira said she could tell you were a good man by what you said and did that night."

Linda slumped back on the pillow, exhausted. Her eyes were barely open and Wake realized that she had strained herself to look cheerful for his benefit.

"Linda, you need to rest. Get some rest, dear. I'll come back later to be with you."

Linda didn't answer but nodded and fell into a wearied half-sleep as Wake kissed her forehead and rose from the cot. He stood up and looked at the girl he loved more than life and watched as she slid into a deep slumber. Walking outside, he spoke to the woman still standing there.

"Ma'am, I want to say thank you for all you did for my wife. I think you saved her life. Linda said your name is Sofira."

The woman looked at her child and then at Wake. She had a quietness that was at once disconcerting and impressive. Her words came slowly and without inflection.

"Yes, Sofira Thomaston. Linda is strong and will be better. She knew the fever before and outlived it. It could not kill her now. It tried."

Wake was taken aback by the bluntness. "Yes, she's a strong person. I remember she told me that she did have a little bit of yellow fever before, when she was younger. Your Indian medicine must have helped her get through this, though, and I am very grateful."

"It is not Indian medicine. I did not make it. It is there for everyone. The earth made it for us all."

Wake considered her words, and took Sofira's hand in his. "Well, whatever it was, I am grateful you helped her. Thank you, Sofira. Thank you so much."

A smile came over her face and she looked into his eyes as her strong hands gently held his. "She loves you greatly, Peter. You and your love were the real medicine that made the fever fall away. She knew you were coming and had to live for you. You should go now and talk with Mr. Newton. Linda will be sleeping. Go and be with your friends here, Peter. Come back later when Linda is awake."

The woman was mesmerizing. Her calm tone and intense dark eyes riveted him to the spot where he stood. She smiled again and walked inside the dwelling, leaving him standing there completely emptied of emotion as Mr. Newton puffed up the pathway and approached him. "Well, young man, I told you back on the beach she was getting better, now didn't I?"

Taking a deep breath, Wake grasped the leathery hand thrust his way and chuckled. "Yes, sir. I believe you did say that, but I was in such a state that I guess I didn't hear it. Thank you for all that everyone here did for Linda."

"Well, son, the young lady hasn't been here long, but it was long enough for us all to love her. Especially that Sofira Indian woman."

"I'm appreciative to everyone here, Mr. Newton. I don't think I could survive without Linda."

Newton changed to a serious look and shook his head. "Hhhmm, well if you're really appreciative then you'll do me the favor of sitting down and telling this old man how the war on the coast north of here is goin' on. And I'll need ya to help me lighten a certain jug of bad Cuban rum that's been a burden to me for a while. What say ya, Captain Wake?"

Wake laughed and held up both hands. "I know when to follow orders, Mr. Newton, and that sounded like an order to me! It would be my pleasure, and there is a lot to tell, sir."

They walked down the path to Newton's thatched hut on the west side of the hill. The sun was starting to descend and the sea breeze had piped up enough to make it pleasant in the shade of a giant gumbo limbo tree that grew next to Newton's dwelling.

Wake sat down on one of the immense roots and leaned back against the base of the tree as Newton emerged from his home with a broad smile on his face and a brown and gray jug in his hand.

Groaning, the old man sat down next to Wake and handed him the jug.

"These tired bones are needin' to taste some of that ol' Cuban rotgut rum, Peter Wake, so don't be taking it all."

Wake took a swig and handed it over to Newton, who tilted it back over his head and swallowed hard. Newton sounded anything but frail when he had finished. "Now I'm ready to hear what's been doin' in the war! Speak onward, Captain Peter Wake!"

Wake looked at the Gulf of Mexico in the far distance past Lacosta Island and reveled as the breeze, cool under the tree, cleansed his soul. He turned to see Newton regarding him intently, waiting. In a way, it was as if his father was there with him, now finally an equal, and waiting to hear a good story from the younger man for a change.

"Well, it was a good sea breeze like this one today, Mr. Newton. We were sailing in company with some other navy schooners north along the coast. Let's see, you may know them, there was the . . . "

Wake's story continued on its course as the afternoon turned into the evening, and the jug eventually emptied.

13 Honor

It had been a bittersweet time at Useppa Island for Wake. He stayed ashore at Sofira's Thomaston's dwelling for two days, mainly watching over Linda as she lay in the cot, alternately sweating and shivering. He was grateful that she was getting stronger but anguished that he would soon have to leave her again. There was no other alternative—he would have to do his duty as a naval officer, though it angered him that he was unable to stay and protect her.

While Wake was ashore, Rork handled the routine of the schooner's crew and their interaction with the other inhabitants of the islands in the area. Fresh fish and some fruit from the locals were a welcome addition to the sailors' provisions, which had long been exhausted of anything tasting better than rancid and sinewy salt pork and beef.

Finally, at a humid sunrise on a Sunday in the third week of September, the crew weighed anchor and sailed away on the morning land breeze. The men on deck were silent as they went through the evolutions of getting the ship under way, watching their captain and slowly shaking their heads in sympathy with him as he grimly obeyed his duty and left his sick wife to recover without him. The breeze was light that day and the *St. James* ghosted away slowly, taking what seemed like an eternity for the jungle-clad island to drop out of sight behind them.

Wake stood at the stern railing and watched the crude thatched hut on the top of the hill until it was indistinguishable from the green trees around it. His mind was focused on those last moments with Linda, when he had knelt beside her cot, holding her to him as close as he dared in her frail condition.

"You'd better go now, Peter. It's getting light outside."

"I hate the thought of leaving you."

"I know that, dear. Believe me that I know that. But your staying here won't accomplish anything. I'm recovering my strength faster now. I'll be fine in a few days. Sofira'll take care of me. Don't worry. You need to concentrate on *St. James* and her crew now."

"I love you so much, Linda. I know there'll come a day when we won't have to say good-bye to each other like this anymore."

"I know, darling. I love you too. Enough to let you do your duty. You need to go, Peter. Please don't drag this out. I just don't have the strength to handle *that.*"

So he left her in the half-gloom and dripping dew of the early morning, more because of her insistence than from his own volition. The scene passed through his mind over and over again as the schooner slid farther away from her on the ebb tide. Not a man in the crew said a word during the time the island was still in sight. It was if they all shared his grief and could not trust themselves to speak, fearing that doing so would lose their precarious grip on self-control. Yellow fever could reach out and take any of them at any time during the season. It was with a sense of quiet relief that Boca Grande was passed to starboard and the open sea was entered. The endless horizon symbolized a freedom from the travails left behind ashore, and the sailors of the naval schooner *St. James* literally breathed easier once they saw it.

Two weeks later, the *St. James* swung on her hook three miles offshore of Key West, waiting for the yellow fever quarantine to be lifted and the yellow jack signal flag to descend from the mast at the naval wharf in the harbor. Water and provisions were running very short, even with the half rations Wake had ordered, and all hands watched the shore every day for any sign they could return.

Wake's report of the action at the Timucuahatchee River had been taken into the squadron offices by the harbor guard cutter, handed over to it by boathook as they lay to windward of the schooner. Receipt of the report was acknowledged by the squadron chief yeoman in a memorandum, which also included an advisement that the quarantine would probably be lifted in a few days and the admiral wanted *St. James* to stay where she was until she could come into port. It went on to report that the squadron's chief surgeon was being conservative, waiting until seven days passed with no new victims reported before lifting the sanctions against going into the harbor.

Rork's normal enthusiasm had been unusually subdued in the days since the *St. James* had left the Timucuahatchee River, silence replacing the humor that he used so effectively to get the crew to accomplish their tasks. He was affected deeply by the suffering and loss of his friend McDougall to yellow fever, and by the melancholy of his other friend, Wake. The bosun was still effective in his position, but the spark had gone. It was one more thing for Wake to worry about as they lay at anchor waiting day after day.

It was Rork who came down into the cabin of his commander with the welcome word that the harbor guard cutter had just sailed by, saying that the quarantine would be lifted at noon that day. Wake looked up from the ink-smudged papers spread on his desk and saw that the news had not cheered the bosun, who was turning to leave.

"Wait, Bosun. I want to ask you something."

Rork nodded and stood quietly looking at his captain.

"Sit down, Rork. Let's talk about how the men are doing."

Rork sat at the chair by the chart table, the concern showing on his face. "Is something wrong with the work o' the men, Captain?"

"Yes, Bosun, there is. One of the petty officers seems to not be himself lately. Brooding, silent—that sort of thing. Not a good sign for a leader of men who've got to do the job we're assigned. The work is getting done, but it's only a matter of time until something bad happens with that man. I'm worried."

Rork leaned back in the chair and shook his head. "Captain, I don't know which petty officer you're speakin' about, sir. Please tell me which one ain't trimmed up proper, an' I'll have him squared away in a admiral's minute."

Wake leaned forward and looked into his friend's eyes. "It's the senior bosun's mate aboard *St. James*, Rork. He's wounded in the heart by the death of his friend, but he needs to mend and come back the way he was. The men of this ship need him, and I need him."

Rork nodded and looked down at the chart on the table, his hand tracing the outline of the coast as he spoke in a quiet voice. "I suppose I *have* been a bit tired lately. I do miss that ol' paddy codger, for some crazy reason. It was grand to have another son o' Eire aboard, ya' know, Captain. Another lad who understood the soul of me home country, so to speak, sir."

Wake sighed as he slowly rolled an ink pen across his desk. "He was a good man and a good gunner."

Rork's tone became hard edged as he nodded again, the hand now clenched into a fist. "A damnable bloody shame, Captain. A shame a man like that had to go the way he did, like some sort o' sick dog, outta his mind and spewin' his guts out. After all the things he'd come through in life. Things you don't know about, sir. Damnable shame."

Wake understood exactly. "I know, Rork. No way for a navy

man to go. Better to die quick from the enemy while standing on your own deck."

"Bloody well right, Captain."

Wake breathed deep and raised his voice slightly. "McDougall was the kind of man who didn't give up or run when times got rough. He'd want us, you and me, to get back to leading this crew through whatever may come our way, and he'd want us to do it with some spirit, Rork. Time for both of us to get past the sadness."

Rork unclenched his hand and let out a sigh of his own, returning Wake's gaze. "Aye, sir. You're right as rain on that. You've had a gale o' problems on your heart too, I know. Don't you worry, your good lady'll be fine on that island with those gentle folks. Better'n here at Key West, with all the hate that's about."

"Yes, she's been spared. Rork, I don't know what I'd do if I lost Linda. I hated leaving, but as you said, they are taking good care of her at Useppa, and that's a comfort."

Rork stood up and spoke with positive inflection for the first time in many days. "By your leave, sir. I've got to go on deck and attend to things. You know how the lads look forward to a bit o' a romp at Key West. In addition to teachin' the mates some little things on small boat navigatin', I've got some work for the others an' best get it done now while we're at sea, an' they're still able to!"

"Very well, Bosun. Get her ready for sailing."

Wake stood and the two men shook hands. "Aye aye, sir. An' much obliged for the good words, sir. You're right, o' course. That ol' gunner wouldn't want to have us failin' the lads, would he?"

"No Rork, he wouldn't want us to waste time feeling sad. He'd want us to get on with it and get this war done and over, at least our part of it. And I suspect he'd want a pint hoisted for him at Key West."

Both men looked at each other and smiled somberly, then went back about their particular business of the moment. For Wake it was writing a letter to his father about James' death, while Rork returned to teaching the junior bosun's mates coastal dead reckoning navigation.

Noon that day was greeted with relief by the men of the *St. James* and the eleven other vessels, both steam and sail, that were anchored off the port. As anticipated, a signal gun was fired at noon and the large faded yellow flag came down the signal mast of the naval wharf on the northwest corner of the island. Another gun was fired at Fort Taylor off the western shore of Key West, and soon several of the vessels in the area fired off a happy round of booming cannon.

Rork looked to Wake for a nod to join in the celebration but was given a shake of the head. "No need to waste the powder, Bosun. The boys'll celebrate enough on liberty."

Instead, the men tackled the anchor rode and halliards with a will and hauled away. Soon the schooner was sailing with the wind on her starboard beam. The trade winds of the winter dry season were starting up again, blowing clean and fresh from the southeast, having come all the way from the middle of the northern coast of Cuba hundreds of miles away. The breathless humidity of the summer months was gradually being displaced by those welcome winds that piped up and gave the air an energy that transferred to the men as well. Even the *St. James* seemed to feel the change in the atmosphere and showed what she was made of on the broad reach, her most favored point of sailing.

Other ships were doing the same, and in the way of sailors, a race quickly developed between the sailing vessels heading into port. The luxuries of the shore provided the prize, but they would have raced anyway. Whenever two sailing vessels were alongside each other the inevitable occurred, each bosun making small adjustments in the sail trim to exact every bit of speed out of his ship. A slow ship was considered an unlucky ship. And no sailor wanted to be on a slow ship.

Wake found himself smiling, even laughing, at the way the men gauged their progress against the competitors and shouted taunts over to them. Even without her hull being cleaned for six months, *St. James* held her own against the others. She didn't win but came in as a respectable third place finisher out of eight schooners and sloops short tacking past the squadron offices and the naval wharf.

The wharf was already crowded with vessels moored alongside, so they anchored out in the harbor amidst a confusing swirl of ships coming up into the wind and backing down on their anchors, sails snapping and thundering as they luffed. Shouted orders and good-natured teasing rang throughout the anchorage as hundreds of men prepared to go ashore on liberty or supply parties.

Bumboats immediately surrounded them, plying everything imaginable to the hungry, thirsty, and lonely sailors. Rork caught Wake's concerned glance and shouted a warning to the schooner's crew not to deal with the men in the boats, knowing that the rum they sold was little more than watered-down fermented sugar at best, and at worst had impurities that could blind or kill. It didn't matter that the sailors had not been paid yet and had no money on them. Those waterside vendors of pleasure would take any items as collateral or barter from the sailors, items that sometimes the men did not themselves own. Temptation was the ruin of many a sailor man, and it was the same in the cold waters of New England and the warm waters of the tropics.

Rork had the schooner's launch swayed out and over with a hand-picked crew, trusted to row ashore for fresh provisions and not get in trouble. Wake decided to ride over to the naval station with the launch and report in to the squadron as soon as possible, in the hope that he would be told to restock the supply of food and water aboard and return up the coast with supplies and dispatches. With any luck, he could be back to Useppa Island and Linda within four days.

Wake had been through yellow fever epidemics before in Key West, but when he came ashore the people of the island looked gaunter this time, weaker and more exhausted. Even with the winds now changing into their invigorating seasonal steadiness and the dampness decreasing, the atmosphere on the island remained subdued. The sentry outside the faded whitewashed walls of the squadron's offices looked as if he was about to fall down with weariness. Wake wondered for a moment if the quarantine had been lifted too soon, that perhaps the sickness was still spreading on the island and among the inhabitants.

A dozen other officers were waiting in the starkly furnished anteroom when Wake entered, looking up and assessing him not as an equal but as a competitor for the attention of the man who controlled their lives, Admiral Loethen. Wake noticed that most of them had an air of self-importance and were probably from larger ships just entered into the harbor, there to report on the events of the coasts and islands from Apalachicola to Cuba and the Bahamas. Self-conscious of the shabby state of even this—his best uniform—he settled into a dilapidated chair in the far corner to begin the long wait while the more senior officers had their audiences with the admiral.

A torn grimy newspaper from Trenton, New Jersey, lay on a table beside him and he picked it up to obtain the latest news of the war raging in Georgia and Virginia. It was dated September 1, 1864, just five weeks ago, and had a banner headline that proclaimed "Democrats Nominate McClellan for President!" with a smaller line underneath advising that a man named Pendleton was nominated for Vice President. Wake had heard of "Little Mac" McClellan, but the other was unknown to him. He wondered who the man was and what qualifications he possessed to help lead the nation during this war. Deciding that it really didn't matter to a naval officer fighting in Florida, he ignored the attendant article on the politics of the presidential race and went to the war news lower on the front page.

The newspaper's correspondents reported via fast telegraph that on just the day before, the Federal army was closing in around Atlanta and had cut the rail line from Macon and thus Confederate General Hood's last supply route into the beleaguered city. Predictions of another imminent and easy victory for General Sherman were touted, but Wake didn't believe them. He had seen with his own eyes the canny resourcefulness of the

Rebels in Florida who had proven so difficult to defeat, and they didn't have the assets of the large Confederate armies in Georgia. Shaking his head slightly, he surveyed the paper further and found New England mentioned in a small article on how the Confederate steam raider *Tallahassee* had made a foray into New England waters, capturing and scuttling the schooners *Mary Howes, Howard, Floral Wreath, Restless,* and *Etta Caroline.* Wake knew the *Etta Caroline* well, having competed against her in the coastal trade. The *Mary Howes* had a reputation as an old slow sailer, cranky and rotted, and he wondered if her owners had secretly welcomed the news as they pressed their claim to the insurers. The paper reported that shipping firms on the New England coast were clamoring to Washington and the navy for protection. It ended by stating that coastal lookouts were being formed to warn vessels in harbors of the approach of the raider, so they would not leave port.

Turning to the inside pages he saw that the temperance movement was gaining momentum and insisting that the army and navy put the movement's clergy in regiments and aboard ships to warn the men in uniform about the evils of spirits and lack of Christian faith. They further demanded that all sales of spirits and ales be banned anywhere near the "lonely boys far from home" to preserve their souls against corruption. Wake wearily wondered if the temperance leaders had ever observed the corrupting influence of seeing one's friends mutilated by the modern weaponry used by both sides in the war. Alcohol seemed a pretty tame malady to Wake, compared to the sights soldiers and sailors had imprinted in their minds.

The news served to make him even more tired as he sat there waiting. He put the paper down on the table and stared at the ceiling, watching a banana spider come in from outside around the top of a window. Bigger than any spider he had ever seen in New England, this one was slowly making his way down the wall toward an obnoxious lieutenant commander who was telling all who would listen that his steamer was stopping in port to repair a boiler, while enroute to Mobile to serve the famous Admiral Farragut and fight the toughest of the Rebs at Fort Morgan on Mobile Bay. Wake glanced over again and saw that several other officers were watching the same spider advance down toward Farragut's future officer. The man talked and they all listened, but with their eyes focused past the man's shoulder on the black and yellow arachnid, now only inches from the hair of the soon-to-be naval hero. Even the anticipation of the officer's reaction when the spider inevitably jumped on him failed to rouse Wake, whose eyelids grew heavier as his breathing became more measured. He was so tired he didn't care about the lieutenant commander or the prowling banana spider. He yawned and shifted in the chair.

He was just starting to doze off with his head leaning back against the wall when he felt a hand tugging at his shoulder and heard a voice quietly call to him. He sat up with a start to see a young embarrassed yeoman standing directly in front of him and some of the other officers in the room attempting to stifle their laughter. A few of the senior ones had looks of disdain, chagrined that a junior officer was being summoned before them. The yeoman led him into the outer office of the admiral's personal clerk and announced his presence to the inner room beyond.

"Captain Wake of the schooner *St. James*, sir."

Just then a flood of curses came echoing from the anteroom, where the pontificating lieutenant commander could be seen through the doorway hopping around, hitting himself in the head and screaming about Key West and its "damnable vermin" that attacked men while they sat in an office. The yeoman, a slightly built lad of maybe eighteen, cast an odd look at Wake, suppressed a smile, and disappeared quickly out of the admiral's office, closing the door behind him.

Wake turned from facing the door and waited for his presence to be acknowledged by Commander Morris and Admiral Loethen, both of whom stood at the window looking out on the harbor. Morris was pointing something out to the admiral, who was in his shirtsleeves. Loethen glanced up upon hearing the officer's antics in the other room, frowned and shook his head woefully, replying something to the commander. Neither man acknowledged Wake's arrival and continued speaking in low tones.

Wake suddenly had the whimsical but illogical thought that the spider was kept there for amusement by the yeomen and that the admiral and commander had seen and heard the trick and subsequent hysterics before. He caught himself smiling, straightened up, and returned his attention to the two men who controlled his future. When they finished their conversation both turned toward Wake. The admiral spoke first.

"Ah yes, . . .Wake of the *St. James.* How good of you to come ashore so soon."

Morris nodded to Wake and motioned toward a chair at the chart table. "Have a seat, Lieutenant Wake. We have something to discuss."

Sitting at the offered chair by the chart table, Wake noticed on top of the pile of charts was an army map of upper Florida, showing both east and west coasts. There were blue lines coming inland from Jacksonville in the east and from the Timucuahatchee River on a bend of the Gulf coast in the west. The blue at that location didn't extend very far. The one from the east didn't either. Red lines were across the paths of both of them.

Morris saw Wake perusing the map. "They haven't gone very far, have they Wake?"

"No, Commander, it appears that they haven't."

Loethen walked to the table and repeatedly stabbed a bony finger at the map's short blue line on the Gulf coast. "Yes, Wake, and it appears they won't anytime soon. After you left the Timookoochee, or whatever they call the damn thing, the New York regiment advanced ten miles and stopped. Yellow jack got 'em. Rebs never had to fire a damned shot. We'll probably have to go back up there and pull 'em off the beach, once the infernal disease stops."

"It was starting to attack us while we were there, sir. Lost several men to it, including a veteran gunner's mate."

Loethen nodded and grimaced. "The squadron suffered mightily too. We've got ships all over our area of operations that have lost men. In some cases many men."

Loethen sat at his desk as Morris took the chair on the other side of the table. Morris pointed at the army map while looking at Wake. "We've read some reports and heard some things about what happened up at the Timucuahatchee River, Lieutenant Wake. The reports and the hearsay don't match up."

Wake noticed that the commander pronounced the river's name correctly. Morris paused and glanced over at the admiral, who spoke next.

"Wake, you've managed to alienate some senior army officers in this squadron's area. Not quite sure exactly how you came about that result, but that's what's happened. There are some ugly rumors going around about what happened up on that coast, with the colonel of the regiment there. Wherley's his name I believe. What light can you shed on what happened there?"

Wake realized that the conversation had turned into an interrogation—a very dangerous interrogation. "I'm not sure what you mean, sir. Things were going relatively well when we left the beachhead and headed south on *St. James*."

Loethen's tone became accusatory and his eyes bored into Wake. "Did you somehow extort the colonel to give up his command?"

"Admiral, the colonel told me he was sick and wanted to leave. He did say he had made some decisions while sick that he regretted. He wanted to return to New York to convalesce. Given the outbreak of yellow fever all along the coast, I'd say he's lucky to get out alive, being unacclimated as he was, sir. The decision to leave was obviously his, sir. I'm just a lieutenant in the navy, what influence could I have over a regimental colonel?"

The room grew quiet when neither man spoke in reply to Wake. Morris looked down at the map. Admiral Loethen shuffled through some papers. Wake saw that he was looking for something. It made him nervous. The admiral found the sheet he was searching for and held it up.

"An army lieutenant named Hammersley wrote a statement that you had threatened and extorted the colonel of that regiment into leaving. Colonel Grosland of the New Jersey artillery regiment, another senior army officer that you angered a while ago, gave me a copy. Would you care to see it?"

Wake struggled to remain calm as his blood heated up. Hammersley. So this was about that cringing fool. Wake could see the army lieutenant in his mind and shook his head. The admiral and commander were watching him. He decided to be blunt.

"Admiral, it doesn't matter whether I see it or not. Hammersley was ashore with us and showed himself to be a fool at best. His word is not important to me. It has no validity."

Loethen put the paper down on his desk. He stared at Wake like a naturalist examining a bug on a pin. "And so you say you don't care about the rumors going around regarding what happened there? You are telling me that what a senior officer in the army has heard is not important? Is that what you are saying to me, Wake?"

Morris looked at Wake and folded his arms as he leaned back in the chair, obviously waiting with interest for the reply.

"Admiral, what the senior army officers feel about me, or hear about me, is obviously important. But there is nothing I can do about it. An army colonel makes his own decisions and cannot be threatened by a mere naval lieutenant. His decisions are his business, sir. Speaking for myself, I am not ashamed of any decision I have made or any action I have taken. I would do them all again, sir."

Loethen and Morris exchanged glances. Morris stood up and walked to the window, contemplating the harbor as he addressed Wake behind him. "Wake, your wife was taken ill with yellow fever. Yes, we know all about your marriage. How is she doing?"

Wake was stunned into silence. They knew. They knew everything. He could feel his heart beating in his chest, blood pounding in his ears, and a warm flush spreading over his face. It was all too much. Everything in his plan for Linda and himself was falling apart. Morris had to repeat his question as he turned back and faced the junior officer. "I said how is she doing, Lieutenant?"

Wake stammered out a reply. "Better, sir. She's doing better. She's recovering."

"And she's at Useppa Island with the refugees?"

"Yes, sir. She's safe at Useppa."

Morris's face took on an aspect of pity as he continued. "Wake, you've become the topic of conversations throughout the squadron and the island since your last departure from here. You've angered many people. The Rebel sympathizers are upset you've run off with the daughter of one of their own, your brother naval officers believe you have lost your senses and cavorted with the enemy, and of course, the senior army commanders here are gunning for you on several accounts. Quite a series of accomplishments for a 'mere naval lieutenant.'"

Loethen spun around and interrupted his second in command. "And so, by marrying the daughter of a well-known traitor in Key West, it would appear that you don't care what the islanders or naval officers say, in addition to not caring about what army officers say. Wake, what exactly do you care about?"

Wake was listening to the remonstrations of his superiors, but his mind was filled with the image of himself and Linda on the beach at the cemetery at sunset, exchanging vows in front of the whole-hearted approval of his brother naval officers and petty officers in the squadron. He could see her face and hear their voices congratulating him. It had been the finest moment in his life. It brought back the self-control he had lost moments earlier. He knew the answer to the admiral's question.

"Honor, sir."

Loethen walked over to where Wake still remained in his chair. The admiral sat down at the table. Morris sighed, quietly left the window and walked out of the room. Loethen's left eyebrow raised slightly and his features hardened as he considered Wake's answer.

"Honor, you say?"

"Yes, sir."

Loethen narrowed his eyes and raised his voice, sounding as if he was bellowing into a gale. "*Explain that*, Lieutenant Wake."

Wake took a shallow breath and spoke, trying to keep his voice controlled despite the anger welling within him. It was all so damned wrong, he thought, as he tried to form the words to convey his point.

"By honor, Admiral, I mean that the sacrifices of the men who are actually fighting the war should never be forgotten or misspent. Their blood is the currency of this war, and we, as the leadership, both in the army and the navy, should never waste or dishonor it on a frivolous military purchase or for some later social bragging rights. My command decisions have always had that as a guiding principal, and always will as long as I have to make those decisions. No one, neither army colonel nor navy admiral, can say that I have wasted lives with that type of dishonor, sir."

Loethen's face softened but his voice was still neutral. "What about your personal life?"

"No apologies for loving and marrying a decent woman, Admiral. It was my honor to marry her, and I hope I can be the kind of husband she deserves. Simple as that, sir."

Loethen sighed and rested his chin on his hand as he examined the junior officer. "I see. Is that all you have to say after what you've done to the image of this squadron? Just some drivel about honor and love?"

Wake was picturing Hammersley cowering in the hut at Claresville as the enemy gunfire was ripping through the village, and whining afterwards, vowing to get the naval lieutenant. Maybe he had after all, Wake thought, as he surveyed the older man across the table.

"Yes, sir. That's it. And I don't consider honor to be drivel, sir."

Loethen made no reply, but remained ominously quiet. He rose and walked to the door, calling in a monotone for the yeoman outside to summon Commander Morris. Afterward, Loethen maintained the uncomfortable silence in the room by sitting at his desk and going through papers, shuffling them into several piles and ignoring the lieutenant sitting eight feet away.

Wake kept still, realizing that he had just sealed his fate by acting arrogantly superior to an admiral in matters of honor. Shaking his head and looking at the floor, he went over what he had just said. The text of what he said was not wrong, he knew that in his heart, but he felt the manner of the delivery had probably offended Admiral Loethen, the most powerful man in Key West. He wondered what decrepit old scow they would assign him to now. Some harbor barge probably. His career was finished, and he would serve out the remainder of the war in a minor role where he could do no more damage to the image of the admiral, the squadron, or the United States Navy. After the war they would cashier him immediately, and his hopes for a life of fulfillment in the navy would be a sad joke for the rest of his life. All because of how he had handled a simple question.

Morris walked in carrying a sheath of papers and laid them on the desk in front of the admiral. A sudden gust of the trade wind rustled the palm trees outside and came through the window to stir the papers Morris had just set down, sending a memorandum off the side of the desk. Morris reached out and caught it, smiling when he saw its title.

"Trade winds are piping up, sir."

Morris reached over and straightened the scattered piles of reports and correspondence on the desk, handing the errant memorandum to Admiral Loethen, saying, "I presume we don't want *that one* to fly out the window, do we Admiral?"

Loethen took the memorandum, smiled as well, and leaned back with his chair tipped against the wall. "No, it wouldn't do for that one to fly out the window, would it? What would young Wake here do then?"

"It just occurred to me, Admiral, that Lieutenant Wake won't have to rely on trade winds anymore. He'll have the luxury of being independent of them."

At the mention of his name, Wake looked over at the desk and tried to see what type of report or memorandum they were speaking about. He couldn't tell but could see their demeanor had changed. Both appeared more relaxed. The admiral motioned to Wake to come over to the desk.

"Step over here, Lieutenant. Don't make an admiral come to you, you young pup. You've already antagonized half the officers on this damned island. Now don't aggravate *me*."

The words were stern but the admiral's manner was not. The man was smiling. Wake came over and stood before the desk, where he said the only thing expected at that point from a junior officer. "Yes, sir."

Loethen handed the memorandum back to Morris. They both looked at Wake, the admiral speaking. "Lieutenant Wake, you have stated your case well. You have also done your duty well. Decisions in our profession have profound consequences. They will always be debated and analyzed by those who never have to make a decision of half the importance. A leader cannot make decisions on what he feels may or may not be politically or socially acceptable a year later. Those factors are far too fickle for the serious decisions we have to make every day. I am therefore quite relieved to hear that you base yours upon the guideposts of honor."

The admiral paused. Morris regarded Wake intently and calmly added his opinion. "Lieutenant, it's refreshing to hear a man who abides by the point of honor, in both his personal and professional lives. An old-fashioned virtue of strength in this time of rather . . . *adaptable* . . . standards."

Wake didn't understand the sudden change in demeanor of his superiors. He didn't understand any of this, but realized he should say something. "Thank you, sir. Thank you both for those kind words."

Loethen shook his head. "Well, you just might not thank us in a moment, Lieutenant. Things are about to change quite a bit for you, wouldn't you say that, Commander Morris?"

"Yes, sir. His situation will change considerably. Give him his orders, sir?"

"Yes, go right on ahead there, Commander, and give our young Mister 'Honor and Love' his new orders."

Morris chuckled and handed Wake the paper he had been holding, the same that had flown off the desk in the gust of the wind. Outside, the breeze was starting to gain in velocity, no longer just a fitful burst but now a steady force making the palm trees swish and flutter. Wake read the memorandum while Admiral Loethen and Commander Morris watched. When he was finished he looked up at the two, a puzzled look betraying his confusion.

"Sir, I don't understand. Is there some sort of mistake here? This orders me to take command of the *Hunt.* She's an armed steam tug. Those usually have been commands for regular officers, or at least volunteer officers with years of steam experience. I'm a volunteer officer and have no steam experience, sir."

Loethen pursed his lips, wrinkled his brow and nodded. "Sit down, Lieutenant. I don't usually take time to explain my decisions for lieutenants, but I think you probably would understand it better than most. Sit down, son."

Wake brought a chair over for himself and sat as Morris did the same next to him.

Loethen continued. "I told you that we've been devastated in this squadron by the yellow jack. One of the ships hit hardest was the *Hunt.* She's been here three months from Philadelphia and had a lieutenant, a master, a third assistant engineer, and two ensigns aboard, along with eighty-two petty officers and men. Now there are but forty-nine effectives among her crew, with none of the officers among them. The officers are all dead except for the engineer, and a third of the ones taken sick by the fever died as well. The remainder of the sick are trying to recuperate in the hospital."

Morris reached forward and touched the orders in Wake's hand. "Lieutenant, the *Hunt* is much more than a tug to us. I had hell to pay to get her assigned down here to us, instead of to the squadron at Charleston. She's a four-year-old seagoing screw steamer with tug capability because of the large towing bitts on her afterdeck. And she's armed with two twelve-pounders, one on either side. With her shallow draft of six feet and speed of ten knots she can be used as a gunboat or a tug. Her versatility is crucial to us."

Wake had seen the *Hunt* one time at anchor in the Key West harbor, but hadn't examined her closely. Several questions came to his mind, but he decided a simple reply was the best. "I see, sir."

Loethen shook his head sadly. "I think you are beginning to, Lieutenant Wake, but let me give you some further information."

"Yes, sir."

"The *Hunt* needs to be ready to get under way as soon as possible. There are several priority assignments waiting, and I don't have any other assets in this squadron with her capabilities. I need that ship, and I need her now."

"I can understand that, sir."

"Good. Her crew is demoralized and has shown some signs of, shall we say, *reluctance.* They are all new to this clime and the onslaught of the yellow fever among them has unmanned them, which, frankly, I can understand. Now they need a commanding officer who can get them past that point and back into the United States Navy and doing their duty. Quickly."

"Yes, sir. Quickly."

Loethen's tone became tense, as if he was about to say something painful. "I've run out of experienced steam line officers, regular or volunteer, to put aboard her. You'll have to learn about steam as you go. I expect you to learn that function rapidly, Wake.

The assistant engineer is a volunteer who is unknown to me. There'll be no time for slowly getting acquainted with running a steamer."

Morris picked a paper off the desk and handed it to Wake. "You'll be shorthanded as well, Lieutenant. There are no other officers to give you right now. But you can take two senior petty officers with you from the *St. James* or whatever ship that's in port right now. You're also getting these ten men," he pointed to a list on the paper just handed to Wake, "to replace the thirty-three lost, dead, and ill, by the sickness aboard her."

Wake was unable to reply beyond the minimum. "Yes, sir."

Admiral Loethen picked up where Morris had ended in the story of the *Hunt.* "She's at anchor now. There's been no fever aboard her for two weeks. Senior man aboard is a bosun's mate by the name of Dane. The harbor boats are loading her with provisions right now, and through the night. You'll go aboard and take command in the morning. By noon at the latest you'll be under way to Jupiter Inlet on the east coast of Florida. The steam gunboat *Epson* is there with a sick crew and unable to work the ship. You'll tow her back here."

"Aye aye, sir."

"Tell the yeoman outside who you want for those two petty officers, and he'll get the orders written up for my signature immediately. *St. James* will go to a new naval master who has just arrived in the squadron."

"Sir, I have a senior bosun's mate who could take command of *St. James* and do an excellent job. Name of Rork, sir."

Morris interrupted. "Rork. He's been with you a while, hasn't he?"

"Yes, sir."

"Has he sat for the examination for ensign?"

"No sir, but he's ready. He is prepared in all aspects for his navigation, seamanship, and gunnery."

Morris shook his head. "Then no, he can't take command. He could make acting ensign possibly, but *St. James* can't be given to an acting ensign, even now."

"Then I'd like to take him with me, sir. And also a gunner's mate named Durlon. He's aboard the *Buker* at anchor right now in the harbor. Saw her as we sailed in today."

Loethen stood up from his desk and called for the yeoman to come into the room. Wake and Morris stood also as the admiral addressed the lieutenant.

"Wake, you've taken some criticism about your personal affairs from some jealous naval officers. You've also received some criticism from certain army quarters. I like your explanation today about all that, so don't you worry about me or the commander here. We think you're the kind of man the squadron needs, particularly at this time. And don't worry about the army. I'll just tell them you're mentally unstable or something and try to get their sympathy. Of course, I would appreciate it if you please don't aggravate them any further. In fact, just stay away from anyone in an army uniform for a while. Now, get that ship and crew ready and get her under way."

Wake's confusion slowed his answer, but he got it said. "Aye aye, sir. Thank you, sir."

The yeoman stood in the corner waiting. Abruptly, the admiral noticed him. "Yeoman, get orders done for Gunner's Mate Durlon on the *Buker*, and Bosun's Mate Rork on the *St. James*, both to be transferred to the *Hunt* immediately. I want those orders sent out to their ships within an hour."

The yeoman acknowledged the order and disappeared out the door. Wake wanted to disappear too, if just to digest this strange turn of events and his new challenge.

"Sir, are there any other orders?"

Loethen looked at Wake, then Morris, and laughed out loud. "Good Lord, Lieutenant, aren't those enough?"

Morris joined him in chuckling and pointed at the door. "The admiral's previous orders were sufficient, Lieutenant. You may go now."

"Aye aye, sir. Thank you, sir."

Wake came to attention, turned on his heel and started to stride from the room when he was stopped by Loethen speaking in a gently paternal manner. "By the way, son, you were right."

Wake faced the older man standing behind the government-issue desk, flanked by wall charts of his geographic area of responsibility. The water-stained charts covered a thousand miles of coastline and islands and had numerous notations written on them. Pins with little flags depicting ships on blockade protruded all over the charts. The admiral, no longer laughing or even smiling, suddenly appeared tired and aged. For the first time since he had entered the office several minutes earlier, Wake was aware that the burdens of command had made the admiral's wrinkles become furrows and his hair thin out and recede. Wake also realized that his eyes were the most different. They had changed considerably over just the last few months. They were weary and dull now, with the lids slanted heavily over the outer corners. They appeared, in this brief study of the admiral, sad and worn out.

Wake remembered when he first arrived in Florida, and the admiral who commanded the squadron at that time, Cantwell Barkley. Old Barkley had taken a fatherly interest in the newly arrived Wake, giving him command of an armed sloop, the *Rosalie.* The admiral later died from yellow fever complications. Now Loethen was taking on the same tired look that Barkley had worn before he got sick. Command could do that to a man, Wake realized, as he replied to the unusual statement of the admiral.

"Right, sir? Right about what?"

"About honor, son. Decisions that are made with honor as a guide don't have to be apologized for, and they're certainly not drivel at all. I needed to be sure of you. Now I am. Continue to make those kinds of decisions, Lieutenant, and may God protect you and your men out there. Now, leave me to my unendingly mundane but necessary chores, son."

Wake felt an empathy and appreciation for the older man who had the lives of thousands of people, both naval and civilian, in his hands. The silence in the room was not uncomfortable to Wake now, but rather it seemed a natural pause that was a type of communication in itself. A silent message of trust.

Wake finally said, "Aye aye, sir."

Loethen nodded and lowered his gaze to the disheveled papers on his desk, then glanced over at Morris, growling an order in a quarterdeck voice. "Commander, how can I control this squadron when I can't even control the papers on my own desk. Get a yeoman in here to make some sort of semblance of order out of this confounded mess."

Loethen noticed Wake standing in the doorway watching him. "Wake, why are you still here? You have things to accomplish. Now go accomplish them!"

Dashing out the door, Wake called, "Aye aye, sir!" over his shoulder to the admiral, as a group of waiting officers in the outer room laughed at the admiral's booming comment and the lieutenant's rapid exit.

Outside the building, past the curious officers and alone in the dwindling sunlight, Wake paused and leaned against a coconut palm and looked out over the anchorage, letting the refreshing breeze wash over him like a cleansing surf. He searched out the *Hunt* lying at anchor on the far side of the harbor. With a tall stack, and two masts without sails that were useful for signaling but not much else, she was certainly different from any other ship he had served aboard, merchant or naval. The distance prevented seeing any detail, but he was intrigued by the concept of the *Hunt* and became impatient to get aboard her and find out how everything worked and what she was really capable of accomplishing. The sun was lowering and the air had lost much of its warmth. He breathed in a deep draught of clean air and wondered at the ever-changing challenges of naval life. It all was so different now, and in his usual methodical manner Wake put the pieces of what had just transpired together in his mind.

One could never become complacent, he thought, for events had a way of transforming life into a completely different equation just when you least expected it. When he had walked into the admiral's office he was concerned for his career over the incident with Colonel Wherley at the Timucuahatchee River. When he walked out of that office, he was consumed by the crucial needs attendant upon assuming a new command, hampered by low manpower and morale.

As he reveled in the slightly cooler air of the shadows and looked out over the glittering waters of the anchorage—starting to change from the fetid windless air of the summer months just past, he thought of what the admiral and commander had said about him not needing the wind anymore. For the first time in his life at sea he would be independent of the wind for motive power and totally dependent upon one of those infernal mechanical contraptions that spoiled the natural beauty of a ship. The smell and dirt and noise would be repulsive. Even the crew would be different, containing many men devoted to maintaining and operating the belching beast in her belly that made her such a dangerous modern warship. Those men were called the "black gang" for the obvious and accurate reason that they were usually filthy from the coal soot and engine grease they worked with. The usual cleanliness of a naval vessel that Wake had always expected would be hard to maintain on a steamer.

He suddenly realized that James had gone from sail to steam in the navy and wondered if his brother had felt the same way when he reported aboard that monitor. He wished James could tell him what to expect. The sad thought of James made him sigh. At least Linda was getting better, and she was definitely safer on Useppa among friends. One less thing for him to worry about while taking on a new command—and a steam command at that. His days under sail were ending.

Wake felt a deep affinity for the *St. James.* She was a schooner man's ship and had performed well in all the trials of the last ten months, but he was ready for his new challenge. It would all be difficult to adjust to, but it was a challenge Wake was beginning to find interesting, as he started walking toward the officers' boat landing by the naval wharf. He was thankful he would have Rork and Durlon as trusted shipmates to help him in that challenge.

The thought of the two veteran petty officers brought questions of what kind of crew he might find aboard the *Hunt* in the morning. He wasn't worried about them—curious but not worried. He was an experienced naval officer now and *Hunt* would be his third command. He knew what to do and had the confidence of his admiral that he would accomplish it. That Loethen had given him command of the *Hunt* over other officers in the squadron Wake considered as a personal debt to the admiral—and he would ensure that debt was paid in full by the success of the armed tug.

"*St. James*," he said to the youngster at the oars as he stepped into a dinghy at the landing.

"Aye, *St. James*, an' a pretty schooner she is, sir," the boy replied, but Wake wasn't listening. He was thinking of the unusual manner he had come to his new command.

The entire situation was ironic to Wake's logical way of thinking. All of this had unfolded because one month ago three hundred miles away from this place he had made a decision fraught with consequence. Wake ran a finger along the scar on the side of his face as he considered it. A point of honor had been the catalyst for that decision—that no one else would die needlessly, wasted through foolish intent or ego, and that Colonel Wherley should be removed from the possibility of showing further tragic idiocy. That the colonel had consented was a minor miracle, but his retaliation was still a distinct problem for the future. If Wherley sought revenge at some point, he would have to deal with it then. Still, the chance was worth it, reasoned Wake as he was rowed out to his final night as the *St. James*'s captain. After all, it wasn't that complicated—his brother James would have understood it perfectly. It was just a simple point of honor.

Wake stowed all of that in the back of his mind, for he had plenty to accomplish aboard the *St. James* this evening before assuming command of the *Hunt* in the morning. Briefing Rork on the day's news was the first item, followed by writing his final reports on the men, armament, rigging, supplies and provisions of the schooner. The last thing he would do tonight might be the most important, he decided. He would write a letter to Linda and share all that had happened to him.

"*St. James*!" called out the boy to the schooner ahead, in the traditional warning to a crew that their captain was approaching. As the dinghy came alongside, Wake saw that Rork was standing at the stern, watching him intently. Wake jumped up to the main chains and climbed to the deck. The bosun flashed a grin as he greeted his commanding officer and friend.

"Aye, Captain. Ye've come just in time for some o' Beech's good apple an' pork stew. The lad concocted it with some salt pork he found in a untainted cask—can your lordship fathom that?—and some o' those dried apple slices the little nip was holdin' onto. A feast for a bishop, I'm thinkin', sir."

"Sounds excellent, Rork! I'm suddenly quite hungry, and I have some important things to talk over with you while we eat. Life is about to get *very* interesting again, Bosun."

Rork's grin expanded to a laugh as his right eyebrow arched. "Oh Mary, Joseph, and Jesus, be with us now in our time o' joy or need! I can tell by that look in your eye, Captain, that you've got some grand news to declare. Interestin' you say? Now *that's* the life for a navy man!"

Wake put his hand on Rork's shoulder. "Rork, this'll definitely be interesting. I can assure you of that. Now let's eat that stew of Beech's, and I'll tell you what tomorrow brings us."

They went below and as they ate Beech's stew in Wake's cabin, they discussed how they would fulfill the new mission given to them. The meal and conversation were finished by the time the sun had set—for both had a lot to do and little time to accomplish it. Writing the reports took more time than Wake anticipated, but it had to be done, and he forced himself to be thorough.

Much later that night Wake set himself to his last task by the dim light of his lamp. He wrote his wife the tremendous news of his next command in his usual straightforward manner, as if he was relating a naval action to the admiral. He also told her of his plans and hopes for their future, but this part of the letter was more animated and hopeful. The sound of the pen scratching its way across the paper suddenly struck Wake, and he imagined Linda trying her best to read the letter—she always joked about his handwriting being almost illegible, that it must be some sort of secret code. When he had written all he could think of, Wake put the folded paper in a navy issue envelope and sealed it with wax. Leaning over the chart table, he carefully extinguished the hanging brass lamp, and crawled utterly exhausted into his berth, knowing that he needed all the rest he could get.

In four hours the sun would rise again, and Lieutenant Peter Wake would be embarking upon the newest challenge of his young naval career—command of a steamer of war.

Robert N. Macomber's Honor Series:

At the Edge of Honor. This nationally acclaimed naval Civil War novel, the first in the Honor series of naval fiction, takes the reader into the steamy world of Key West and the Caribbean in 1863 and introduces Peter Wake, the reluctant New England volunteer officer who finds himself battling the enemy on the coasts of Florida, sinister intrigue in Spanish Havana and the British Bahamas, and social taboos in Key West when he falls in love with the daughter of a Confederate zealot. (hb, pb)

Point of Honor. Winner of the Florida Historical Society's 2003 Patrick Smith Award for Best Florida Fiction. In this second book in the Honor series, it is 1864 and Lt. Peter Wake, United States Navy, assisted by his indomitable Irish bosun, Sean Rork, commands the naval schooner St. James. He searches for army deserters in the Dry Tortugas, finds an old nemesis during a standoff with the French Navy on the coast of Mexico, starts a drunken tavern riot in Key West, and confronts incompetent Federal army officers during an invasion of upper Florida. (hb, pb)

Honorable Mention. This third book in the Honor series of naval fiction covers the tumultuous end of the Civil War in Florida and the Caribbean. Lt. Peter Wake is now in command of the steamer USS Hunt, and quickly plunges into action, chasing a strange vessel during a tropical storm off Cuba, confronting death to liberate an escaping slave ship, and coming face to face with the enemy's most powerful ocean warship in Havana's harbor. Finally, when he tracks down a colony of former Confederates in Puerto Rico, Wake becomes involved in a deadly twist of irony. (hb)

A Dishonorable Few. Fourth in the Honor series. It is 1869 and the United States is painfully recovering from the Civil War. Lt. Peter Wake heads to turbulent Central America to deal with a former American naval officer turned renegade mercenary. As the action unfolds in Colombia and Panama, Wake realizes that his most dangerous adversary may be a man on his own ship, forcing Wake to make a decision that will lead to his court-martial in Washington when the mission has finally ended. (hb)

An Affair of Honor. Fifth in the Honor series. It's December 1873 and Lt. Peter Wake is the executive officer of the USS *Omaha* on patrol in the West Indies, eager to return home. Fate, however, has other plans. He runs afoul of the Royal Navy in Antigua and then is sent off to Europe, where he finds himself embroiled in a Spanish civil war. But his real test comes when he and Sean Rork are sent on a mission in northern Africa. (hb)

A Different Kind of Honor. In this sixth novel in the Honor series, it's 1879 and Lt. Cmdr. Peter Wake, U.S.N., is on assignment as the American naval observer to the War of the Pacific along the west coast of South America. During this mission Wake will witness history's first battle between ocean-going ironclads, ride the world's first deep-diving submarine, face his first machine guns in combat, and run for his life in the Catacombs of the Dead in Lima. (hb)

The Honored Dead. Seventh in the series. On what at first appears to be a simple mission for the U.S. president in French Indochina in 1883, naval intelligence officer Lt. Cmdr. Peter Wake encounters opium warlords, Chinese-Malay pirates, and French gangsters. (hb)

The Darkest Shade of Honor. Eighth in the series. It's 1886 and Wake, now of the U.S. Navy's Office of Naval Intelligence, meets rising politico Theodore Roosevelt in New York City. Wake is assigned to uncover Cuban revolutionary activities between Florida and Cuba. He meets José Martí, finds himself engulfed in the most catastrophic event in Key West history, and must make a decision involving the very darkest shade of honor. (hb)

Honor Bound. Ninth in the series. In 1888 Wake, U.S. Navy intelligence agent, meets a woman from his past who begs him to find her missing son. Wake sets off across Florida, through the Bahamian islands, and deep into the dank jungles of Haiti. Overcoming storms, mutiny, and shipwreck, Wake discovers the hidden lair of an anarchist group planning to wreak havoc around the world—unless he stops it.

For a complete catalog, visit our website at www.pineapplepress.com. Or write to Pineapple Press, P.O. Box 3889, Sarasota, Florida 34230-3889, or call (800) 746-3275.

CPSIA information can be obtained at www.ICGtesting.com
Printed in the USA
BVOW05s1753121114

374718BV00004B/5/P